D1098006

· THE ·
JUNIOR VISUAL
DICTIONARY
ENGLISH·FRENCH

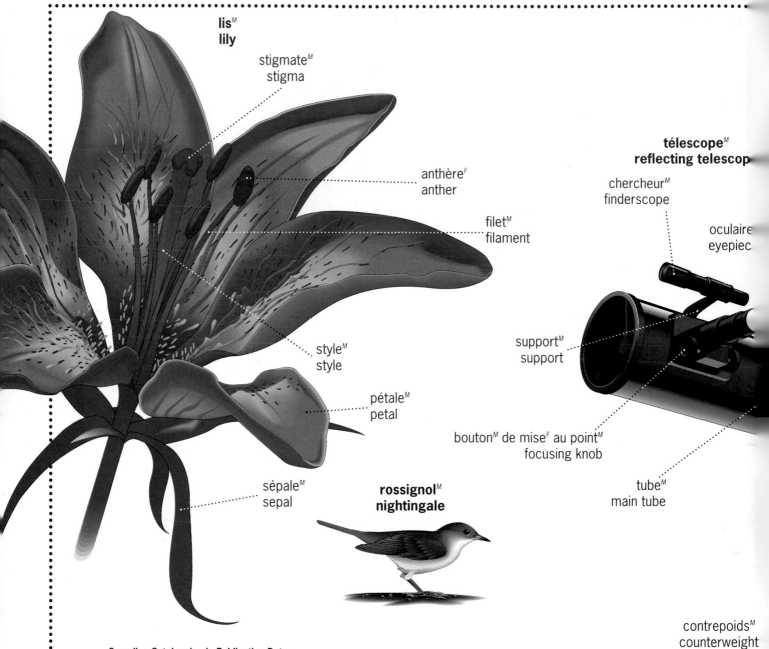

lis^M
lily

stigmate^M
stigma

anthère^F
anther

filet^M
filament

style^M
style

pétale^M
petal

sépale^M
sepal

rossignol^M
nightingale

télescope^M
reflecting telescop

chercheur^M
finderscope

oculaire^M
eyepiec

support^M
support

bouton^M de mise^F au point^M
focusing knob

tube^M
main tube

contrepoids^M
counterweight

Canadian Cataloguing in Publication Data

Corbeil, Jean-Claude, 1932-
The junior visual dictionary : English-French

ISBN: 2-89037-991-4

1. Picture dictionaries, English - Juvenile literature. 2. Picture dictionaries, French - Juvenile literature.
3. English language - Dictionaries, Juvenile - French. 4. French language - Dictionaries, Juvenile - English.
I. Archambault, Ariane, 1936-   II. Title.

PE1629.C67   1999   j423'.41   C99-940624-8E

Created and produced by QA International
a division of Éditions Québec Amérique Inc.
329, rue de la Commune Ouest, Montréal (Québec) H2Y 2Z7.
Tel. : 514-499-3000 Fax : 514-499-3010
www.qa-international.com

Copyright © 1999 Éditions Québec Amérique Inc.

All rights reserved. No part of this publication may be reproduced or
transmitted in any form or by any means, electronic or mechanical, including
photocopying, recording or by any information storage and retrieval system,
without permission in writing from the Publisher.

Printed and bound in Canada.

We acknowledge the financial support of the Government of Canada
through the Book Publishing Industry Development Program (BPIDP)
for our publishing activities.

Canadä

We would also like to thank SODEC for its financial support.

10 9 8 7 6 5 4 3 2 1   02 01 00 99

JEAN-CLAUDE CORBEIL • ARIANE ARCHAMBAULT

• THE •
JUNIOR VISUAL
DICTIONARY
ENGLISH • FRENCH

Authors
Jean-Claude Corbeil
Ariane Archambault

Director of Computer Graphics
François Fortin

Art Directors
Jean-Louis Martin
François Fortin

Graphic Designer
Anne Tremblay

Computer Graphics Designers
Marc Lalumière
Jean-Yves Ahern
Rielle Lévesque
Anne Tremblay

Jacques Perrault
Jocelyn Gardner
Christiane Beauregard
Michel Blais
Stéphane Roy
Alice Comtois
Benoît Bourdeau

Computer Programming
Yves Ferland
Daniel Beaulieu

Data Capture
Serge D'Amico

Page Make-up
Lucie Mc Brearty
Pascal Goyette

Technical Support
Gilles Archambault

Production
Tony O'Riley

QA INTERNATIONAL

THEMES AND SUBJECTS

SKY

EARTH

VEGETABLE KINGDOM

FRUITS AND VEGETABLES

GARDENING

ANIMAL KINGDOM

HUMAN BODY

ARCHITECTURE

HOUSE

DO-IT-YOURSELF

CLOTHING

PERSONAL ARTICLES

COMMUNICATIONS

5

LE SYSTÈME^M SOLAIRE
SOLAR SYSTEM

planètes^F et satellites^M
planets and moons

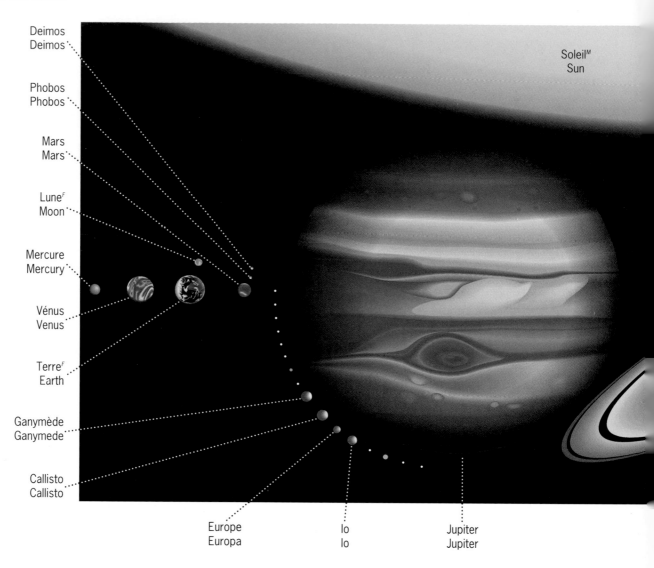

Deimos
Deimos

Phobos
Phobos

Mars
Mars

Lune^F
Moon

Mercure
Mercury

Vénus
Venus

Terre^F
Earth

Ganymède
Ganymede

Callisto
Callisto

Soleil^M
Sun

Europe
Europa

Io
Io

Jupiter
Jupiter

orbites^F des planètes^F
orbits of the planets

astéroïdes^M
asteroid belt

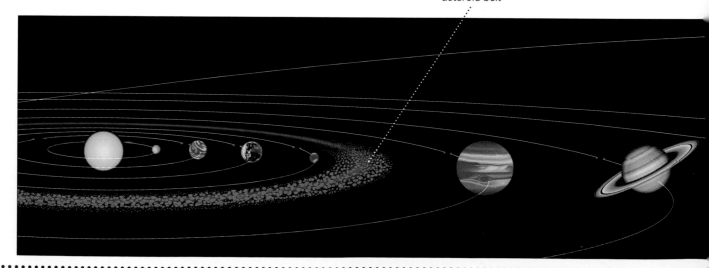

LE SYSTÈME^M SOLAIRE
SOLAR SYSTEM

6

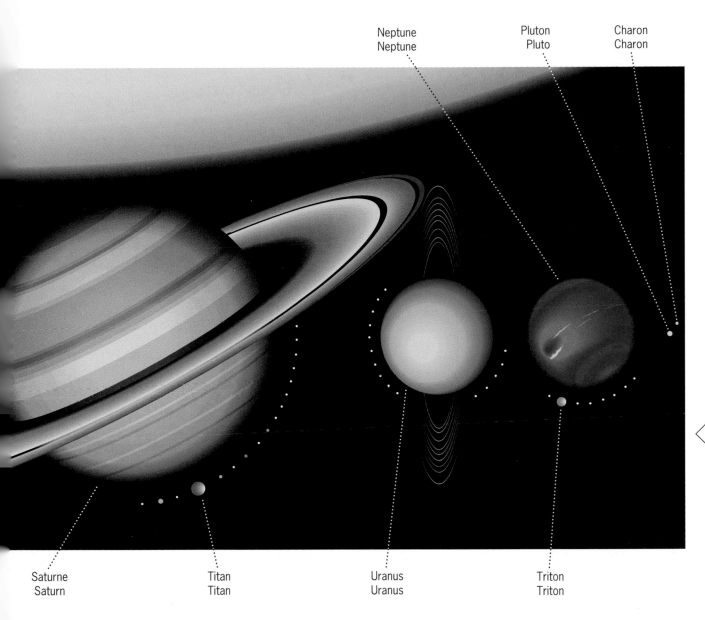

Neptune
Neptune

Pluton
Pluto

Charon
Charon

Saturne
Saturn

Titan
Titan

Uranus
Uranus

Triton
Triton

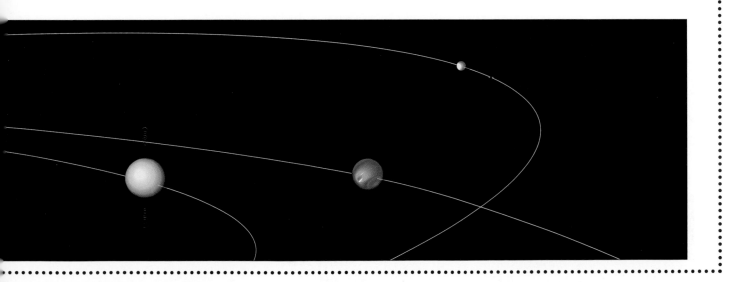

8

LE SOLEIL^M
SUN

structure^F **du Soleil**^M
structure of the Sun

zone^F de radiation^F
radiation zone

zone^F de convection^F
convection zone

surface^F solaire
Sun's surface

couronne^F
corona

protubérance^F
prominence

tache^F
sunspot

noyau^M
core

éruption^F
flare

LA LUNE^F
MOON

baie^F
bay

falaise^F
cliff

océan^M
ocean

lac^M
lake

mer^F
sea

chaîne^F de montagnes^F
mountain range

cratère^M
crater

rempart^M
wall

cirque^M
cirque

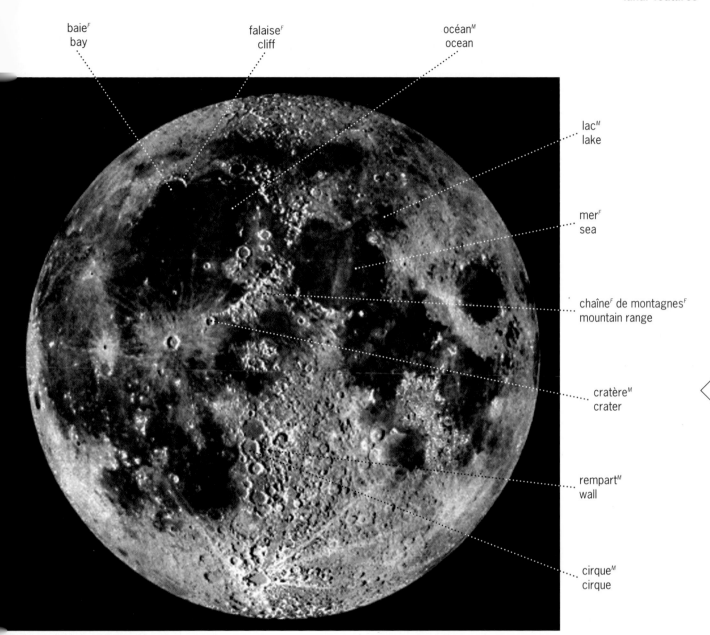

PHASES^F DE LA LUNE^F
PHASES OF THE MOON

premier croissant^M
new crescent

Lune^F gibbeuse croissante
waxing gibbous Moon

Lune^F gibbeuse décroissante
waning gibbous Moon

dernier croissant^M
old crescent

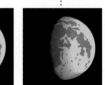

nouvelle Lune^F
new Moon

premier quartier^M
first quarter

pleine Lune^F
full Moon

dernier quartier^M
last quarter

LA COMÈTE^F
COMET

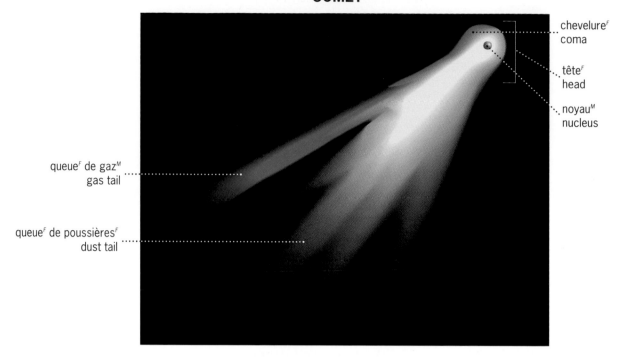

chevelure^F
coma

tête^F
head

noyau^M
nucleus

queue^F de gaz^M
gas tail

queue^F de poussières^F
dust tail

L'ÉCLIPSE^F DE SOLEIL^M
SOLAR ECLIPSE

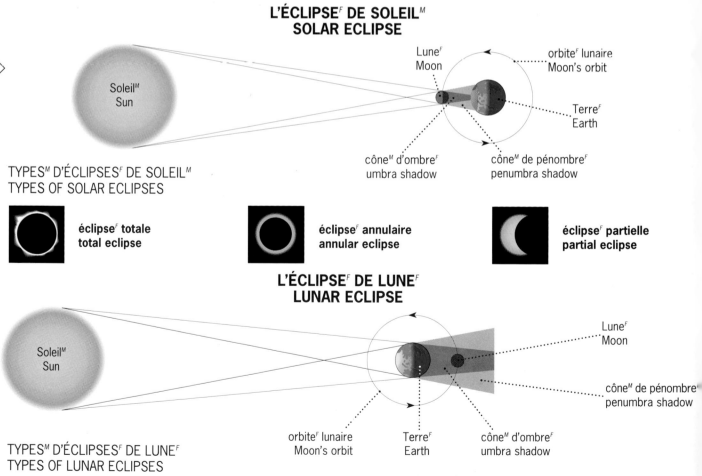

Soleil^M
Sun

Lune^F
Moon

orbite^F lunaire
Moon's orbit

Terre^F
Earth

cône^M d'ombre^F
umbra shadow

cône^M de pénombre^F
penumbra shadow

TYPES^M D'ÉCLIPSES^F DE SOLEIL^M
TYPES OF SOLAR ECLIPSES

éclipse^F totale
total eclipse

éclipse^F annulaire
annular eclipse

éclipse^F partielle
partial eclipse

L'ÉCLIPSE^F DE LUNE^F
LUNAR ECLIPSE

Soleil^M
Sun

Lune^F
Moon

cône^M de pénombre^F
penumbra shadow

orbite^F lunaire
Moon's orbit

Terre^F
Earth

cône^M d'ombre^F
umbra shadow

TYPES^M D'ÉCLIPSES^F DE LUNE^F
TYPES OF LUNAR ECLIPSES

éclipse^F partielle
partial eclipse

éclipse^F totale
total eclipse

LE TÉLESCOPE^M
REFLECTING TELESCOPE

chercheur^M
finderscope

oculaire^M
eyepiece

tube^M
main tube

bouton^M de mise^F au point^M
focusing knob

cercle^M de déclinaison^F
declination setting scale

vis^F de blocage^M (azimut^M)
azimuth clamp

cercle^M d'ascension^F droite
right ascension setting scale

vis^F de blocage^M (latitude^F)
altitude clamp

réglage^M micrométrique (azimut^M)
azimuth fine adjustment

réglage^M micrométrique (latitude^F)
altitude fine adjustment

coupe^F d'un télescope^M
cross section of a reflecting telescope

oculaire^M
eyepiece

tube^M
main tube

miroir^M primaire parabolique
main mirror

miroir^M plan
flat mirror

lumière^F
light

LA LUNETTE^F ASTRONOMIQUE
REFRACTING TELESCOPE

support^M
support

tube^M porte-oculaire^M
eyepiece holder

oculaire^M coudé
star diagonal

fourche^F
fork

trépied^M
tripod

plateau^M pour accessoires^M
tripod accessories shelf

lentille^F objectif^M
objective lens

pare-soleil^M
dew shield

bride^F de fixation^F
cradle

contrepoids^M
counterweight

coupe^F d'une lunette^F astronomique
cross section of a refracting telescope

oculaire^M
eyepiece

lentille^F objectif^M
objective lens

tube^M
main tube

lumière^F
light

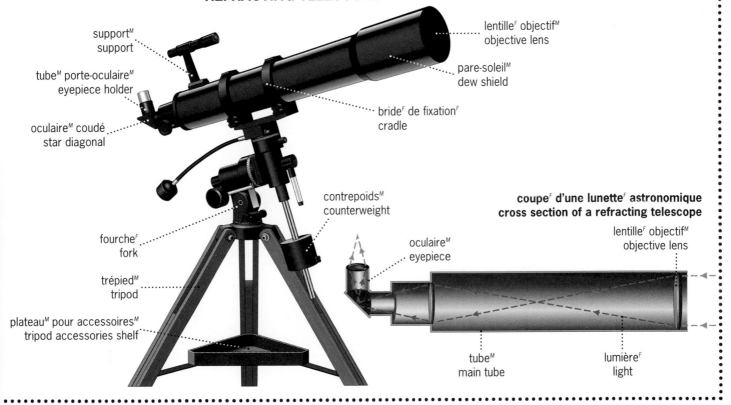

LES COORDONNÉES^F TERRESTRES
EARTH COORDINATE SYSTEM

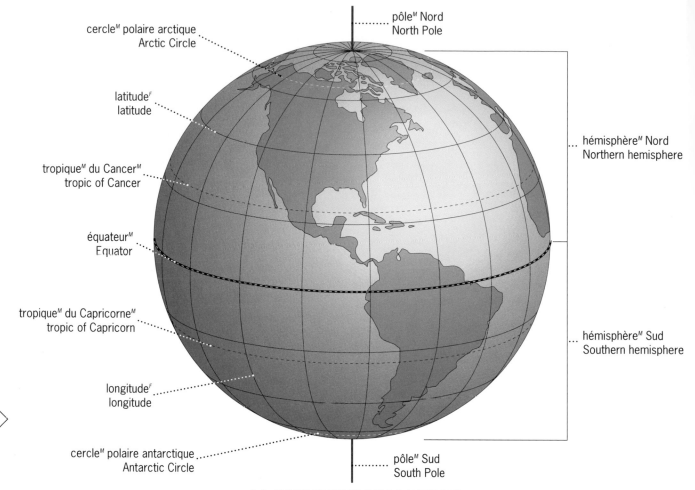

cercle^M polaire arctique
Arctic Circle

pôle^M Nord
North Pole

latitude^F
latitude

hémisphère^M Nord
Northern hemisphere

tropique^M du Cancer^M
tropic of Cancer

équateur^M
Equator

tropique^M du Capricorne^M
tropic of Capricorn

hémisphère^M Sud
Southern hemisphere

longitude^F
longitude

cercle^M polaire antarctique
Antarctic Circle

pôle^M Sud
South Pole

LA STRUCTURE^F DE LA TERRE^F
STRUCTURE OF THE EARTH

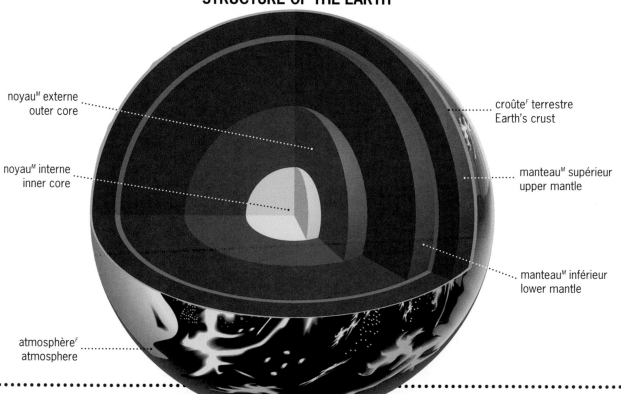

noyau^M externe
outer core

croûte^F terrestre
Earth's crust

noyau^M interne
inner core

manteau^M supérieur
upper mantle

manteau^M inférieur
lower mantle

atmosphère^F
atmosphere

LES COORDONNÉES^F TERRESTRES
EARTH COORDINATE SYSTEM

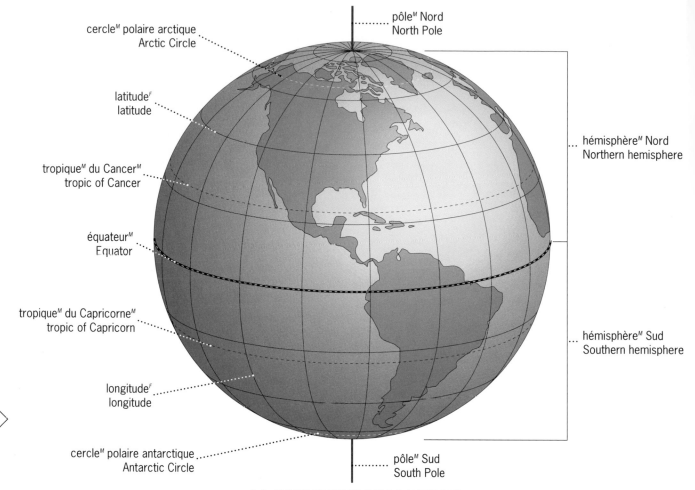

cercle^M polaire arctique
Arctic Circle

pôle^M Nord
North Pole

latitude^F
latitude

hémisphère^M Nord
Northern hemisphere

tropique^M du Cancer^M
tropic of Cancer

équateur^M
Equator

tropique^M du Capricorne^M
tropic of Capricorn

hémisphère^M Sud
Southern hemisphere

longitude^F
longitude

cercle^M polaire antarctique
Antarctic Circle

pôle^M Sud
South Pole

LA STRUCTURE^F DE LA TERRE^F
STRUCTURE OF THE EARTH

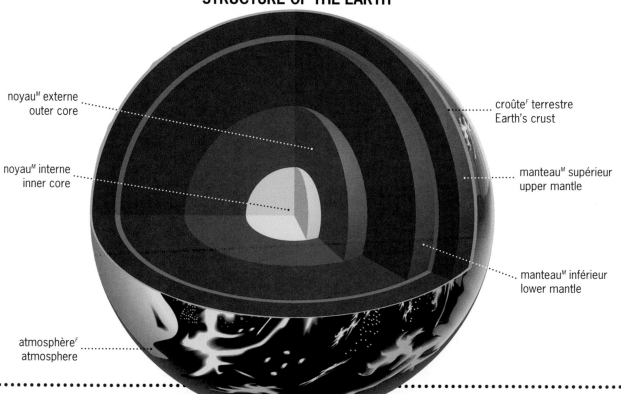

noyau^M externe
outer core

croûte^F terrestre
Earth's crust

noyau^M interne
inner core

manteau^M supérieur
upper mantle

manteau^M inférieur
lower mantle

atmosphère^F
atmosphere

LE SÉISME^M
EARTHQUAKE

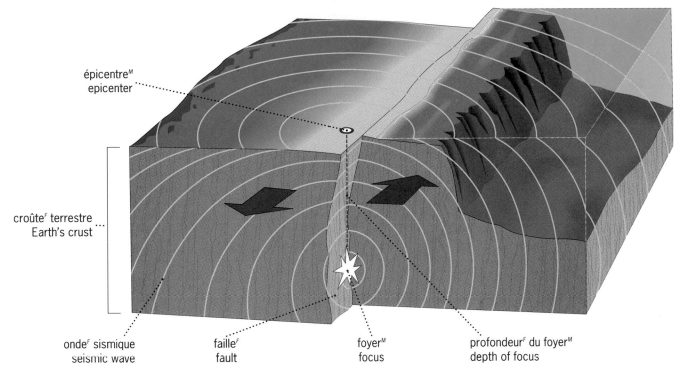

épicentre^M
epicenter

croûte^F terrestre
Earth's crust

onde^F sismique
seismic wave

faille^F
fault

foyer^M
focus

profondeur^F du foyer^M
depth of focus

LA GROTTE^F
CAVE

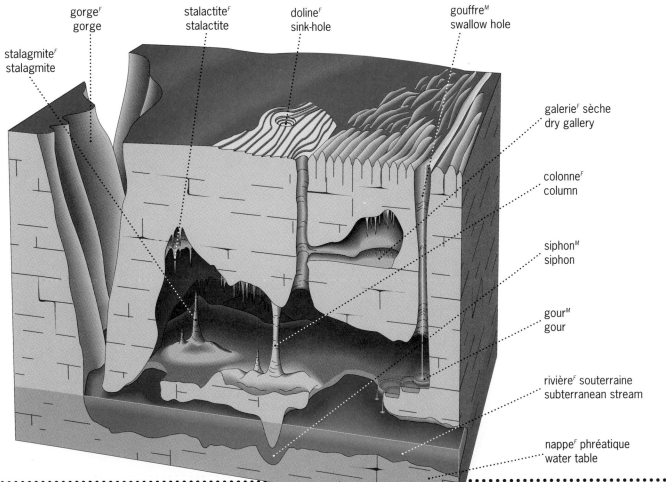

gorge^F
gorge

stalactite^F
stalactite

doline^F
sink-hole

gouffre^M
swallow hole

stalagmite^F
stalagmite

galerie^F sèche
dry gallery

colonne^F
column

siphon^M
siphon

gour^M
gour

rivière^F souterraine
subterranean stream

nappe^F phréatique
water table

LA CONFIGURATION^F DU LITTORAL^M
COASTAL FEATURES

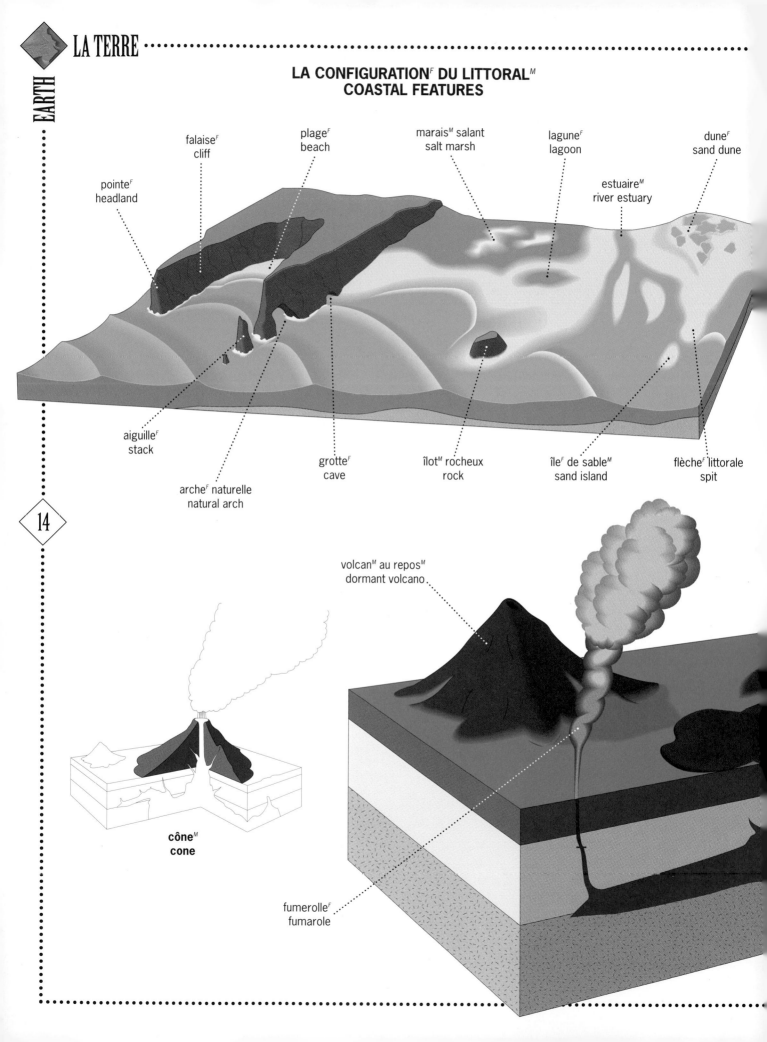

pointe^F
headland

falaise^F
cliff

plage^F
beach

marais^M salant
salt marsh

lagune^F
lagoon

dune^F
sand dune

estuaire^M
river estuary

aiguille^F
stack

arche^F naturelle
natural arch

grotte^F
cave

îlot^M rocheux
rock

île^F de sable^M
sand island

flèche^F littorale
spit

14

volcan^M au repos^M
dormant volcano

cône^M
cone

fumerolle^F
fumarole

LE VOLCAN^M
VOLCANO

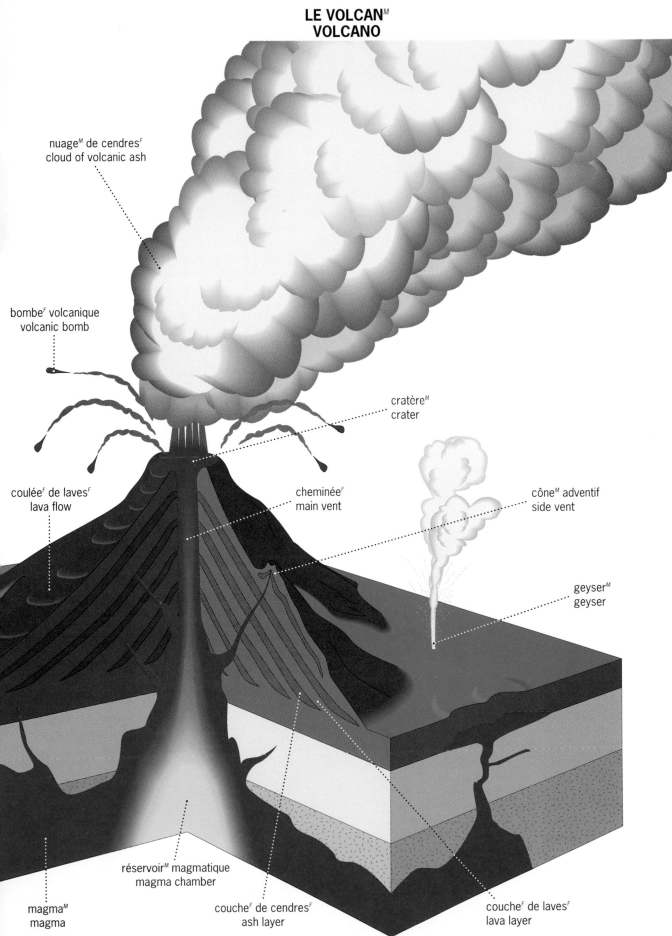

nuage^M de cendres^F
cloud of volcanic ash

bombe^F volcanique
volcanic bomb

coulée^F de laves^F
lava flow

cratère^M
crater

cheminée^F
main vent

cône^M adventif
side vent

geyser^M
geyser

réservoir^M magmatique
magma chamber

magma^M
magma

couche^F de cendres^F
ash layer

couche^F de laves^F
lava layer

LE GLACIER^M
GLACIER

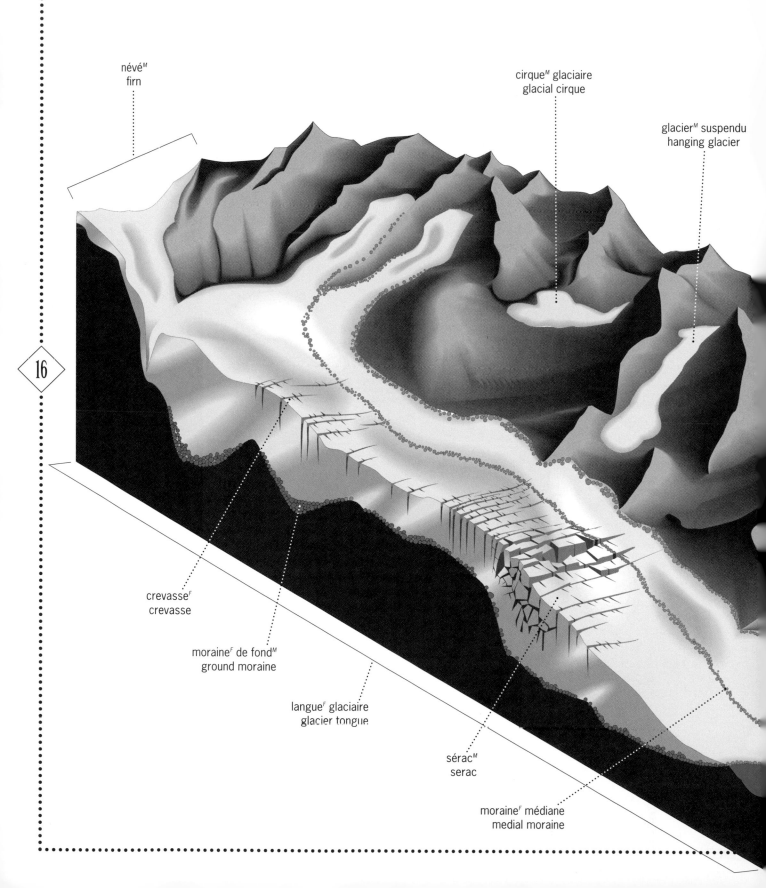

névé^M
firn

cirque^M glaciaire
glacial cirque

glacier^M suspendu
hanging glacier

16

crevasse^F
crevasse

moraine^F de fond^M
ground moraine

langue^F glaciaire
glacier tongue

sérac^M
serac

moraine^F médiane
medial moraine

**LA MONTAGNE^F
MOUNTAIN**

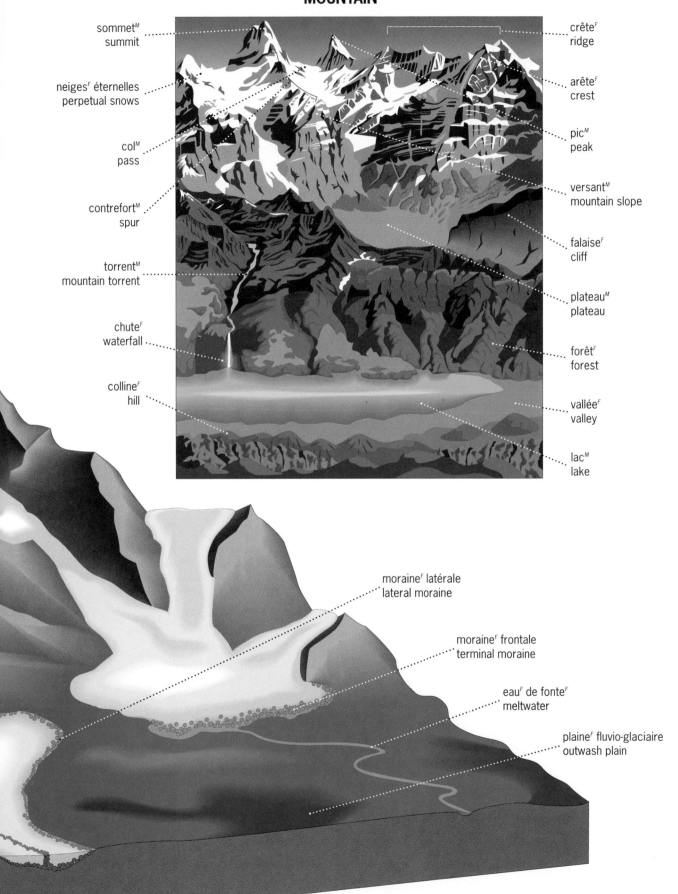

sommet^M
summit

neiges^F éternelles
perpetual snows

col^M
pass

contrefort^M
spur

torrent^M
mountain torrent

chute^F
waterfall

colline^F
hill

crête^F
ridge

arête^F
crest

pic^M
peak

versant^M
mountain slope

falaise^F
cliff

plateau^M
plateau

forêt^F
forest

vallée^F
valley

lac^M
lake

moraine^F latérale
lateral moraine

moraine^F frontale
terminal moraine

eau^F de fonte^F
meltwater

plaine^F fluvio-glaciaire
outwash plain

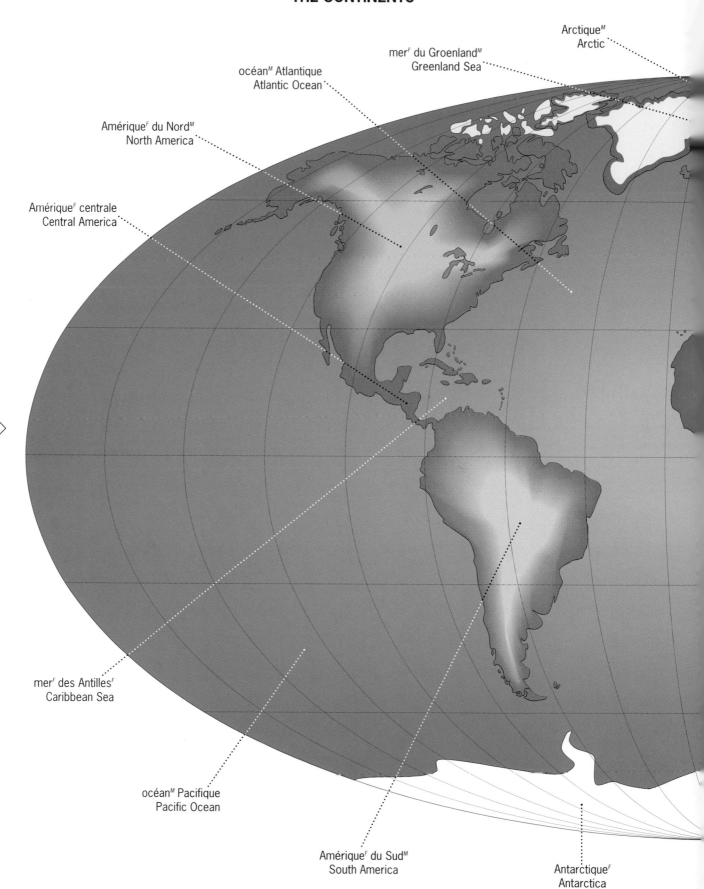

LA CONFIGURATION[F] DES CONTINENTS[M]
THE CONTINENTS

Arctique[M]
Arctic

mer[F] du Groenland[M]
Greenland Sea

océan[M] Atlantique
Atlantic Ocean

Amérique[F] du Nord[M]
North America

Amérique[F] centrale
Central America

mer[F] des Antilles[F]
Caribbean Sea

océan[M] Pacifique
Pacific Ocean

Amérique[F] du Sud[M]
South America

Antarctique[F]
Antarctica

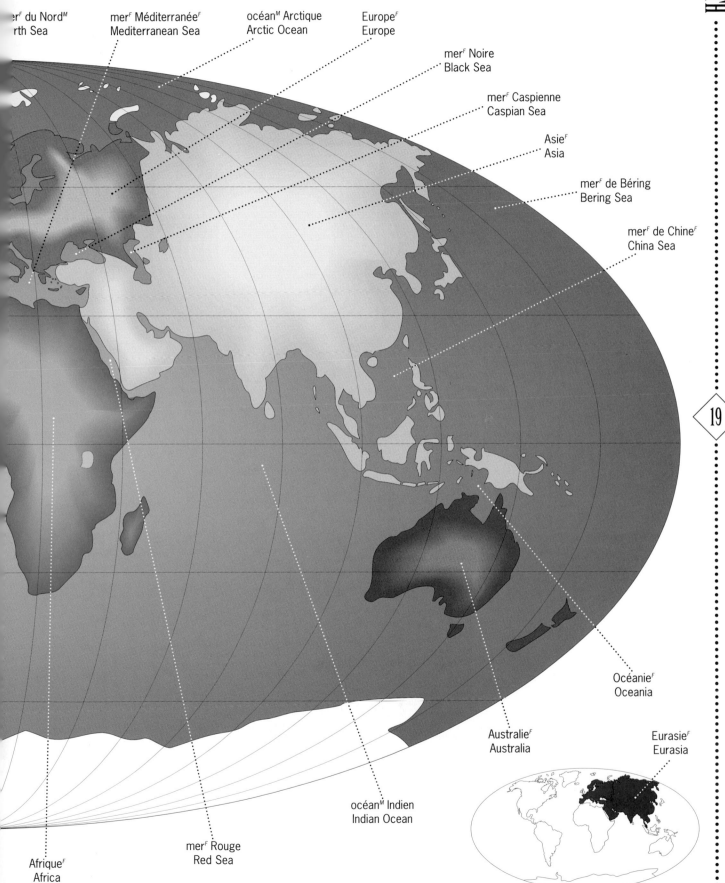

mer[F] du Nord[M]
rth Sea

mer[F] Méditerranée[F]
Mediterranean Sea

océan[M] Arctique
Arctic Ocean

Europe[F]
Europe

mer[F] Noire
Black Sea

mer[F] Caspienne
Caspian Sea

Asie[F]
Asia

mer[F] de Béring
Bering Sea

mer[F] de Chine[F]
China Sea

Océanie[F]
Oceania

Australie[F]
Australia

Eurasie[F]
Eurasia

océan[M] Indien
Indian Ocean

mer[F] Rouge
Red Sea

Afrique[F]
Africa

19

LE CYCLE^M DES SAISONS^F
SEASONS OF THE YEAR

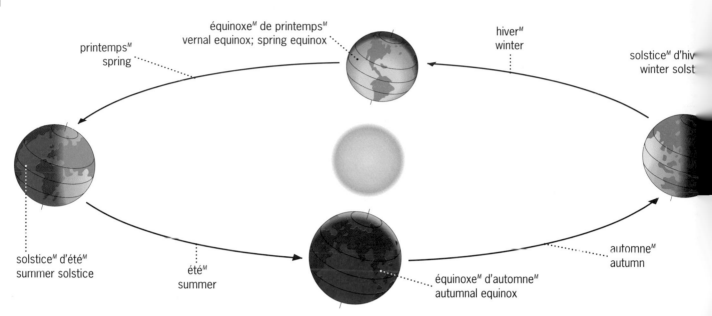

équinoxe^M de printemps^M
vernal equinox; spring equinox

hiver^M
winter

solstice^M d'hiv
winter solst

printemps^M
spring

solstice^M d'été^M
summer solstice

été^M
summer

automne^M
autumn

équinoxe^M d'automne^M
autumnal equinox

LA STRUCTURE^F DE LA BIOSPHÈR
STRUCTURE OF THE BIOSPHER

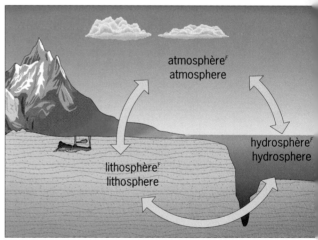

atmosphère^F
atmosphere

hydrosphère^F
hydrosphere

lithosphère^F
lithosphere

LE PAYSAGE^M VÉGÉTAL SELON L'ALTITUDE^F
ELEVATION ZONES AND VEGETATION

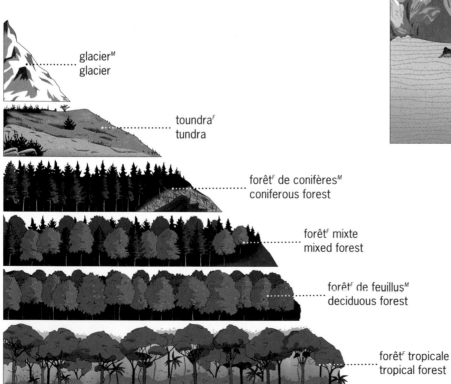

glacier^M
glacier

toundra^F
tundra

forêt^F de conifères^M
coniferous forest

forêt^F mixte
mixed forest

forêt^F de feuillus^M
deciduous forest

forêt^F tropicale
tropical forest

LES CLIMATS^M DU MONDE^M
CLIMATES OF THE WORLD

climats^M tropicaux
tropical climates

forêt^F tropicale
tropical rain forest

savane^F
tropical savanna

steppe^F
steppe

désert^M
desert

climats^M tempérés
temperate climates

humide, à été^M long
humid - long summer

humide, à été^M court
humid - short summer

océanique
marine

climats^M polaires
polar climates

toundra^F
polar tundra

calotte^F glaciaire
polar ice cap

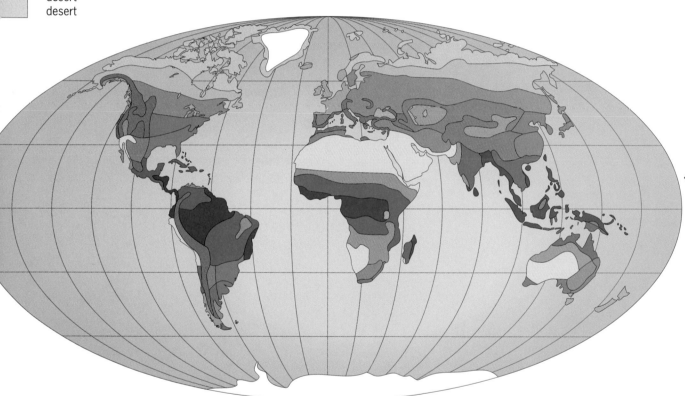

climats^M subtropicaux
subtropical climates

méditerranéen
Mediterranean subtropical

subtropical humide
humid subtropical

subtropical sec
dry subtropical

climats^M continentaux
continental climates

continental aride
dry continental - arid

continental semi-aride
dry continental - semiarid

climats^M de montagne^F
highland climates

climats^M de montagne^F
highland climates

climats^M subarctiques
subarctic climates

climats^M subarctiques
subarctic climates

LE TEMPS^M
WEATHER

brume^F
mist

brouillard^M
fog

rosée^F
dew

verglas^M
glazed frost

ciel^M **d'orage**^M
stormy sky

22

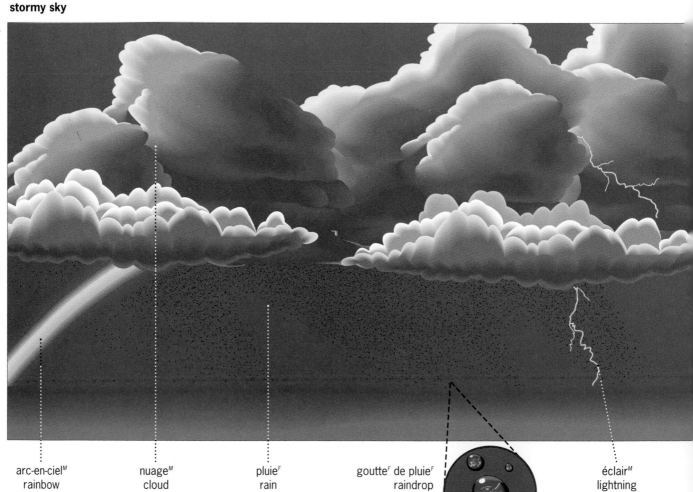

arc-en-ciel^M
rainbow

nuage^M
cloud

pluie^F
rain

goutte^F de pluie^F
raindrop

éclair^M
lightning

LES INSTRUMENTS^M DE MESURE^F MÉTÉOROLOGIQUE
METEOROLOGICAL MEASURING INSTRUMENTS

SURE^F DE LA DIRECTION^F DU VENT^M
ASURE OF WIND DIRECTION

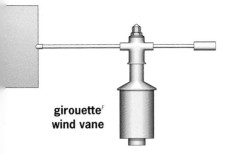

girouette^F
wind vane

MESURE^F DE LA VITESSE^F DU VENT^M
MEASURE OF WIND STRENGTH

anémomètre^M
anemometer

MESURE^F DE L'HUMIDITÉ^F
MEASURE OF HUMIDITY

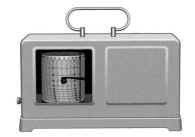

hygromètre^M enregistreur
hygrograph

SURE^F DE LA PLUVIOSITÉ^F
EASURE OF RAINFALL

pluviomètre^M enregistreur
rain gauge recorder

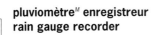

appareil^M enregistreur
recording unit

récipient^M collecteur
collecting vessel

pluviomètre^M à lecture^F directe
direct-reading rain gauge

entonnoir^M collecteur
collecting funnel

éprouvette^F graduée
measuring tube

collier^M de serrage^M
tightening band

récipient^M
container

support^M
support

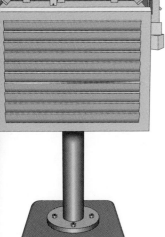

abri^M météorologique
instrument shelter

MESURE^F DE LA TEMPÉRATURE^F
MEASURE OF TEMPERATURE

thermomètre^M à minima^M
minimum thermometer

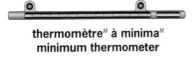

thermomètre^M à maxima^M
maximum thermometer

baromètre^M à mercure^M
mercury barometer

MESURE^F DE LA PRESSION^F
MEASURE OF AIR PRESSURE

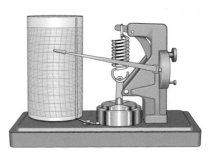

baromètre^M enregistreur
barograph

LA CARTOGRAPHIE^F
CARTOGRAPHY

hémisphères^M
hemispheres

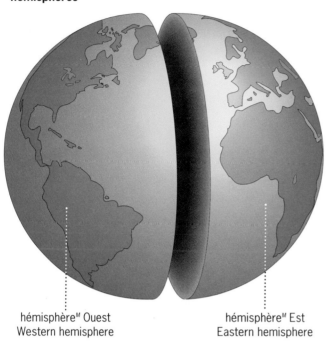

hémisphère^M Ouest
Western hemisphere

hémisphère^M Est
Eastern hemisphere

hémisphère^M Nord
Northern hemisphere

hémisphère^M Sud
Southern hemispher

24 DIVISIONS^F CARTOGRAPHIQUES
GRID SYSTEM

latitude^F
lines of latitude

cercle^M polaire arctique
Arctic Circle

tropique^M du Cancer^M
tropic of Cancer

équateur^M
Equator

tropique^M du Capricorne^M
tropic of Capricorn

parallèle^M
parallel

longitude^F
lines of longitude

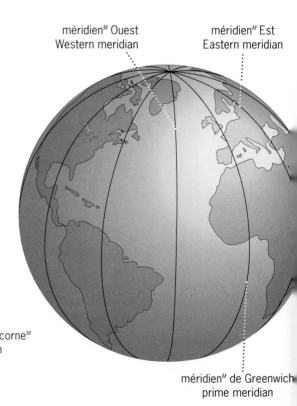

méridien^M Ouest
Western meridian

méridien^M Est
Eastern meridian

méridien^M de Greenwich
prime meridian

PROJECTIONS^F CARTOGRAPHIQUES
MAP PROJECTIONS

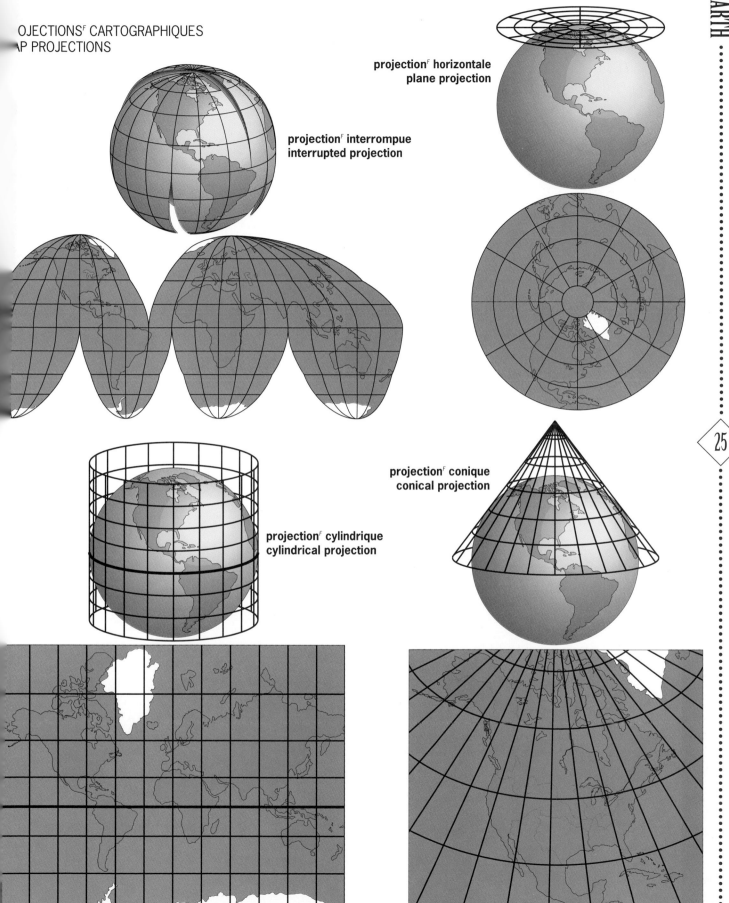

projection^F horizontale
plane projection

projection^F interrompue
interrupted projection

projection^F cylindrique
cylindrical projection

projection^F conique
conical projection

LA CARTOGRAPHIE^F
CARTOGRAPHY

carte^F politique
political map

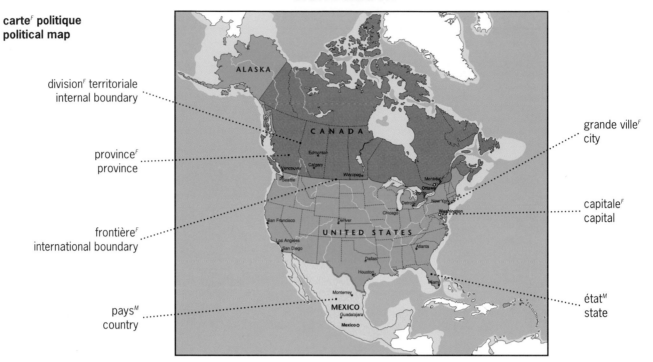

division^F territoriale
internal boundary

province^F
province

frontière^F
international boundary

pays^M
country

grande ville^F
city

capitale^F
capital

état^M
state

carte^F physique
physical map

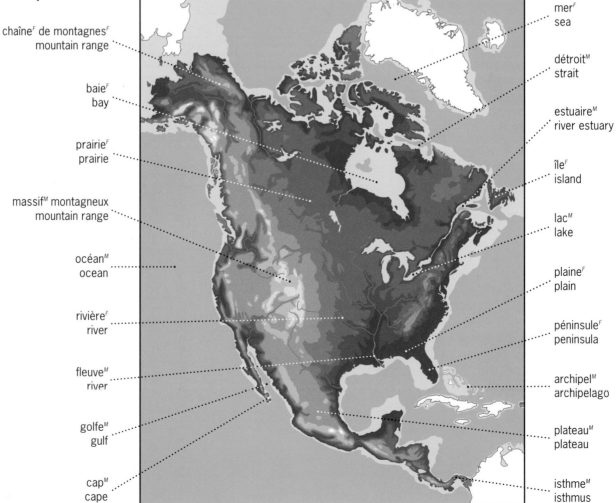

chaîne^F de montagnes^F
mountain range

baie^F
bay

prairie^F
prairie

massif^M montagneux
mountain range

océan^M
ocean

rivière^F
river

fleuve^M
river

golfe^M
gulf

cap^M
cape

mer^F
sea

détroit^M
strait

estuaire^M
river estuary

île^F
island

lac^M
lake

plaine^F
plain

péninsule^F
peninsula

archipel^M
archipelago

plateau^M
plateau

isthme^M
isthmus

carte^F routière
road map

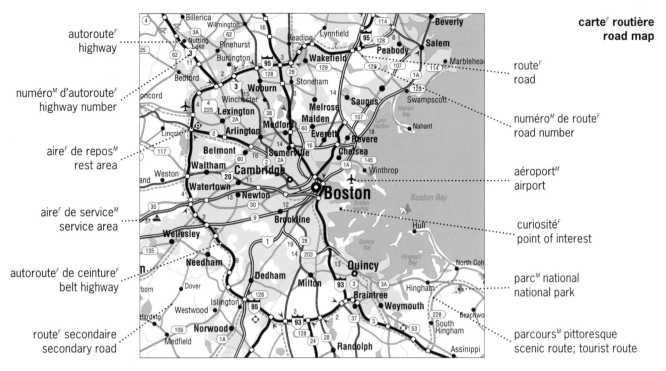

autoroute^F
highway

numéro^M d'autoroute^F
highway number

aire^F de repos^M
rest area

aire^F de service^M
service area

autoroute^F de ceinture^F
belt highway

route^F secondaire
secondary road

route^F
road

numéro^M de route^F
road number

aéroport^M
airport

curiosité^F
point of interest

parc^M national
national park

parcours^M pittoresque
scenic route; tourist route

**LA ROSE^F DES VENTS^M
COMPASS CARD**

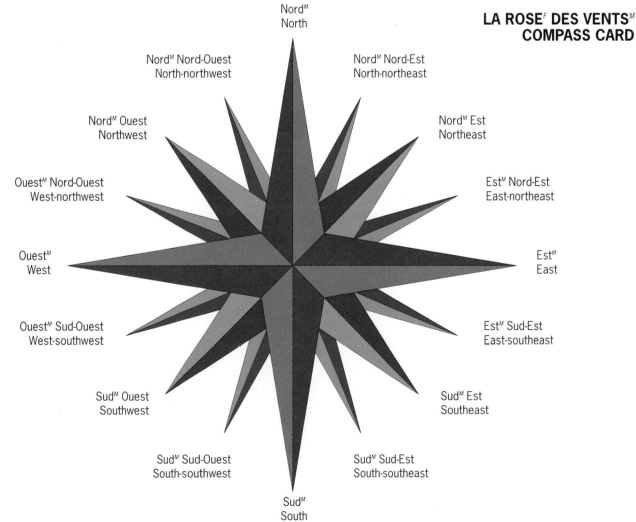

Nord^M
North

Nord^M Nord-Ouest
North-northwest

Nord^M Nord-Est
North-northeast

Nord^M Ouest
Northwest

Nord^M Est
Northeast

Ouest^M Nord-Ouest
West-northwest

Est^M Nord-Est
East-northeast

Ouest^M
West

Est^M
East

Ouest^M Sud-Ouest
West-southwest

Est^M Sud-Est
East-southeast

Sud^M Ouest
Southwest

Sud^M Est
Southeast

Sud^M Sud-Ouest
South-southwest

Sud^M Sud-Est
South-southeast

Sud^M
South

L'ÉCOLOGIE[F]
ECOLOGY

effet[M] de serre[F]
greenhouse effect

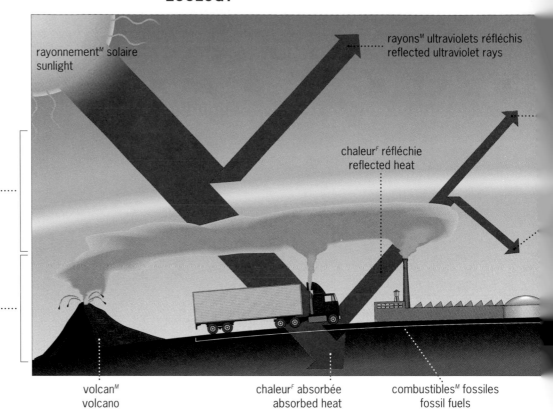

rayonnement[M] solaire
sunlight

rayons[M] ultraviolets réfléchis
reflected ultraviolet rays

chaleur[F] réfléchie
reflected heat

stratosphère[F]
stratosphere

troposphère[F]
troposphere

volcan[M]
volcano

chaleur[F] absorbée
absorbed heat

combustibles[M] fossiles
fossil fuels

chaîne[F] alimentaire
food chain

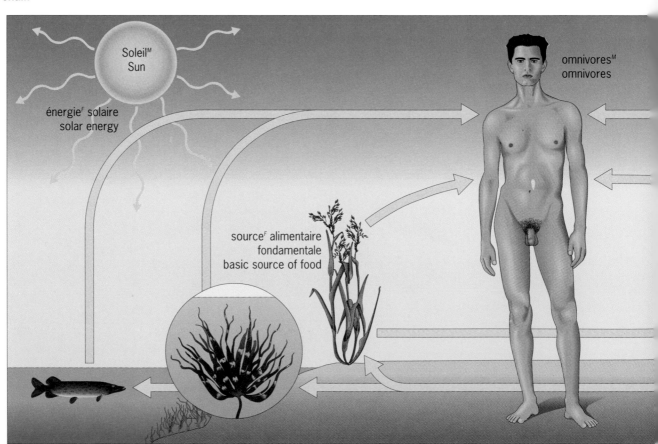

Soleil[M]
Sun

omnivores[M]
omnivores

énergie[F] solaire
solar energy

source[F] alimentaire
fondamentale
basic source of food

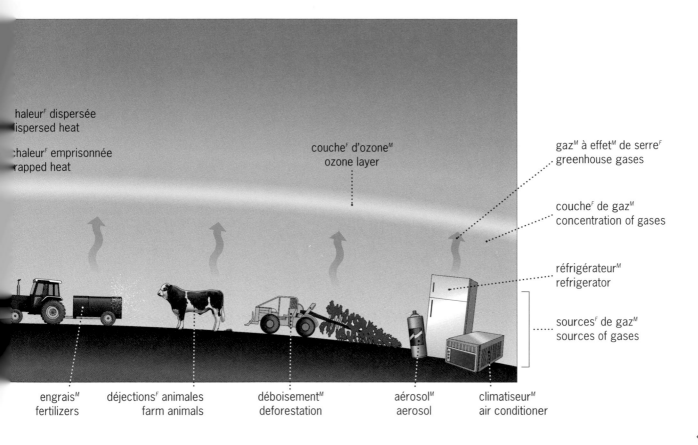

haleur^F dispersée
ispersed heat

haleur^F emprisonnée
rapped heat

couche^F d'ozone^M
ozone layer

gaz^M à effet^M de serre^F
greenhouse gases

couche^F de gaz^M
concentration of gases

réfrigérateur^M
refrigerator

sources^F de gaz^M
sources of gases

engrais^M
fertilizers

déjections^F animales
farm animals

déboisement^M
deforestation

aérosol^M
aerosol

climatiseur^M
air conditioner

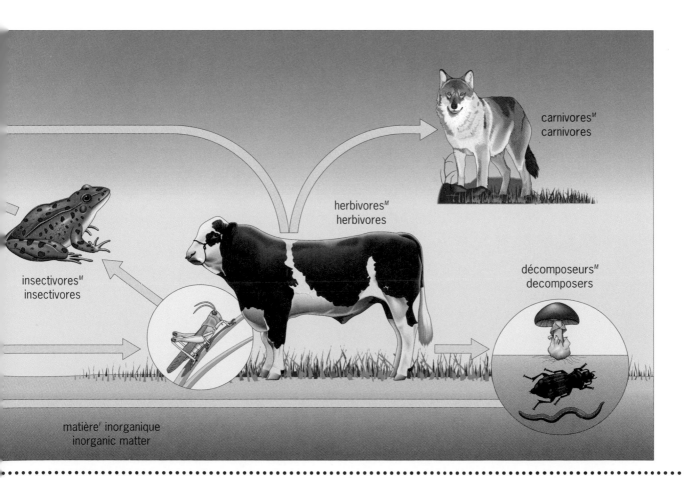

carnivores^M
carnivores

herbivores^M
herbivores

décomposeurs^M
decomposers

insectivores^M
insectivores

matière^F inorganique
inorganic matter

L'ÉCOLOGIE*F*
ECOLOGY

pollution*F* de l'air*M*
atmospheric pollution

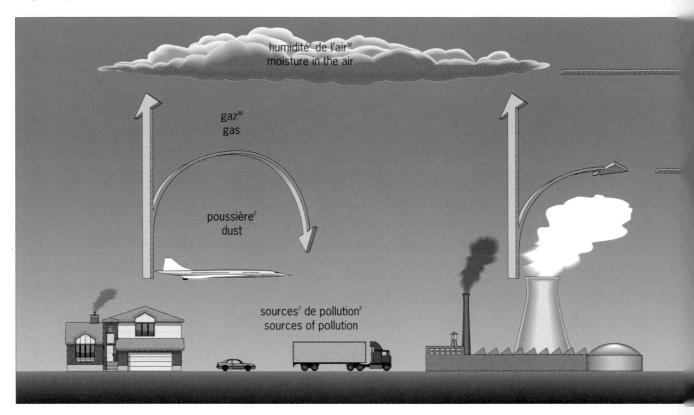

humidité*F* de l'air*M*
moisture in the air

gaz*M*
gas

poussière*F*
dust

sources*F* de pollution*F*
sources of pollution

cycle*M* de l'eau*F*
water cycle

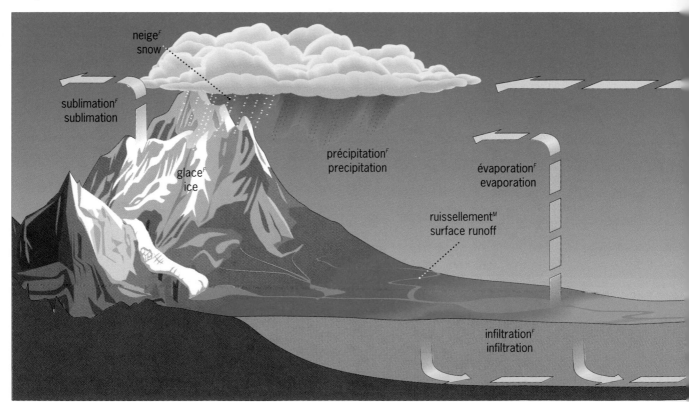

neige*F*
snow

sublimation*F*
sublimation

glace*F*
ice

précipitation*F*
precipitation

évaporation*F*
evaporation

ruissellement*M*
surface runoff

infiltration*F*
infiltration

L'ÉCOLOGIE*F*
ECOLOGY

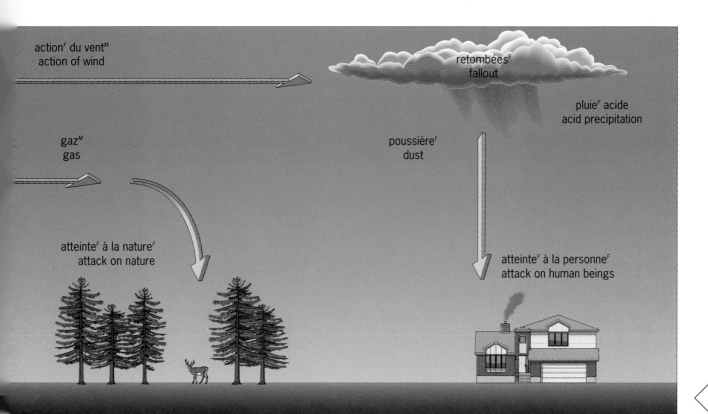

action^F du vent^M
action of wind

retombées^F
fallout

pluie^F acide
acid precipitation

gaz^M
gas

poussière^F
dust

atteinte^F à la nature^F
attack on nature

atteinte^F à la personne^F
attack on human beings

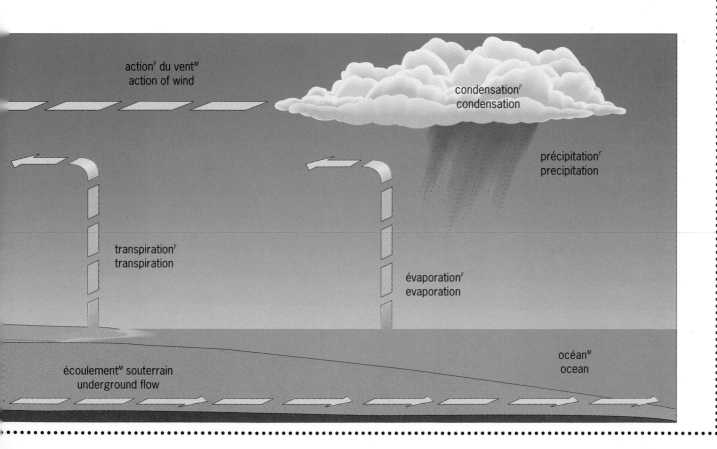

action^F du vent^M
action of wind

condensation^F
condensation

précipitation^F
precipitation

transpiration^F
transpiration

évaporation^F
evaporation

océan^M
ocean

écoulement^M souterrain
underground flow

L'ÉCOLOGIE^F
ECOLOGY

pollution^F des aliments^M au sol^M
food pollution on ground

pluie^F acide
acid rain

pollution^F agricole
farm pollution

pollution^F industrielle
industrial pollution

pollution^F des aliments^M dans l'eau^F
food pollution in water

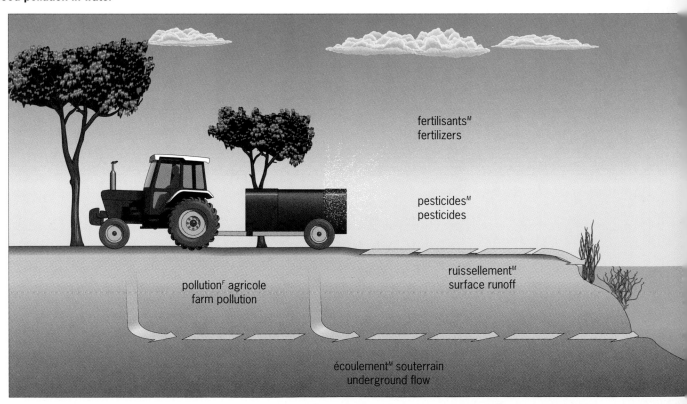

fertilisants^M
fertilizers

pesticides^M
pesticides

ruissellement^M
surface runoff

pollution^F agricole
farm pollution

écoulement^M souterrain
underground flow

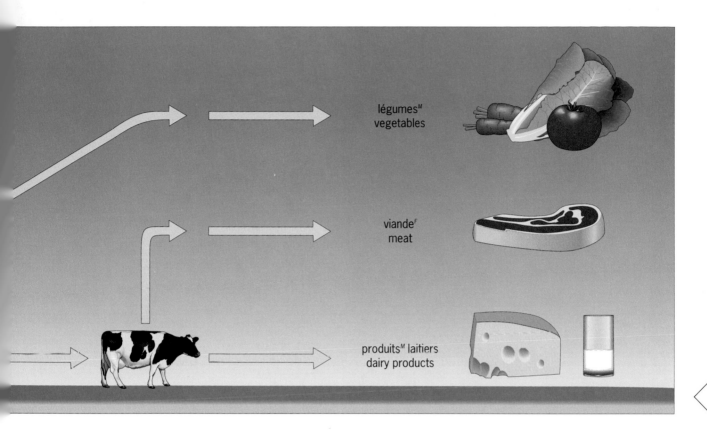

légumes^M
vegetables

viande^F
meat

produits^M laitiers
dairy products

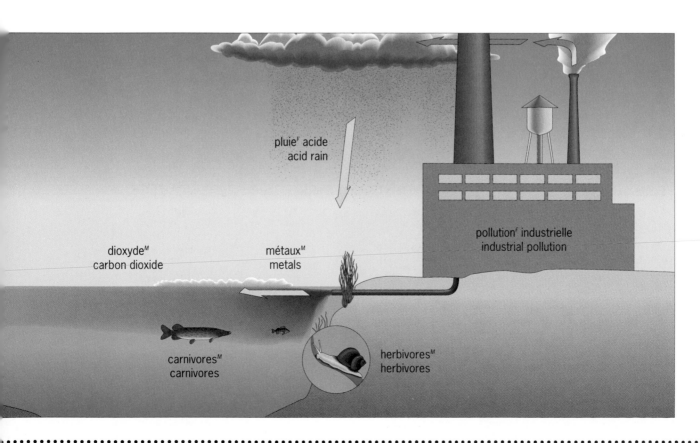

pluie^F acide
acid rain

pollution^F industrielle
industrial pollution

dioxyde^M
carbon dioxide

métaux^M
metals

carnivores^M
carnivores

herbivores^M
herbivores

VEGETABLE KINGDOM

34

LA PLANTE^F ET SON MILIEU^M
PLANT AND SOIL

LE PROFIL^M DU SOL^M
SOIL PROFILE

LA GERMINATIO
GERMINATIO

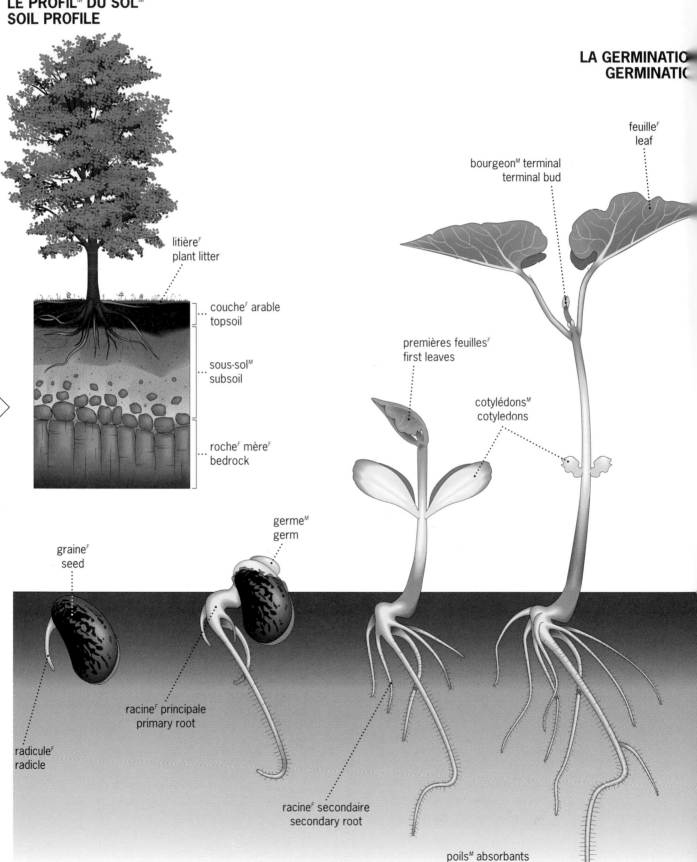

litière^F
plant litter

couche^F arable
topsoil

sous-sol^M
subsoil

roche^F mère^F
bedrock

feuille^F
leaf

bourgeon^M terminal
terminal bud

premières feuilles^F
first leaves

cotylédons^M
cotyledons

germe^M
germ

graine^F
seed

racine^F principale
primary root

radicule^F
radicle

racine^F secondaire
secondary root

poils^M absorbants
root hairs

LE CHAMPIGNON[M]
MUSHROOM

structure[F] d'un champignon[M]
structure of a mushroom

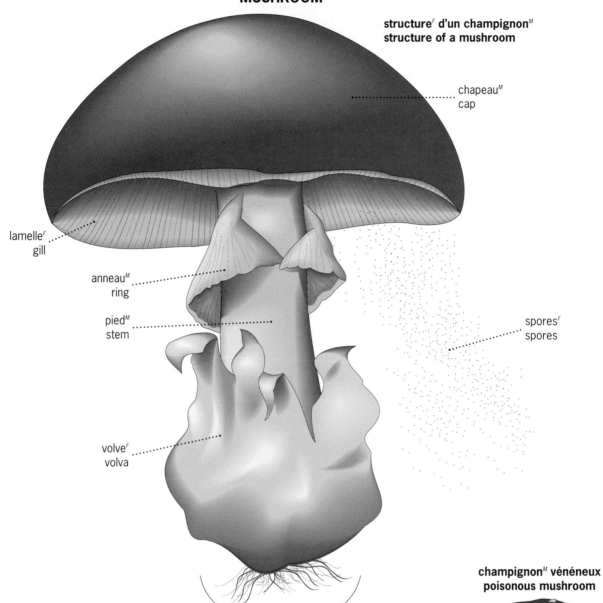

chapeau[M]
cap

lamelle[F]
gill

anneau[M]
ring

pied[M]
stem

spores[F]
spores

volve[F]
volva

mycélium[M]
mycelium

champignon[M] vénéneux
poisonous mushroom

champignon[M] comestible
edible mushroom

champignon[M] de couche[F]
cultivated mushroom

champignon[M] mortel
deadly mushroom

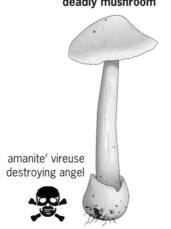

amanite[F] vireuse
destroying angel

fausse oronge[F]
fly agaric

LA STRUCTURE^F D'UNE PLANTE^F
STRUCTURE OF A PLANT

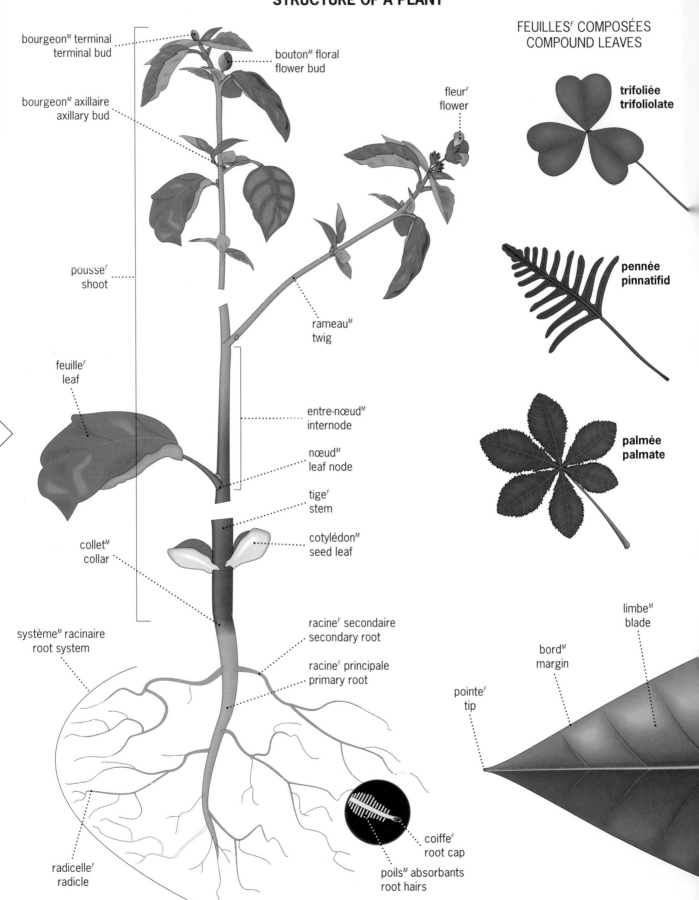

bourgeon^M terminal
terminal bud

bouton^M floral
flower bud

bourgeon^M axillaire
axillary bud

fleur^F
flower

pousse^F
shoot

rameau^M
twig

feuille^F
leaf

entre-nœud^M
internode

nœud^M
leaf node

tige^F
stem

collet^M
collar

cotylédon^M
seed leaf

système^M racinaire
root system

racine^F secondaire
secondary root

racine^F principale
primary root

radicelle^F
radicle

coiffe^F
root cap

poils^M absorbants
root hairs

FEUILLES^F COMPOSÉES
COMPOUND LEAVES

**trifoliée
trifoliolate**

**pennée
pinnatifid**

**palmée
palmate**

limbe^M
blade

bord^M
margin

pointe^F
tip

FEUILLES^F SIMPLES
SIMPLE LEAVES

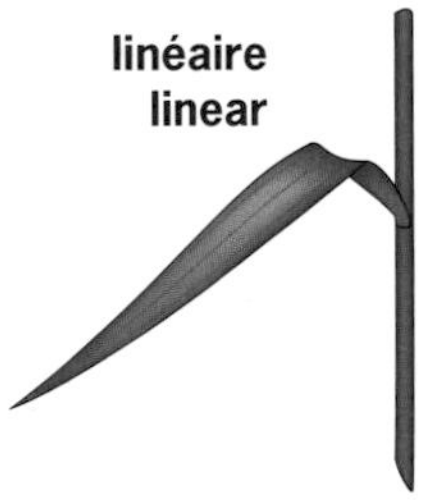

BORD^M D'UNE FEUILLE^F
LEAF MARGINS

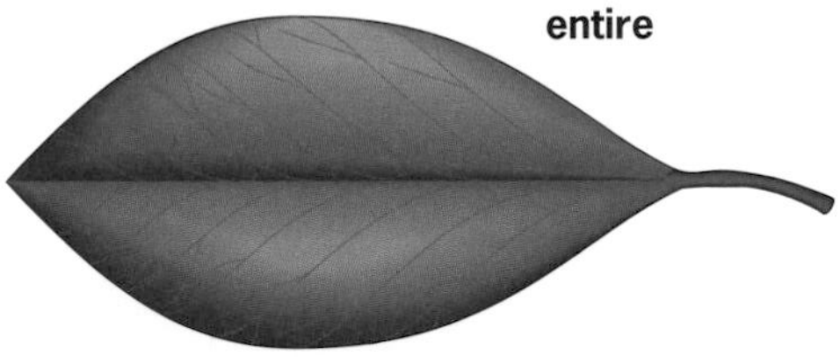

linéaire
linear

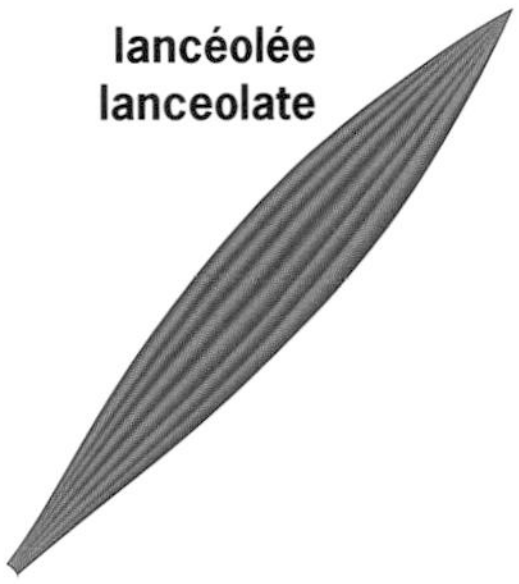

entier
entire

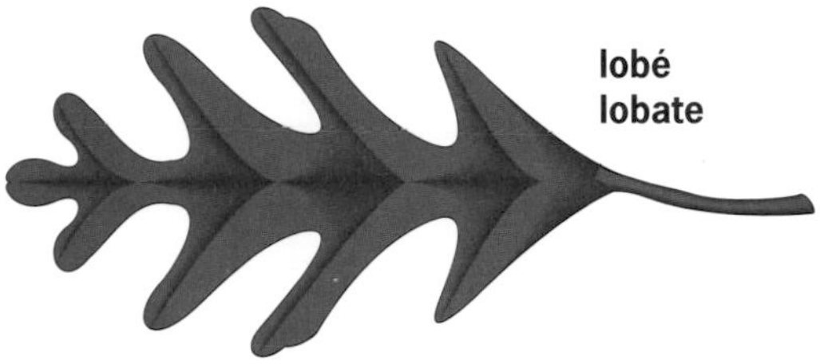

cilié
ciliate

lancéolée
lanceolate

lobé
lobate

crénelé
crenate

arrondie
orbiculate

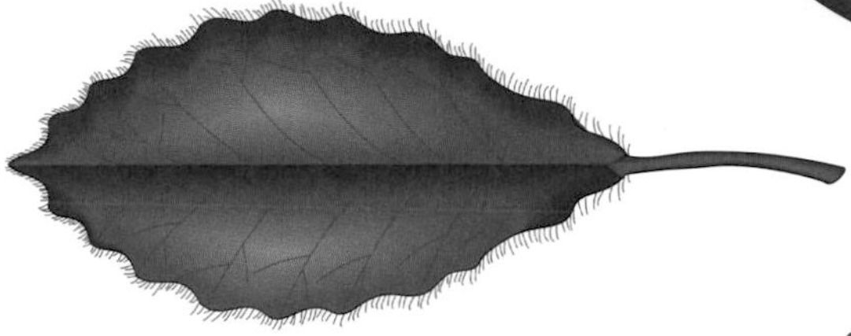

denté
dentate

nervure^F secondaire
vein

nervure^F principale
midrib

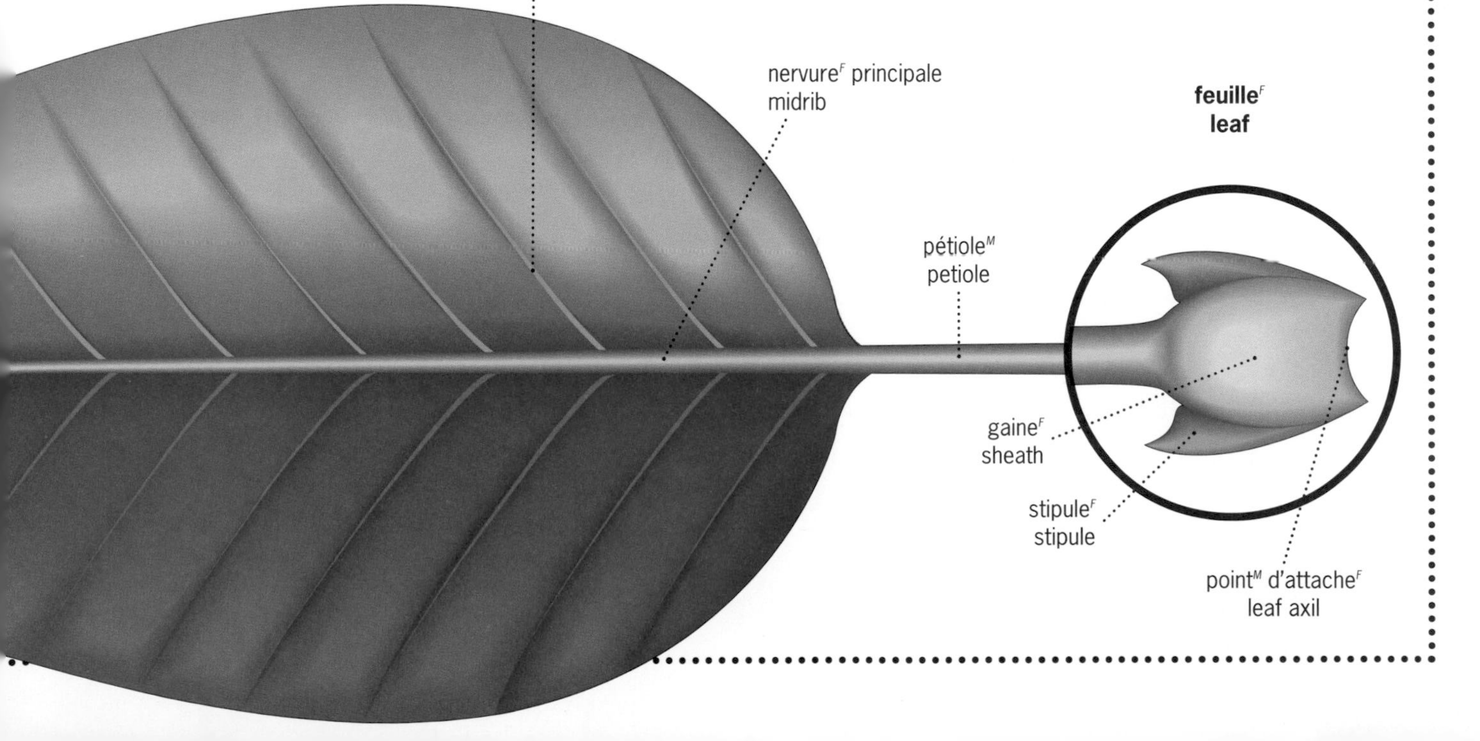

feuille^F
leaf

pétiole^M
petiole

gaine^F
sheath

stipule^F
stipule

point^M d'attache^F
leaf axil

VEGETABLE KINGDOM

LES FLEURS^F
FLOWERS

structure^F d'une fleur^F
structure of a flower

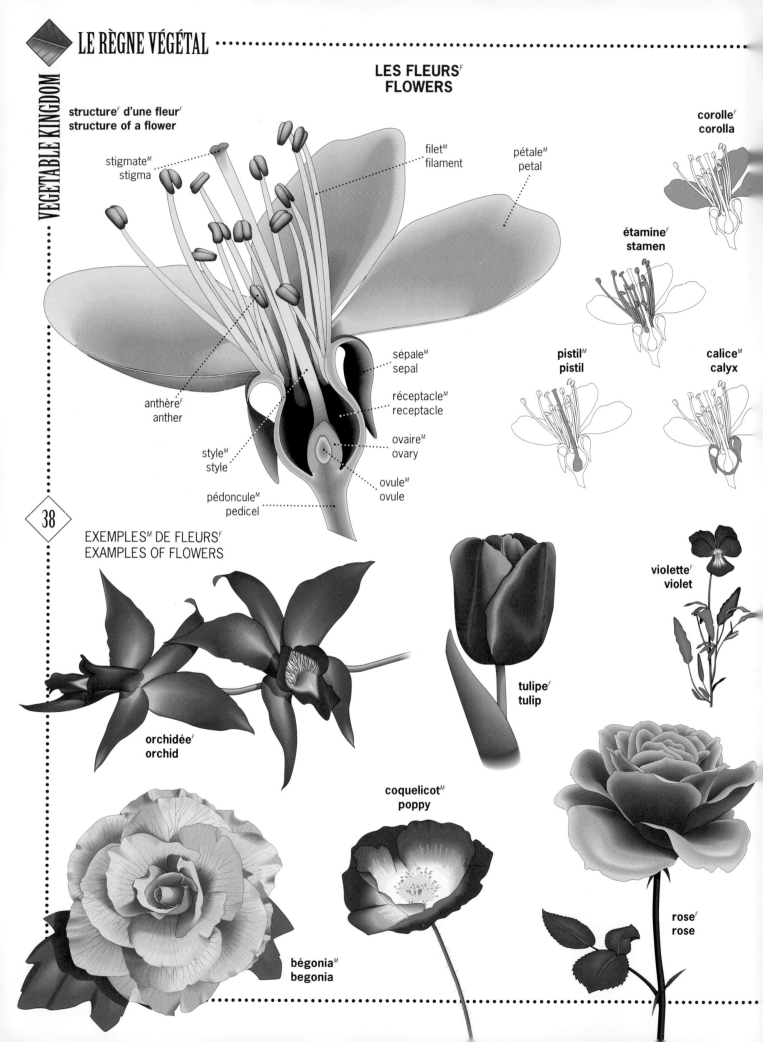

stigmate^M
stigma

filet^M
filament

pétale^M
petal

corolle^F
corolla

étamine^F
stamen

sépale^M
sepal

réceptacle^M
receptacle

pistil^M
pistil

calice^M
calyx

anthère^F
anther

ovaire^M
ovary

style^M
style

ovule^M
ovule

pédoncule^M
pedicel

38

EXEMPLES^M DE FLEURS^F
EXAMPLES OF FLOWERS

violette^F
violet

orchidée^F
orchid

tulipe^F
tulip

coquelicot^M
poppy

rose^F
rose

bégonia^M
begonia

lis^M
lily

tournesol^M
sunflower

muguet^M
lily of the valley

39

crocus^M
crocus

œillet^M
carnation

jonquille^F
daffodil

L'ARBRE[M]
TREE

structure[F] d'un arbre[M]
structure of a tree

ramure[F]
branches

feuillage[M]
foliage

cime[F]
top

houppier[M]
crown

rameau[M]
branch

ramille[F]
twig

branche[F] maîtresse
limb

racine[F] pivotante
taproot

tronc[M]
trunk

racine[F] traçante
shallow root

chevelu[M]
root-hair zone

radicelle[F]
radicle

souche[F]
stump

rejet[M]
shoot

coupe[F] transversale du tronc[M]
cross section of a trunk

cerne[M] annuel
annual ring

moelle[F]
pith

écorce[F]
outer bark

liber[M]
inner bark

bois[M] de cœur[M]
heartwood

cambium[M]
cambium

aubier[M]
sapwood

EMPLES^M D'ARBRES^M
AMPLES OF TREES

peuplier^M
poplar

chêne^M
oak

érable^M
maple

palmier^M
palm tree

saule^M pleureur
weeping willow

bouleau^M
birch

42

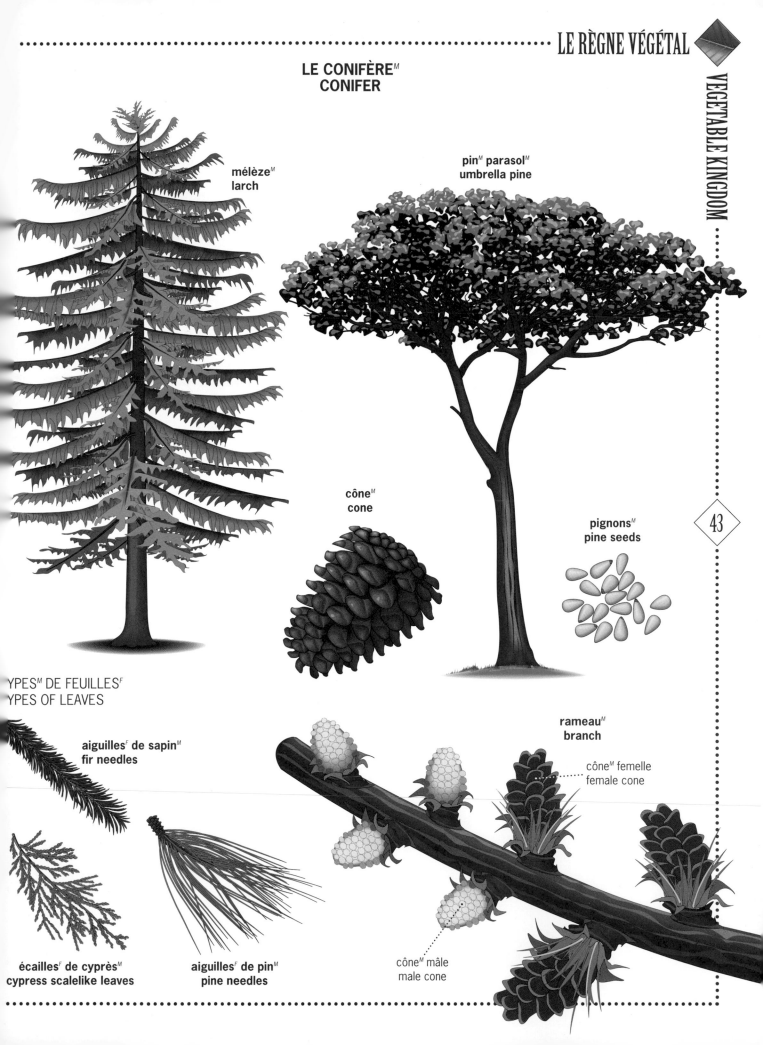

LE CONIFÈRE^M
CONIFER

mélèze^M
larch

pin^M **parasol**^M
umbrella pine

cône^M
cone

pignons^M
pine seeds

YPES^M DE FEUILLES^F
YPES OF LEAVES

rameau^M
branch

aiguilles^F **de sapin**^M
fir needles

cône^M **femelle**
female cone

écailles^F **de cyprès**^M
cypress scalelike leaves

aiguilles^F **de pin**^M
pine needles

cône^M **mâle**
male cone

LES FRUITS^M CHARNUS: LES BAIES^F
FLESHY FRUITS: BERRY FRUITS

coupe^F d'une baie^F
section of a berry

PRINCIPALES VARIÉTÉS^F DE BA
MAJOR TYPES OF BERR

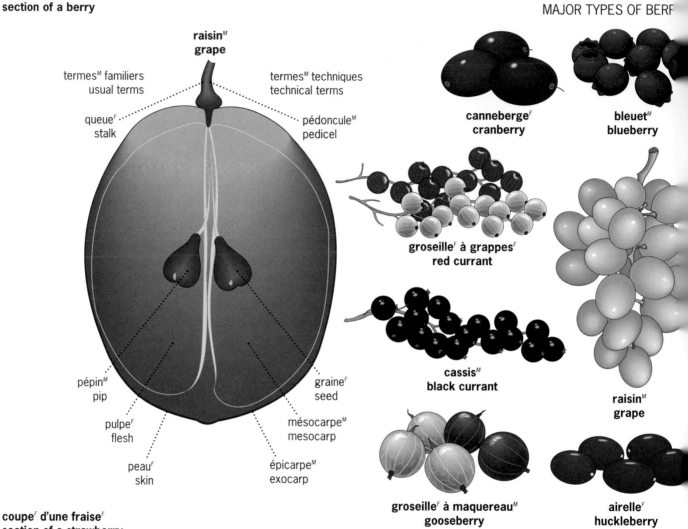

raisin^M
grape

termes^M familiers
usual terms

termes^M techniques
technical terms

queue^F
stalk

pédoncule^M
pedicel

pépin^M
pip

graine^F
seed

pulpe^F
flesh

mésocarpe^M
mesocarp

peau^F
skin

épicarpe^M
exocarp

canneberge^F
cranberry

bleuet^M
blueberry

groseille^F à grappes^F
red currant

cassis^M
black currant

raisin^M
grape

groseille^F à maquereau^M
gooseberry

airelle^F
huckleberry

coupe^F d'une fraise^F
section of a strawberry

coupe^F d'une framboi
section of a raspber

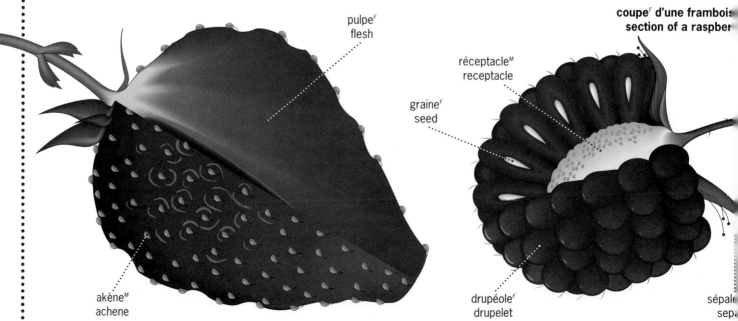

pulpe^F
flesh

réceptacle^M
receptacle

graine^F
seed

akène^M
achene

drupéole^F
drupelet

sépale
sepa

LES FRUITS^M CHARNUS À NOYAU^M
FLESHY STONE FRUITS

coupe^F d'un fruit^M à noyau^M
section of a stone fruit

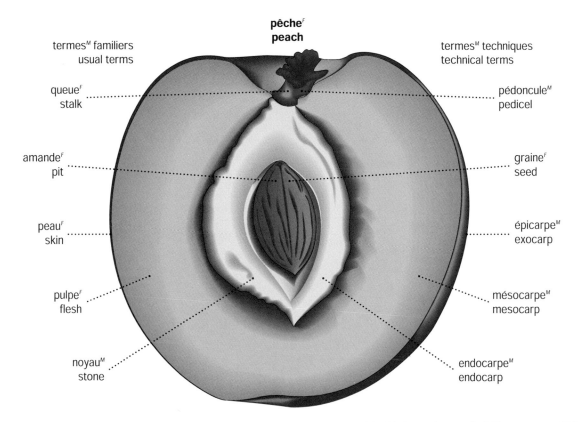

pêche^F
peach

termes^M familiers
usual terms

termes^M techniques
technical terms

queue^F
stalk

pédoncule^M
pedicel

amande^F
pit

graine^F
seed

peau^F
skin

épicarpe^M
exocarp

pulpe^F
flesh

mésocarpe^M
mesocarp

noyau^M
stone

endocarpe^M
endocarp

PRINCIPALES VARIÉTÉS^F DE FRUITS^M À NOYAU^M
MAJOR TYPES OF STONE FRUITS

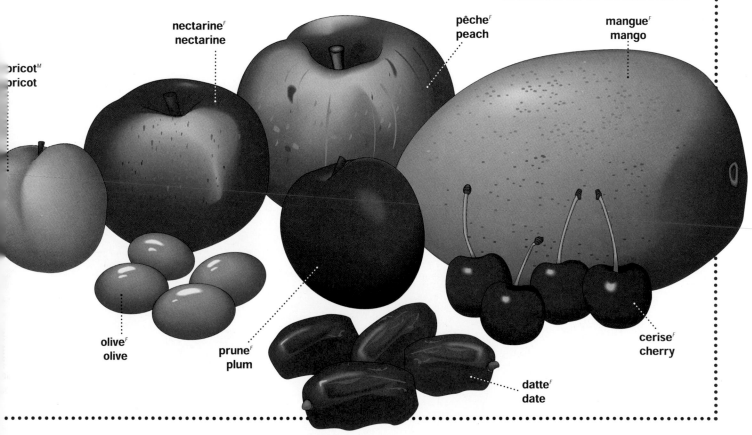

nectarine^F
nectarine

pêche^F
peach

mangue^F
mango

pricot^M
pricot

olive^F
olive

prune^F
plum

datte^F
date

cerise^F
cherry

LES FRUITS^M CHARNUS À PÉPINS^M
FLESHY POME FRUITS

coupe^F d'un fruit^M à pépins^M
section of a pome fruit

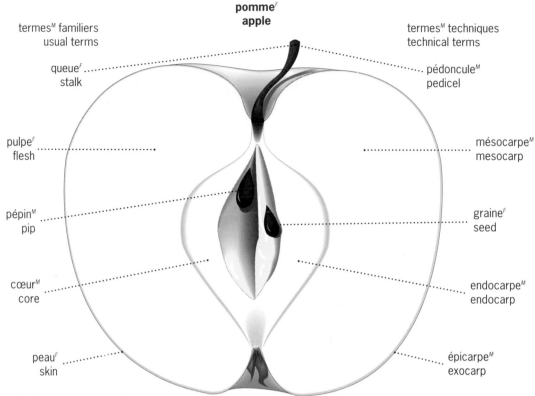

pomme^F
apple

termes^M familiers
usual terms

termes^M techniques
technical terms

queue^F ⋯⋯
stalk

pédoncule^M
pedicel

pulpe^F ⋯⋯
flesh

mésocarpe^M
mesocarp

pépin^M ⋯⋯
pip

graine^F
seed

cœur^M
core

endocarpe^M
endocarp

peau^F ⋯⋯
skin

épicarpe^M
exocarp

PRINCIPALES VARIÉTÉS^F DE FRUITS^M À PÉPINS^M
MAJOR TYPES OF POME FRUITS

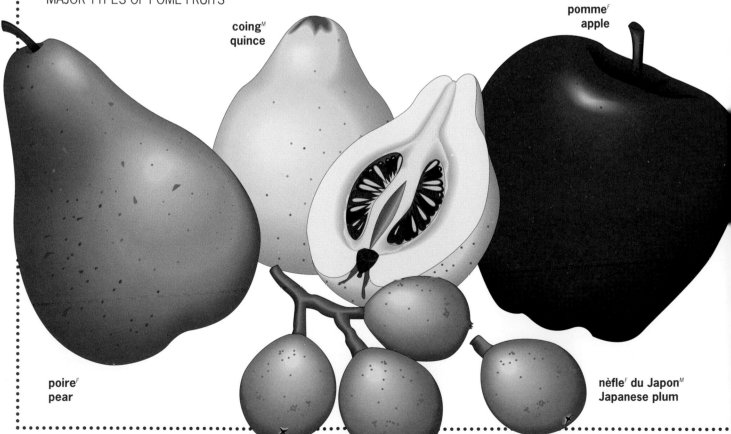

coing^M
quince

pomme^F
apple

poire^F
pear

nèfle^F du Japon^M
Japanese plum

LES FRUITS^M CHARNUS: LES AGRUMES^M
FLESHY FRUITS: CITRUS FRUITS

coupe^F d'un agrume^M
section of a citrus fruit

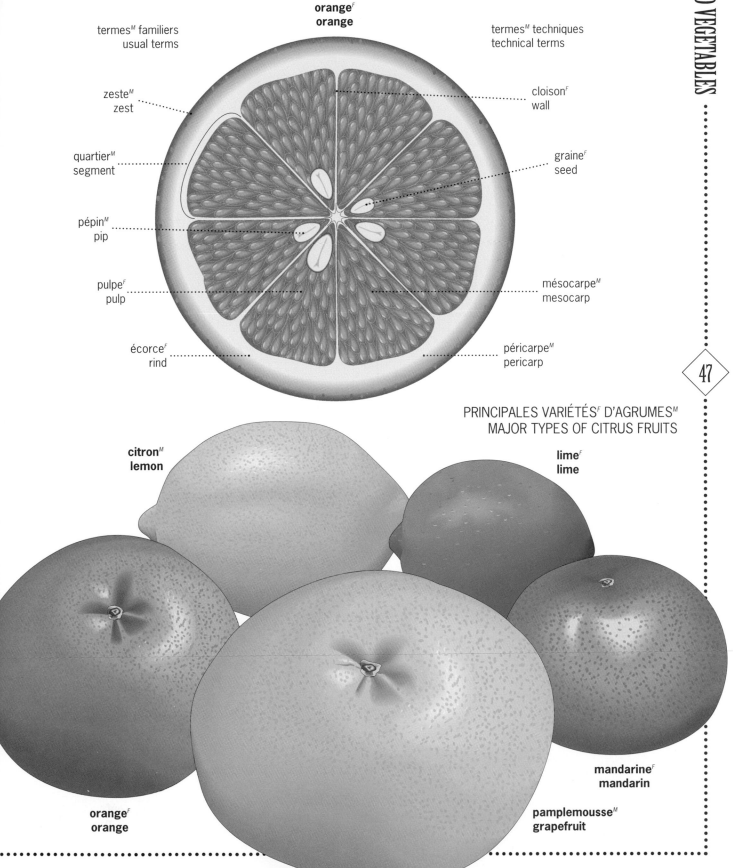

orange^F
orange

termes^M familiers
usual terms

termes^M techniques
technical terms

zeste^M
zest

cloison^F
wall

quartier^M
segment

graine^F
seed

pépin^M
pip

pulpe^F
pulp

mésocarpe^M
mesocarp

écorce^F
rind

péricarpe^M
pericarp

PRINCIPALES VARIÉTÉS^F D'AGRUMES^M
MAJOR TYPES OF CITRUS FRUITS

citron^M
lemon

lime^F
lime

mandarine^F
mandarin

orange^F
orange

pamplemousse^M
grapefruit

LES FRUITS ET LÉGUMES

LES FRUITS^M TROPICAUX
TROPICAL FRUITS

PRINCIPAUX FRUITS^M TROPICAUX
MAJOR TYPES OF TROPICAL FRUITS

litchi^M
litchi

kiwi^M
kiwi

goyave^F
guava

kaki^M
Japanese persimmon

figue^F **de Barbarie**
Indian fig

chérimole^F
cherimoya

figue^F
fig

papaye^F
papaya

grenade^F
pomegranate

banane^F
banana

ananas^M
pineapple

avocat^M
avocado

48

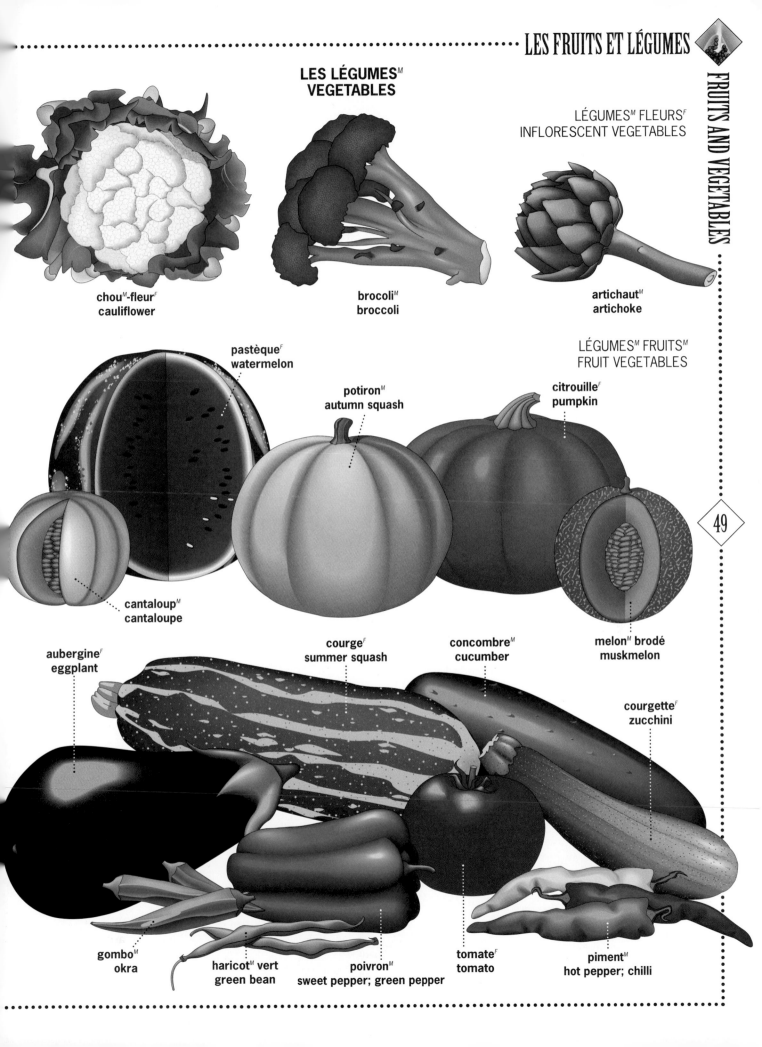

LES LÉGUMES^M
VEGETABLES

LÉGUMES^M FLEURS^F
INFLORESCENT VEGETABLES

chou^M-fleur^F
cauliflower

brocoli^M
broccoli

artichaut^M
artichoke

LÉGUMES^M FRUITS^M
FRUIT VEGETABLES

pastèque^F
watermelon

potiron^M
autumn squash

citrouille^F
pumpkin

cantaloup^M
cantaloupe

melon^M brodé
muskmelon

aubergine^F
eggplant

courge^F
summer squash

concombre^M
cucumber

courgette^F
zucchini

gombo^M
okra

haricot^M vert
green bean

poivron^M
sweet pepper; green pepper

tomate^F
tomato

piment^M
hot pepper; chilli

49

LES LÉGUMES^M
VEGETABLES

coupe^F d'un bulbe^M
section of a bulb

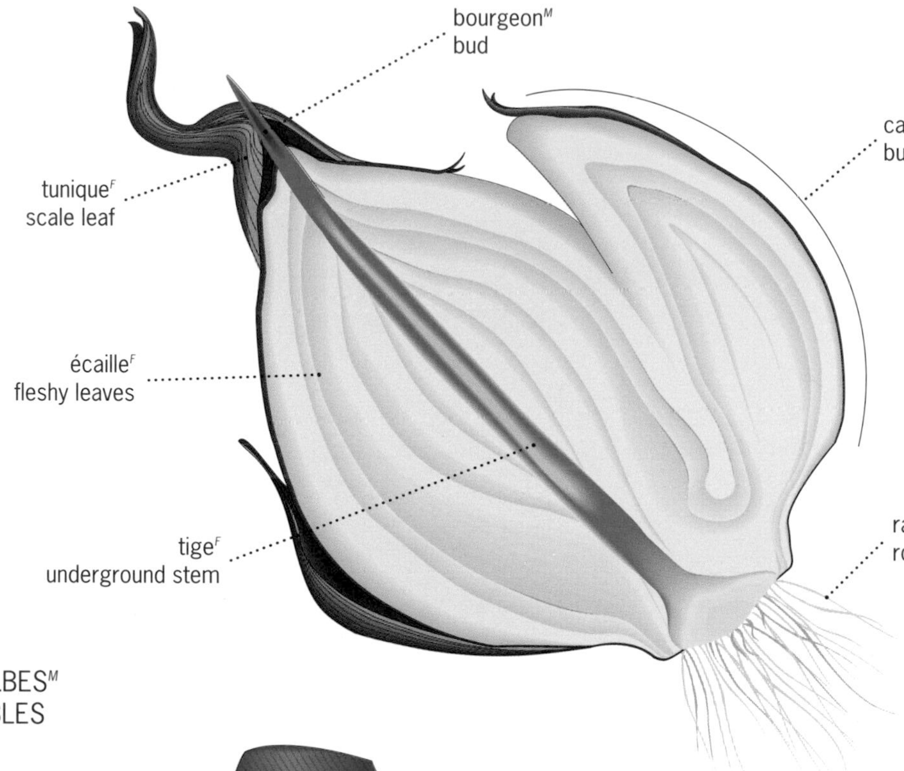

bourgeon^M
bud

caïeu^M
bulbil

tunique^F
scale leaf

écaille^F
fleshy leaves

racine^F
root

tige^F
underground stem

LÉGUMES^M BULBES^M
BULB VEGETABLES

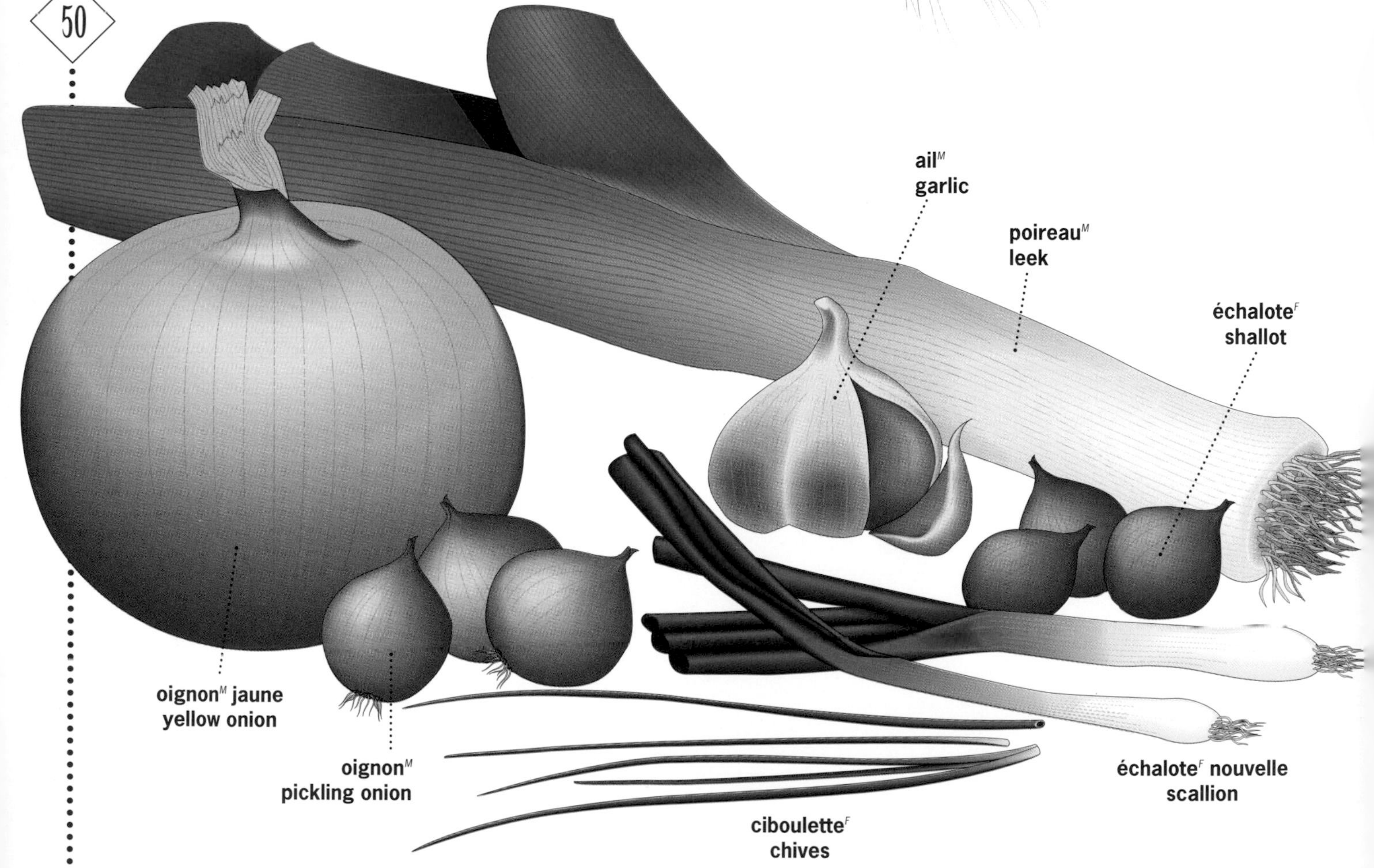

ail^M
garlic

poireau^M
leek

échalote^F
shallot

oignon^M jaune
yellow onion

oignon^M
pickling onion

ciboulette^F
chives

échalote^F nouvelle
scallion

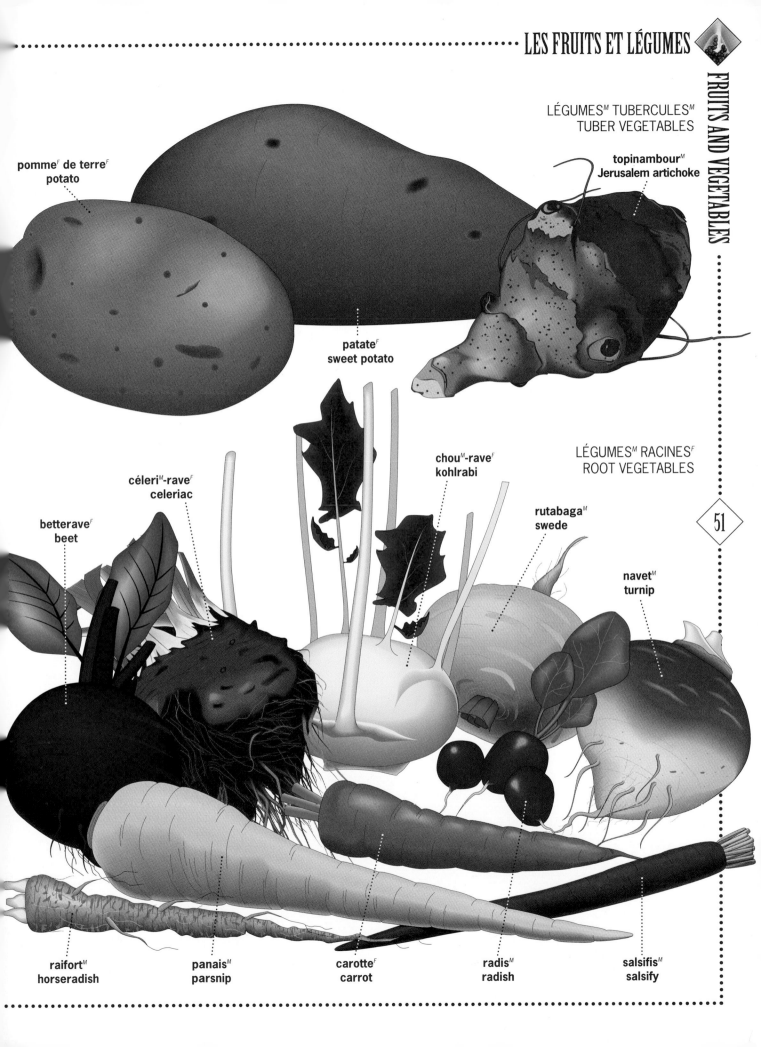

LÉGUMES^M TUBERCULES^M
TUBER VEGETABLES

pomme^F de terre^F
potato

topinambour^M
Jerusalem artichoke

patate^F
sweet potato

chou^M-rave^F
kohlrabi

LÉGUMES^M RACINES^F
ROOT VEGETABLES

céleri^M-rave^F
celeriac

rutabaga^M
swede

betterave^F
beet

navet^M
turnip

51

raifort^M
horseradish

panais^M
parsnip

carotte^F
carrot

radis^M
radish

salsifis^M
salsify

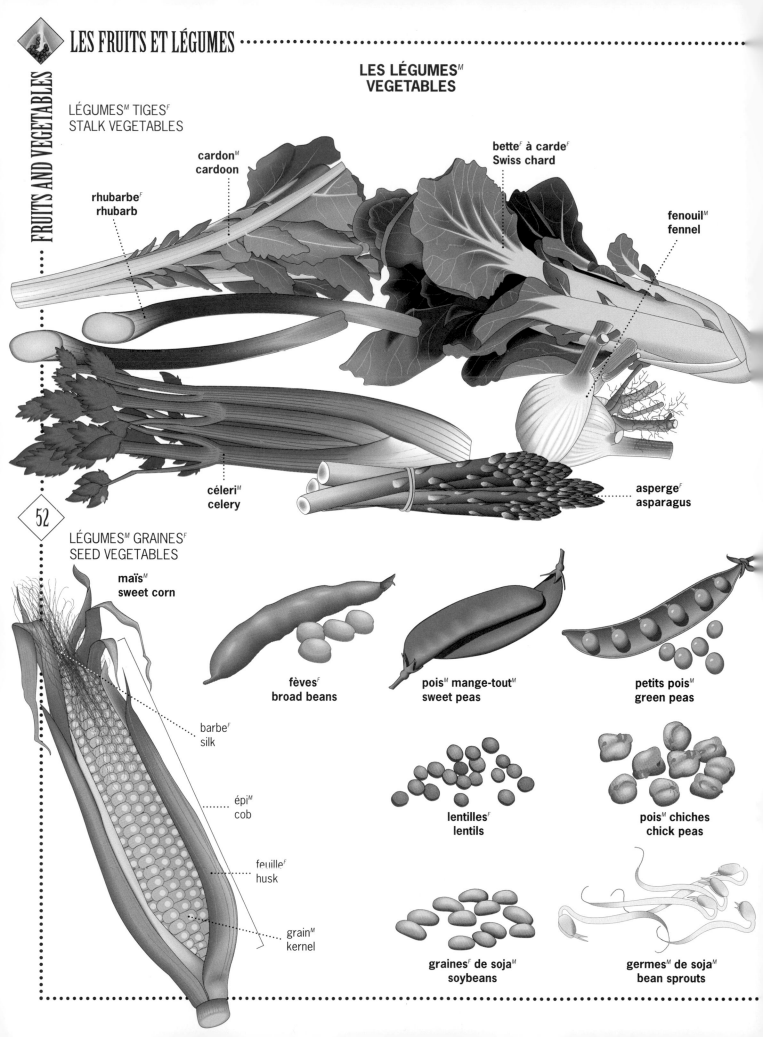

FRUITS AND VEGETABLES

LES LÉGUMES^M
VEGETABLES

LÉGUMES^M TIGES^F
STALK VEGETABLES

cardon^M
cardoon

bette^F **à carde**^F
Swiss chard

fenouil^M
fennel

rhubarbe^F
rhubarb

céleri^M
celery

asperge^F
asparagus

52

LÉGUMES^M GRAINES^F
SEED VEGETABLES

maïs^M
sweet corn

fèves^F
broad beans

pois^M **mange-tout**^M
sweet peas

petits pois^M
green peas

barbe^F
silk

épi^M
cob

feuille^F
husk

grain^M
kernel

lentilles^F
lentils

pois^M **chiches**
chick peas

graines^F **de soja**^M
soybeans

germes^M **de soja**^M
bean sprouts

LÉGUMES^M FEUILLES^F
LEAF VEGETABLES

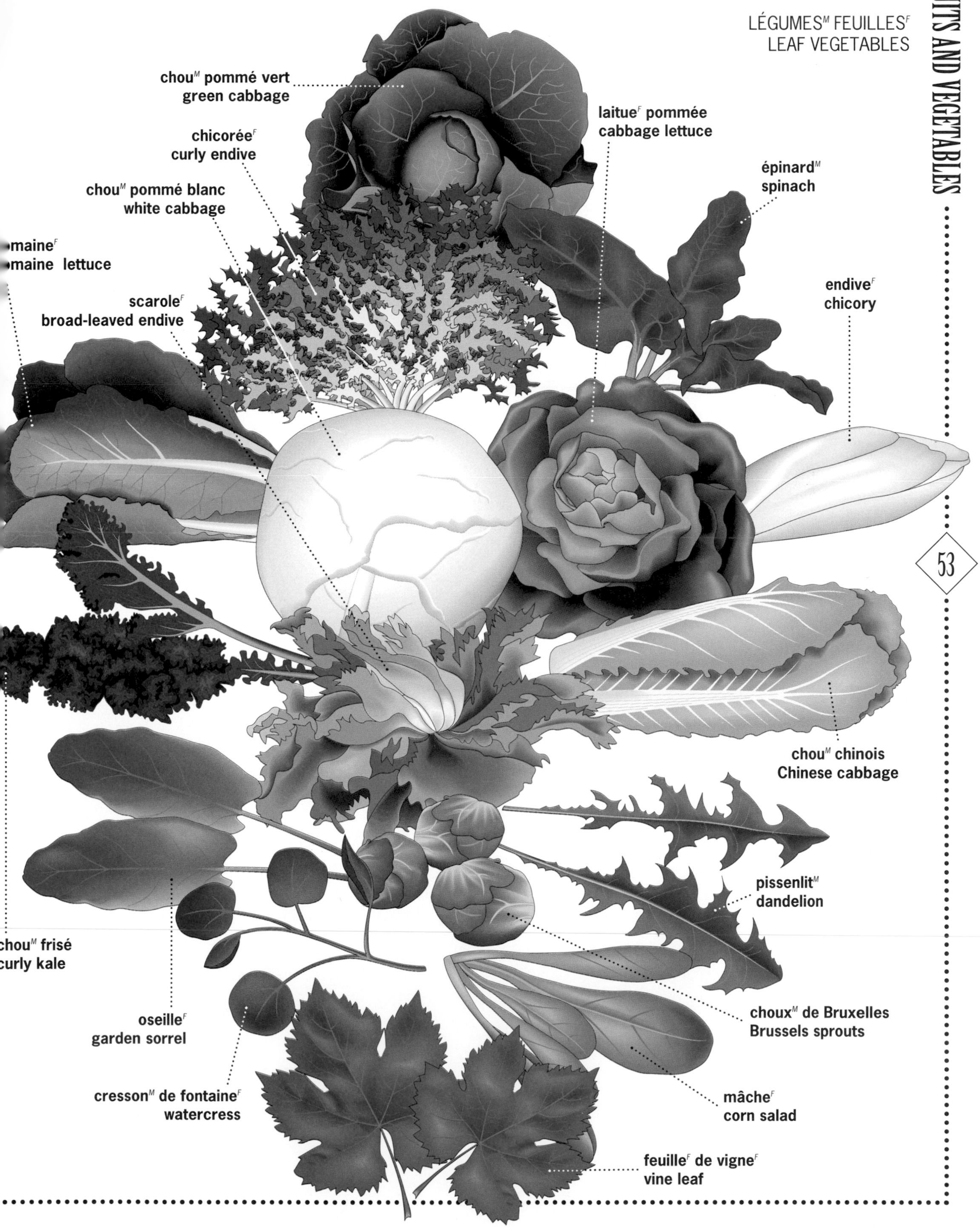

chou^M pommé vert
green cabbage

laitue^F pommée
cabbage lettuce

chicorée^F
curly endive

épinard^M
spinach

chou^M pommé blanc
white cabbage

maine^F
maine lettuce

endive^F
chicory

scarole^F
broad-leaved endive

chou^M chinois
Chinese cabbage

chou^M frisé
curly kale

pissenlit^M
dandelion

oseille^F
garden sorrel

choux^M de Bruxelles
Brussels sprouts

cresson^M de fontaine^F
watercress

mâche^F
corn salad

feuille^F de vigne^F
vine leaf

53

LE JARDINAGE^F
GARDENING

transplantoir^M
trowel

fourche^F **à fleurs**^F
hand fork

griffe^F **à fleurs**^F
hand cultivator

sécateur^M
pruning shears

tondeuse^F **à gazon**^M
lawnmower

sélecteur^M de régime^M
speed control

clé^F de contact^M
ignition key

guidon^M
handle

poignée^F de sécurité^F
safety handle

arrosoir
watering can

bac^M de ramassage^M
grassbox

démarreur^M manuel
starter

moteur^M
motor

déflecteur^M
deflector

carter^M
casing

54

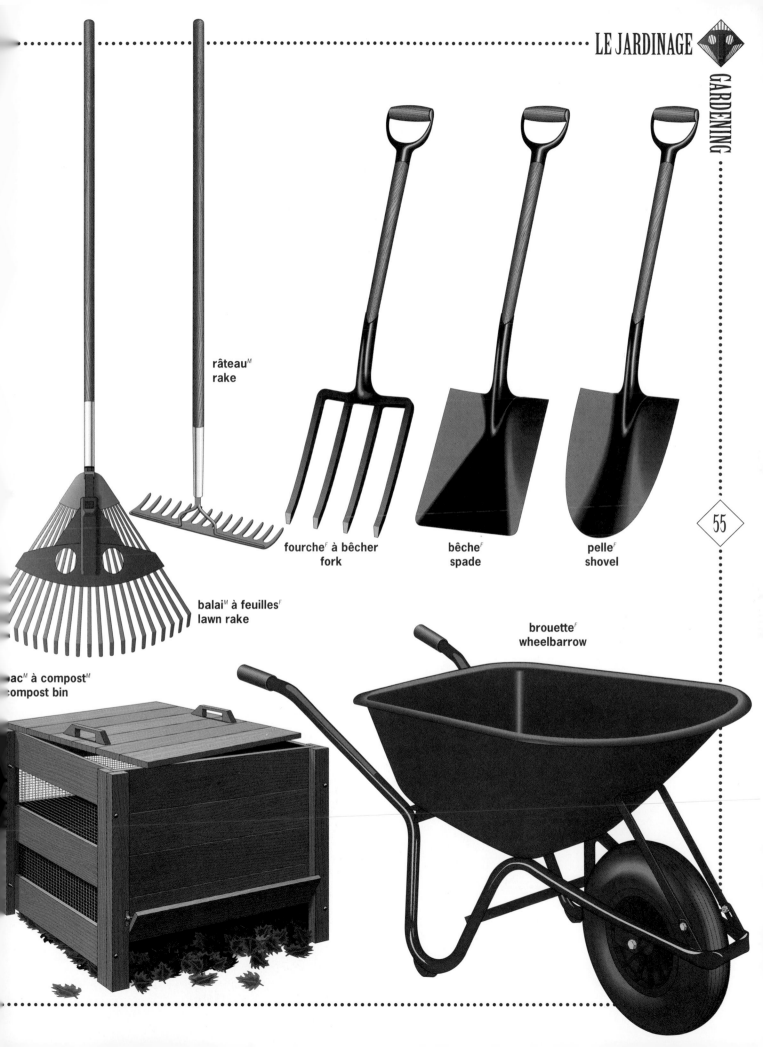

râteau^M
rake

fourche^F à bêcher
fork

bêche^F
spade

pelle^F
shovel

balai^M à feuilles^F
lawn rake

bac^M à compost^M
compost bin

brouette^F
wheelbarrow

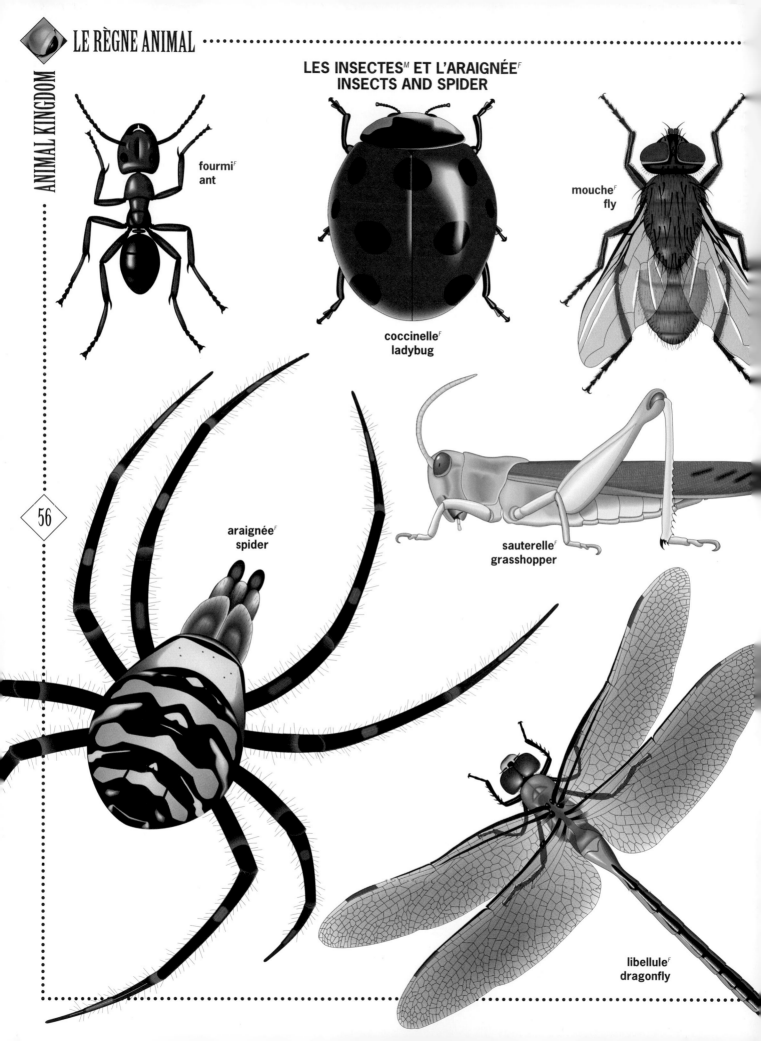

LES INSECTES^M ET L'ARAIGNÉE^F
INSECTS AND SPIDER

fourmi^F
ant

coccinelle^F
ladybug

mouche^F
fly

araignée^F
spider

sauterelle^F
grasshopper

56

libellule^F
dragonfly

LE PAPILLON^M
BUTTERFLY

chrysalide^F
chrysalis

nille^F
erpillar

œil^M simple
simple eye

mandibule^F
mandible

patte^F ambulatoire
walking leg

atte^F ventouse
proleg

aile^F antérieure
forewing

nervure^F
wing vein

cellule^F
cell

aile^F postérieure
hind wing

thorax^M
thorax

tête^F
head

57

antenne^F
antenna

palpe^M labial
labial palp

œil^M composé
compound eye

trompe^F
proboscis

patte^F antérieure
foreleg

patte^F médiane
middle leg

griffe^F
claw

abdomen^M
abdomen

patte^F postérieure
hind leg

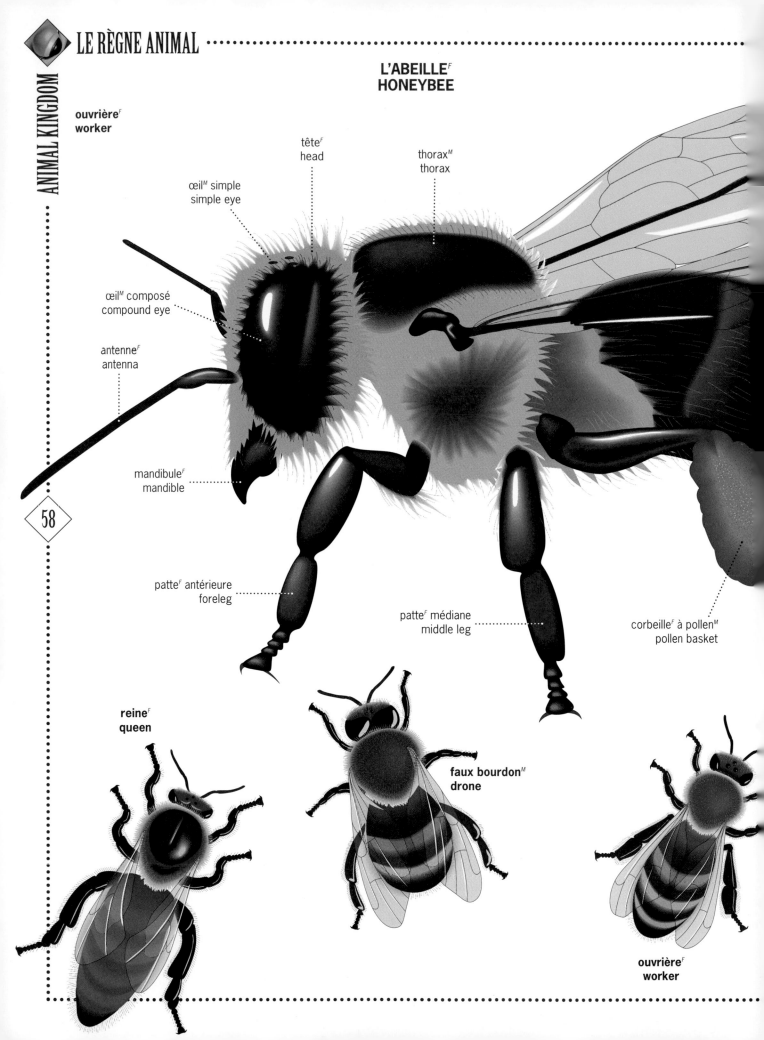

L'ABEILLE^F
HONEYBEE

ouvrière^F
worker

tête^F
head

thorax^M
thorax

œil^M simple
simple eye

œil^M composé
compound eye

antenne^F
antenna

mandibule^F
mandible

58

patte^F antérieure
foreleg

patte^F médiane
middle leg

corbeille^F à pollen^M
pollen basket

reine^F
queen

faux bourdon^M
drone

ouvrière^F
worker

ouvrière^F
worker

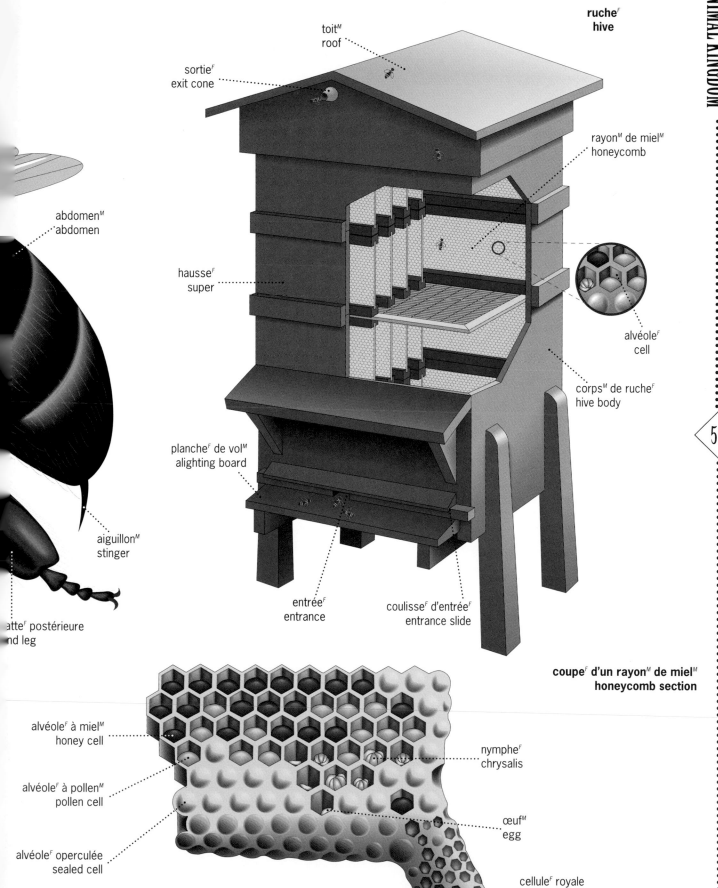

ruche^F
hive

toit^M
roof

sortie^F
exit cone

rayon^M de miel^M
honeycomb

abdomen^M
abdomen

hausse^F
super

alvéole^F
cell

corps^M de ruche^F
hive body

aiguillon^M
stinger

planche^F de vol^M
alighting board

atte^F postérieure
nd leg

entrée^F
entrance

coulisse^F d'entrée^F
entrance slide

coupe^F **d'un rayon**^M **de miel**^M
honeycomb section

alvéole^F à miel^M
honey cell

nymphe^F
chrysalis

alvéole^F à pollen^M
pollen cell

œuf^M
egg

alvéole^F operculée
sealed cell

cellule^F royale
queen cell

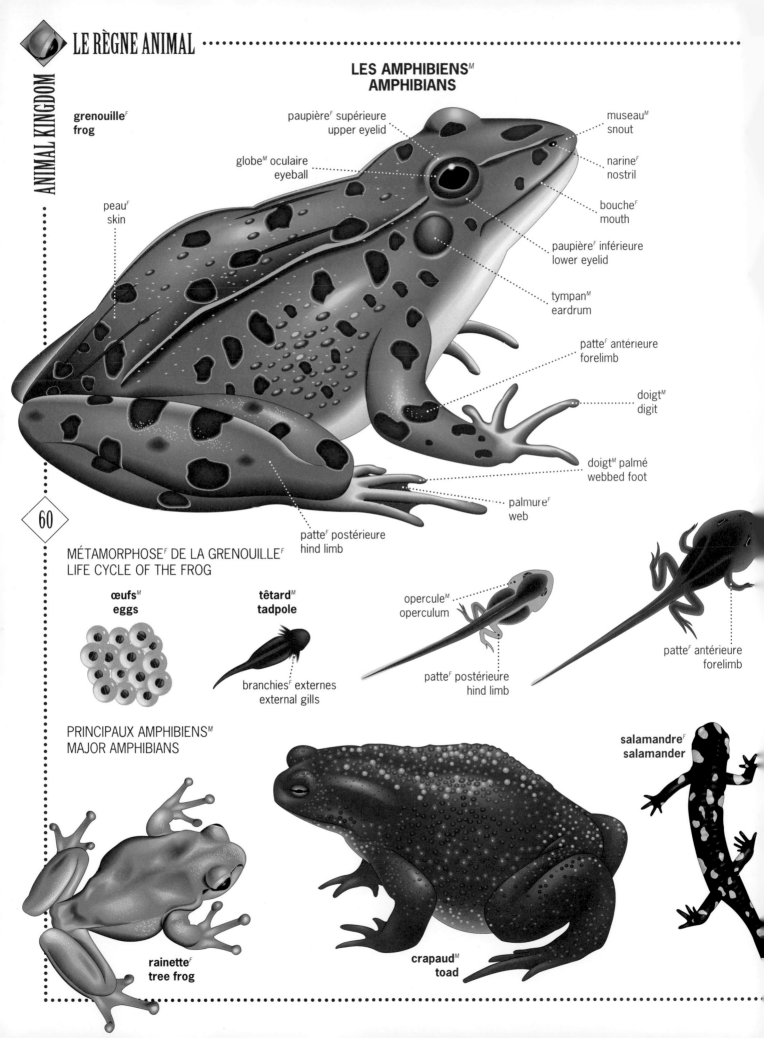

LES AMPHIBIENS^M
AMPHIBIANS

grenouille^F
frog

paupière^F supérieure
upper eyelid

museau^M
snout

globe^M oculaire
eyeball

narine^F
nostril

peau^F
skin

bouche^F
mouth

paupière^F inférieure
lower eyelid

tympan^M
eardrum

patte^F antérieure
forelimb

doigt^M
digit

doigt^M palmé
webbed foot

palmure^F
web

patte^F postérieure
hind limb

60

MÉTAMORPHOSE^F DE LA GRENOUILLE^F
LIFE CYCLE OF THE FROG

œufs^M
eggs

têtard^M
tadpole

opercule^M
operculum

branchies^F externes
external gills

patte^F postérieure
hind limb

patte^F antérieure
forelimb

PRINCIPAUX AMPHIBIENS^M
MAJOR AMPHIBIANS

salamandre^F
salamander

rainette^F
tree frog

crapaud^M
toad

LES CRUSTACÉS^M
CRUSTACEANS

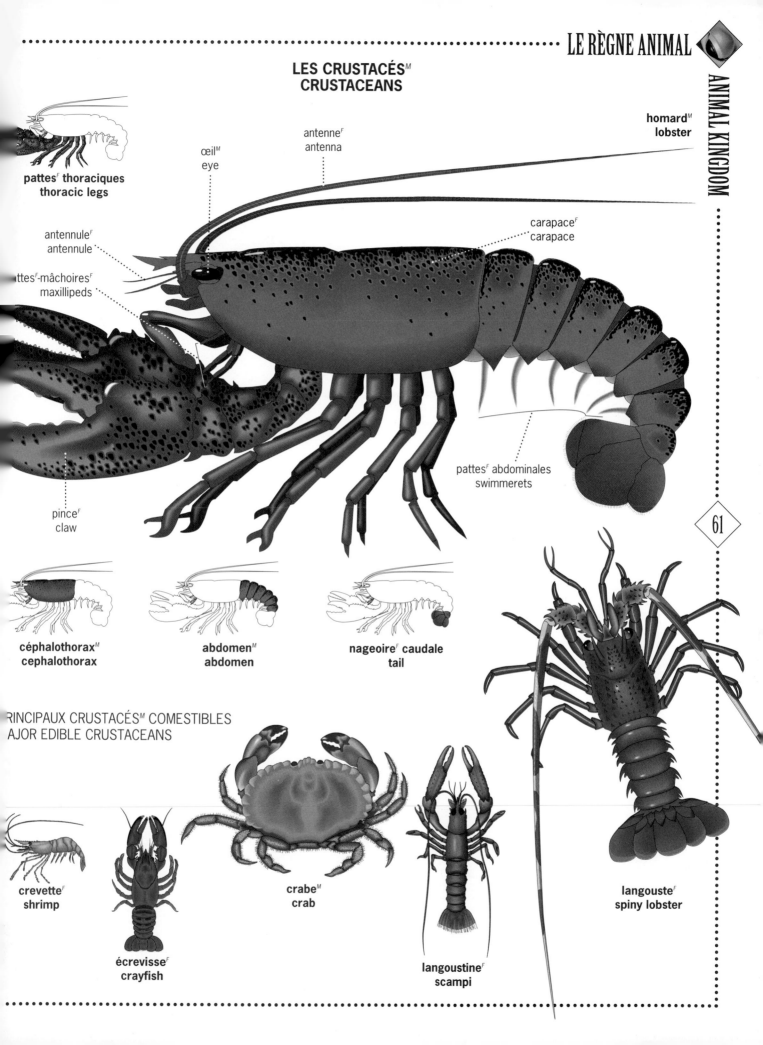

pattes^F thoraciques
thoracic legs

œil^M
eye

antenne^F
antenna

homard^M
lobster

antennule^F
antennule

carapace^F
carapace

pattes^F-mâchoires^F
maxillipeds

pattes^F abdominales
swimmerets

pince^F
claw

céphalothorax^M
cephalothorax

abdomen^M
abdomen

nageoire^F caudale
tail

61

RINCIPAUX CRUSTACÉS^M COMESTIBLES
AJOR EDIBLE CRUSTACEANS

crevette^F
shrimp

écrevisse^F
crayfish

crabe^M
crab

langoustine^F
scampi

langouste^F
spiny lobster

LES POISSONS^M
FISHES

MORPHOLOGIE^F
MORPHOLOGY

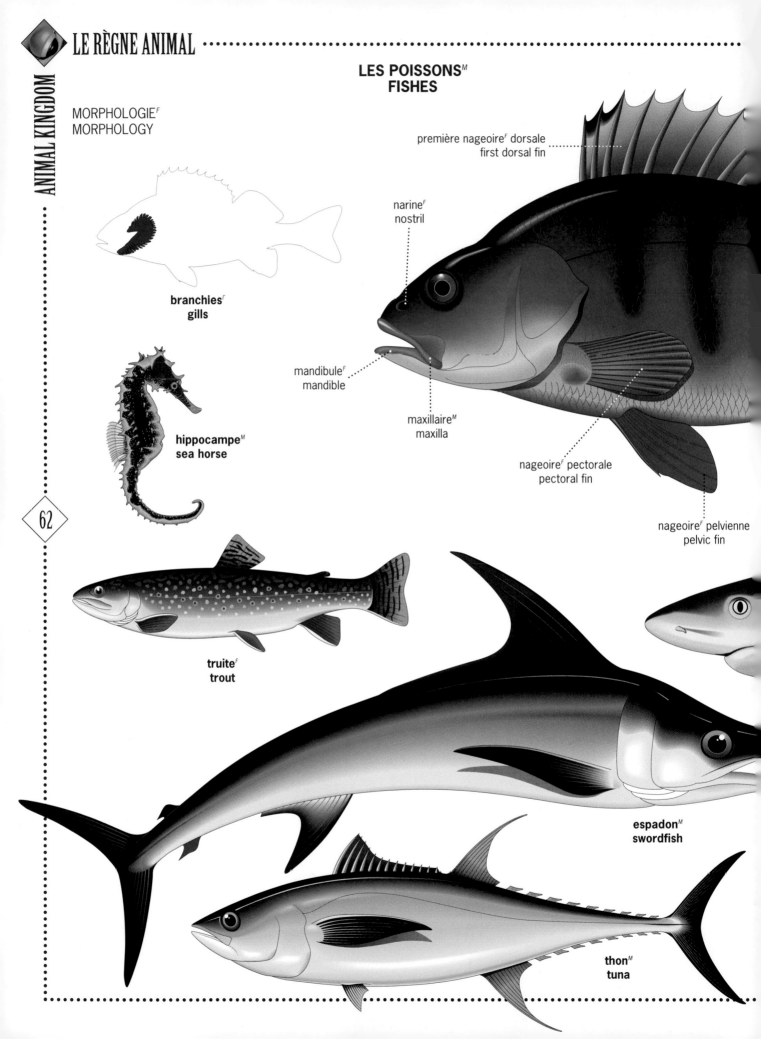

première nageoire^F dorsale
first dorsal fin

narine^F
nostril

branchies^F
gills

mandibule^F
mandible

maxillaire^M
maxilla

nageoire^F pectorale
pectoral fin

nageoire^F pelvienne
pelvic fin

hippocampe^M
sea horse

truite^F
trout

espadon^M
swordfish

thon^M
tuna

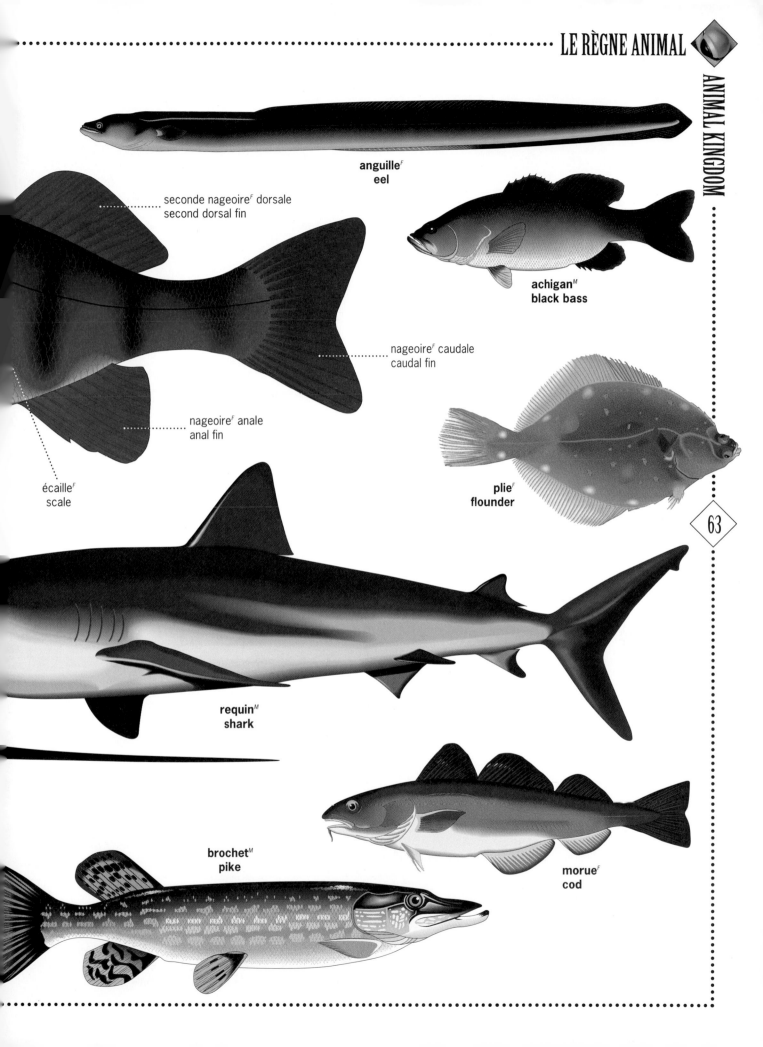

anguille^F
eel

seconde nageoire^F dorsale
second dorsal fin

achigan^M
black bass

nageoire^F caudale
caudal fin

nageoire^F anale
anal fin

plie^F
flounder

écaille^F
scale

63

requin^M
shark

brochet^M
pike

morue^F
cod

ANIMAL KINGDOM

LES REPTILES^M
REPTILES

tortue^F
turtle

tympan^M
eardrum

cou^M
neck

paupière^F
eyelid

œil^M
eye

bec^M corné
horny beak

écaille^F
scale

patte^F
leg

carapace^F
shell

dossière^F
carapace

plastron^M
plastron

griffe^F
claw

64

tête^F **de serpent**^{M} **venimeux**
venomous snake's head

maxillaire^M basculant
movable maxillary

conduit^M de la glande^F
venom-conducting tube

canal^M à venin^M
venom canal

crochet^M à venin^M
fang

glande^F à venin^M
venom gland

glotte^F
glottis

dent^F
tooth

fourreau^M de la langue^F
tongue sheath

langue^F bifide
forked tongue

cobra^M
cobra

crocodile^M
crocodile

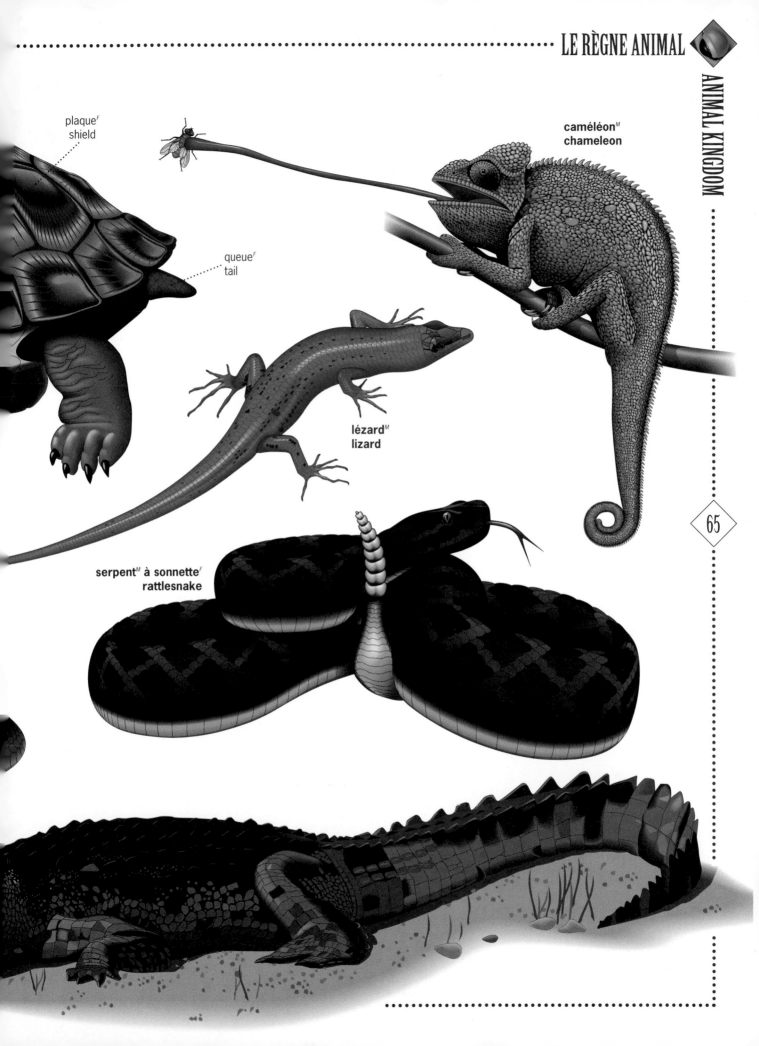

plaque^F
shield

queue^F
tail

caméléon^M
chameleon

lézard^M
lizard

serpent^M à sonnette^F
rattlesnake

LE CHAT^M
CAT

sourcils^M
whiskers

paupière^F supérieure
upper eyelid

paupière^F inférieure
lower eyelid

paupière^F interne
nictitating membrane

moustaches^F
whiskers

lèvre^F
lip

cils^M
eyelashes

pupille^F
pupil

truffe^F
nose leather

museau^M
muzzle

LE CHIEN^M
DOG

stop^M
stop

museau^M
muzzle

babines^F
flews

joue^F
cheek

garrot^M
withers

dos^M
back

MORPHOLOGIE^F
MORPHOLOGY

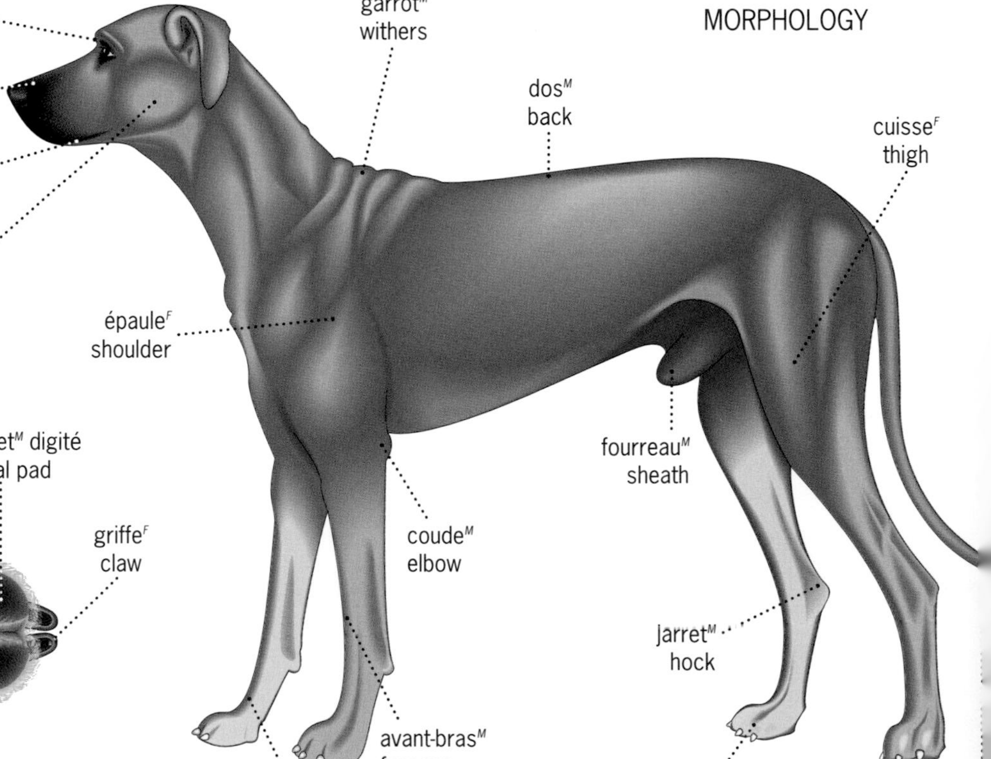

cuisse^F
thigh

**patte^F antérieure
dog's forepaw**

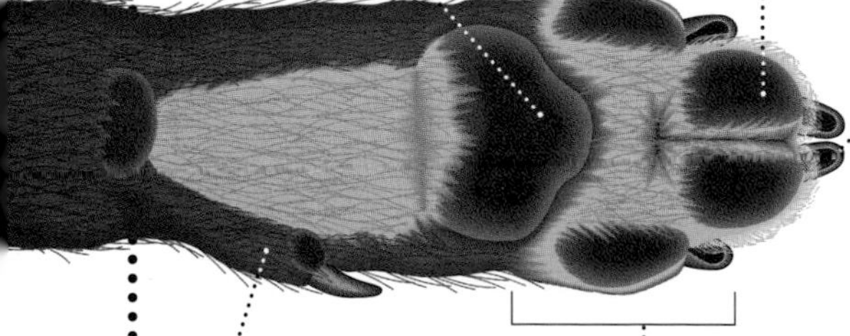

coussinet^M palmaire
palmar pad

coussinet^M digité
digital pad

griffe^F
claw

épaule^F
shoulder

fourreau^M
sheath

coude^M
elbow

Jarret^M
hock

ergot^M
dewclaw

orteil^M
toe

avant-bras^M
forearm

poignet^M
wrist

orteil^M
toe

queue
ta

LE CHEVAL^M
HORSE

toupet^M
forelock

chanfrein^M
nose

naseau^M
nostril

bout^M du nez^M
muzzle

lèvre^F
lip

crinière^F
mane

garrot^M
withers

dos^M
back

rein^M
loin

queue^F
tail

flanc^M
flank

croupe^F
croup

encolure^F
neck

épaule^F
shoulder

poitrail^M
chest

bras^M
arm

coude^M
elbow

genou^M
knee

châtaigne^F
chestnut

boulet^M
fetlock joint

couronne^F
coronet

fanon^M
fetlock

ventre^M
belly

fourreau^M
sheath

cuisse^F
thigh

jambe^F
gaskin

paturon^M
pastern

sabot^M
hoof

jarret^M
hock

canon^M
cannon

67

LES ANIMAUX^M DE LA FERME^F
FARM ANIMALS

poule^F
hen

poussin^M
chick

coq^M
rooster; cock

canard^M
duck

oie^F
goose

dindon^M
turkey

vache^F
cow

veau^M
calf

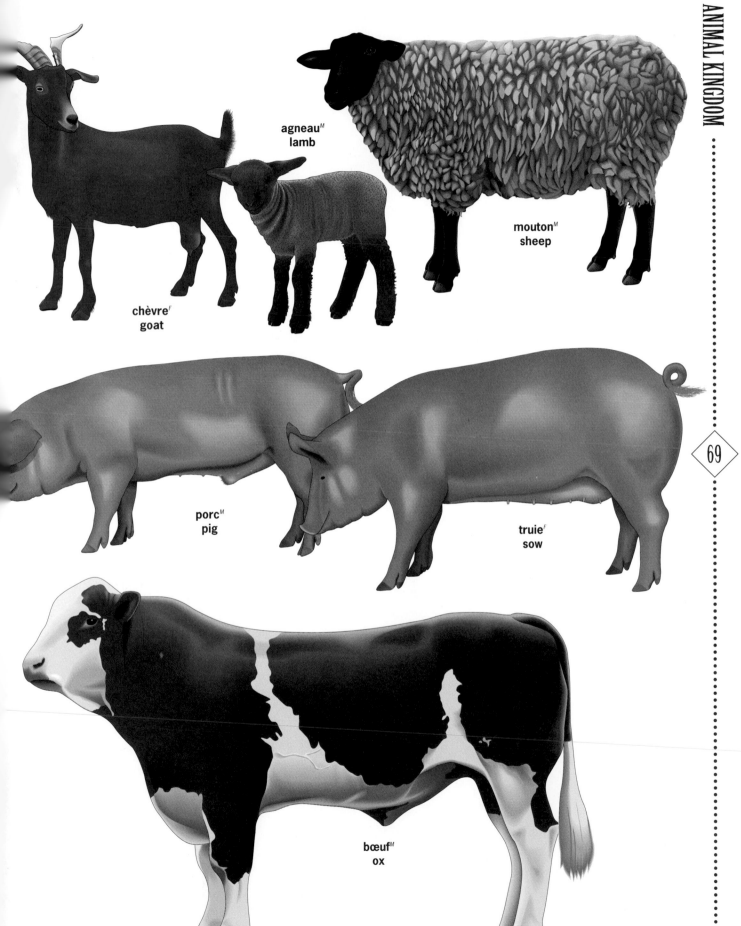

agneau^M
lamb

mouton^M
sheep

chèvre^F
goat

porc^M
pig

truie^F
sow

bœuf^M
ox

LES TYPES^M DE MÂCHOIRES^F
TYPES OF JAWS

mâchoire^F de rongeur^M
rodent's jaw

castor^M
beaver

prémolaire^F
premolar

incisive^F
incisor

molaire^F
molar

barre^F
diastema

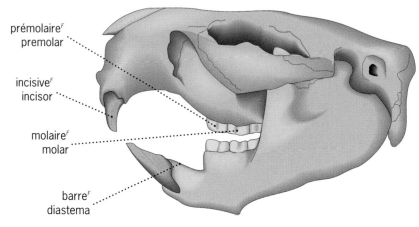

mâchoire^F de carnivore^M
carnivore's jaw

lion^M
lion

prémolaire^F
premolar

incisive^F
incisor

canine^F
canine

molaire^F
molar

carnassière^F
carnassial

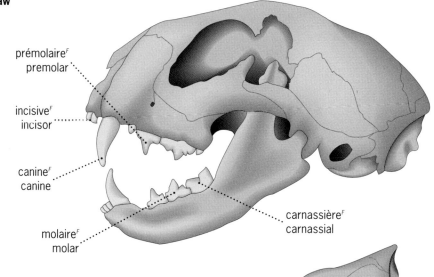

mâchoire^F d'herbivore^M
herbivore's jaw

cheval^M
horse

molaire^F
molar

prémolaire^F
premolar

canine^F
canine

incisive^F
incisor

barre^F
diastema

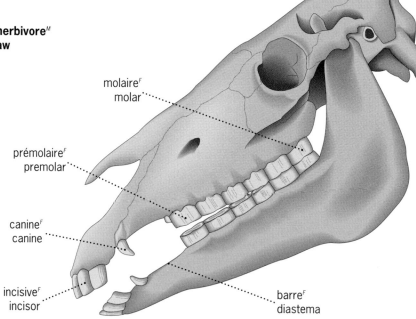

LES PRINCIPAUX TYPES^M DE CORNES^F
MAJOR TYPES OF HORNS

cornes^F de mouflon^M
horns of mouflon

cornes^F de girafe^F
horns of giraffe

cornes^F de rhinocéros^M
horns of rhinoceros

LES PRINCIPAUX TYPES^M DE DÉFENSES^F
MAJOR TYPES OF TUSKS

défenses^F de morse^M
tusks of walrus

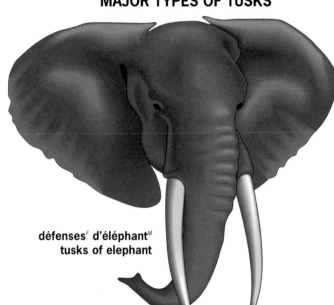

défenses^F d'éléphant^M
tusks of elephant

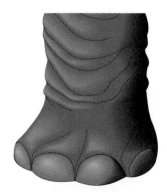

défenses^F de phacochère^M
tusks of wart hog

LES TYPES^M DE SABOTS^M
TYPES OF HOOFS

sabot^M à 1 doigt^M
one-toe hoof

sabot^M à 2 doigts^M
two-toed hoof

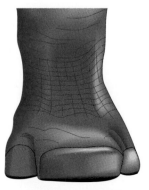

sabot^M à 3 doigts^M
three-toed hoof

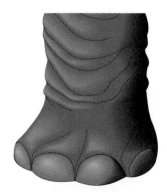

sabot^M à 4 doigts^M
four-toed hoof

LES ANIMAUX^M SAUVAGES
WILD ANIMALS

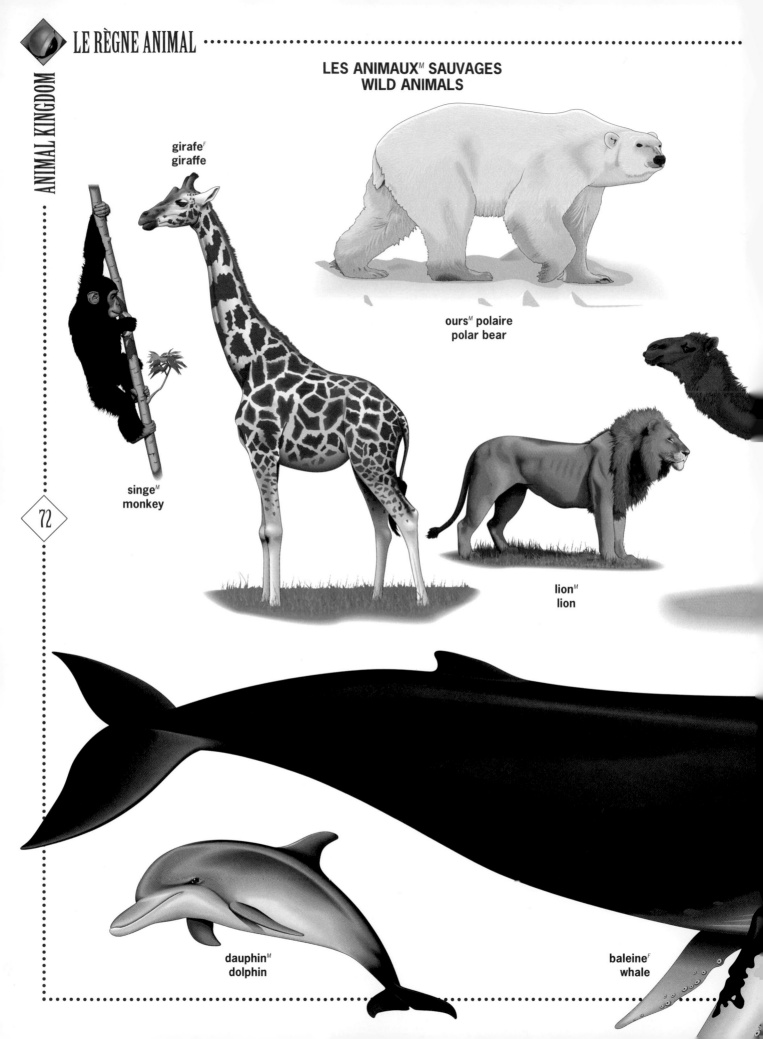

girafe^F
giraffe

ours^M polaire
polar bear

singe^M
monkey

lion^M
lion

dauphin^M
dolphin

baleine^F
whale

72

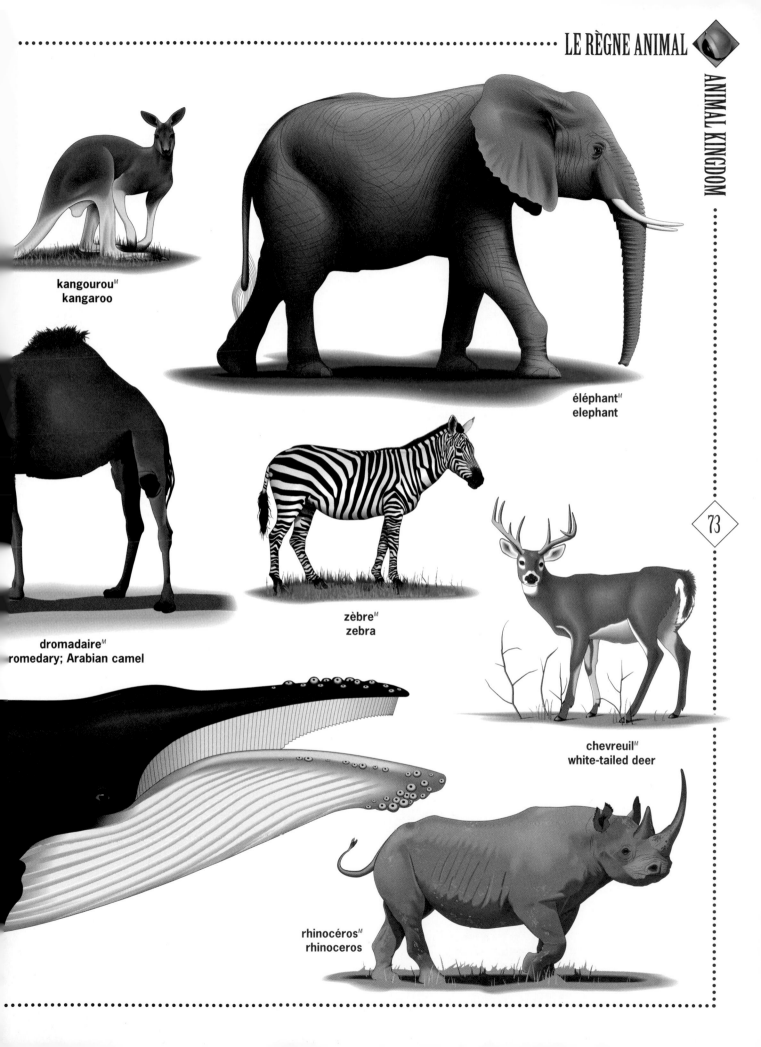

kangourou^M
kangaroo

éléphant^M
elephant

dromadaire^M
dromedary; Arabian camel

zèbre^M
zebra

chevreuil^M
white-tailed deer

rhinocéros^M
rhinoceros

L'OISEAU^M
BIRD

PRINCIPAUX TYPES^M DE BECS^M
PRINCIPAL TYPES OF BILLS

MORPHOLO
MORPHOLO

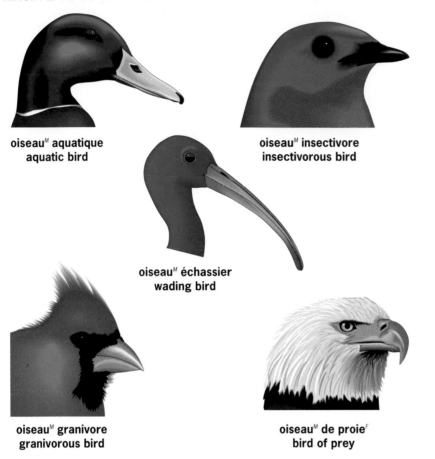

oiseau^M aquatique
aquatic bird

oiseau^M insectivore
insectivorous bird

oiseau^M échassier
wading bird

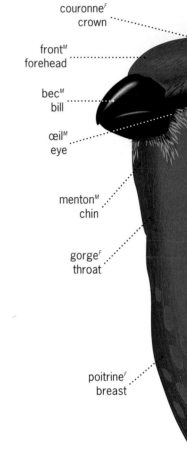

couronne^F
crown

front^M
forehead

bec^M
bill

œil^M
eye

menton^M
chin

gorge^F
throat

poitrine^F
breast

oiseau^M granivore
granivorous bird

oiseau^M de proie^F
bird of prey

PRINCIPAUX TYPES^M DE PATTES^F
PRINCIPAL TYPES OF FEET

oiseau^M de proie^F
bird of prey

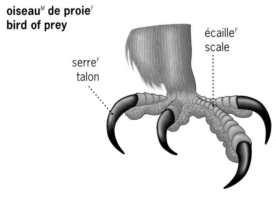

écaille^F
scale

serre^F
talon

oiseau^M aquatique
aquatic bird

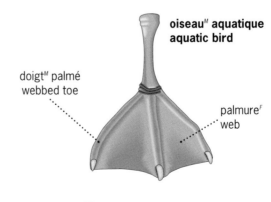

doigt^M palmé
webbed toe

palmure^F
web

abdomen^M
abdomen

oiseau^M aquatique
aquatic bird

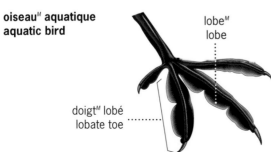

lobe^M
lobe

doigt^M lobé
lobate toe

oiseau^M percheur
perching bird

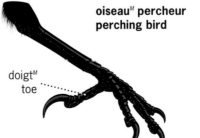

doigt^M médian
middle toe

doigt^M
toe

doigt^M externe
outer toe

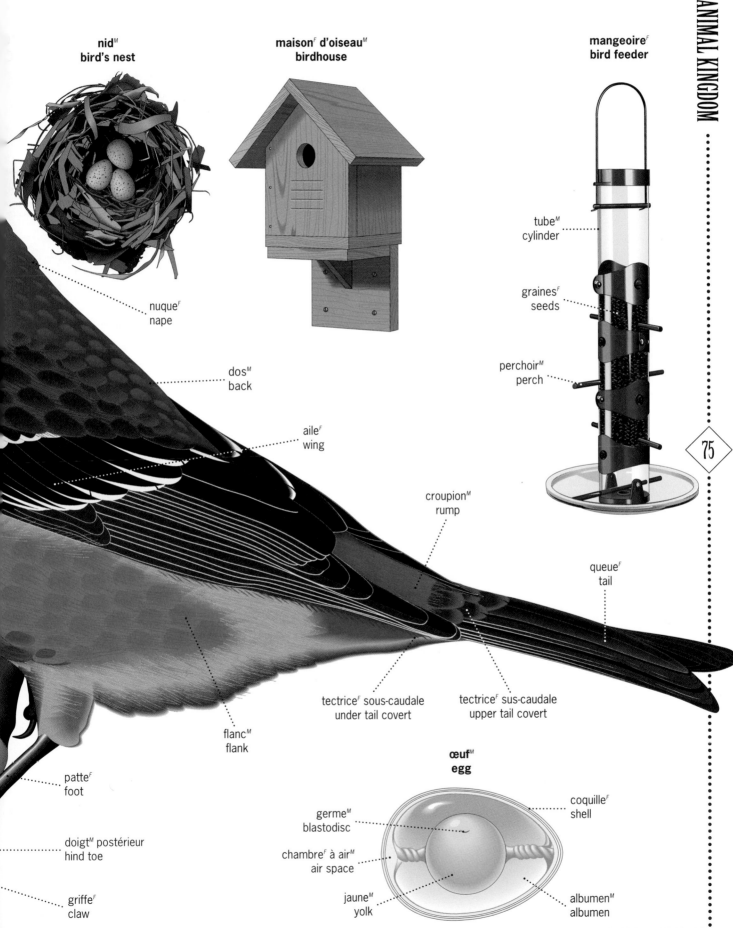

nid^M
bird's nest

maison^F **d'oiseau**^M
birdhouse

mangeoire^F
bird feeder

tube^M
cylinder

graines^F
seeds

perchoir^M
perch

nuque^F
nape

dos^M
back

aile^F
wing

croupion^M
rump

queue^F
tail

tectrice^F sous-caudale
under tail covert

tectrice^F sus-caudale
upper tail covert

flanc^M
flank

patte^F
foot

doigt^M postérieur
hind toe

griffe^F
claw

œuf^M
egg

germe^M
blastodisc

chambre^F à air^M
air space

jaune^M
yolk

coquille^F
shell

albumen^M
albumen

EXEMPLES^M D'OISEAUX^M
EXAMPLES OF BIRDS

corbeau^M
crow

perroquet^M
parrot

cigogne^F
stork

hirondelle^F
swallow

flamant^M
flamingo

autruche^F
ostrich

76

rouge-gorge[M]
robin

geai[M]
blue jay

hibou[M]
owl

rossignol[M]
nightingale

colibri[M]
hummingbird

paon[M]
peacock

LE CORPS^M, VUE^F DE FACE^F
HUMAN BODY, ANTERIOR VIEW

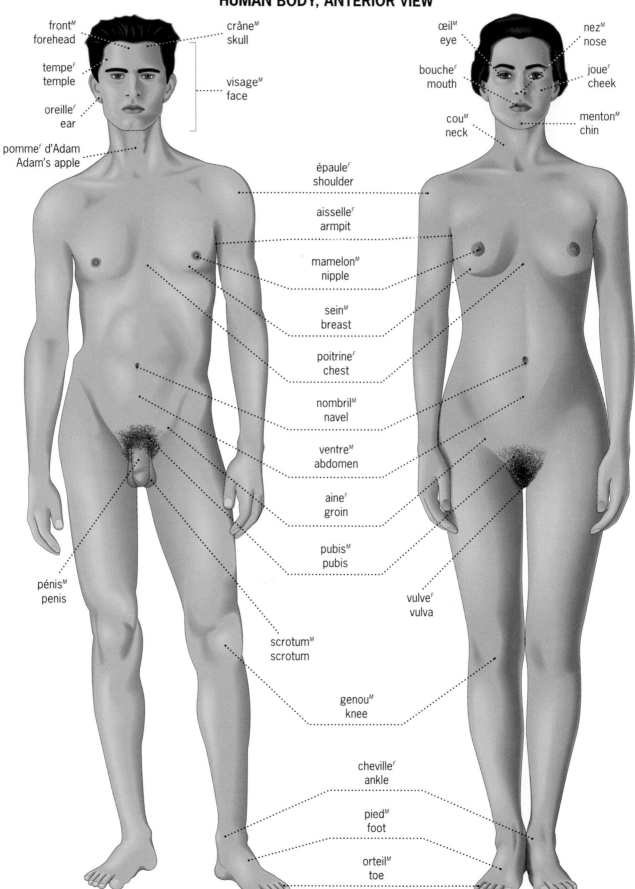

front^M
forehead

tempe^F
temple

oreille^F
ear

pomme^F d'Adam
Adam's apple

crâne^M
skull

visage^M
face

œil^M
eye

bouche^F
mouth

cou^M
neck

nez^M
nose

joue^F
cheek

menton^M
chin

épaule^F
shoulder

aisselle^F
armpit

mamelon^M
nipple

sein^M
breast

poitrine^F
chest

nombril^M
navel

ventre^M
abdomen

aine^F
groin

pubis^M
pubis

pénis^M
penis

vulve^F
vulva

scrotum^M
scrotum

genou^M
knee

cheville^F
ankle

pied^M
foot

orteil^M
toe

LE CORPS^M, VUE^F DE DOS^M
HUMAN BODY, POSTERIOR VIEW

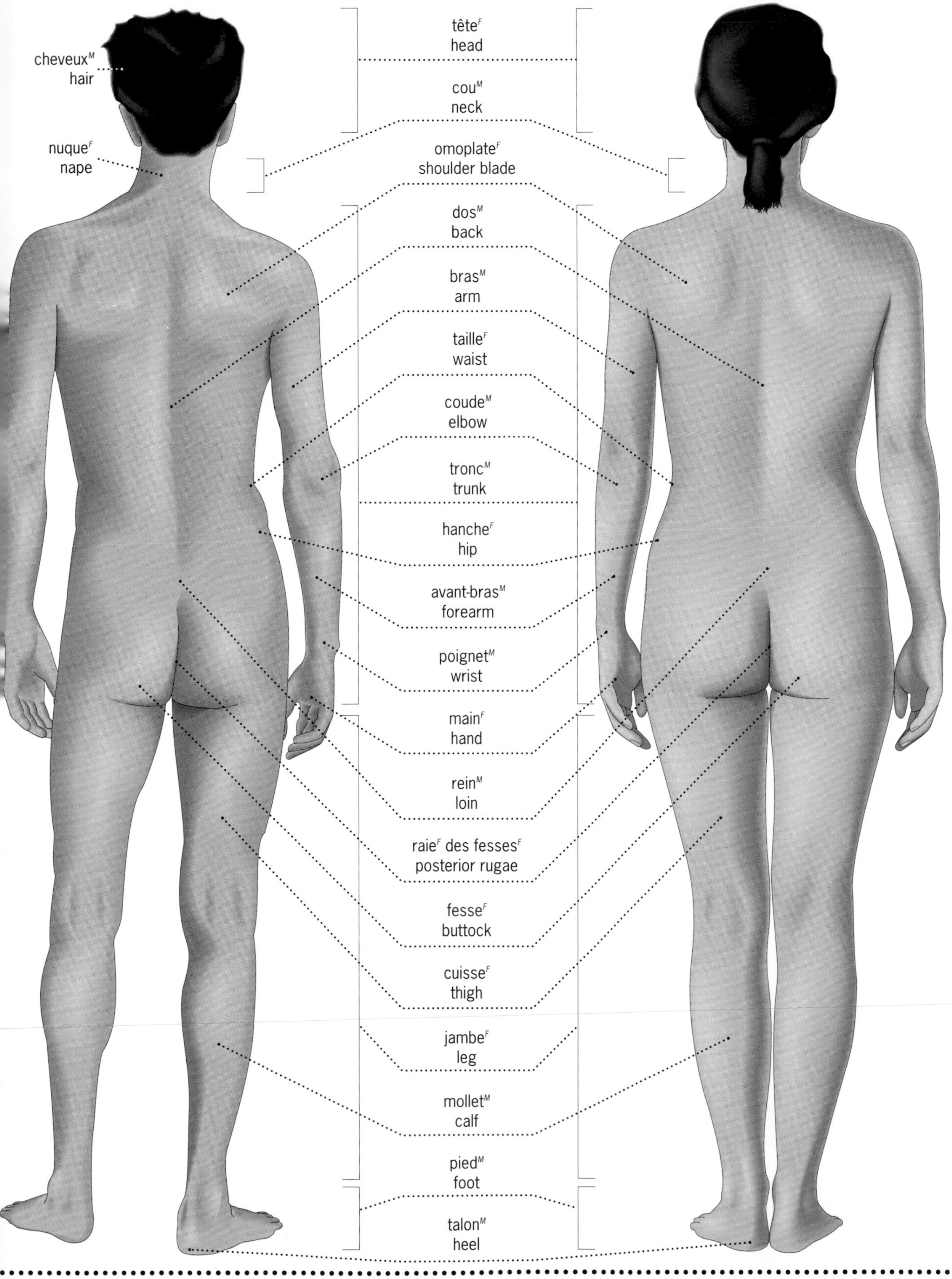

cheveux^M
hair

nuque^F
nape

tête^F
head

cou^M
neck

omoplate^F
shoulder blade

dos^M
back

bras^M
arm

taille^F
waist

coude^M
elbow

tronc^M
trunk

hanche^F
hip

avant-bras^M
forearm

poignet^M
wrist

main^F
hand

rein^M
loin

raie^F des fesses^F
posterior rugae

fesse^F
buttock

cuisse^F
thigh

jambe^F
leg

mollet^M
calf

pied^M
foot

talon^M
heel

LE SQUELETTE^M
SKELETON

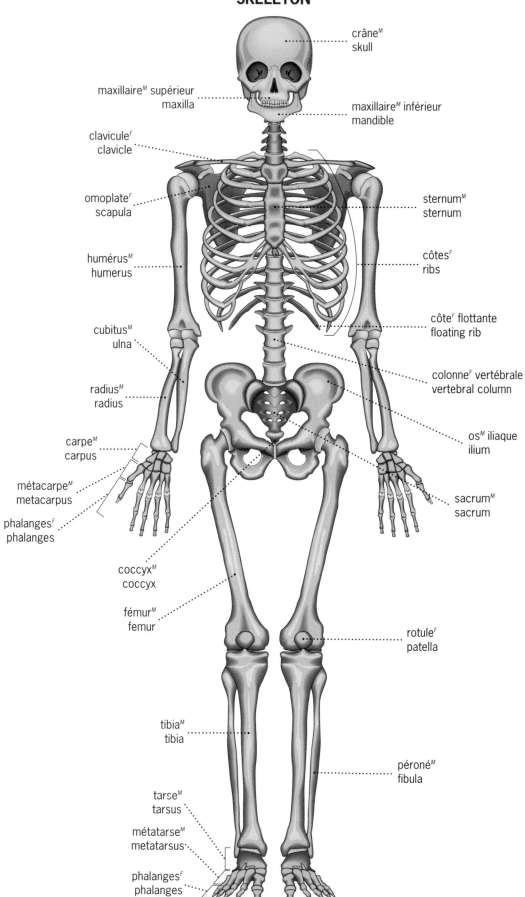

crâne^M
skull

maxillaire^M supérieur
maxilla

maxillaire^M inférieur
mandible

clavicule^F
clavicle

omoplate^F
scapula

sternum^M
sternum

côtes^F
ribs

humérus^M
humerus

côte^F flottante
floating rib

cubitus^M
ulna

colonne^F vertébrale
vertebral column

radius^M
radius

os^M iliaque
ilium

carpe^M
carpus

métacarpe^M
metacarpus

sacrum^M
sacrum

phalanges^F
phalanges

coccyx^M
coccyx

fémur^M
femur

rotule^F
patella

tibia^M
tibia

péroné^M
fibula

tarse^M
tarsus

métatarse^M
metatarsus

phalanges^F
phalanges

L'ANATOMIE^F HUMAINE
HUMAN ANATOMY

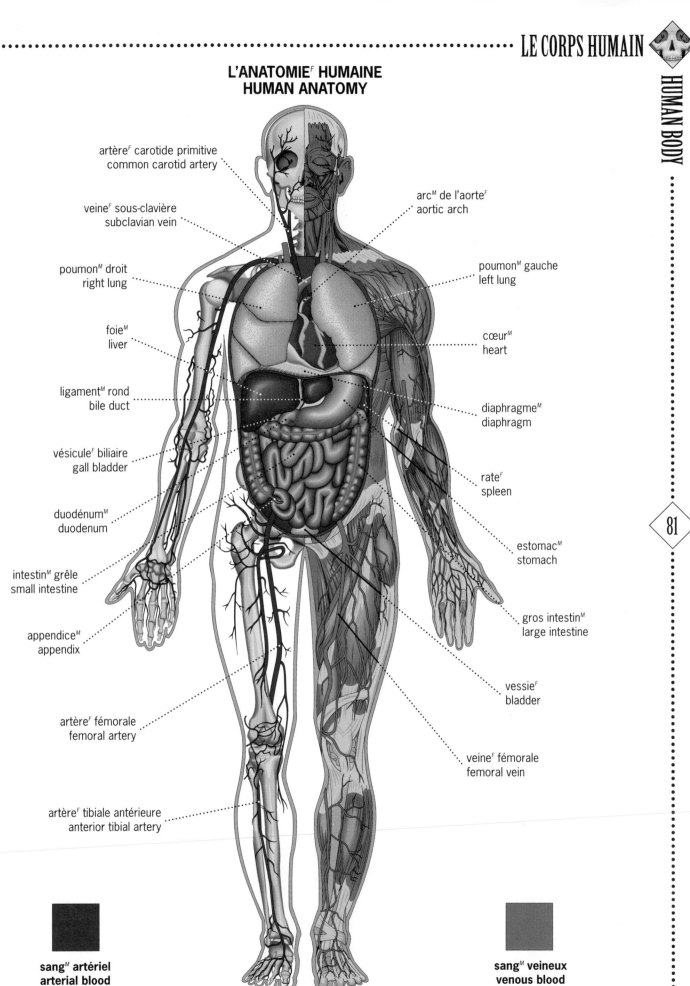

artère^F carotide primitive
common carotid artery

veine^F sous-clavière
subclavian vein

poumon^M droit
right lung

foie^M
liver

ligament^M rond
bile duct

vésicule^F biliaire
gall bladder

duodénum^M
duodenum

intestin^M grêle
small intestine

appendice^M
appendix

artère^F fémorale
femoral artery

artère^F tibiale antérieure
anterior tibial artery

arc^M de l'aorte^F
aortic arch

poumon^M gauche
left lung

cœur^M
heart

diaphragme^M
diaphragm

rate^F
spleen

estomac^M
stomach

gros intestin^M
large intestine

vessie^F
bladder

veine^F fémorale
femoral vein

**sang^M artériel
arterial blood**

**sang^M veineux
venous blood**

LE SENS*M* DE LA VUE*F*: L'ŒIL*M*
EYE: THE ORGAN OF SIGHT

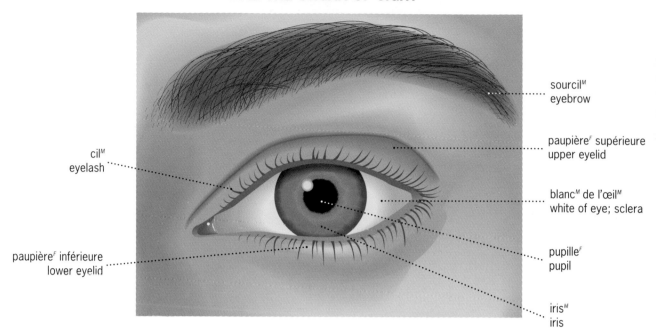

sourcil*M*
eyebrow

paupière*F* supérieure
upper eyelid

cil*M*
eyelash

blanc*M* de l'œil*M*
white of eye; sclera

paupière*F* inférieure
lower eyelid

pupille*F*
pupil

iris*M*
iris

LE SENS*M* DU TOUCHER*M*: LA MAIN*F*
HAND: THE ORGAN OF TOUCH

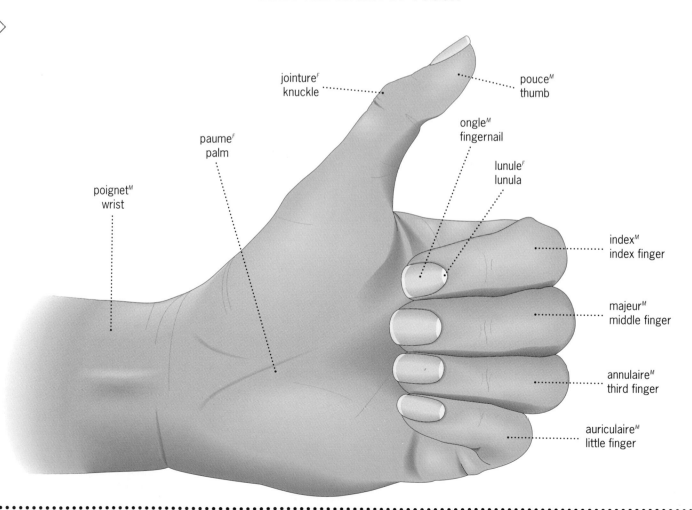

jointure*F*
knuckle

pouce*M*
thumb

ongle*M*
fingernail

paume*F*
palm

lunule*F*
lunula

poignet*M*
wrist

index*M*
index finger

majeur*M*
middle finger

annulaire*M*
third finger

auriculaire*M*
little finger

LE SENS^M DE L'OUÏE^F: L'OREILLE^F
EAR: THE ORGAN OF HEARING

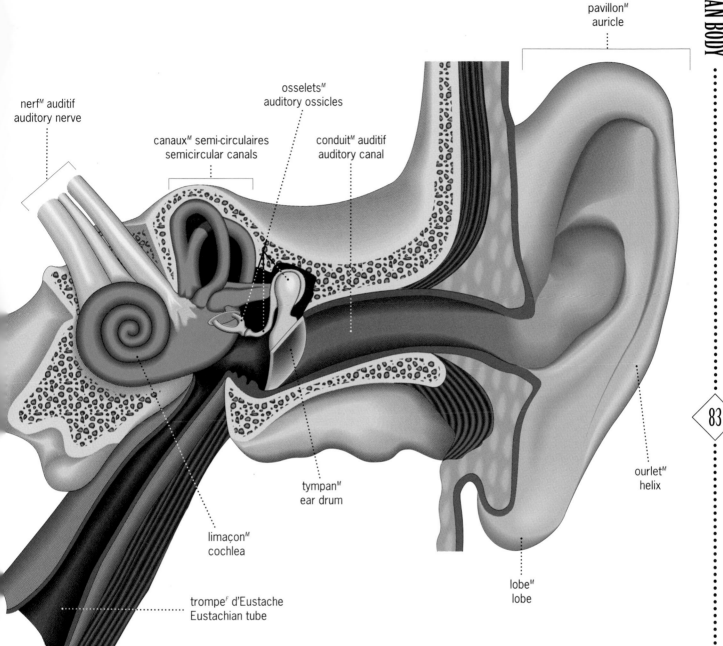

pavillon^M
auricle

nerf^M auditif
auditory nerve

osselets^M
auditory ossicles

canaux^M semi-circulaires
semicircular canals

conduit^M auditif
auditory canal

ourlet^M
helix

tympan^M
ear drum

limaçon^M
cochlea

lobe^M
lobe

trompe^F d'Eustache
Eustachian tube

83

PARTIES^F DE L'OREILLE^F
PARTS OF THE EAR

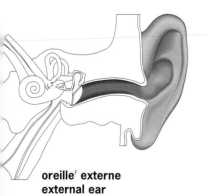

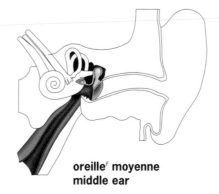

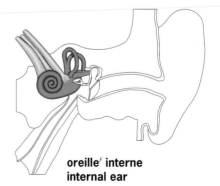

oreille^F externe
external ear

oreille^F moyenne
middle ear

oreille^F interne
internal ear

LE SENS^M DE L'ODORAT^M: LE NEZ^M
NOSE: THE ORGAN OF SMELL

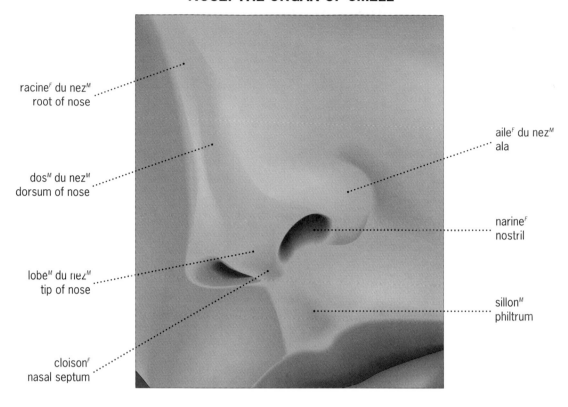

racine^F du nez^M
root of nose

dos^M du nez^M
dorsum of nose

lobe^M du nez^M
tip of nose

cloison^F
nasal septum

aile^F du nez^M
ala

narine^F
nostril

sillon^M
philtrum

84

LE SENS^M DU GOÛT^M: LA BOUCHE^F
MOUTH: THE ORGAN OF TASTE

perception^F des saveurs^F
taste sensations

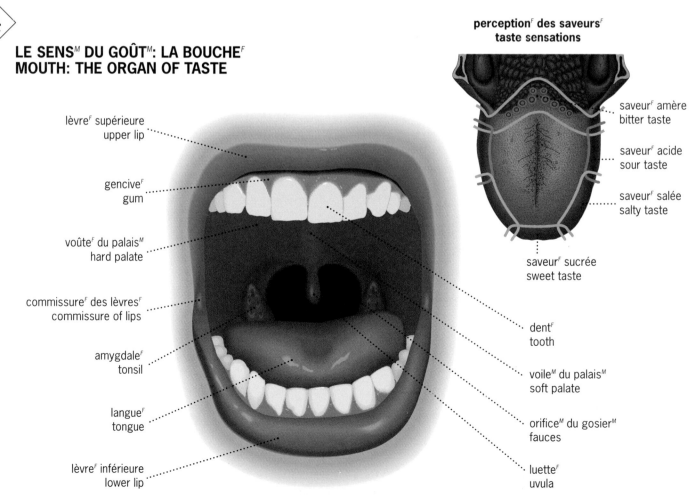

lèvre^F supérieure
upper lip

gencive^F
gum

voûte^F du palais^M
hard palate

commissure^F des lèvres^F
commissure of lips

amygdale^F
tonsil

langue^F
tongue

lèvre^F inférieure
lower lip

saveur^F amère
bitter taste

saveur^F acide
sour taste

saveur^F salée
salty taste

saveur^F sucrée
sweet taste

dent^F
tooth

voile^M du palais^M
soft palate

orifice^M du gosier^M
fauces

luette^F
uvula

LA DENTURE^F HUMAINE
HUMAN DENTURE

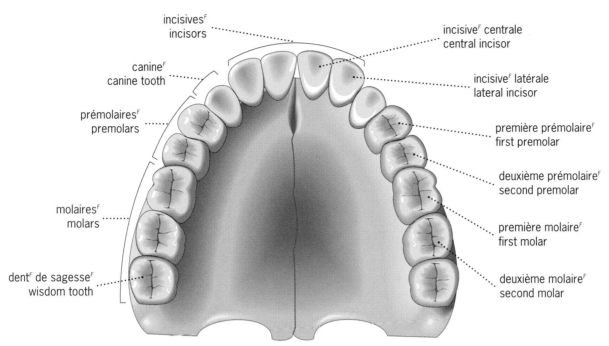

incisives^F
incisors

incisive^F centrale
central incisor

canine^F
canine tooth

incisive^F latérale
lateral incisor

prémolaires^F
premolars

première prémolaire^F
first premolar

deuxième prémolaire^F
second premolar

molaires^F
molars

première molaire^F
first molar

dent^F de sagesse^F
wisdom tooth

deuxième molaire^F
second molar

coupe^F d'une molaire^F
cross section of a molar

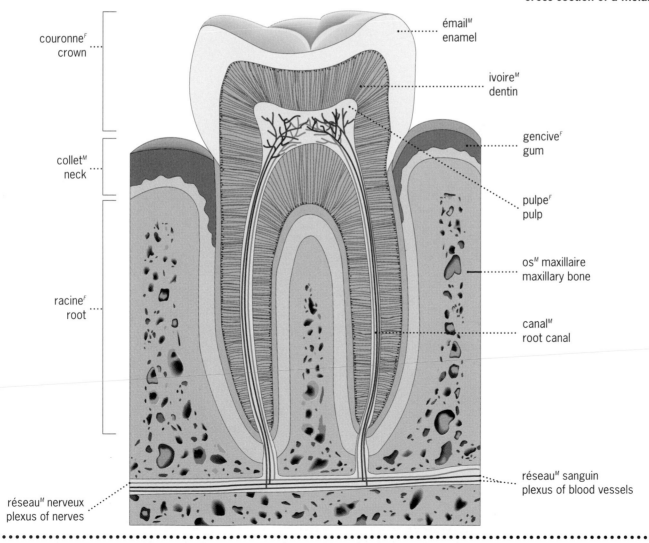

couronne^F
crown

émail^M
enamel

ivoire^M
dentin

collet^M
neck

gencive^F
gum

pulpe^F
pulp

os^M maxillaire
maxillary bone

racine^F
root

canal^M
root canal

réseau^M sanguin
plexus of blood vessels

réseau^M nerveux
plexus of nerves

85

LES MAISONS^F TRADITIONNELLES
TRADITIONAL HOUSES

igloo^M
igloo

wigwam^M
wigwam

isba^F
log cabin

case^F
mud hut

maison^F sur pilotis^M
house on stilts

tipi^M
tepee

hutte[F]
hut

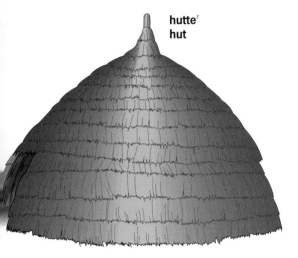

yourte[F]
yurt

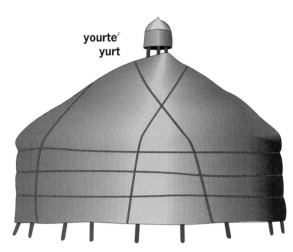

LA MOSQUÉE[F]
MOSQUE

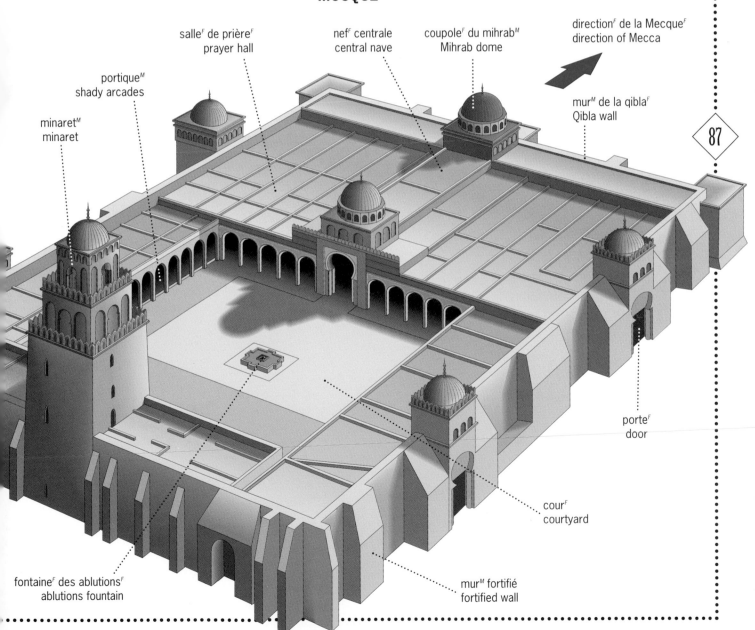

salle[F] de prière[F]
prayer hall

nef[F] centrale
central nave

coupole[F] du mihrab[M]
Mihrab dome

direction[F] de la Mecque[F]
direction of Mecca

portique[M]
shady arcades

mur[M] de la qibla[F]
Qibla wall

minaret[M]
minaret

porte[F]
door

cour[F]
courtyard

fontaine[F] des ablutions[F]
ablutions fountain

mur[M] fortifié
fortified wall

L'ARCHITECTURE

LE CHÂTEAU^M FORT
CASTLE

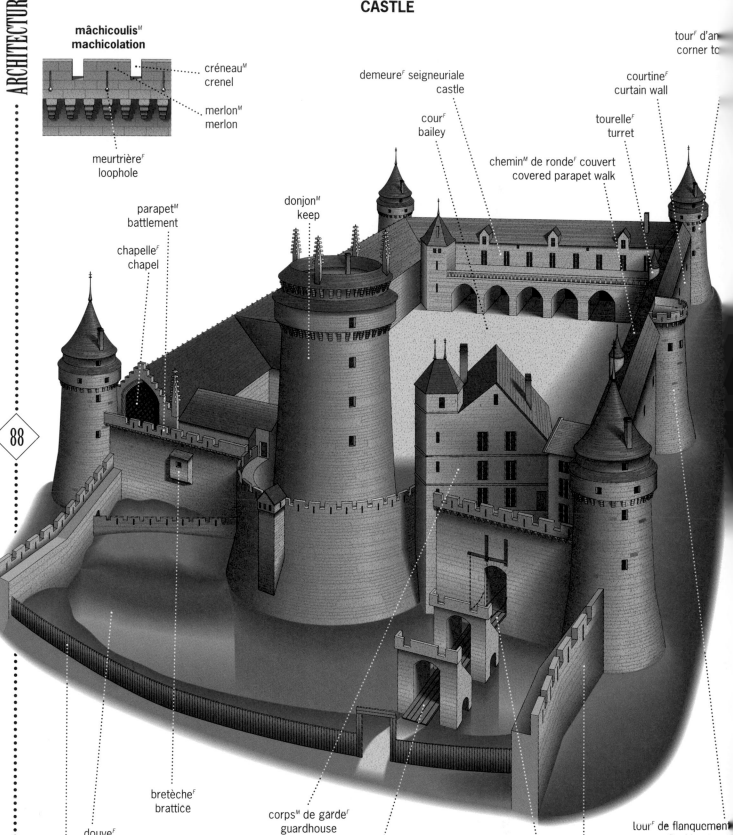

mâchicoulis^M
machicolation

créneau^M
crenel

merlon^M
merlon

meurtrière^F
loophole

demeure^F seigneuriale
castle

cour^F
bailey

chemin^M de ronde^F couvert
covered parapet walk

tour^F d'an...
corner to...

courtine^F
curtain wall

tourelle^F
turret

parapet^M
battlement

chapelle^F
chapel

donjon^M
keep

tour^F de flanquement
flanking towe...

bretèche^F
brattice

corps^M de garde^F
guardhouse

douve^F
moat

passerelle^F
footbridge

pont-levis^M
drawbridge

rempart^M
rampart

palissade^F
stockade

LA CATHÉDRALE^F GOTHIQUE
GOTHIC CATHEDRAL

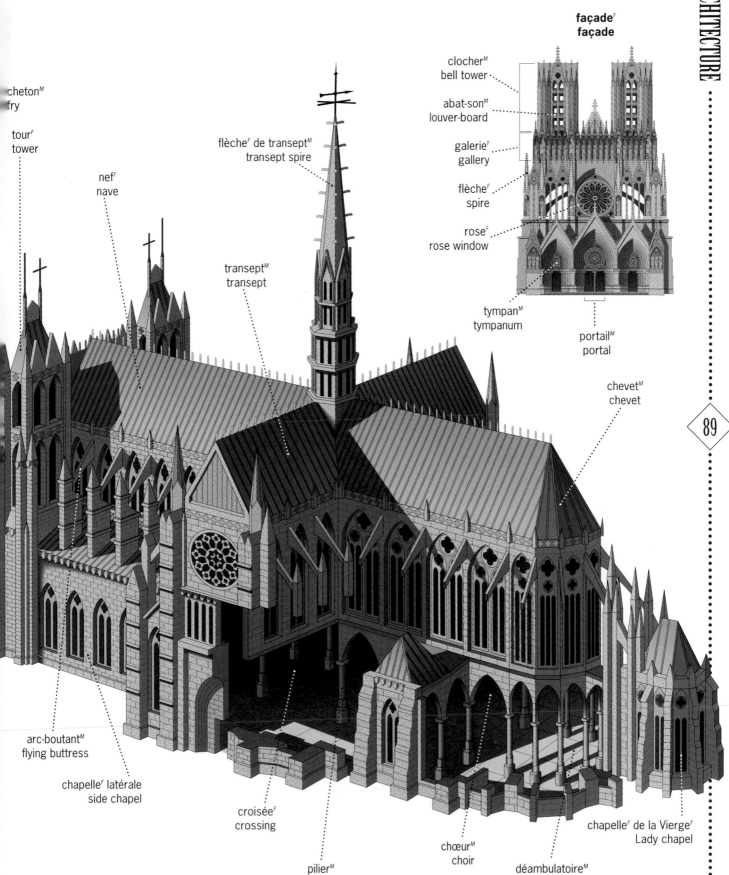

façade^F
façade

clocher^M
bell tower

abat-son^M
louver-board

galerie^F
gallery

flèche^F
spire

rose^F
rose window

tympan^M
tympanum

portail^M
portal

cheton^M
fry

tour^F
tower

nef^F
nave

flèche^F de transept^M
transept spire

transept^M
transept

chevet^M
chevet

arc-boutant^M
flying buttress

chapelle^F latérale
side chapel

croisée^F
crossing

pilier^M
pillar

chœur^M
choir

déambulatoire^M
ambulatory

chapelle^F de la Vierge^F
Lady chapel

LE CENTRE-VILLE^M
DOWNTOWN

espace^M vert
square

parc^M
park

cathédrale^F
cathedral

palais^M des congrès^M
convention center

gare^F
railroad station

tour^F à bureaux^M
office tower

terre-plein^M
median strip

planétarium^M
planetarium

voie^F ferrée
railroad

îlot^M refuge^M
traffic island

boulevard^M
boulevard

rue^F
street

rampe^F de livraison^F
delivery ramp

autoroute^F
freeway

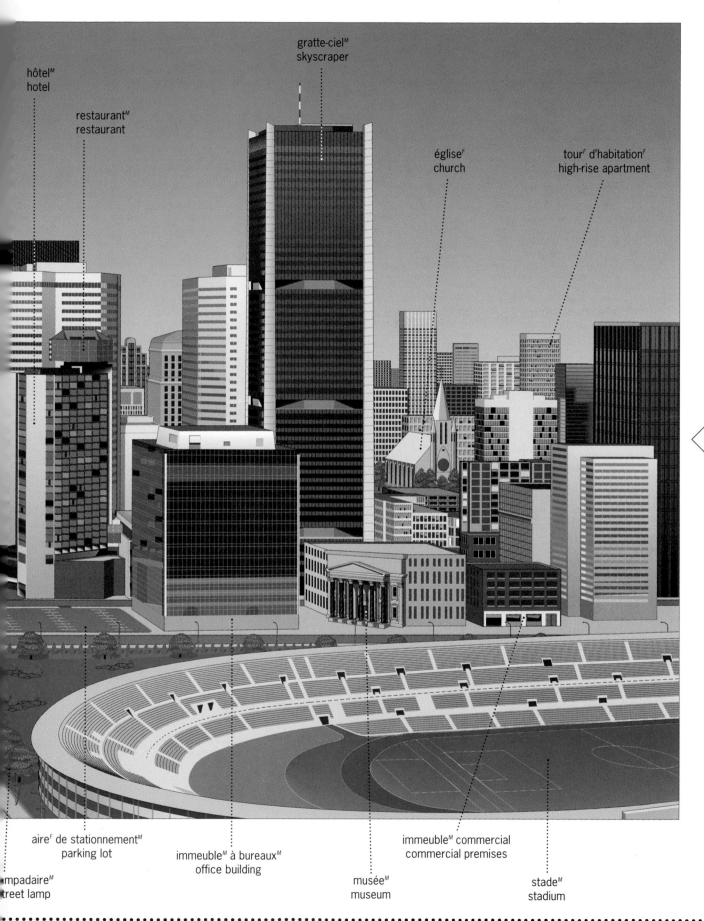

hôtel^M
hotel

restaurant^M
restaurant

gratte-ciel^M
skyscraper

église^F
church

tour^F d'habitation^F
high-rise apartment

aire^F de stationnement^M
parking lot

immeuble^M à bureaux^M
office building

immeuble^M commercial
commercial premises

mpadaire^M
treet lamp

musée^M
museum

stade^M
stadium

LA MAISON^F
HOUSE

extérieur^M d'une maison^F
exterior of a house

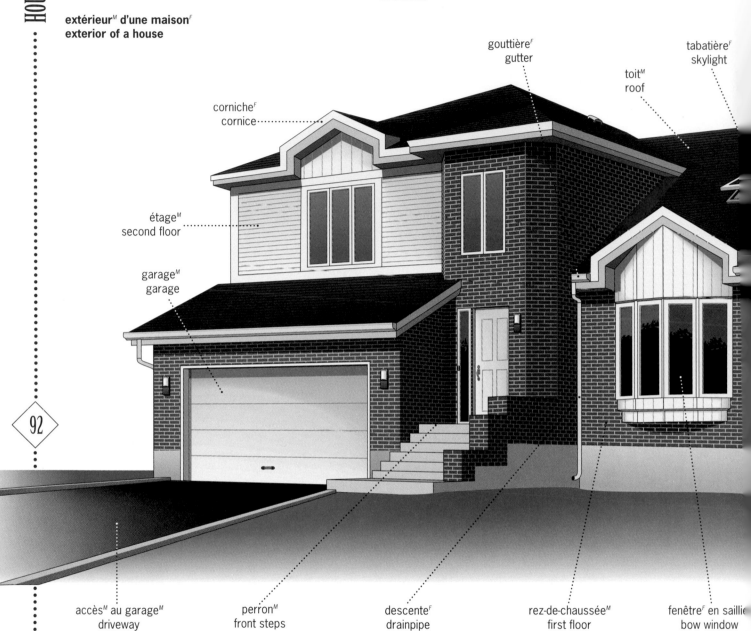

gouttière^F
gutter

tabatière^F
skylight

toit^M
roof

corniche^F
cornice

étage^M
second floor

garage^M
garage

accès^M au garage^M
driveway

perron^M
front steps

descente^F
drainpipe

rez-de-chaussée^M
first floor

fenêtre^F en saillie
bow window

92

TYPES^M DE PORTES^F
TYPES OF DOORS

porte^F classique
conventional door

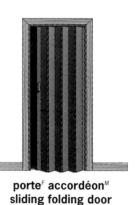

porte^F accordéon^M
sliding folding door

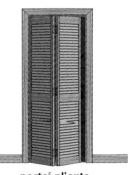

porte^F pliante
folding door

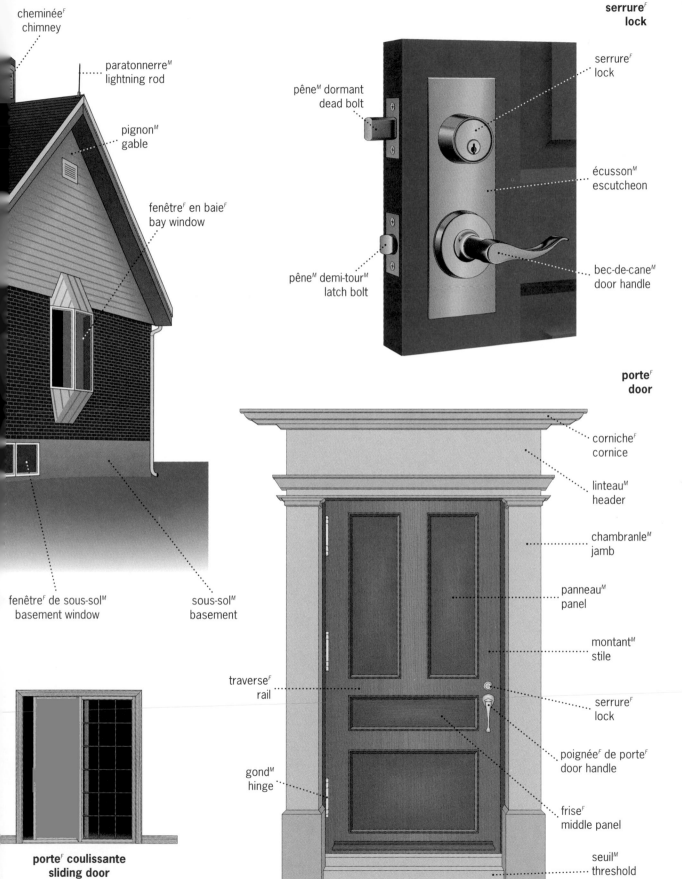

cheminée^F
chimney

paratonnerre^M
lightning rod

pignon^M
gable

fenêtre^F en baie^F
bay window

fenêtre^F de sous-sol^M
basement window

sous-sol^M
basement

serrure^F
lock

pêne^M dormant
dead bolt

pêne^M demi-tour^M
latch bolt

serrure^F
lock

écusson^M
escutcheon

bec-de-cane^M
door handle

porte^F
door

corniche^F
cornice

linteau^M
header

chambranle^M
jamb

panneau^M
panel

montant^M
stile

serrure^F
lock

poignée^F de porte^F
door handle

frise^F
middle panel

seuil^M
threshold

traverse^F
rail

gond^M
hinge

porte^F coulissante
sliding door

HOUSE

LA FENÊTRE^F
WINDOW

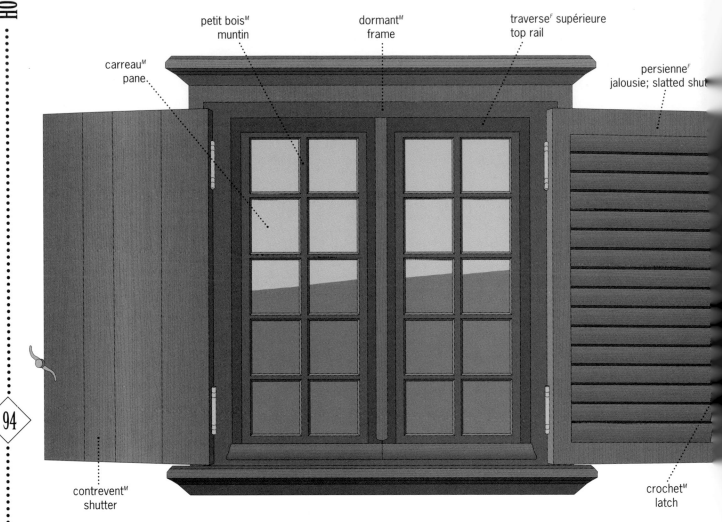

petit bois^M
muntin

dormant^M
frame

traverse^F supérieure
top rail

carreau^M
pane.

persienne^F
jalousie; slatted shut

contrevent^M
shutter

crochet^M
latch

TYPES^M DE FENÊTRES^F
TYPES OF WINDOWS

fenêtre^F à la française^F
casement window (inward opening)

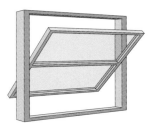

fenêtre^F à l'anglaise^F
casement window (outward opening)

fenêtre^F basculante
horizontal pivoting window

fenêtre^F coulissante
sliding window

fenêtre^F en accordéon^M
sliding folding window

fenêtre^F pivotante
vertical pivoting window

fenêtre^F à guillotine^F
sash window

fenêtre^F à jalousies^F
louvred window

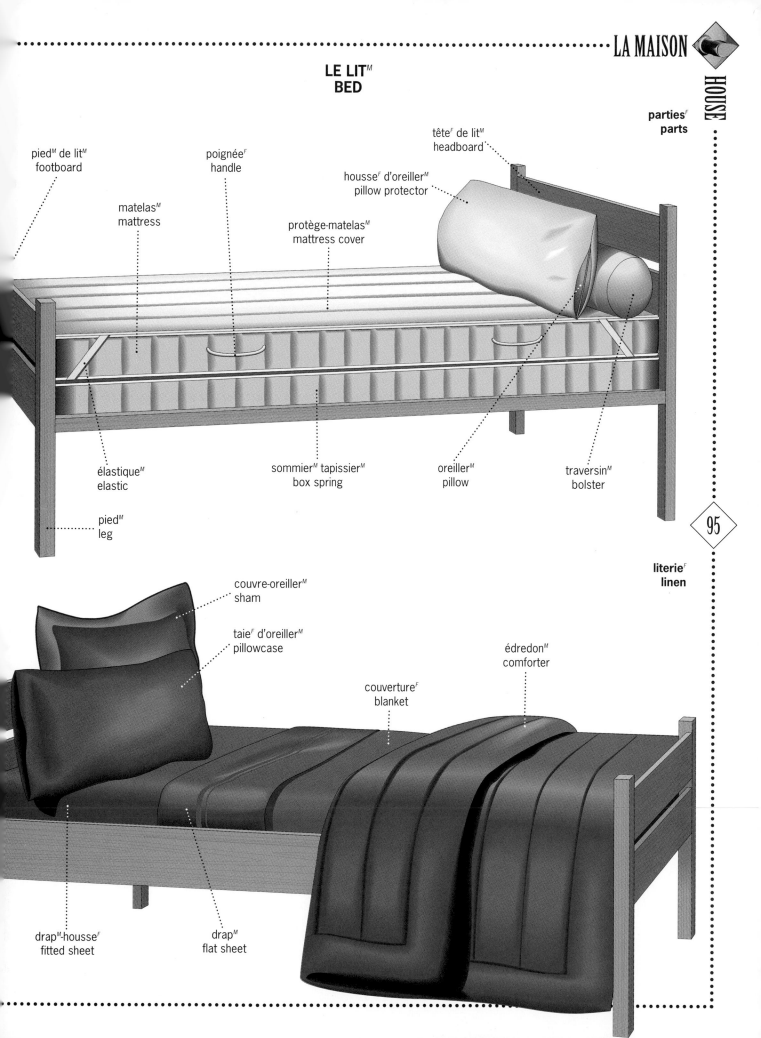

LE LIT^M
BED

pied^M de lit^M
footboard

poignée^F
handle

tête^F de lit^M
headboard

housse^F d'oreiller^M
pillow protector

matelas^M
mattress

protège-matelas^M
mattress cover

élastique^M
elastic

sommier^M tapissier^M
box spring

oreiller^M
pillow

traversin^M
bolster

pied^M
leg

95

literie^F
linen

couvre-oreiller^M
sham

taie^F d'oreiller^M
pillowcase

édredon^M
comforter

couverture^F
blanket

drap^M-housse^F
fitted sheet

drap^M
flat sheet

LES SIÈGES^M
SEATS

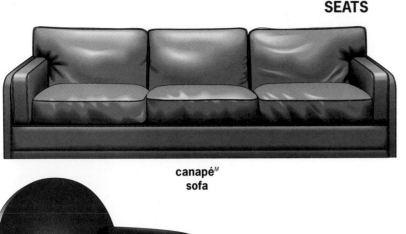

canapé^M
sofa

causeuse^F
loveseat

fauteuil^M club^M
armchair

pouf^M
footstool

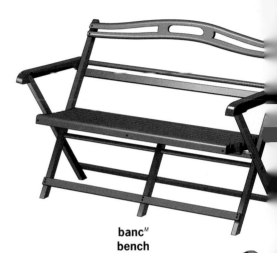

banc^M
bench

tabouret-bar^M
bar stool

tabouret^M
stool

chaise^F longue
chaise longue

chaise^F pliante
folding chair

chaise^F berçante
rocking chair

chaises^F empilables
stacking chairs

LES SIÈGES^M ET LA TABLE^F
TABLE AND CHAIRS

chaise^F
side chair

oreille^F
ear

traverse^F
rail

dossier^M
back

montant^M
stile

siège^M
seat

ceinture^F
apron

barreau^M
spindle

pied^M
leg

piètement^M
support

fauteuil^M
armchair

bras^M
arm

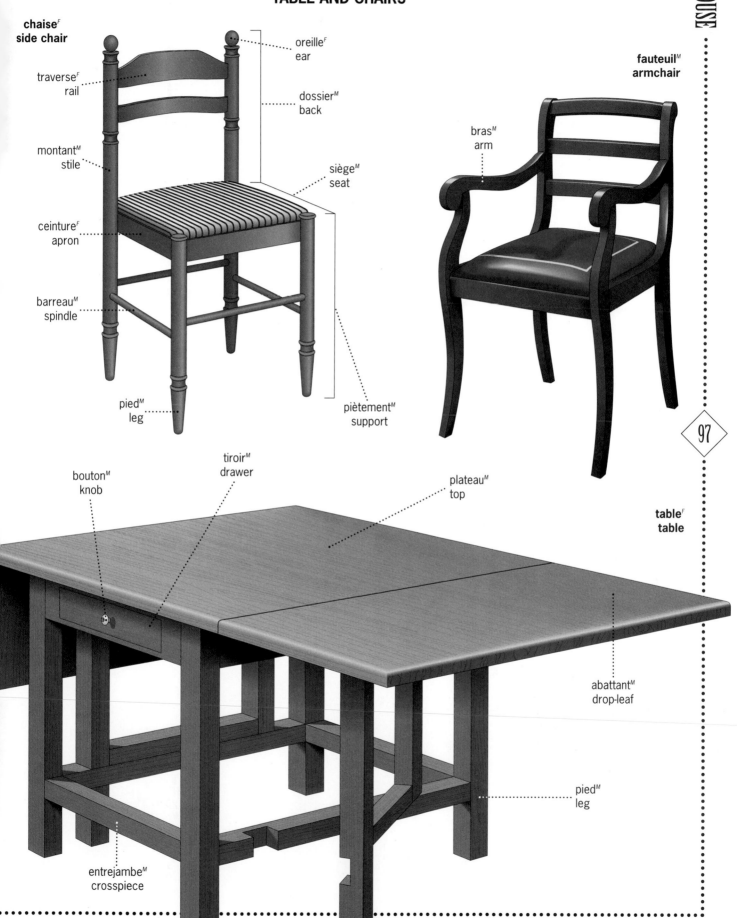

97

bouton^M
knob

tiroir^M
drawer

plateau^M
top

table^F
table

abattant^M
drop-leaf

pied^M
leg

entrejambe^M
crosspiece

LES LUMINAIRES^M
LIGHTS

spot^M
track lighting

rail^M d'éclairage^M
track

transformateur^M
transformer

lampadaire^M
floor lamp

plafonnier^M
ceiling fixture

lampe^F **de table**^F
table lamp

abat-jour^M
shade

pied^M
stand

suspension^F
hanging pendant

applique^F
wall fixture

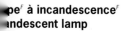
L'ÉCLAIRAGE^M
LIGHTING

pe^F à incandescence^F
ndescent lamp

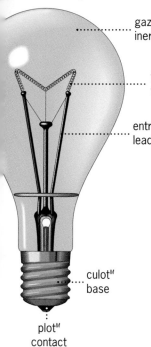

gaz^M inerte
inert gas

filament^M
filament

entrée^F de courant^M
lead-in wire

culot^M
base

plot^M
contact

ampoule^F
bulb

culot^M à vis^F
screw base

culot^M à baïonnette^F
bayonet base

lampe^F à économie^F d'énergie^F
energy saving bulb

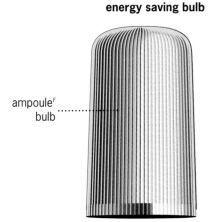

ampoule^F
bulb

tube^M fluorescent
fluorescent tube

boîtier^M
housing

culot^M
base

99

npe^F à halogène^M
gsten-halogen lamp

broche^F
pin

culot^M
base

tube^M fluorescent
fluorescent tube

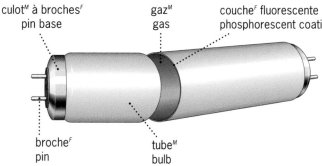

culot^M à broches^F
pin base

gaz^M
gas

couche^F fluorescente
phosphorescent coating

broche^F
pin

tube^M
bulb

fiche^F européenne
European plug

couvercle^M
cover

broche^F
pin

fiche^F américaine
American plug

lame^F
pin

prise^F de terre^F
grounding terminal

interrupteur^M
switch

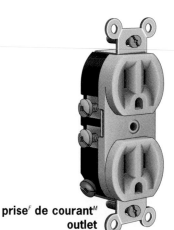

prise^F de courant^M
outlet

LES VERRES^M
GLASSWARE

coupe^F
champagne glass

verre^M à vin^M blanc
white wine glass

verre^M à vin^M rouge
red wine glass

flûte^F
champagne flute

verre^M ordinaire
tumbler; glass

chope^F
beer mug

carafon^M
carafe

carafe^F
decanter

LA VAISSELLE^F
DINNERWARE

tasse^F à café^M
coffee cup

tasse^F à thé^M
cup

chope^F à café^M
mug

crémier^M
creamer

sucrier^M
sugar bowl

poivrière^F
pepper shaker

salière^F
salt shaker

beurrier^M
butter dish

bol^M
cereal bowl

assiette^F creuse
soup bowl

assiette^F plate
dinner plate

assiette^F à salade^F
salad plate

assiette^F à dessert^M
bread and butter plate; side plate

bol^M à salade^F
salad dish

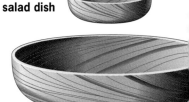

saladier^M
salad bowl

théière^F
teapot

cafetière^F à piston^M
coffee plunger

soupière^F
soup tureen

pichet^M
water pitcher

LE COUVERT^M
SILVERWARE

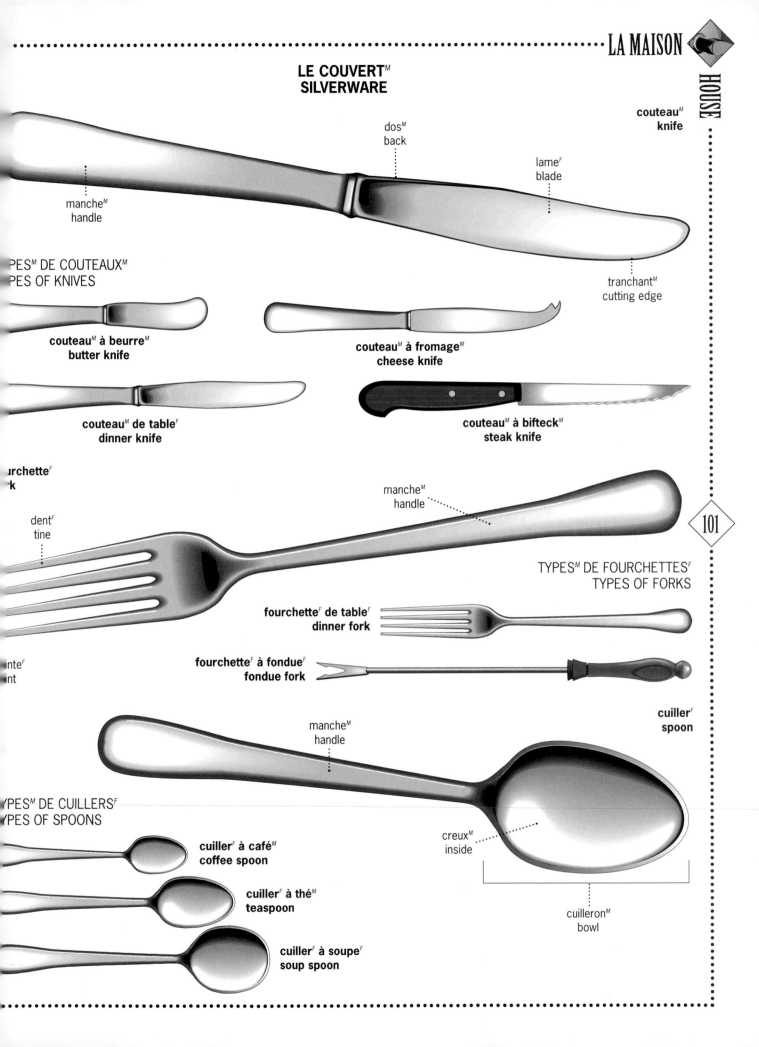

couteau^M
knife

dos^M
back

lame^F
blade

manche^M
handle

tranchant^M
cutting edge

PES^M DE COUTEAUX^M
PES OF KNIVES

couteau^M à beurre^M
butter knife

couteau^M à fromage^M
cheese knife

couteau^M de table^F
dinner knife

couteau^M à bifteck^M
steak knife

urchette^F
k

dent^F
tine

manche^M
handle

TYPES^M DE FOURCHETTES^F
TYPES OF FORKS

fourchette^F de table^F
dinner fork

inte^F
nt

fourchette^F à fondue^F
fondue fork

cuiller^F
spoon

manche^M
handle

PES^M DE CUILLERS^F
PES OF SPOONS

creux^M
inside

cuiller^F à café^M
coffee spoon

cuiller^F à thé^M
teaspoon

cuilleron^M
bowl

cuiller^F à soupe^F
soup spoon

101

LES USTENSILES^M DE CUISINE^F
KITCHEN UTENSILS

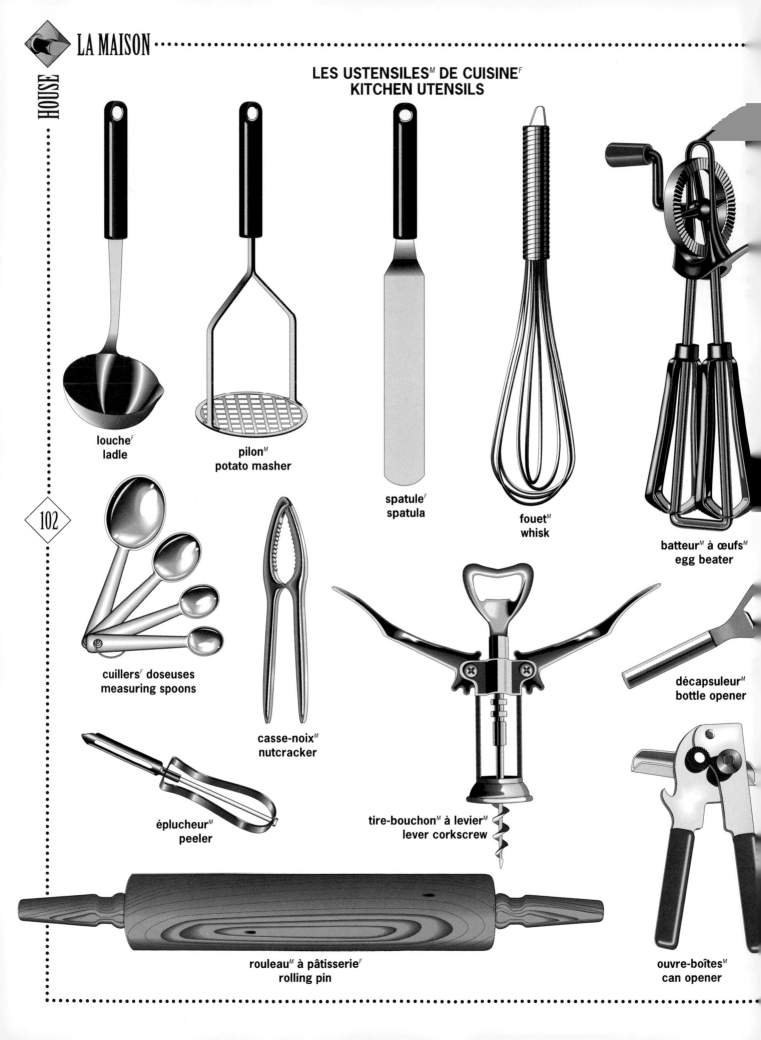

louche^F
ladle

pilon^M
potato masher

spatule^F
spatula

fouet^M
whisk

batteur^M à œufs^M
egg beater

102

cuillers^F doseuses
measuring spoons

casse-noix^M
nutcracker

décapsuleur^M
bottle opener

éplucheur^M
peeler

tire-bouchon^M à levier^M
lever corkscrew

rouleau^M à pâtisserie^F
rolling pin

ouvre-boîtes^M
can opener

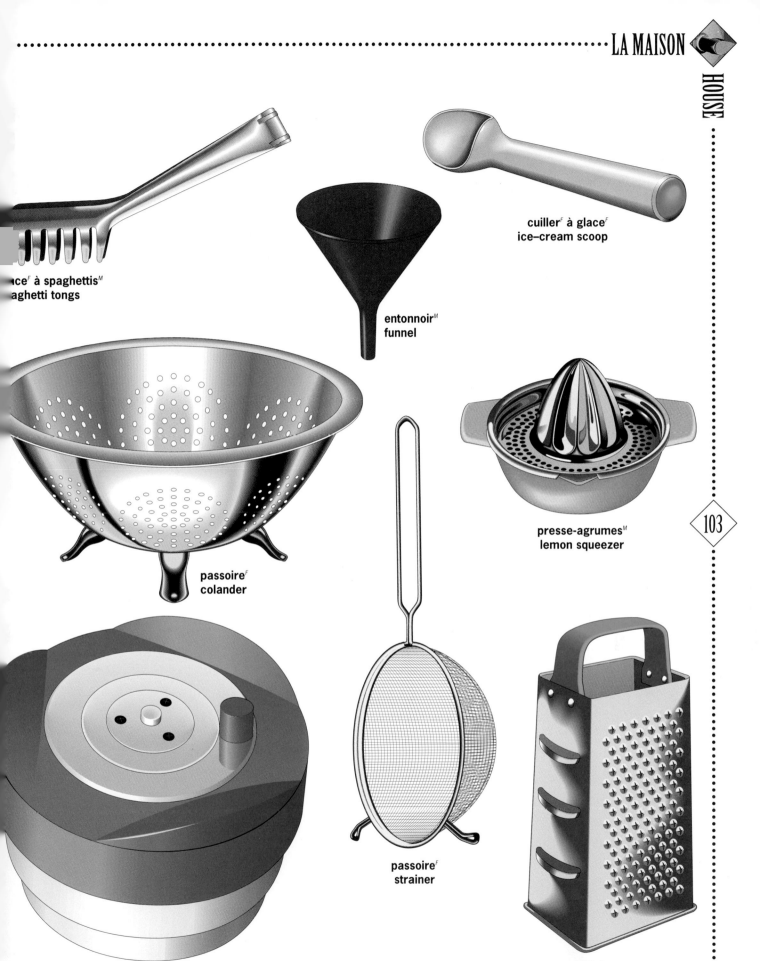
cuiller^F à glace^F
ice–cream scoop

entonnoir^M
funnel

ace^F à spaghettis^M
aghetti tongs

presse-agrumes^M
lemon squeezer

103

passoire^F
colander

passoire^F
strainer

essoreuse^F à salade^F
salad spinner

râpe^F
grater

LA BATTERIE^F DE CUISINE^F
COOKING UTENSILS

poêle^F à frire
frying pan

sauteuse^F
sauté pan

marmite^F
stockpot; casserole

service^M à fondue^F
fondue set

wok^M
wok

caquelon^M
fondue pot

réchaud^M
burner

bain-marie^M
double boiler

casserole^F
saucepan

étuveuse^F
vegetable steame

plats^M à four^M
roasting pans

autocuiseur^M
pressure cooker

régulateur^M de pression^F
pressure regulator

soupape^F
safety valve

LES APPAREILS^M ÉLECTROMÉNAGERS
KITCHEN APPLIANCES

...etière^F filtre^M
...omatic drip coffee maker

réservoir^M
reservoir

panier^M
basket

verseuse^F
carafe

plaque^F chauffante
warming plate

interrupteur^M
on-off switch

**bouilloire^F
kettle**

**batteur^M à main^F
hand mixer**

éjecteur^M de fouets^M
beater ejector

commande^F de vitesse^F
speed control

fouet^M
beater

...élangeur^M
...ender

**mélangeur^M à main^F
hand blender**

récipient^M
container

couteau^M
cutting blade

bouton^M-poussoir^M
push button

**grille-pain^M
toaster**

fente^F
slot

manette^F
lever

thermostat^M
temperature control

LE RÉFRIGÉRATEUR^M
REFRIGERATOR

bac^M à glaçons^M
ice cube tray

congélateur^M
freezer compartment

commande^F de température^F
thermostat control

œufrier^M
egg tray

casier^M à beurre^M
butter compartment

casier^M laitier
dairy compartment

bac^M à légumes^M
crisper

réfrigérateur^M
refrigerator compartment

barre^F de retenue^F
guard rail

bac^M à viande^F
meat tray

tablette^F de verre^M
glass cover

clayette^F
shelf

porte^F étagère^F
storage door

LES APPAREILS^M DE CUISSON^F
COOKING APPLIANCES

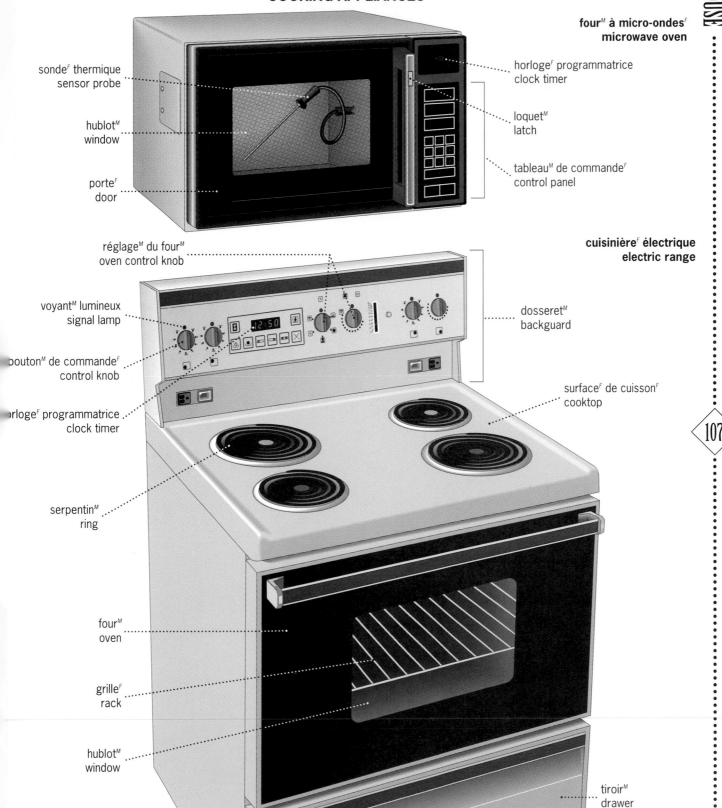

four^M à micro-ondes^F
microwave oven

sonde^F thermique
sensor probe

hublot^M
window

porte^F
door

horloge^F programmatrice
clock timer

loquet^M
latch

tableau^M de commande^F
control panel

réglage^M du four^M
oven control knob

voyant^M lumineux
signal lamp

bouton^M de commande^F
control knob

horloge^F programmatrice
clock timer

serpentin^M
ring

cuisinière^F électrique
electric range

dosseret^M
backguard

surface^F de cuisson^F
cooktop

four^M
oven

grille^F
rack

hublot^M
window

tiroir^M
drawer

LES OUTILS^M DE BRICOLAGE^M
CARPENTRY TOOLS

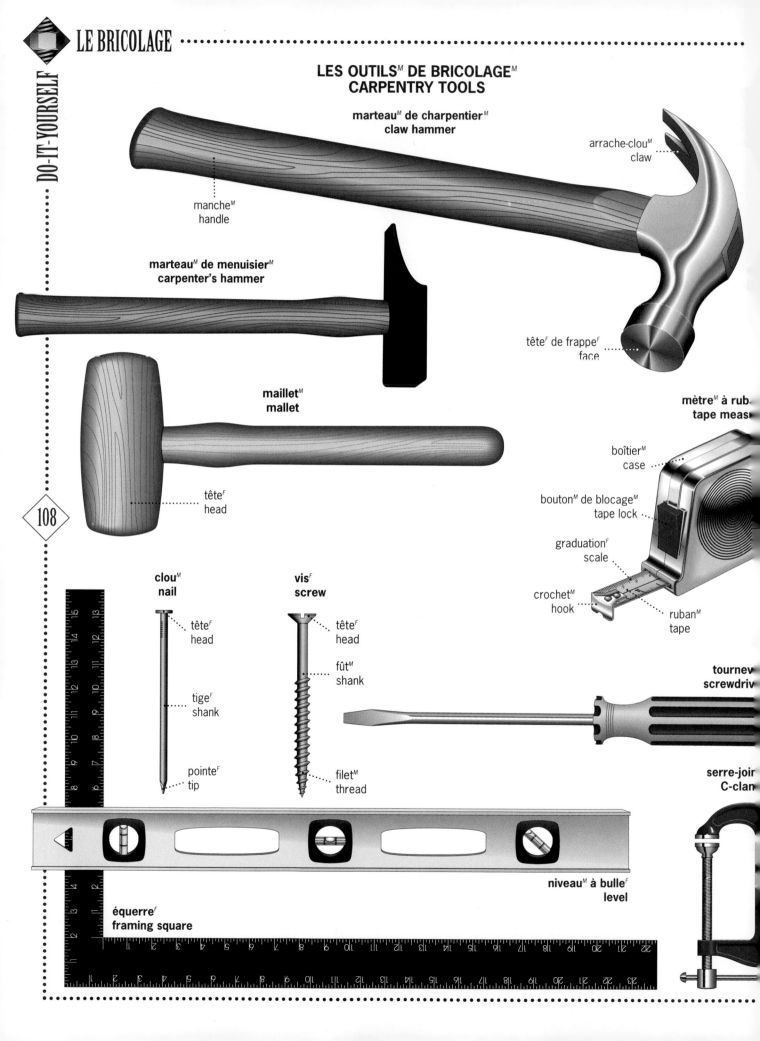

marteau^M **de charpentier**^M
claw hammer

arrache-clou^M
claw

manche^M
handle

marteau^M **de menuisier**^M
carpenter's hammer

tête^F de frappe^F
face

maillet^M
mallet

mètre^M à rub...
tape meas...

boîtier^M
case

bouton^M de blocage^M
tape lock

tête^F
head

graduation^F
scale

crochet^M
hook

ruban^M
tape

clou^M
nail

vis^F
screw

tête^F
head

tête^F
head

fût^M
shank

tournev...
screwdriv...

tige^F
shank

pointe^F
tip

filet^M
thread

serre-joir...
C-clam...

niveau^M à bulle^F
level

équerre^F
framing square

108

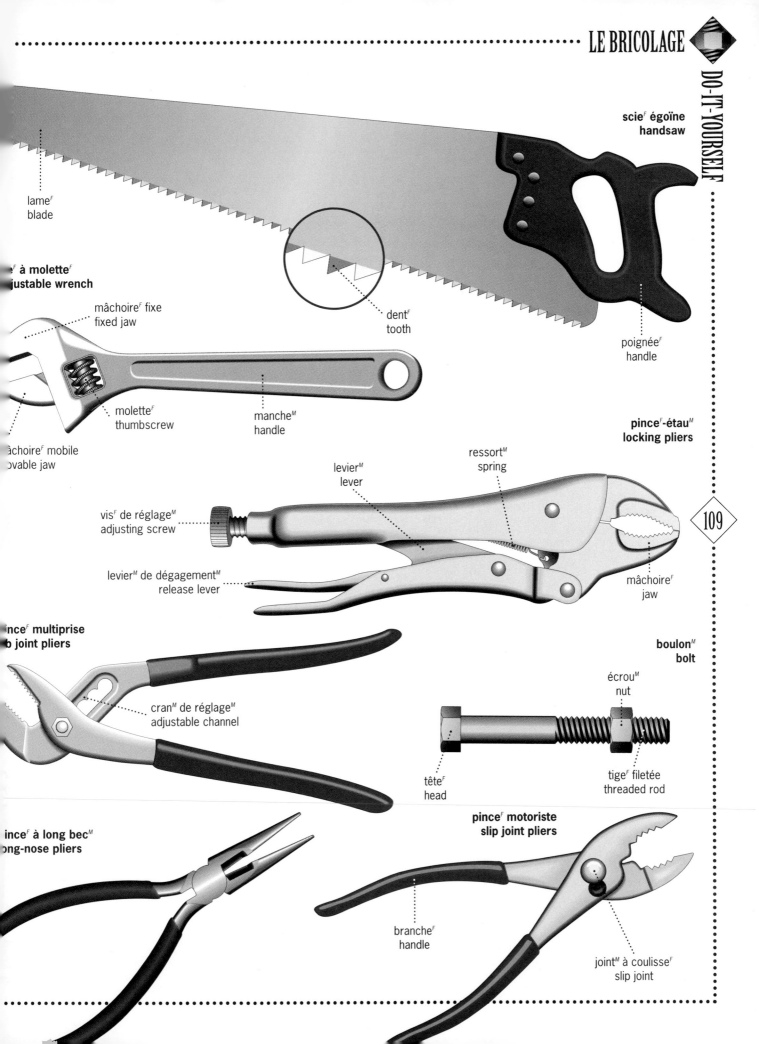

scie^F égoïne
handsaw

lame^F
blade

dent^F
tooth

poignée^F
handle

é^F à molette^F
djustable wrench

mâchoire^F fixe
fixed jaw

molette^F
thumbscrew

manche^M
handle

âchoire^F mobile
ovable jaw

pince^F-étau^M
locking pliers

levier^M
lever

ressort^M
spring

vis^F de réglage^M
adjusting screw

levier^M de dégagement^M
release lever

mâchoire^F
jaw

109

ince^F multiprise
b joint pliers

cran^M de réglage^M
adjustable channel

boulon^M
bolt

écrou^M
nut

tête^F
head

tige^F filetée
threaded rod

ince^F à long bec^M
ong-nose pliers

pince^F motoriste
slip joint pliers

branche^F
handle

joint^M à coulisse^F
slip joint

LES OUTILS^M ÉLECTRIQUES
ELECTRIC TOOLS

perceuse^F électrique
electric drill

mèche^F hélicoï
auger

boîtier^M
housing

blocage^M de l'interrupteur^M
switch lock

mandrin^M
chuck

foret^M hélicoïdal
twist drill

mors^M
jaw

poignée^F auxiliaire
auxiliary handle

interrupteur^M
switch

clé^F de mandrin^M
chuck key

poignée^F-pistolet^M
pistol grip handle

câble^M
cable

fiche^F
plug

110

scie^F circulaire
circular saw

poignée^F
handle

protège-lame^M
blade guard

interrupteur^M
trigger switch

lame^F de scie^F circulai
circular saw bla

inclinaison^F de la lame^F
blade tilting mechanism

pointe^F
tip

moteur^M
motor

bouton^M-guide^M
knob handle

lame^F
blade

semelle^F
base plate

dent^F
tooth

LA PEINTURE^F D'ENTRETIEN^M
PAINTING UPKEEP

leau^M à peinture^F
nt roller

bac^M
tray

grattoir^M
scraper

lame^F
blade

échelle^F coulissante
extension ladder

armature^F
roller frame

manche^M
handle

pinceau^M
brush

manchon^M
roller cover

soies^F
bristles

cabeau^M
epladder

montant^M
side rail

poulie^F
pulley

dispositif^M de blocage^M
locking device

échelon^M
rung

marchepied^M
platform ladder

corde^F de tirage^M
hoisting rope

patin^M antidérapant
anti-slip shoe

LES VÊTEMENTS

LES VÊTEMENTS^M D'HOMME^M
MEN'S CLOTHING

chemise^F
shirt

col^M
collar

pointe^F de col^M
collar point

patte^F de boutonnage^M
placket

poche^F poitrine^F
breast pocket

devant^M
front

poignet^M
cuff

bouton^M
button

pan^M
shirttail

bretel
suspend

coulisse^F
adjustment slide

boutonnière^F
button loop

patte^F
leather end

pince^F
suspender clip

cravate^F
tie

pan^M arrière
rear apron

tour^M de cou^M
neck end

passant^M
loop

pan^M avant
front apron

pantalon^M
pants

ceinture^F montée
waistband

poche^F
pocket

braguette^F
fly

ceinture^F
belt

boucle^F de ceinture^F
frame

cran^M
punch hole

passant^M
belt carrier

ardillon^M
tongue

pli^M
crease

gilet^M **athlétique**
tank top; undershirt

caleçon^M
boxer shorts

slip^M **ouvert**
briefs

braguette^F
fly

enfourchure^F
crotch

ceinture^F élastique
waistband

revers^M
cuff

veston^M **croisé**
double-breasted jacket

col^M
collar

doublure^F
lining

pochette^F
breast welt pocket

manche^F
sleeve

poche^F-ticket^M
concealed pocket

rabat^M
flap

poche^F plaquée
patch pocket

duffle-coat^M
duffle coat

capuchon^M
hood

brandebourg^M
frog

bûchette^F
toggle fastening

casquette^F
cap

calotte^F
crown

visière^F
peak

tuque^F
stocking cap

casquette^F **norvégienne**
hunting cap

cache-oreilles^M abattant
ear flap

113

blouson^M **court**
jacket

bouton-pression^M
snap fastener

ceinture^F élastique
elastic waistband

blouson^M **long**
windbreacker

ceinture^F montée
waistband

cordon^M coulissant
drawstring

LES VÊTEMENTS^M DE FEMME^F
WOMEN'S CLOTHING

toque^F
toque

bonnet^M
knitted hat

cagoule^F
balaclava

visière^F
peak

béret^M
beret

tailleur^M
suit

chemisier^M **classique**
blouse

caban^M
double-breasted jacket

veste^F
jacket

jupe^F
skirt

manteau^M
overcoat

poncho^M
poncho

robe^F**-polo**^M
dress

114

jean^M
jeans

fuseau^M
ski pants

short^M
shorts

bermuda^M
Bermuda shorts

sous-pied^M
footstrap

jupe^F **droite**
straight skirt

jupe^F**-culotte**^F
culottes

jupe^F **plissée**
pleated skirt

LES VÊTEMENTS^M DE FEMME^F
WOMEN'S CLOTHING

pyjama^M
pajamas

soutien-gorge^M
bra

bretelle^F ·······
shoulder strap

bonnet^M ·······
cup

culotte^F
pants

jupon^M
half-slip

peignoir^M
bathrobe

116

LES TRICOTS^M
SWEATERS

ras-de-cou^M
crew neck sweater

col^M roulé
turtleneck

cardigan^M
cardigan

polo^M
polo shirt

gilet^M de laine^F
V-neck cardigan

117

débardeur^M
slipover

bride^F de suspension^F
hanger loop

manche^F
sleeve

encolure^F en V
V-neck

bouton^M
button

poche^F
pocket

bord^M-côte^F
ribbing

LES GANTS^M ET LES BAS^M
GLOVES AND STOCKINGS

gants^M
gloves

doigt^M
glove finger

pouce^M
thumb

paume^F
palm

bouton^M pression^F
snap fastener

baguette^F
stitching

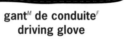

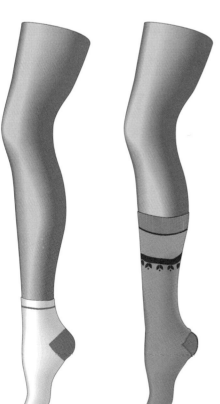

gant^M de conduite^F
driving glove

mitaine^F
mitten

chausse
s

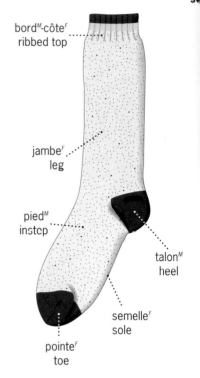

bord^M-côte^F
ribbed top

jambe^F
leg

pied^M
instep

talon^M
heel

semelle^F
sole

pointe^F
toe

118

collant^M
tights

socquette^F
ankle sock

chaussette^F
sock

mi-bas^M
knee-high sock

bas^M
stocking

LES CHAUSSURES^F
SHOES

brodequin^M
heavy duty boot

ballerine^F
ballerina

sandale^F
slingback

cuissarde^F
thigh-boot

escarpin^M
pump

tennis^M
tennis shoe

espadrille^F
espadrille

flâneur^M
loafer

119

socque^M
clog

mocassin^M
moccasin

botte^F
boot

bottine^F
ankle boot

LES VÊTEMENTS

TENUEF **D'EXERCICE**M
SPORTSWEAR

VÊTEMENTSM D'EXERCICEM
EXERCISE WEAR

débardeurM
tank top

maillotM **de bain**M
swimsuit

justaucorpsM
leotard

SURVÊTEMENTSM
TRACK SUIT

pullM **d'entraînement**M
sweatshirt

anorakM
windbreaker

pullM **à capuche**F
hooded sweatshirt

pantalonM
pants

pantalonM **molleton**M
sweatpants

VÊTEMENTS^M D'EXERCICE^M
EXERCISE WEAR

collant^M sans pied^M
footless tights

jambière^F
leg-warmer

slip^M de bain^M
swimming trunks

short^M boxeur^M
boxer shorts

chaussure^F de sport^M
running shoe

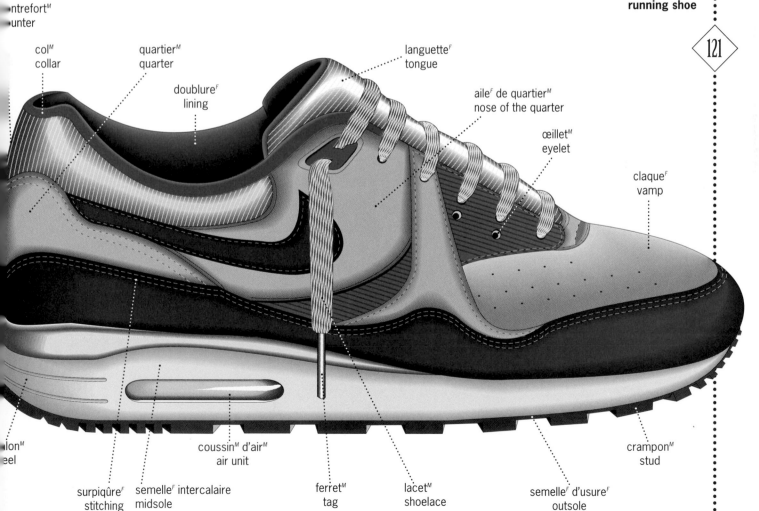

∎ntrefort^M
∎unter

col^M
collar

quartier^M
quarter

doublure^F
lining

languette^F
tongue

aile^F de quartier^M
nose of the quarter

œillet^M
eyelet

claque^F
vamp

∎lon^M
∎eel

coussin^M d'air^M
air unit

ferret^M
tag

lacet^M
shoelace

crampon^M
stud

surpiqûre^F
stitching

semelle^F intercalaire
midsole

semelle^F d'usure^F
outsole

L'HYGIÈNE^F DENTAIRE
DENTAL CARE

brosse^F à dents^F
toothbrush

stimulateur^M de gencives^F
stimulator tip

manche^M
handle

poils^M
bristles

soie^F denta
dental flo

tête^F
head

dentifrice^M
toothpaste

LA COIFFURE^F
HAIRDRESSING

peigne^M à tige^F
tail comb

démêloir^M
rake comb

sèche-cheveux^M
hair-dryer

ventilateur^M
fan

sélecteur^M de température^F
heat selector switch

corps^M
barrel

heat air

chal. air

brosse^F pneumatique
hairbrush

peigne^M afro
Afro pick

sélecteur^M de vitesse^F
speed selector switch

interrupteur^M
on-off switch

grille^F de sortie^F d'air^M
air-outlet grille

buse^F
air concentrator

poignée^F
handle

122

LES ARTICLES^M DE MAROQUINERIE^F
LEATHER GOODS

c^M seau^M
awstring bag

et^M de serrage^M
wstring

sac^M à dos^M
knapsack

porte-clés^M
key case

portefeuille^M
wallet

bandoulière^F
shoulder strap

porte-monnaie^M
purse

poche^F frontale
front pocket

LES LUNETTES^F

verre^M
glass lens

pont^M
bridge

barre^F
bar

cercle^M
rim

plaquette^F
nose pad

branche^F
temple

123

LE PARAPLUIE^M
UMBRELLA

toile^F
canopy

embout^M de baleine^F
tip

rayon^M
spreader

coulant^M
ring

attache^F
tie

parapluie^M télescopique
telescopic umbrella

manche^M
shank

fourreau^M
cover

baleine^F
rib

ferret^M
tab

poignée^F
handle

COMMUNICATIONS

LES COMMUNICATIONS^F PAR TÉLÉPHONE^M
COMMUNICATION BY TELEPHONE

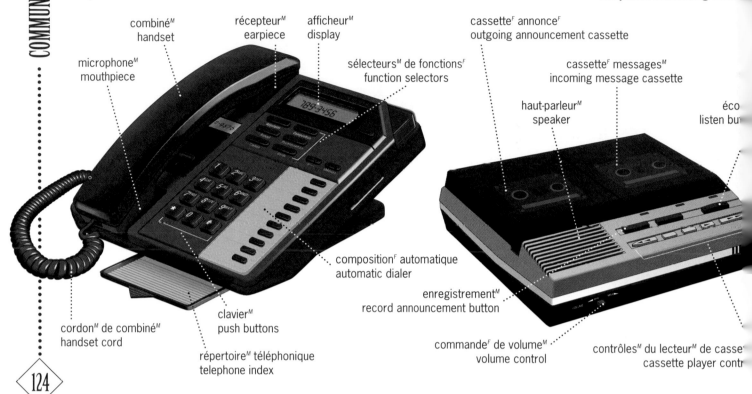

poste^M téléphonique
telephone set

combiné^M
handset

récepteur^M
earpiece

afficheur^M
display

microphone^M
mouthpiece

sélecteurs^M de fonctions^F
function selectors

cordon^M de combiné^M
handset cord

clavier^M
push buttons

composition^F automatique
automatic dialer

répertoire^M téléphonique
telephone index

répondeur^M téléphoni...
telephone answering mach...

cassette^F annonce^F
outgoing announcement cassette

cassette^F messages^M
incoming message cassette

haut-parleur^M
speaker

éco...
listen bu...

enregistrement^M
record announcement button

commande^F de volume^M
volume control

contrôles^M du lecteur^M de casse...
cassette player contr...

124

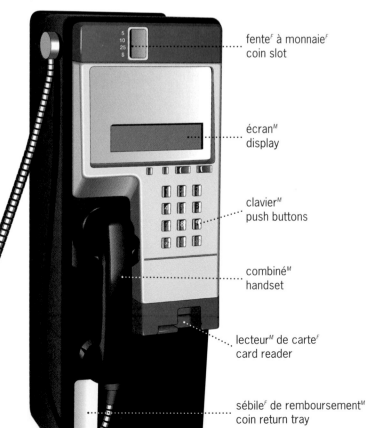

téléphone^M public
pay phone

fente^F à monnaie^F
coin slot

écran^M
display

clavier^M
push buttons

combiné^M
handset

lecteur^M de carte^F
card reader

sébile^F de remboursement^M
coin return tray

poste^M à clavier^M
push-button telephone

téléphone^M cellulaire portatif
portable cellular telephone

poste^M sans cordon^M
cordless telephone

LA PHOTOGRAPHIE^F
PHOTOGRAPHY

griffe^F porte-accessoires^M
accessory shoe

appareil^M à visée^F reflex mono-objectif^M
single lens reflex (slr) camera

rebobinage^M
film rewind button

contact^M électrique
hot-shoe contact

mode^M d'entraînement^M du film^M
film advance button

écran^M de contrôle^M
control panel

...cteur^M de fonctions^F
control dial

mode^M d'exposition^F
exposure button

sensibilité^F du film^M
film speed

prise^F de télécommande^F
remote control terminal

boîtier^M
camera body

bague^F de mise^F au point^M
focus setting ring

déclencheur^M
shutter release button

objectif^M
objective lens

appareil^M à télémètre^M couplé
compact camera

flash^M électronique
electronic flash

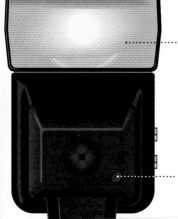

réflecteur^M
flashtube

perforation^F
perforation

cassette^F de pellicule^F
cassette film

cellule^F photoélectrique
photoelectric cell

amorce^F
film leader

Polaroid®^M
Polaroid® Land camera

pied^M de fixation^F
mounting foot

...ppareil^M petit-format
...ocket camera

cartouche^F de pellicule^F
cartridge film

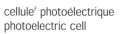

film^M-pack^M
film pack

LA TÉLÉVISION^F
TELEVISION

téléviseur^M
television set

coffret^M
cabinet

écran^M
screen

capteur^M de télécomma...
remote control sensor

interrupteur^M d'alimenta...
on/off button

lampes^F témoins^M
indicators

boutons^M de réglage^M
tuning controls

télécommande^F
remote control

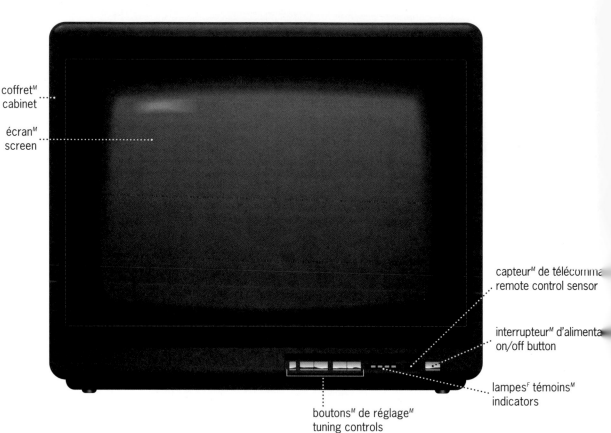

mode^M télévision^F
TV mode

réglage^M du volume^M
volume control

mode^M magnétoscope^M
VCR mode

sélecteur^M télé^F/vidéo^F
TV/video button

sélection^F des canaux^M
channel selector controls

interrupteur^M du télévise...
TV on/off button

commandes^F de préréglage^M
preset buttons

recherche^F des canaux^M
channel scan buttons

commandes^F du magnétoscope^M
VCR controls

interrupteur^M du magnétoscop...
VCR on/off button

ralenti^M
slow-motion

rebobinage^M
rewind

enregistrement^M
record

avance^F rapide
fast forward

pause^F/arrêt^M sur l'image^F
pause

lecture^F
play

arrêt^M
stop

LA VIDÉO^F
VIDEO

interrupteur^M d'alimentation^F
on/off button

affichage^M des données^F
data display

commandes^F de préréglage^M
preset buttons

magnétoscope^M
videocassette recorder

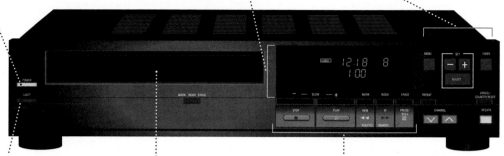

commande^F d'éjection^F de la cassette^F
cassette eject switch

logement^M de la cassette^F
cassette compartment

commandes^F de fonctions^F
controls

caméra^F **vidéo**
video camera

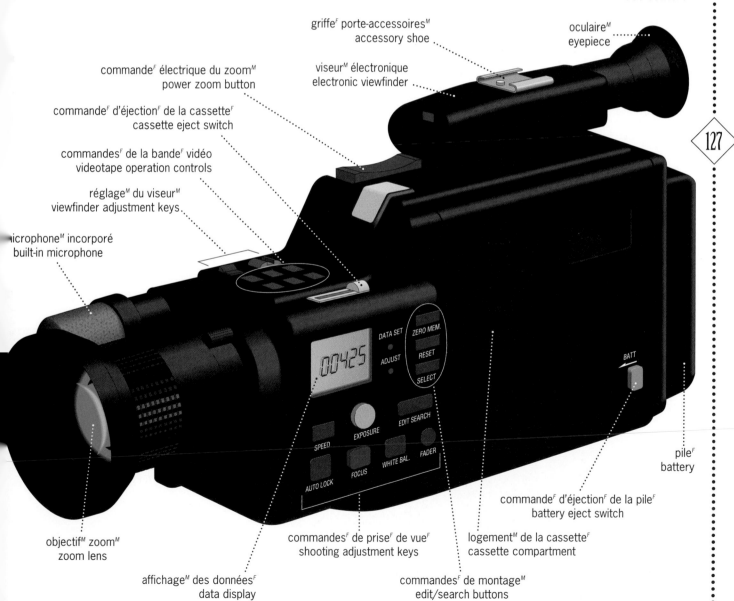

griffe^F porte-accessoires^M
accessory shoe

oculaire^M
eyepiece

commande^F électrique du zoom^M
power zoom button

viseur^M électronique
electronic viewfinder

commande^F d'éjection^F de la cassette^F
cassette eject switch

commandes^F de la bande^F vidéo
videotape operation controls

réglage^M du viseur^M
viewfinder adjustment keys

microphone^M incorporé
built-in microphone

127

pile^F
battery

commande^F d'éjection^F de la pile^F
battery eject switch

objectif^M zoom^M
zoom lens

affichage^M des données^F
data display

commandes^F de prise^F de vue^F
shooting adjustment keys

logement^M de la cassette^F
cassette compartment

commandes^F de montage^M
edit/search buttons

LES COMMUNICATIONS

LA CHAÎNE^F STÉRÉO
STEREO SYSTEM

COMPOSANTES^F D'UN SYSTÈME^M
SYSTEM COMPONENTS

tuner^M
tuner

antenne^F FM
FM antenna

antenne^F AM
AM antenna

platine^F tourne-disque^M
turntable

lecteur^M de disque^M compact
compact disk player

amplificateur^M
amplifier

platine^F cassette^F
cassette tape deck

égalisateur^M graphique
graphic equalizer

enceinte^F acoustique
loudspeakers

canal^M gauche
left channel

canal^M droit
right channel

haut-parleur^M d'aigus^M
tweeter

casque^M d'écout
headphone

haut-parleur^M de médium^M
midrange

coussinet^M
ear cushion

serre-tête^M
headband

haut-parleur^M de graves^M
woofer

membrane^F
diaphragm; cone

glissière^F d'ajustement^M
adjusting band

treillis^M
speaker cover

écouteur^M
earphone

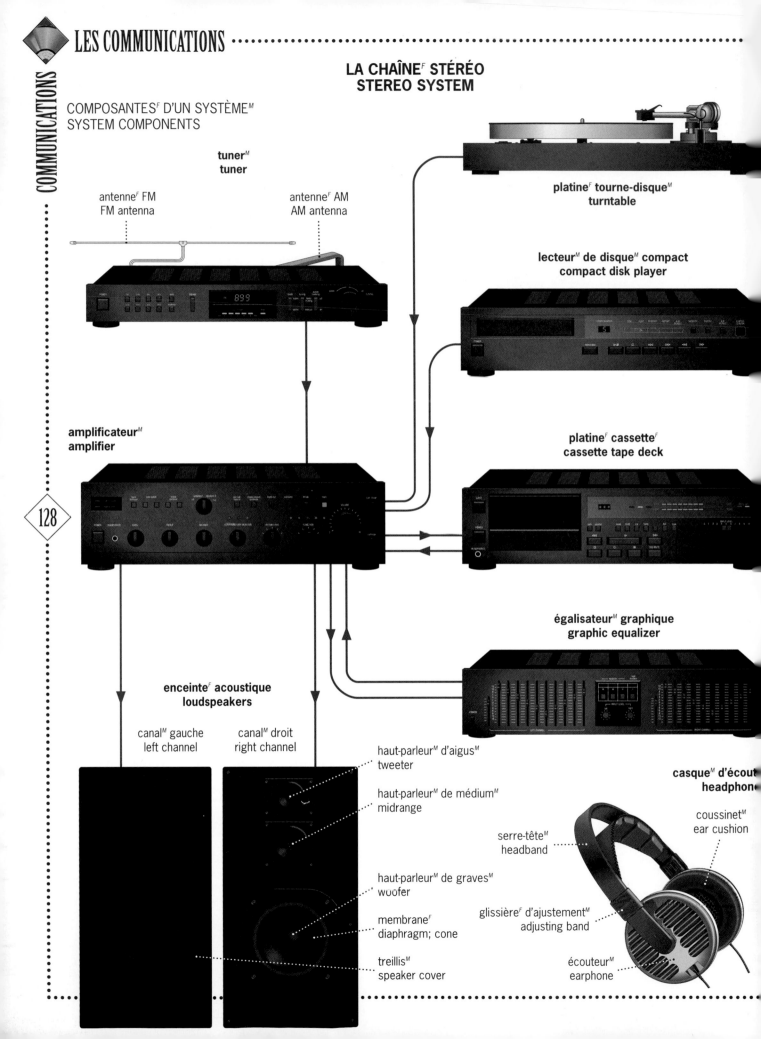

LES APPAREILS^M DE SON^M PORTATIFS
PORTABLE SOUND SYSTEMS

radiocassette^F
portable CD AM/FM cassette recorder

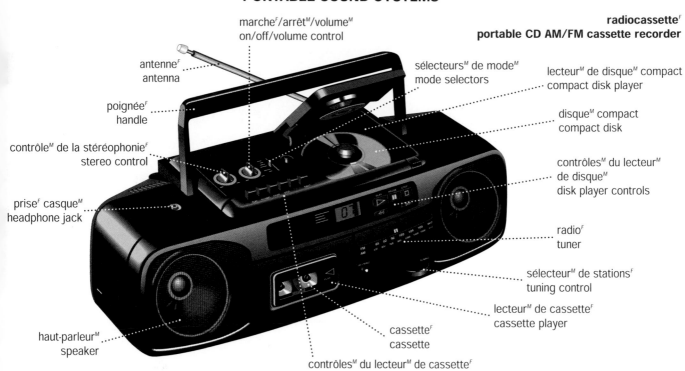

marche^F/arrêt^M/volume^M
on/off/volume control

antenne^F
antenna

sélecteurs^M de mode^M
mode selectors

poignée^F
handle

lecteur^M de disque^M compact
compact disk player

disque^M compact
compact disk

contrôle^M de la stéréophonie^F
stereo control

contrôles^M du lecteur^M
de disque^M
disk player controls

prise^F casque^M
headphone jack

radio^F
tuner

sélecteur^M de stations^F
tuning control

lecteur^M de cassette^F
cassette player

haut-parleur^M
speaker

cassette^F
cassette

contrôles^M du lecteur^M de cassette^F
cassette player controls

baladeur^M
personal AM/FM cassette player; Walkman®

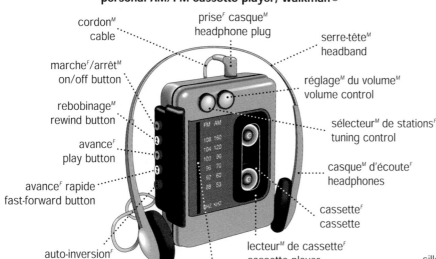

cordon^M
cable

prise^F casque^M
headphone plug

serre-tête^M
headband

marche^F/arrêt^M
on/off button

réglage^M du volume^M
volume control

rebobinage^M
rewind button

sélecteur^M de stations^F
tuning control

avance^F
play button

casque^M d'écoute^F
headphones

avance^F rapide
fast-forward button

cassette^F
cassette

auto-inversion^F
auto reverse

lecteur^M de cassette^F
cassette player

radio^F
tuner

disque^M compact
compact disk

surface^F pressée
pressed area

début^M de lecture^F
reading start

bande^F d'identification^F technique
technical identification band

disque^M
record

sillon^M de départ^M
spiral-in groove

plage^F de séparation^F
spiral

surface^F gravée
band

sillon^M de sortie^F
tail-out groove

étiquette^F
label

trou^M central
centre hole

cassette^F
cassette

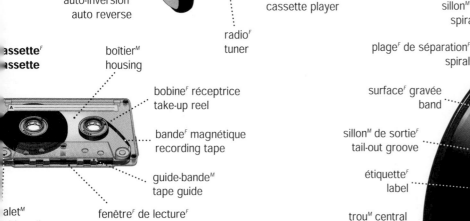

boîtier^M
housing

bobine^F réceptrice
take-up reel

bande^F magnétique
recording tape

guide-bande^M
tape guide

galet^M
guide roller

fenêtre^F de lecture^F
playing window

L'AUTOMOBILE^F
CAR

carrosserie^F
body

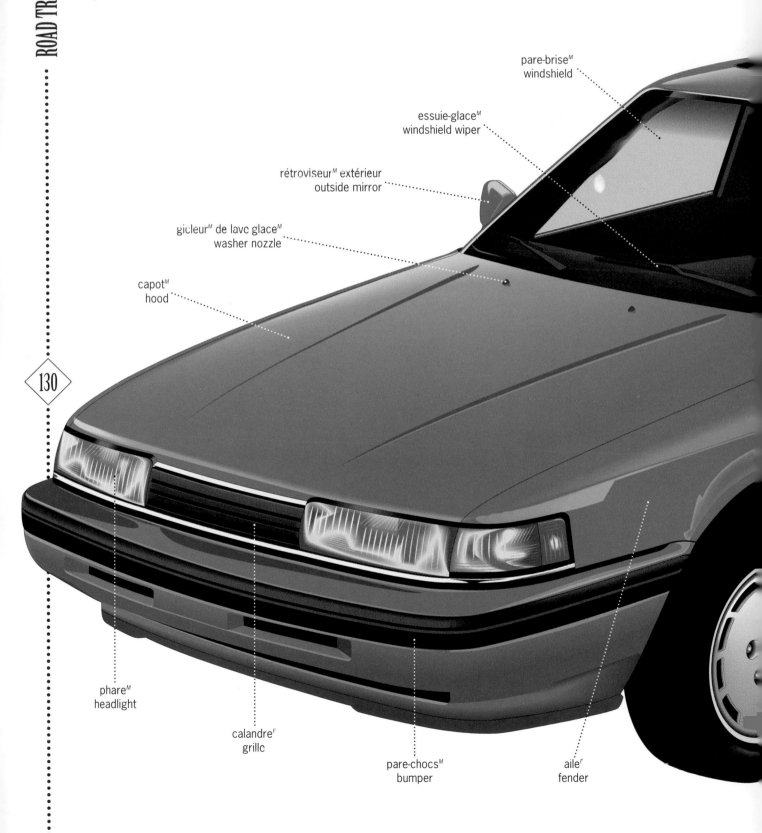

pare-brise^M
windshield

essuie-glace^M
windshield wiper

rétroviseur^M extérieur
outside mirror

gicleur^M de lave glace^M
washer nozzle

capot^M
hood

130

phare^M
headlight

calandre^F
grille

pare-chocs^M
bumper

aile^F
fender

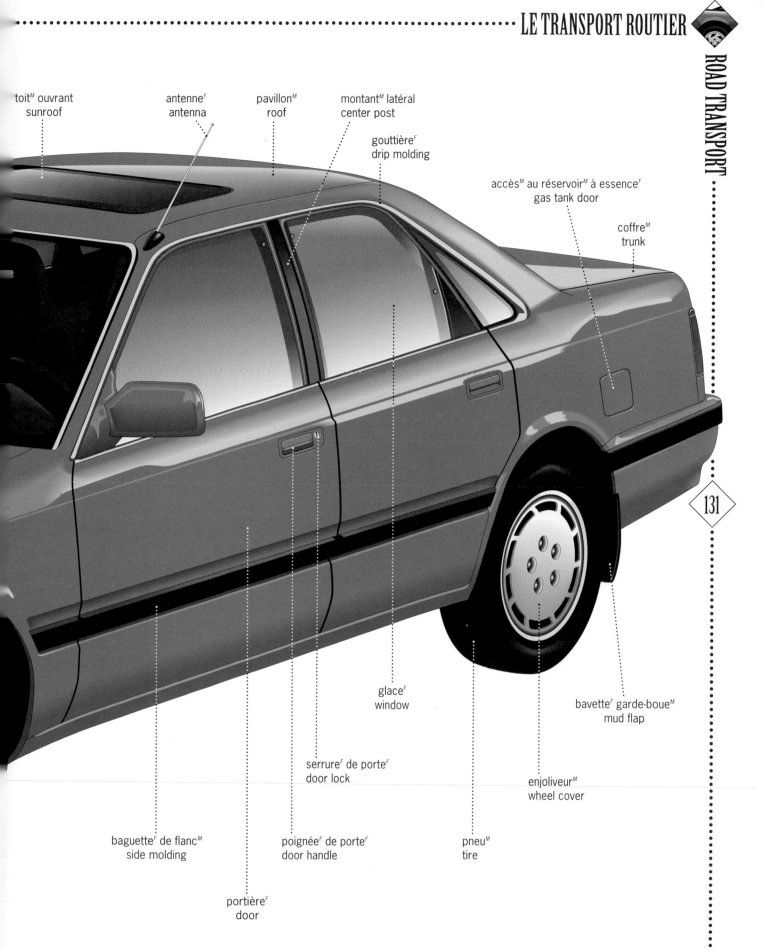

toit^M ouvrant
sunroof

antenne^F
antenna

pavillon^M
roof

montant^M latéral
center post

gouttière^F
drip molding

accès^M au réservoir^M à essence^F
gas tank door

coffre^M
trunk

glace^F
window

bavette^F garde-boue^M
mud flap

serrure^F de porte^F
door lock

enjoliveur^M
wheel cover

baguette^F de flanc^M
side molding

poignée^F de porte^F
door handle

pneu^M
tire

portière^F
door

L'AUTOMOBILE[F]
CAR

tableau[M] de bord[M]
dashboard

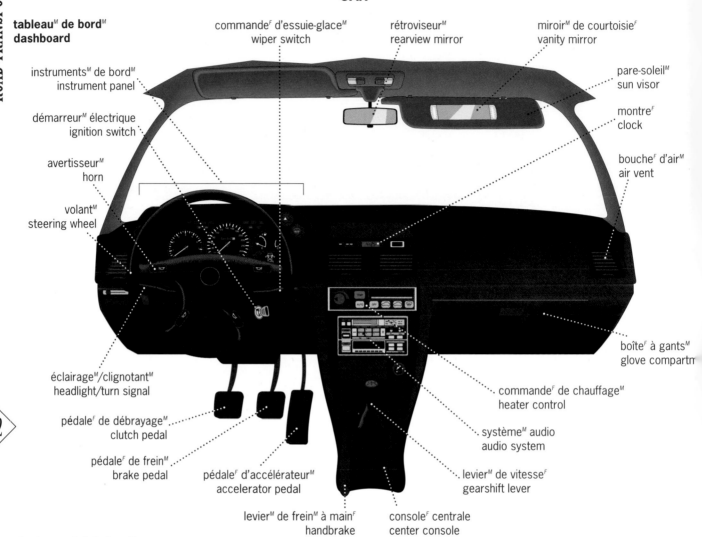

commande[F] d'essuie-glace[M]
wiper switch

rétroviseur[M]
rearview mirror

miroir[M] de courtoisie[F]
vanity mirror

instruments[M] de bord[M]
instrument panel

pare-soleil[M]
sun visor

démarreur[M] électrique
ignition switch

montre[F]
clock

avertisseur[M]
horn

bouche[F] d'air[M]
air vent

volant[M]
steering wheel

boîte[F] à gants[M]
glove compartm

éclairage[M]/clignotant[M]
headlight/turn signal

commande[F] de chauffage[M]
heater control

pédale[F] de débrayage[M]
clutch pedal

système[M] audio
audio system

pédale[F] de frein[M]
brake pedal

levier[M] de vitesse[F]
gearshift lever

pédale[F] d'accélérateur[M]
accelerator pedal

levier[M] de frein[M] à main[F]
handbrake

console[F] centrale
center console

instruments[M] de bord[M]
instrument panel

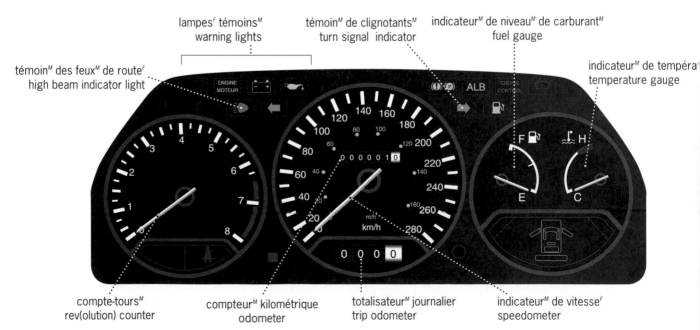

lampes[F] témoins[M]
warning lights

témoin[M] de clignotants[M]
turn signal indicator

indicateur[M] de niveau[M] de carburant[M]
fuel gauge

témoin[M] des feux[M] de route[F]
high beam indicator light

indicateur[M] de tempéra
temperature gauge

compte-tours[M]
rev(olution) counter

compteur[M] kilométrique
odometer

totalisateur[M] journalier
trip odometer

indicateur[M] de vitesse[F]
speedometer

LES FEUX^M CAR LIGHTS

feux^M avant
front lights

feux^M de croisement^M
low beam

feux^M clignotants
turn signal

feux^M de gabarit^M
side light

feux^M de route^F
high beam

feux^M de brouillard^M
fog light

feux^M arrière
rear lights

feux^M clignotants
turn signal

feux^M rouges arrière
tail light

feux^M de gabarit^M
side light

feux^M stop^M
brake light

feux^M de recul^M
backup light

feu^M de plaque^F
license plate light

feu^M stop^M
brake light

LES TYPES^M DE CARROSSERIES^F
TYPES OF CAR BODIES

voiture^F sport^M
sports car

coach^M
two-door sedan

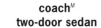

trois-portes^F
hatchback

camionnette^F
pickup truck

cabriolet^M
convertible

berline^F
four-door sedan

familiale^F
station wagon

véhicule^M tout-terrain^M
multipurpose vehicle

fourgonnette^F
minivan

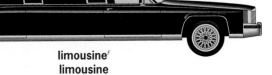

limousine^F
limousine

LE CAMIONNAGE^M
TRUCKING

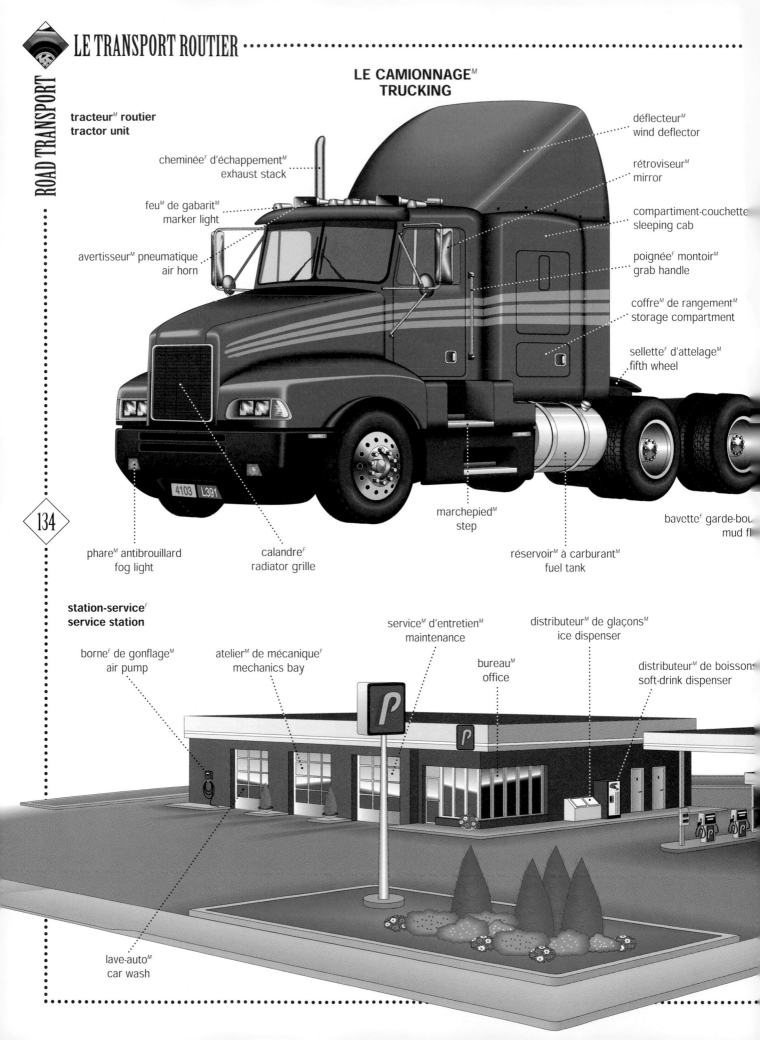

tracteur^M routier
tractor unit

cheminée^F d'échappement^M
exhaust stack

feu^M de gabarit^M
marker light

avertisseur^M pneumatique
air horn

déflecteur^M
wind deflector

rétroviseur^M
mirror

compartiment-couchette
sleeping cab

poignée^F montoir^M
grab handle

coffre^M de rangement^M
storage compartment

sellette^F d'attelage^M
fifth wheel

marchepied^M
step

bavette^F garde-bou
mud fl

phare^M antibrouillard
fog light

calandre^F
radiator grille

réservoir^M à carburant^M
fuel tank

station-service^F
service station

borne^F de gonflage^M
air pump

atelier^M de mécanique^F
mechanics bay

service^M d'entretien^M
maintenance

distributeur^M de glaçons^M
ice dispenser

bureau^M
office

distributeur^M de boissons
soft-drink dispenser

lave-auto^M
car wash

LA MOTO^F
MOTORCYCLE

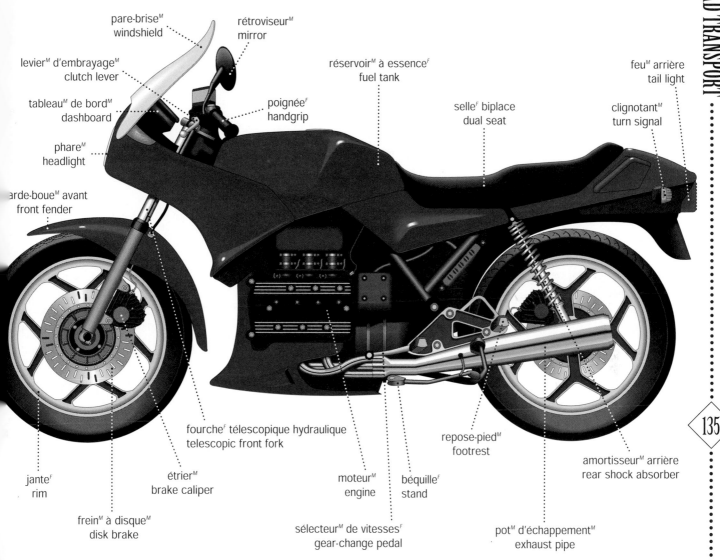

pare-brise^M
windshield

rétroviseur^M
mirror

réservoir^M à essence^F
fuel tank

feu^M arrière
tail light

levier^M d'embrayage^M
clutch lever

poignée^F
handgrip

selle^F biplace
dual seat

clignotant^M
turn signal

tableau^M de bord^M
dashboard

phare^M
headlight

garde-boue^M avant
front fender

fourche^F télescopique hydraulique
telescopic front fork

repose-pied^M
footrest

amortisseur^M arrière
rear shock absorber

jante^F
rim

étrier^M
brake caliper

moteur^M
engine

béquille^F
stand

frein^M à disque^M
disk brake

sélecteur^M de vitesses^F
gear-change pedal

pot^M d'échappement^M
exhaust pipe

disque^M
disk

135

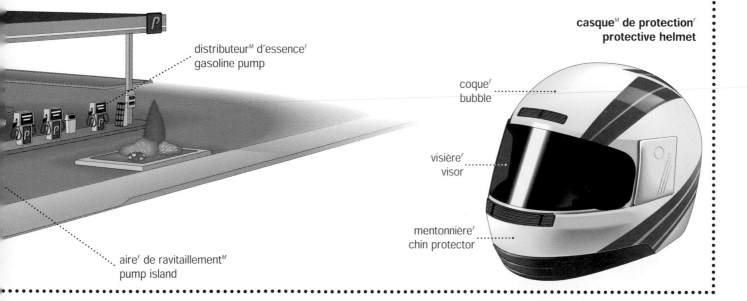

distributeur^M d'essence^F
gasoline pump

casque^M de protection^F
protective helmet

coque^F
bubble

visière^F
visor

mentonnière^F
chin protector

aire^F de ravitaillement^M
pump island

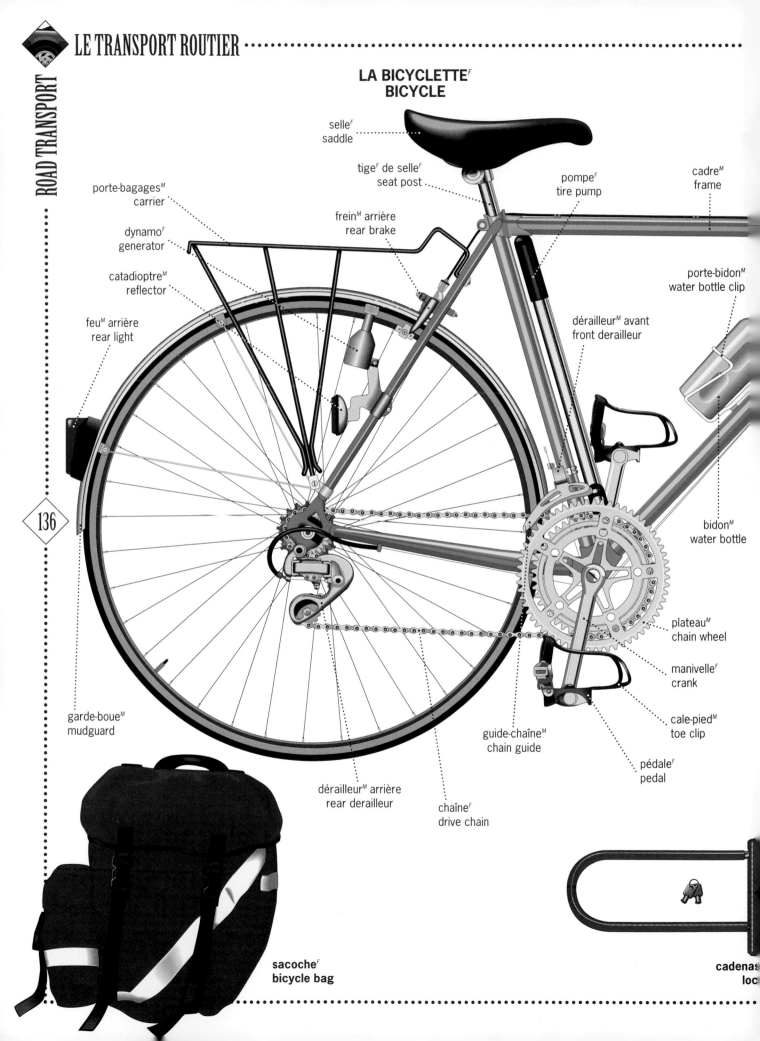

LA BICYCLETTE[F]
BICYCLE

selle[F]
saddle

tige[F] de selle[F]
seat post

pompe[F]
tire pump

cadre[M]
frame

porte-bagages[M]
carrier

frein[M] arrière
rear brake

dynamo[F]
generator

porte-bidon[M]
water bottle clip

catadioptre[M]
reflector

dérailleur[M] avant
front derailleur

feu[M] arrière
rear light

bidon[M]
water bottle

plateau[M]
chain wheel

manivelle[F]
crank

garde-boue[M]
mudguard

cale-pied[M]
toe clip

guide-chaîne[M]
chain guide

pédale[F]
pedal

dérailleur[M] arrière
rear derailleur

chaîne[F]
drive chain

sacoche[F]
bicycle bag

cadenas[M]
lock

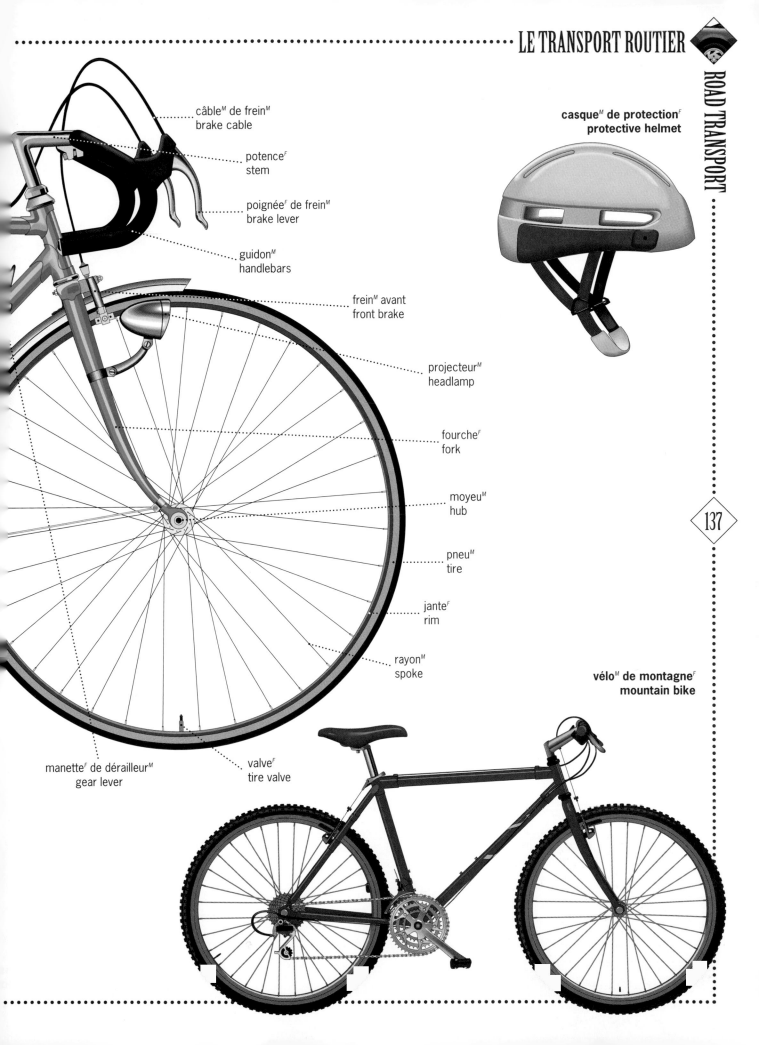

câble^M de frein^M
brake cable

potence^F
stem

poignée^F de frein^M
brake lever

guidon^M
handlebars

frein^M avant
front brake

projecteur^M
headlamp

fourche^F
fork

moyeu^M
hub

pneu^M
tire

jante^F
rim

rayon^M
spoke

manette^F de dérailleur^M
gear lever

valve^F
tire valve

casque^M de protection^F
protective helmet

vélo^M de montagne^F
mountain bike

LA LOCOMOTIVE^F DIESEL-ÉLECTRIQUE
DIESEL-ELECTRIC LOCOMOTIVE

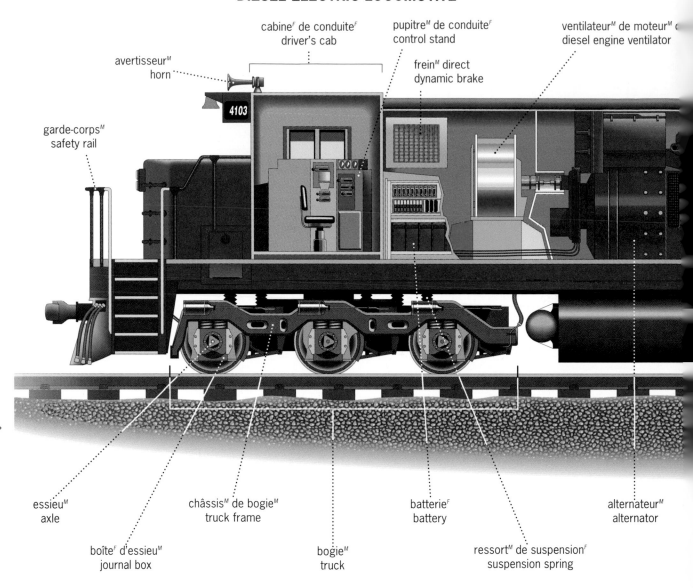

cabine^F de conduite^F
driver's cab

pupitre^M de conduite^F
control stand

ventilateur^M de moteur^M
diesel engine ventilator

avertisseur^M
horn

frein^M direct
dynamic brake

garde-corps^M
safety rail

4103

essieu^M
axle

châssis^M de bogie^M
truck frame

batterie^F
battery

alternateur^M
alternator

boîte^F d'essieu^M
journal box

bogie^M
truck

ressort^M de suspension^F
suspension spring

LES TYPES^M DE WAGONS^M
TYPES OF FREIGHT CARS

wagon^M à bestiaux^M
livestock car

wagon^M-trémie^F
hopper car

wagon^M couvert
box car

wagon^M porte-automobiles^M
automobile car

wagon^M porte-conteneurs^M
container car

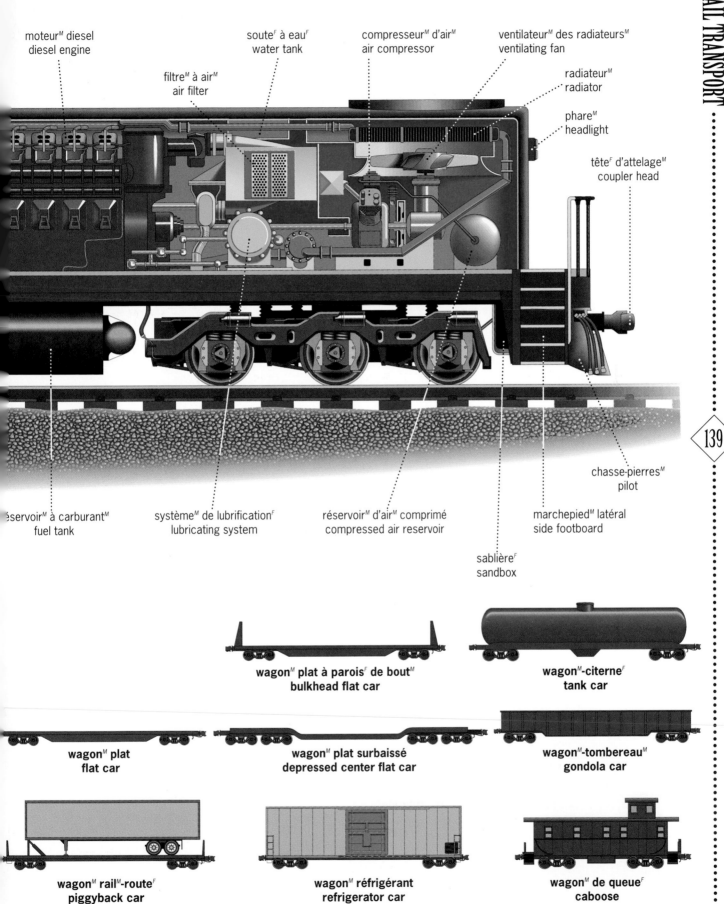

moteur^M diesel
diesel engine

filtre^M à air^M
air filter

soute^F à eau^F
water tank

compresseur^M d'air^M
air compressor

ventilateur^M des radiateurs^M
ventilating fan

radiateur^M
radiator

phare^M
headlight

tête^F d'attelage^M
coupler head

réservoir^M à carburant^M
fuel tank

système^M de lubrification^F
lubricating system

réservoir^M d'air^M comprimé
compressed air reservoir

marchepied^M latéral
side footboard

chasse-pierres^M
pilot

sablière^F
sandbox

wagon^M plat à parois^F de bout^M
bulkhead flat car

wagon^M-citerne^F
tank car

wagon^M plat
flat car

wagon^M plat surbaissé
depressed center flat car

wagon^M-tombereau^M
gondola car

wagon^M rail^M-route^F
piggyback car

wagon^M réfrigérant
refrigerator car

wagon^M de queue^F
caboose

LE PASSAGE^M À NIVEAU^M
HIGHWAY CROSSING

sonnerie^F de passage^M à niveau^M
highway crossing bell

croix^F de Saint-André
crossbuck sign

mât^M
mast

visière^F
visor

feu^M clignotant
flashing light; warning light

écran^M de visibilité^F
signal background plate

2

panneau^M nombre^M de voies^F
number of tracks sign

feu^M de lisse^F
gate arm lamp

contrepoids^M
counterweight

lisse^F
gate arm

support^M de lisse^F
gate arm support

commande^F de barrières^F
crossing gate mechanism

base^F
base

LE TRAIN^M À GRANDE VITESSE^F (T.G.V.)
HIGH-SPEED TRAIN

140

caténaire^F
catenary

pantographe^M
pantograph

cabine^F de conduite^F
driver's cab

motrice^F
power car

phare^M central
headlight

projecteur^M
headlight

feu^M de position^F
position light

compartime
voyageurs
passenger

chasse-pierres^M
pilot

ballast^M
ballast

selle^F de rail^M
tie plate

traverse^F
tie

rail^M
rail

LE QUATRE-MÂTS[M] BARQUE[F]
FOUR-MASTED BARK

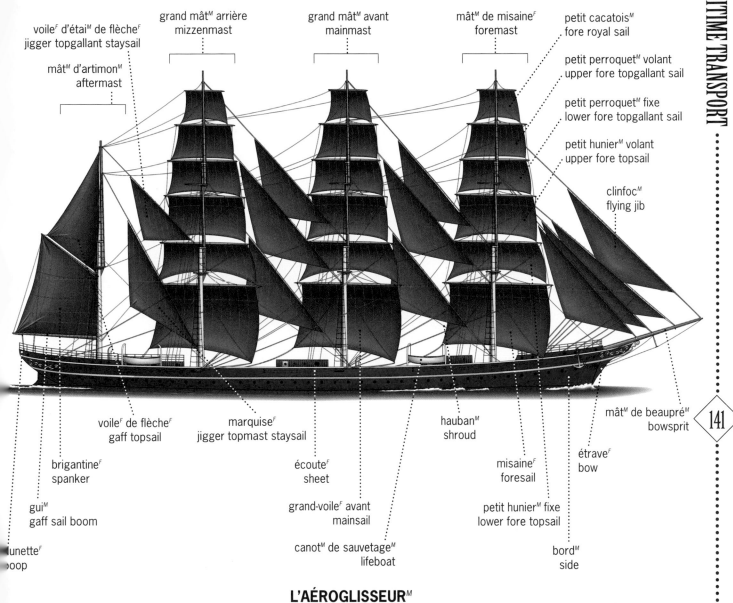

voile[F] d'étai[M] de flèche[F]
jigger topgallant staysail

mât[M] d'artimon[M]
aftermast

grand mât[M] arrière
mizzenmast

grand mât[M] avant
mainmast

mât[M] de misaine[F]
foremast

petit cacatois[M]
fore royal sail

petit perroquet[M] volant
upper fore topgallant sail

petit perroquet[M] fixe
lower fore topgallant sail

petit hunier[M] volant
upper fore topsail

clinfoc[M]
flying jib

voile[F] de flèche[F]
gaff topsail

marquise[F]
jigger topmast staysail

hauban[M]
shroud

mât[M] de beaupré[M]
bowsprit

brigantine[F]
spanker

écoute[F]
sheet

misaine[F]
foresail

étrave[F]
bow

gui[M]
gaff sail boom

grand-voile[F] avant
mainsail

petit hunier[M] fixe
lower fore topsail

bord[M]
side

unette[F]
poop

canot[M] de sauvetage[M]
lifeboat

L'AÉROGLISSEUR[M]
HOVERCRAFT

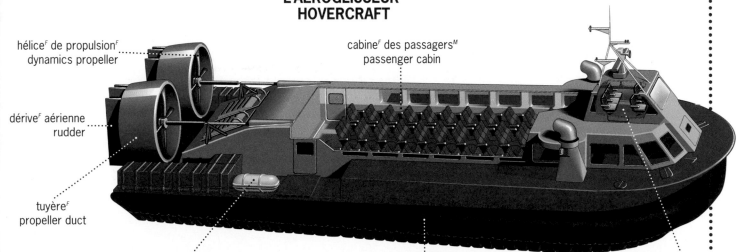

hélice[F] de propulsion[F]
dynamics propeller

cabine[F] des passagers[M]
passenger cabin

dérive[F] aérienne
rudder

tuyère[F]
propeller duct

canot[M] pneumatique de sauvetage[M]
life raft

jupe[F] souple
flexible skirt

cabine[F] de pilotage[M]
control deck

LE PAQUEBOT^M
CRUISE LINER

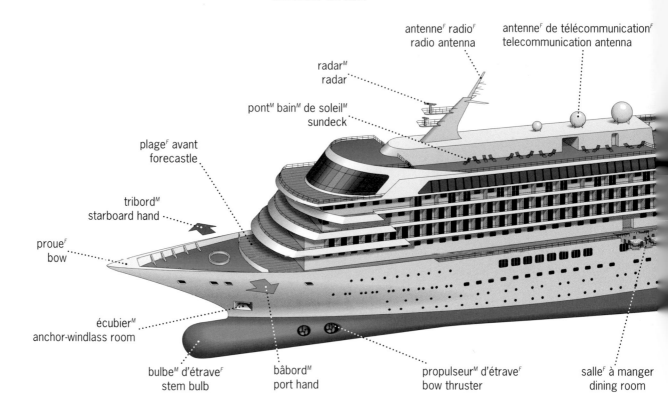

antenne^F radio^F
radio antenna

antenne^F de télécommunication^F
telecommunication antenna

radar^M
radar

pont^M bain^M de soleil^M
sundeck

plage^F avant
forecastle

tribord^M
starboard hand

proue^F
bow

écubier^M
anchor-windlass room

bulbe^M d'étrave^F
stem bulb

bâbord^M
port hand

propulseur^M d'étrave^F
bow thruster

salle^F à manger
dining room

LE PORT^M MARITIME
HARBOR

terminal^M de vrac^M
bulk terminal

portique^M de chargement^M
de conteneurs^M
container-loading bridge

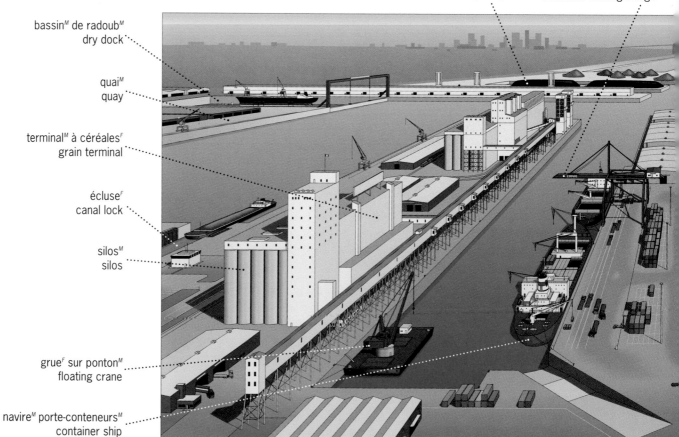

bassin^M de radoub^M
dry dock

quai^M
quay

terminal^M à céréales^F
grain terminal

écluse^F
canal lock

silos^M
silos

grue^F sur ponton^M
floating crane

navire^M porte-conteneurs^M
container ship

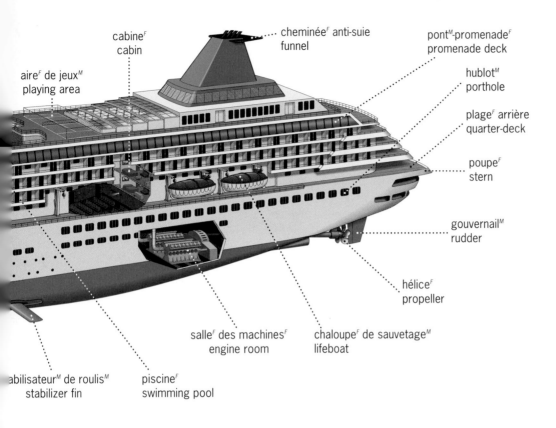

aire^F de jeux^M
playing area

cabine^F
cabin

cheminée^F anti-suie
funnel

pont^M-promenade^F
promenade deck

hublot^M
porthole

plage^F arrière
quarter-deck

poupe^F
stern

gouvernail^M
rudder

hélice^F
propeller

chaloupe^F de sauvetage^M
lifeboat

salle^F des machines^F
engine room

piscine^F
swimming pool

stabilisateur^M de roulis^M
stabilizer fin

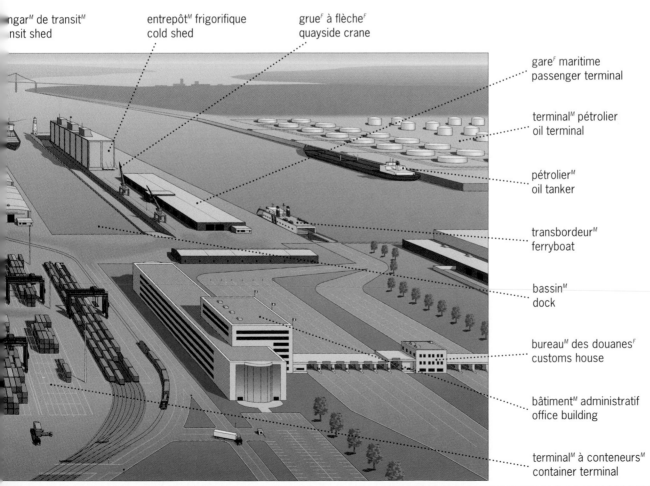

hangar^M de transit^M
transit shed

entrepôt^M frigorifique
cold shed

grue^F à flèche^F
quayside crane

gare^F maritime
passenger terminal

terminal^M pétrolier
oil terminal

pétrolier^M
oil tanker

transbordeur^M
ferryboat

bassin^M
dock

bureau^M des douanes^F
customs house

bâtiment^M administratif
office building

terminal^M à conteneurs^M
container terminal

LE TRANSPORT AÉRIEN

L'AVION^M
PLANE

TYPES^M DE VOILURES^F
TYPES OF WING SHAPES

voilure^F droite
straight wing

aile^F à géométrie^F variable
variable geometry wing

voilure^F en flèche^F
swept-back wing

voilure^F trapézoïdale
tapered wing

voilure^F delta^M
delta wing

avion^M long-courrier^M
long-range jet

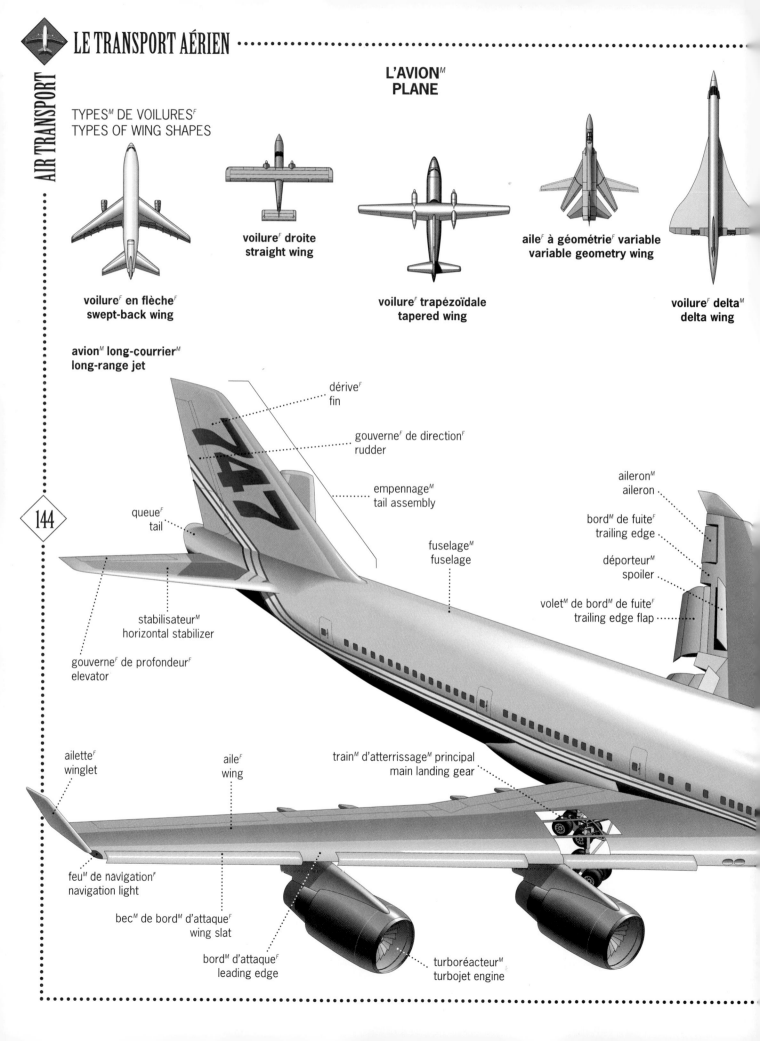

144

dérive^F
fin

gouverne^F de direction^F
rudder

empennage^M
tail assembly

queue^F
tail

fuselage^M
fuselage

aileron^M
aileron

bord^M de fuite^F
trailing edge

déporteur^M
spoiler

volet^M de bord^M de fuite^F
trailing edge flap

stabilisateur^M
horizontal stabilizer

gouverne^F de profondeur^F
elevator

ailette^F
winglet

aile^F
wing

train^M d'atterrissage^M principal
main landing gear

feu^M de navigation^F
navigation light

bec^M de bord^M d'attaque^F
wing slat

bord^M d'attaque^F
leading edge

turboréacteur^M
turbojet engine

L'HÉLICOPTÈRE^M
HELICOPTER

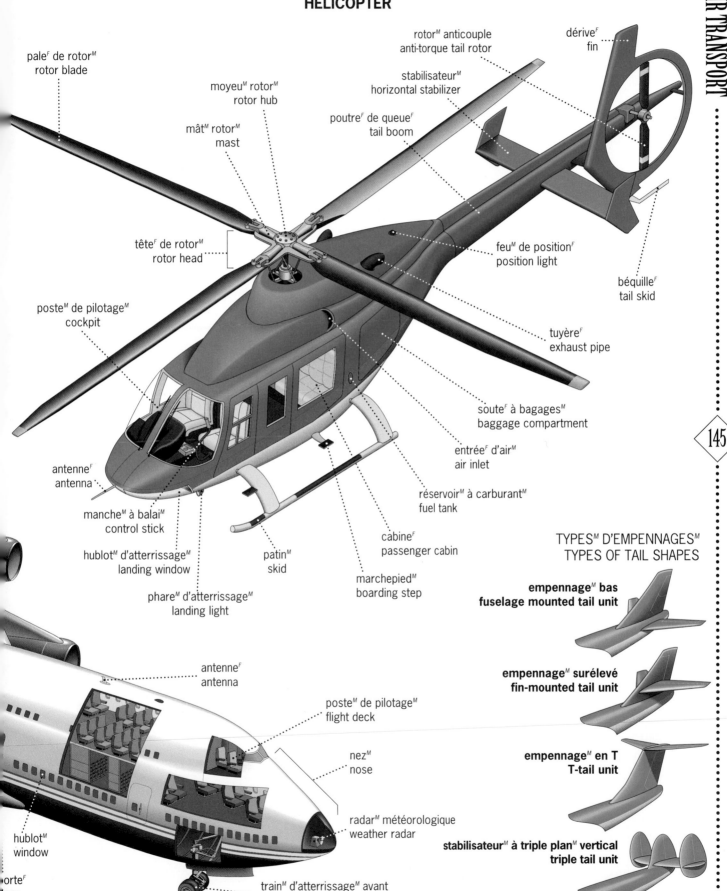

pale^F de rotor^M
rotor blade

moyeu^M rotor^M
rotor hub

mât^M rotor^M
mast

tête^F de rotor^M
rotor head

rotor^M anticouple
anti-torque tail rotor

stabilisateur^M
horizontal stabilizer

poutre^F de queue^F
tail boom

dérive^F
fin

feu^M de position^F
position light

béquille^F
tail skid

poste^M de pilotage^M
cockpit

tuyère^F
exhaust pipe

soute^F à bagages^M
baggage compartment

entrée^F d'air^M
air inlet

antenne^F
antenna

réservoir^M à carburant^M
fuel tank

manche^M à balai^M
control stick

cabine^F
passenger cabin

hublot^M d'atterrissage^M
landing window

patin^M
skid

phare^M d'atterrissage^M
landing light

marchepied^M
boarding step

antenne^F
antenna

poste^M de pilotage^M
flight deck

nez^M
nose

hublot^M
window

radar^M météorologique
weather radar

orte^F
oor

train^M d'atterrissage^M avant
nose landing gear

145

TYPES^M D'EMPENNAGES^M
TYPES OF TAIL SHAPES

empennage^M bas
fuselage mounted tail unit

empennage^M surélevé
fin-mounted tail unit

empennage^M en T
T-tail unit

stabilisateur^M à triple plan^M vertical
triple tail unit

L'AÉROPORT^M
AIRPORT

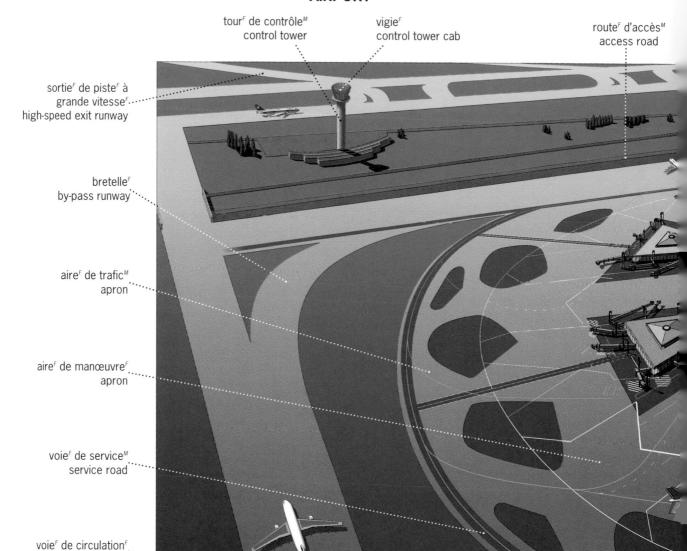

tour^F de contrôle^M
control tower

vigie^F
control tower cab

route^F d'accès^M
access road

sortie^F de piste^F à
grande vitesse^F
high-speed exit runway

bretelle^F
by-pass runway

aire^F de trafic^M
apron

aire^F de manœuvre^F
apron

voie^F de service^M
service road

voie^F de circulation^F
runway

146

ÉQUIPEMENTS^M AÉROPORTUAIRES
AIRPORT GROUND EQUIPMENT

barre^F de tractage^M
tow bar

tracteur^M de piste^F
tow tractor

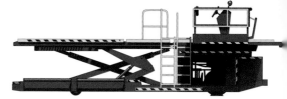

plate-forme^F élévatrice automotrice
container/pallet loader

escalier^M d'accès^M
universal step

convoyeur^M à bagages^M
baggage conveyor

cale^F
wheel chock

hangar^M
maintenance hangar

aire^F de stationnement^M
parking area

aérogare^F de passagers^M
passenger terminal

quai^M d'embarquement^M
boarding walkway

aérogare^F satellite^M
radial passenger
loading area

passerelle^F télescopique
telescopic corridor

aire^F de service^M
service area

marques^F de circulation^F
runway line

147

remorque^F à bagages^M
baggage trailer

tracteur^M
tow tractor

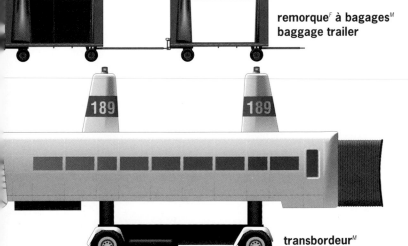

camion^M **commissariat**^M
catering vehicle

transbordeur^M
passenger transfer vehicle

LA NAVETTE^F SPATIALE
SPACE SHUTTLE

navette^F spatiale au décollage^M
space shuttle at takeoff

réservoir^M externe
external tank

parachute^M
booster parachute

fusée^F à propergol^M solide
solid rocket booster

navette^F
shuttle

tuyère^F
nozzle

navette^F spatiale en orbite^F
space shuttle in orbit

gouvernail^M
rudder

moteur^M de manœuvre^F
maneuvering engine

moteurs^M principaux
main engines

réservoirs^M
fuel tanks

volet^M
body flap

élevon^M
elevon

instruments^M scientifiques
scientific instruments

hublot^M d'observation^F
observation window

sas^M
hatch

tuiles^F
insulation tiles

aile^F
wing

laboratoire^M spatial
spacelab

panneau^M de refroidissement^M
radiator panel

porte^F de la soute^F
cargo bay door

148

LE SCAPHANDRE^M SPATIAL
SPACESUIT

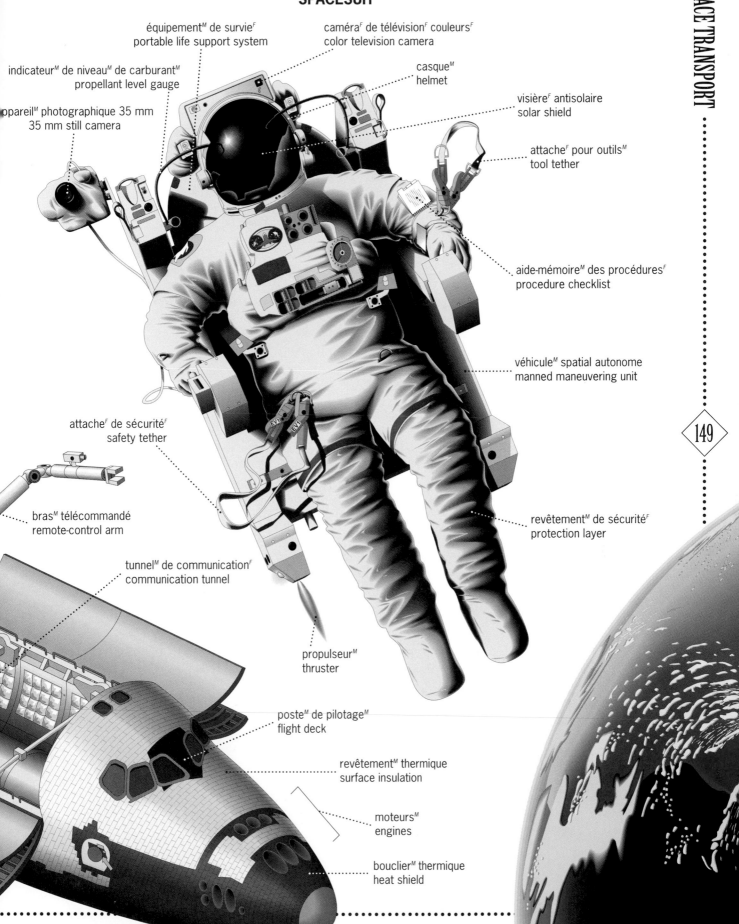

équipement^M de survie^F
portable life support system

caméra^F de télévision^F couleurs^F
color television camera

casque^M
helmet

indicateur^M de niveau^M de carburant^M
propellant level gauge

visière^F antisolaire
solar shield

appareil^M photographique 35 mm
35 mm still camera

attache^F pour outils^M
tool tether

aide-mémoire^M des procédures^F
procedure checklist

véhicule^M spatial autonome
manned maneuvering unit

attache^F de sécurité^F
safety tether

bras^M télécommandé
remote-control arm

revêtement^M de sécurité^F
protection layer

tunnel^M de communication^F
communication tunnel

propulseur^M
thruster

poste^M de pilotage^M
flight deck

revêtement^M thermique
surface insulation

moteurs^M
engines

bouclier^M thermique
heat shield

LES FOURNITURES^F SCOLAIRES
SCHOOL SUPPLIES

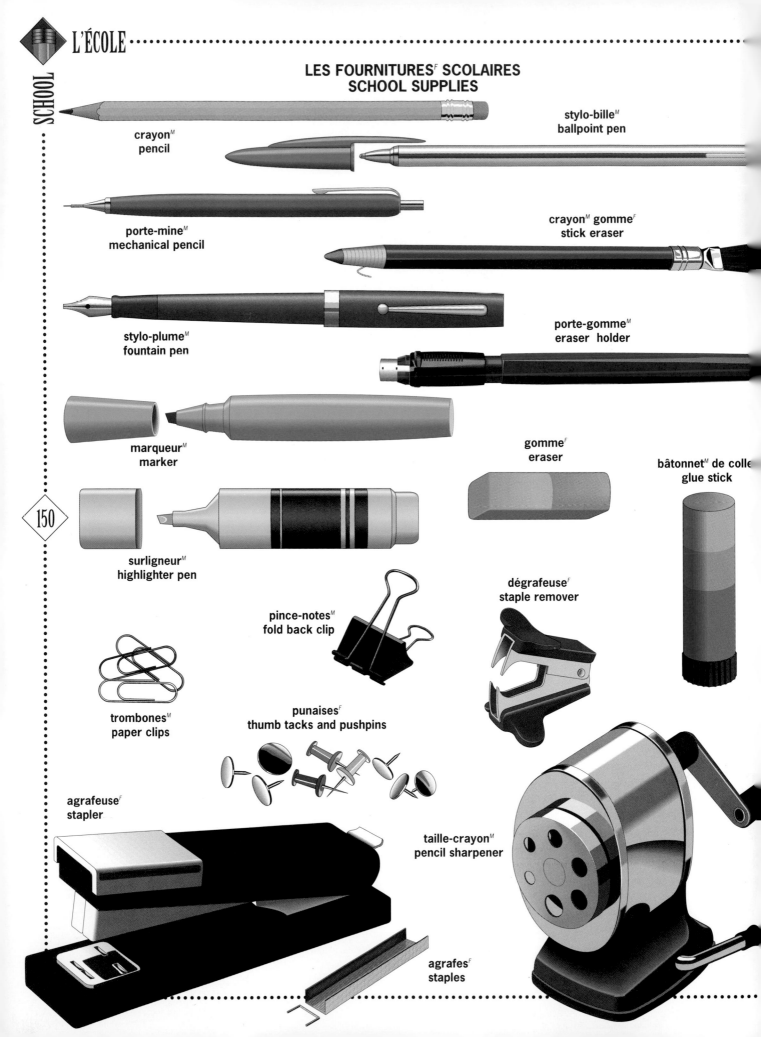

crayon^M
pencil

stylo-bille^M
ballpoint pen

porte-mine^M
mechanical pencil

crayon^M gomme^F
stick eraser

stylo-plume^M
fountain pen

porte-gomme^M
eraser holder

marqueur^M
marker

gomme^F
eraser

bâtonnet^M de colle
glue stick

surligneur^M
highlighter pen

pince-notes^M
fold back clip

dégrafeuse^F
staple remover

trombones^M
paper clips

punaises^F
thumb tacks and pushpins

agrafeuse^F
stapler

taille-crayon^M
pencil sharpener

agrafes^F
staples

150

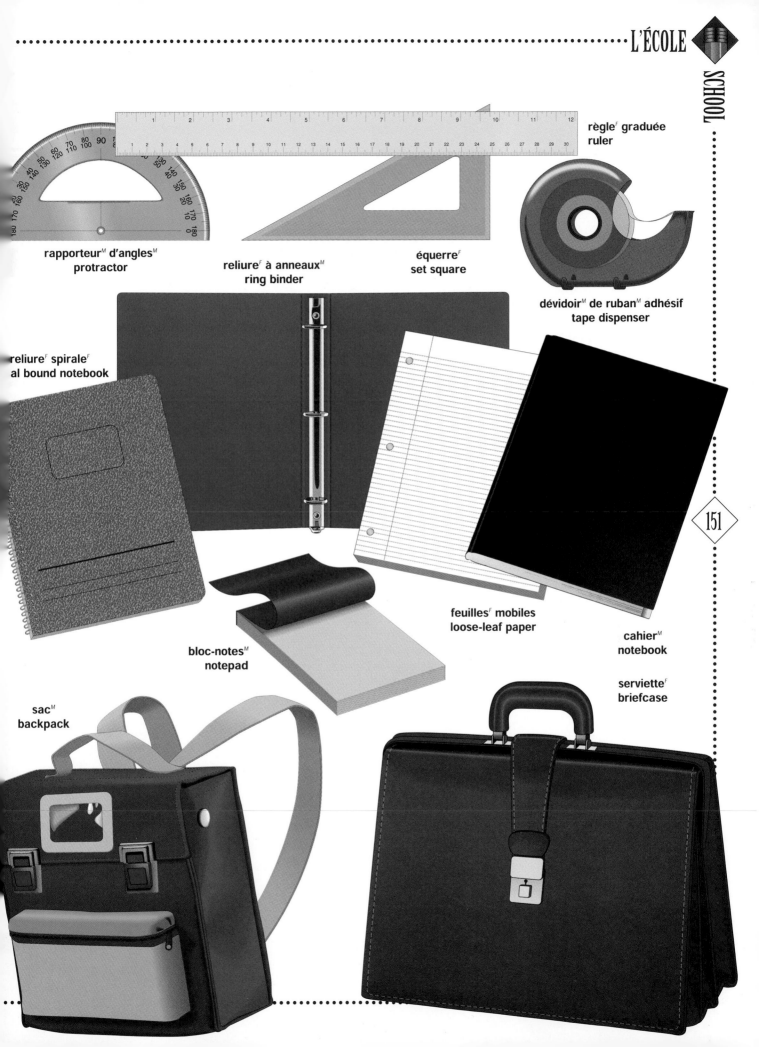

règle^F graduée
ruler

rapporteur^M d'angles^M
protractor

reliure^F à anneaux^M
ring binder

équerre^F
set square

dévidoir^M de ruban^M adhésif
tape dispenser

reliure^F spirale^F
al bound notebook

feuilles^F mobiles
loose-leaf paper

cahier^M
notebook

bloc-notes^M
notepad

serviette^F
briefcase

sac^M
backpack

151

LE MATÉRIEL^M SCOLAIRE
SCHOOL EQUIPMENT

tableau^M noir
blackboard

rétroprojecteur^M
overhead projector

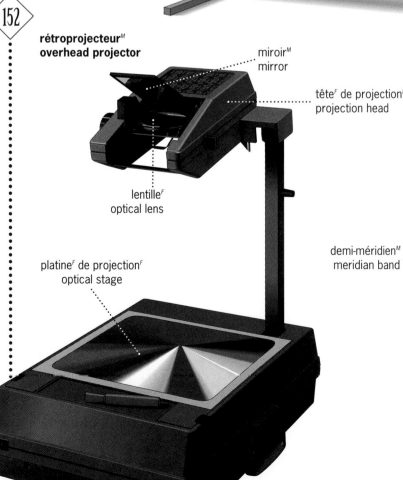

miroir^M
mirror

tête^F de projection^F
projection head

lentille^F
optical lens

platine^F de projection^F
optical stage

globe^M terrestre
globe of Earth

demi-méridien^M
meridian band

globe^M
globe

support^M
base

axe^M de rotation^F
axis of rotation

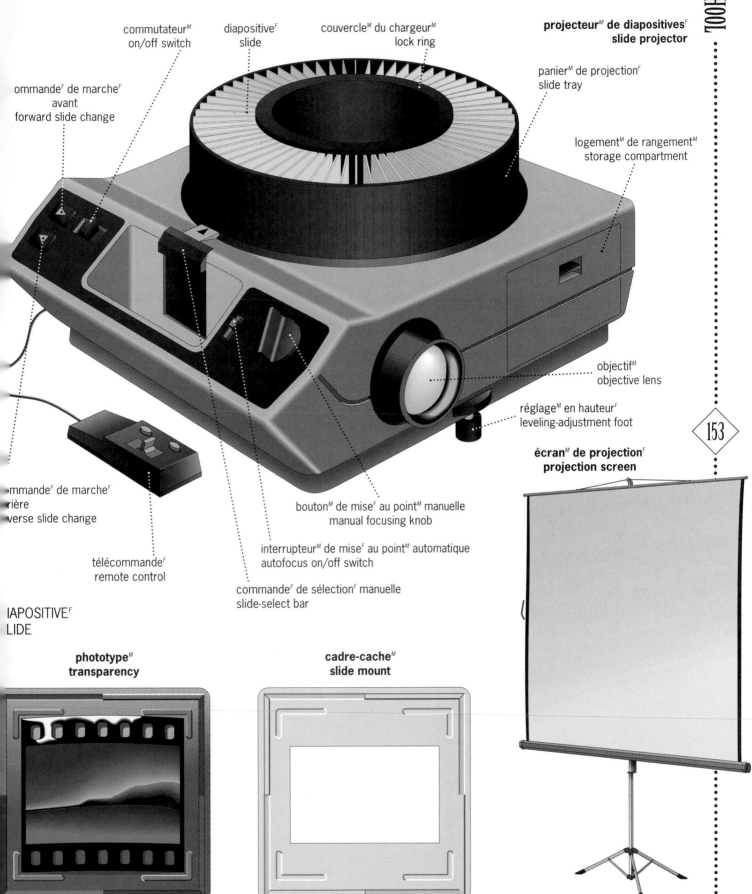

commutateur^M
on/off switch

diapositive^F
slide

couvercle^M du chargeur^M
lock ring

**projecteur^M de diapositives^F
slide projector**

ommande^F de marche^F
avant
forward slide change

panier^M de projection^F
slide tray

logement^M de rangement^M
storage compartment

objectif^M
objective lens

réglage^M en hauteur^F
leveling-adjustment foot

153

**écran^M de projection^F
projection screen**

•mmande^F de marche^F
rière
verse slide change

bouton^M de mise^F au point^M manuelle
manual focusing knob

interrupteur^M de mise^F au point^M automatique
autofocus on/off switch

télécommande^F
remote control

commande^F de sélection^F manuelle
slide-select bar

IAPOSITIVE^F
LIDE

**phototype^M
transparency**

**cadre-cache^M
slide mount**

LE MATÉRIEL^M SCOLAIRE
SCHOOL EQUIPMENT

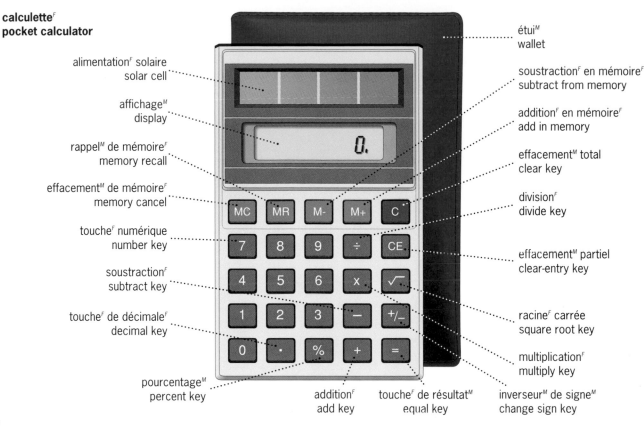

calculette^F
pocket calculator

étui^M
wallet

alimentation^F solaire
solar cell

soustraction^F en mémoire^F
subtract from memory

affichage^M
display

addition^F en mémoire^F
add in memory

rappel^M de mémoire^F
memory recall

effacement^M total
clear key

effacement^M de mémoire^F
memory cancel

division^F
divide key

touche^F numérique
number key

effacement^M partiel
clear-entry key

soustraction^F
subtract key

racine^F carrée
square root key

touche^F de décimale^F
decimal key

multiplication^F
multiply key

pourcentage^M
percent key

addition^F
add key

touche^F de résultat^M
equal key

inverseur^M de signe^M
change sign key

micro-ordinateur^M
personal computer

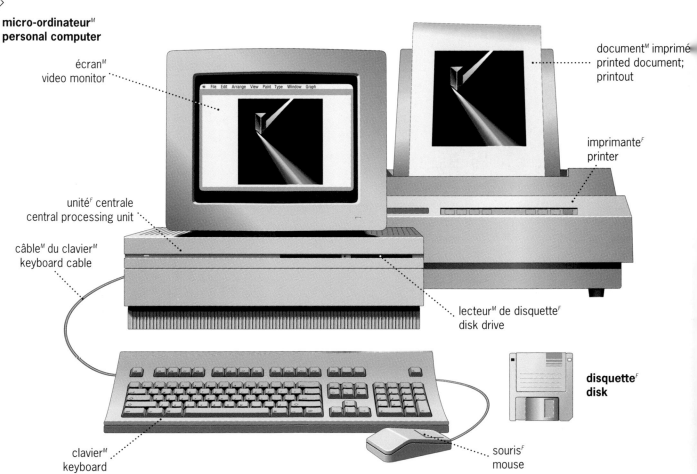

écran^M
video monitor

document^M imprimé
printed document;
printout

imprimante^F
printer

unité^F centrale
central processing unit

câble^M du clavier^M
keyboard cable

lecteur^M de disquette^F
disk drive

disquette^F
disk

clavier^M
keyboard

souris^F
mouse

loupe^F
magnifying glass

oculaire^M
eyepiece

microscope^M
microscope

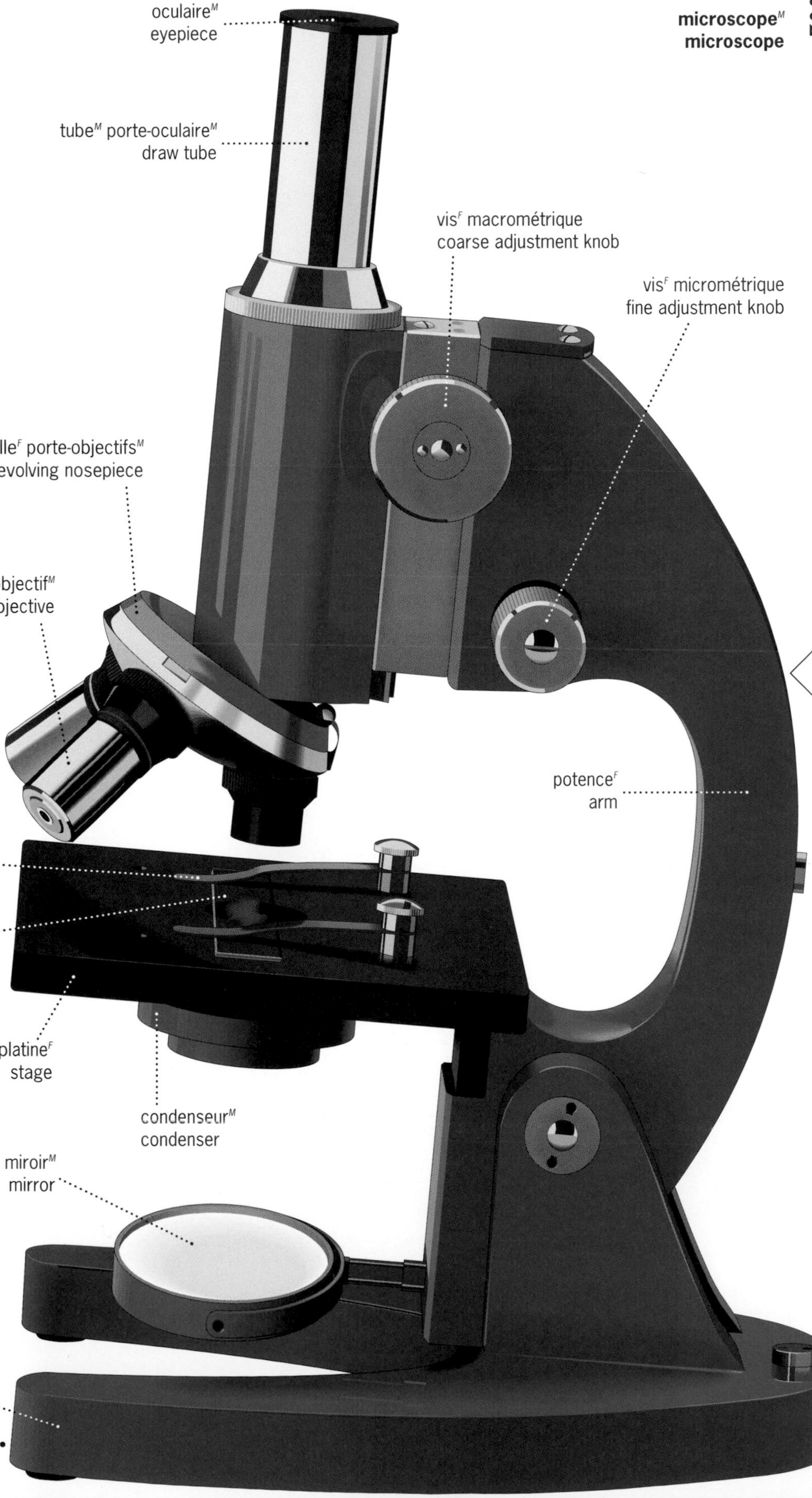

tube^M porte-oculaire^M
draw tube

vis^F macrométrique
coarse adjustment knob

vis^F micrométrique
fine adjustment knob

tourelle^F porte-objectifs^M
revolving nosepiece

objectif^M
objective

potence^F
arm

éprouvette^F
test tube

valet^M
stage clip

lame^F porte-objet^M
glass slide

platine^F
stage

condenseur^M
condenser

miroir^M
mirror

pied^M
base

155

LA GÉOMÉTRIE^F
GEOMETRY

SURFACES^F
PLANE SURFACES

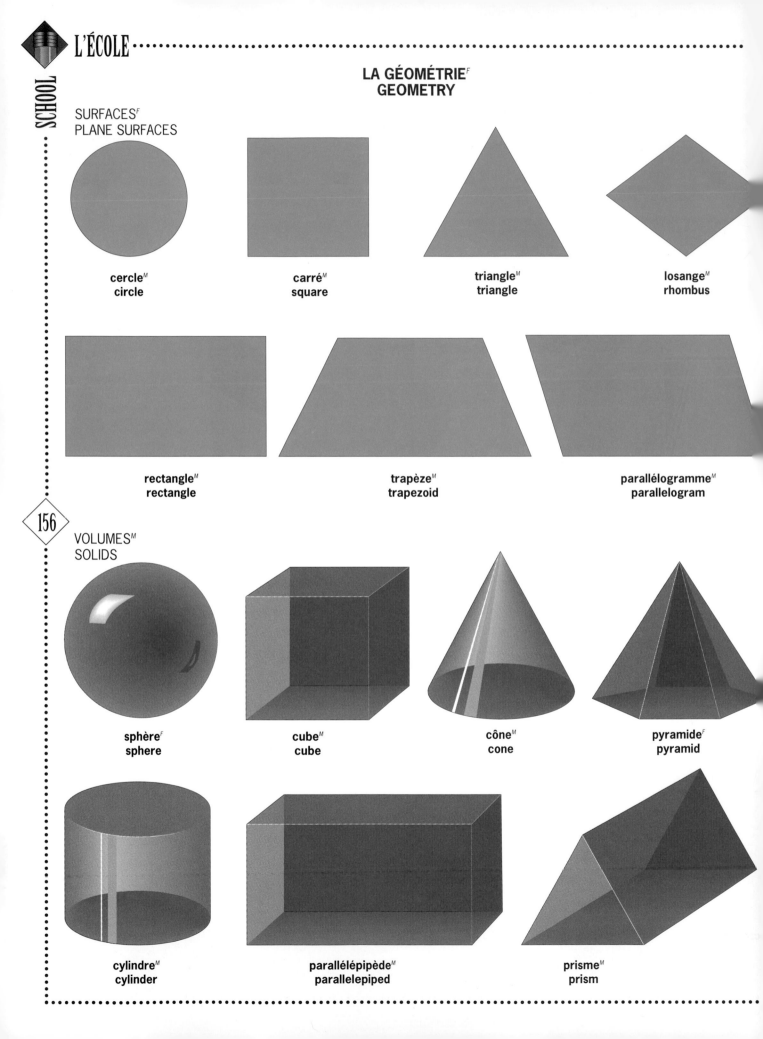

cercle^M
circle

carré^M
square

triangle^M
triangle

losange^M
rhombus

rectangle^M
rectangle

trapèze^M
trapezoid

parallélogramme^M
parallelogram

VOLUMES^M
SOLIDS

sphère^F
sphere

cube^M
cube

cône^M
cone

pyramide^F
pyramid

cylindre^M
cylinder

parallélépipède^M
parallelepiped

prisme^M
prism

LE DESSIN^M
DRAWING

couleurs^F secondaires
secondary colors

couleurs^F primaires
primary colors

couleurs^F tertiaires
tertiary colors

CERCLE^M DES COULEURS^F
COLOR CIRCLE

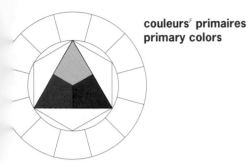

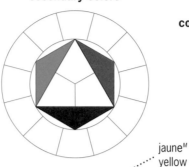

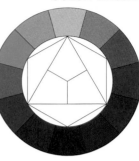

jaune^M
yellow

jaune^M vert
yellow-green

jaune^M orangé
orange-yellow

vert^M
green

orange^M
orange

bleu^M vert
blue-green

rouge^M orangé
orange-red

bleu^M
blue

rouge^M
red

bleu^M violet
violet-blue

rouge^M violet
red- violet

violet^M
violet

pinceau^M
paintbrush

brosse^F
flat brush

crayons^M de couleur^F
colored pencils

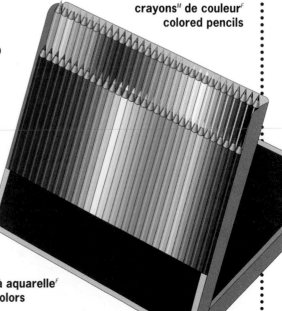

crayons^M de cire^F
wax crayons

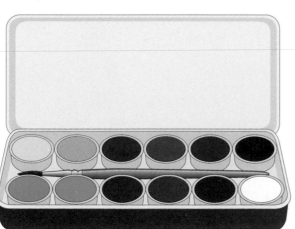

boîte^F à aquarelle^F
watercolors

LES INSTRUMENTS^M TRADITIONNELS
TRADITIONAL MUSICAL INSTRUMENTS

balalaïka^F
balalaika

mandoline^F
mandolin

cithare^F
zither

caisse^F de résonance^F
soundboard

lyre^F
lyre

caisse^F triangulaire
triangular body

cordes^F d'accompagnement^M
open strings

cordes^F de mélodie^F
melody strings

cornemu...
bagpip...

158

flûte^F de Pan
panpipes

tuyau^M d'insufflation
blowpipe; mouthpipe

bourdon^M
drone pipe

banjo^M
banjo

caisse^F bombée
pear-shaped body

caisse^F circulaire
circular body

harmonica^M
harmonica

soufflet^M
bellows

accordéon^M
accordion

clavier^M chant^M
treble keyboard

clavier^M accompagnement^M
bass keyboard

sac^M
windbag

registre^M des aigus^M
treble register

registre^M des basses^F
bass register

chalumeau^M
chanter

LES INSTRUMENTS^M À CLAVIER^M
KEYBOARD INSTRUMENTS

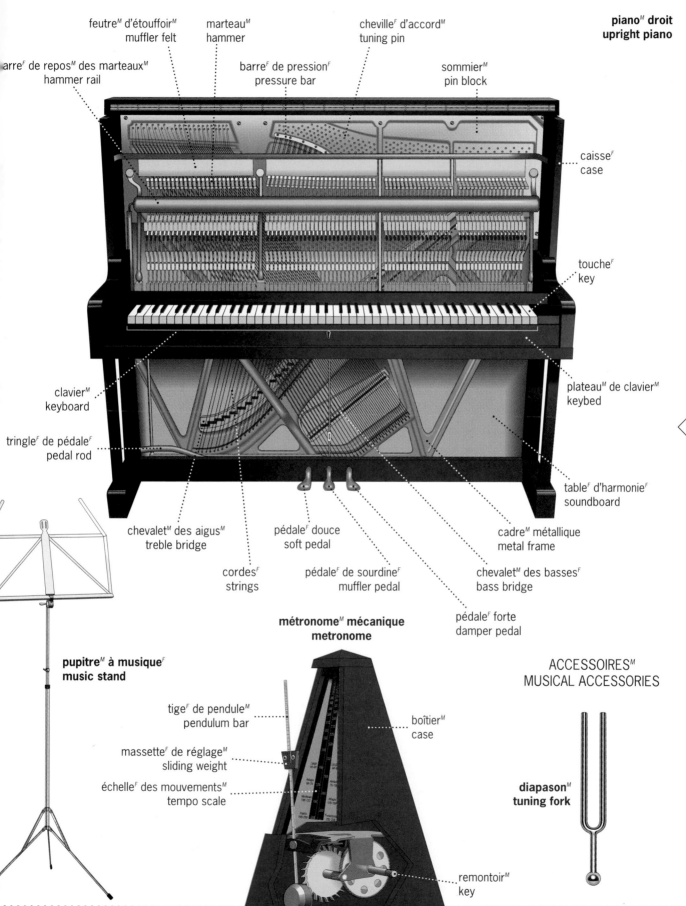

feutre^M d'étouffoir^M
muffler felt

marteau^M
hammer

cheville^F d'accord^M
tuning pin

**piano^M droit
upright piano**

barre^F de repos^M des marteaux^M
hammer rail

barre^F de pression^F
pressure bar

sommier^M
pin block

caisse^F
case

touche^F
key

clavier^M
keyboard

plateau^M de clavier^M
keybed

tringle^F de pédale^F
pedal rod

table^F d'harmonie^F
soundboard

chevalet^M des aigus^M
treble bridge

pédale^F douce
soft pedal

cadre^M métallique
metal frame

cordes^F
strings

pédale^F de sourdine^F
muffler pedal

chevalet^M des basses^F
bass bridge

pédale^F forte
damper pedal

**pupitre^M à musique^F
music stand**

**métronome^M mécanique
metronome**

ACCESSOIRES^M
MUSICAL ACCESSORIES

tige^F de pendule^M
pendulum bar

boîtier^M
case

massette^F de réglage^M
sliding weight

échelle^F des mouvements^M
tempo scale

**diapason^M
tuning fork**

remontoir^M
key

159

LA NOTATION^F MUSICALE
MUSICAL NOTATION

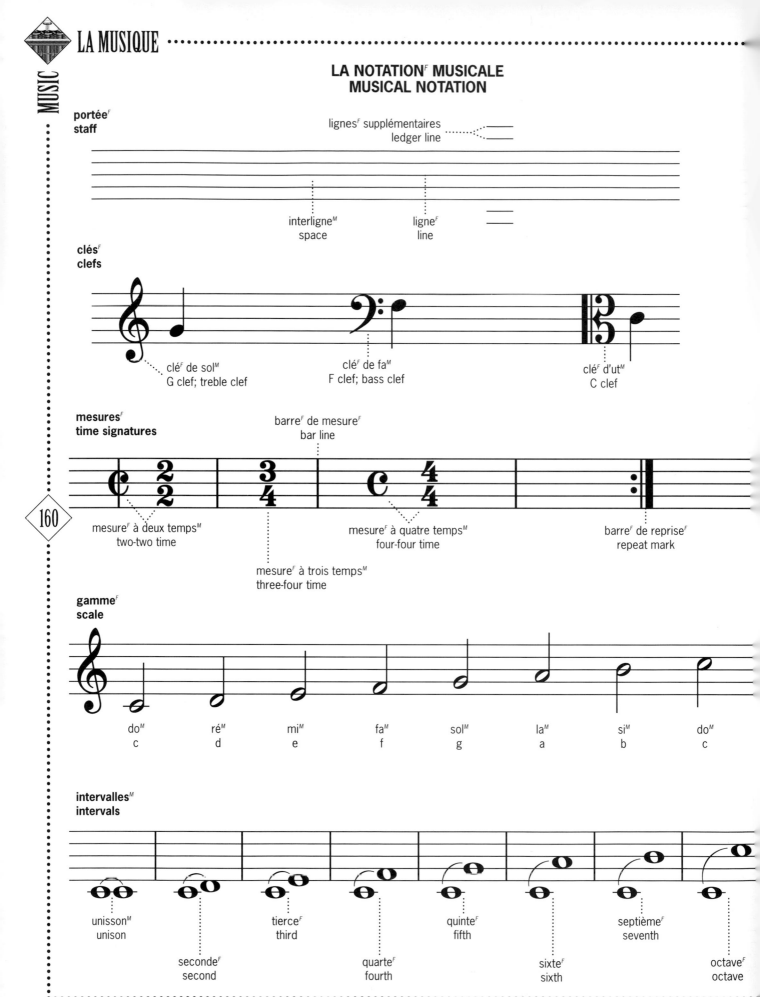

portée^F
staff

lignes^F supplémentaires
ledger line

interligne^M
space

ligne^F
line

clés^F
clefs

clé^F de sol^M
G clef; treble clef

clé^F de fa^M
F clef; bass clef

clé^F d'ut^M
C clef

mesures^F
time signatures

barre^F de mesure^F
bar line

mesure^F à deux temps^M
two-two time

mesure^F à quatre temps^M
four-four time

barre^F de reprise^F
repeat mark

mesure^F à trois temps^M
three-four time

gamme^F
scale

do^M
c

ré^M
d

mi^M
e

fa^M
f

sol^M
g

la^M
a

si^M
b

do^M
c

intervalles^M
intervals

unisson^M
unison

seconde^F
second

tierce^F
third

quarte^F
fourth

quinte^F
fifth

sixte^F
sixth

septième^F
seventh

octave^F
octave

valeur^F des notes^F / note symbols

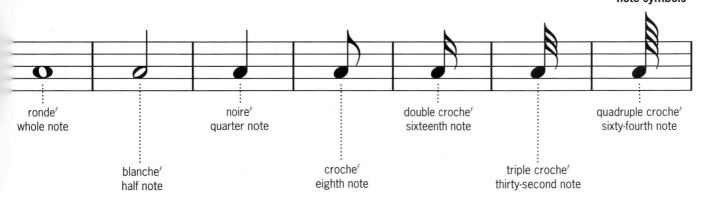

ronde^F / whole note

blanche^F / half note

noire^F / quarter note

croche^F / eighth note

double croche^F / sixteenth note

triple croche^F / thirty-second note

quadruple croche^F / sixty-fourth note

valeur^F des silences^M / rest symbols

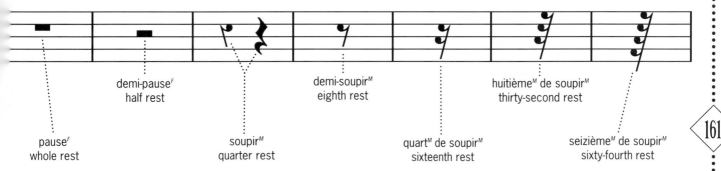

pause^F / whole rest

demi-pause^F / half rest

soupir^M / quarter rest

demi-soupir^M / eighth rest

quart^M de soupir^M / sixteenth rest

huitième^M de soupir^M / thirty-second rest

seizième^M de soupir^M / sixty-fourth rest

altérations^F / accidentals

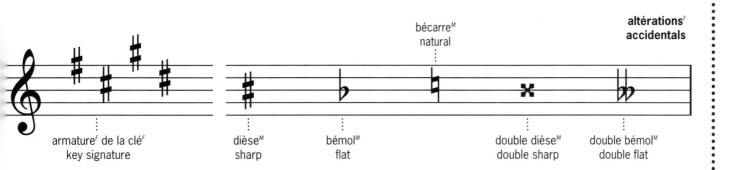

bécarre^M / natural

armature^F de la clé^F / key signature

dièse^M / sharp

bémol^M / flat

double dièse^M / double sharp

double bémol^M / double flat

ornements^M / ornaments

appoggiature^F / appoggiatura

trille^M / trill

gruppetto^M / turn

mordant^M / mordent

161

LES INSTRUMENTS^M À CORDES^F
STRINGED INSTRUMENTS

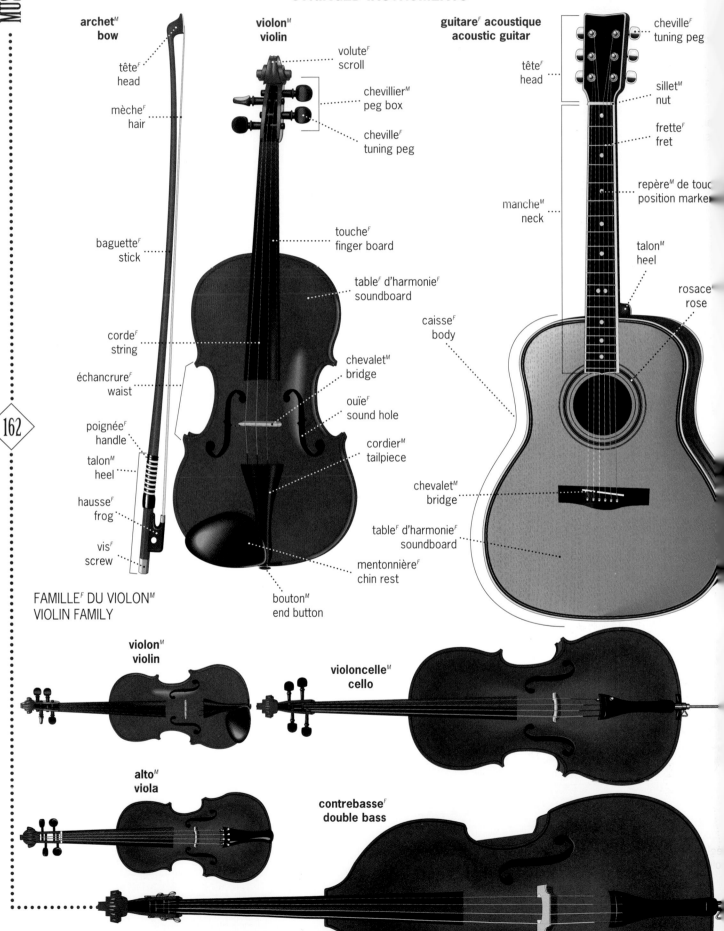

archet^M
bow

tête^F
head

mèche^F
hair

baguette^F
stick

corde^F
string

échancrure^F
waist

poignée^F
handle

talon^M
heel

hausse^F
frog

vis^F
screw

violon^M
violin

volute^F
scroll

chevillier^M
peg box

cheville^F
tuning peg

touche^F
finger board

table^F d'harmonie^F
soundboard

chevalet^M
bridge

ouïe^F
sound hole

cordier^M
tailpiece

mentonnière^F
chin rest

bouton^M
end button

guitare^F acoustique
acoustic guitar

cheville^F
tuning peg

tête^F
head

sillet^M
nut

frette^F
fret

repère^M de touc
position marker

manche^M
neck

talon^M
heel

rosace^F
rose

caisse^F
body

chevalet^M
bridge

table^F d'harmonie^F
soundboard

FAMILLE^F DU VIOLON^M
VIOLIN FAMILY

violon^M
violin

violoncelle^M
cello

alto^M
viola

contrebasse^F
double bass

guitareF **électrique**
electric guitar

cro^M de fréquences^F aiguës
treble pickup

nsemble^M du chevalet^M
bridge assembly

aisse^F pleine
solid body

micro^M de fréquences^F moyennes
midrange pickup

micro^M de fréquences^F graves
bass pickup

repère^M de touche^F
position marker

frette^F
fret

touche^F
finger board

mécanique^F d'accordage^M
tuning peg

plaque^F de protection^F
pickguard

levier^M de vibrato^M
vibrato arm

sélecteur^M de micro^M
pickup selector

réglage^M de la tonalité^F
tone controls

réglage^M du volume^M
volume control

sillet^M
nut

tête^F
head

manche^M
neck

ck^M de sortie^F
tput jack

163

guitareF **basse**
bass guitar

aisse^F
dy

chevalet^M
bridge

micro^M
pickups

bouton^M fixe-courroie
strap system

mécanique^F d'accordage^M
tuning peg

sillet^M
nut

frette^F
fret

contrôle^M de tonalité^F des graves^F
bass tone control

contrôle^M de tonalité^F des aigus^M
treble tone control

réglage^M de la balance^F
balancer

églage^M du volume^M
olume control

manche^M
neck

repère^M de touche^F
position marker

touche^F
finger board

tête^F
head

LES INSTRUMENTS^M À VENT^M
WIND INSTRUMENTS

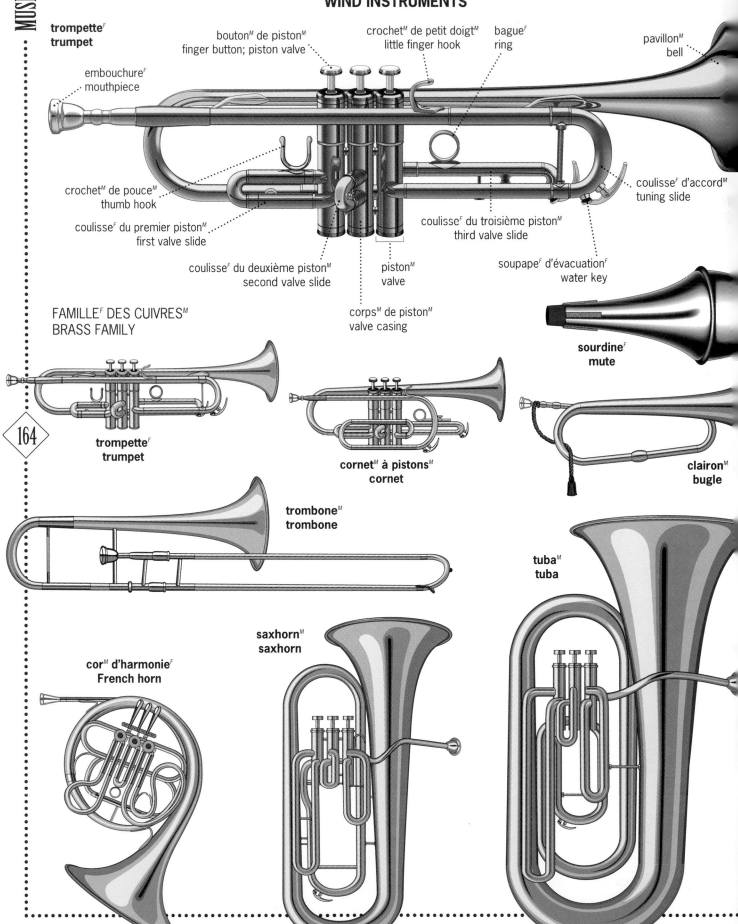

trompette^F
trumpet

bouton^M de piston^M
finger button; piston valve

crochet^M de petit doigt^M
little finger hook

bague^F
ring

pavillon^M
bell

embouchure^F
mouthpiece

crochet^M de pouce^M
thumb hook

coulisse^F du premier piston^M
first valve slide

coulisse^F du deuxième piston^M
second valve slide

piston^M
valve

corps^M de piston^M
valve casing

coulisse^F du troisième piston^M
third valve slide

soupape^F d'évacuation^F
water key

coulisse^F d'accord^M
tuning slide

FAMILLE^F DES CUIVRES^M
BRASS FAMILY

trompette^F
trumpet

cornet^M **à pistons**^M
cornet

sourdine^F
mute

clairon^M
bugle

trombone^M
trombone

tuba^M
tuba

saxhorn^M
saxhorn

cor^M **d'harmonie**^F
French horn

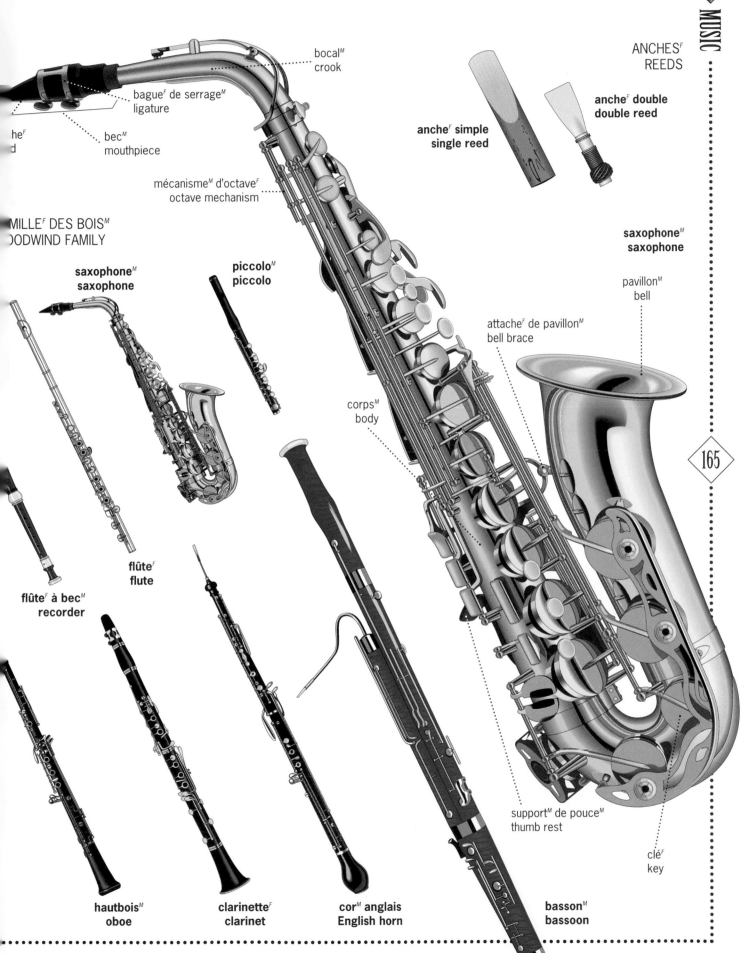

bocal^M
crook

bague^F de serrage^M
ligature

bec^M
mouthpiece

he^F
d

mécanisme^M d'octave^F
octave mechanism

ANCHES^F
REEDS

anche^F simple
single reed

anche^F double
double reed

saxophone^M
saxophone

pavillon^M
bell

attache^F de pavillon^M
bell brace

corps^M
body

MILLE^F DES BOIS^M
OODWIND FAMILY

saxophone^M
saxophone

piccolo^M
piccolo

flûte^F
flute

flûte^F à bec^M
recorder

support^M de pouce^M
thumb rest

clé^F
key

hautbois^M
oboe

clarinette^F
clarinet

cor^M anglais
English horn

basson^M
bassoon

165

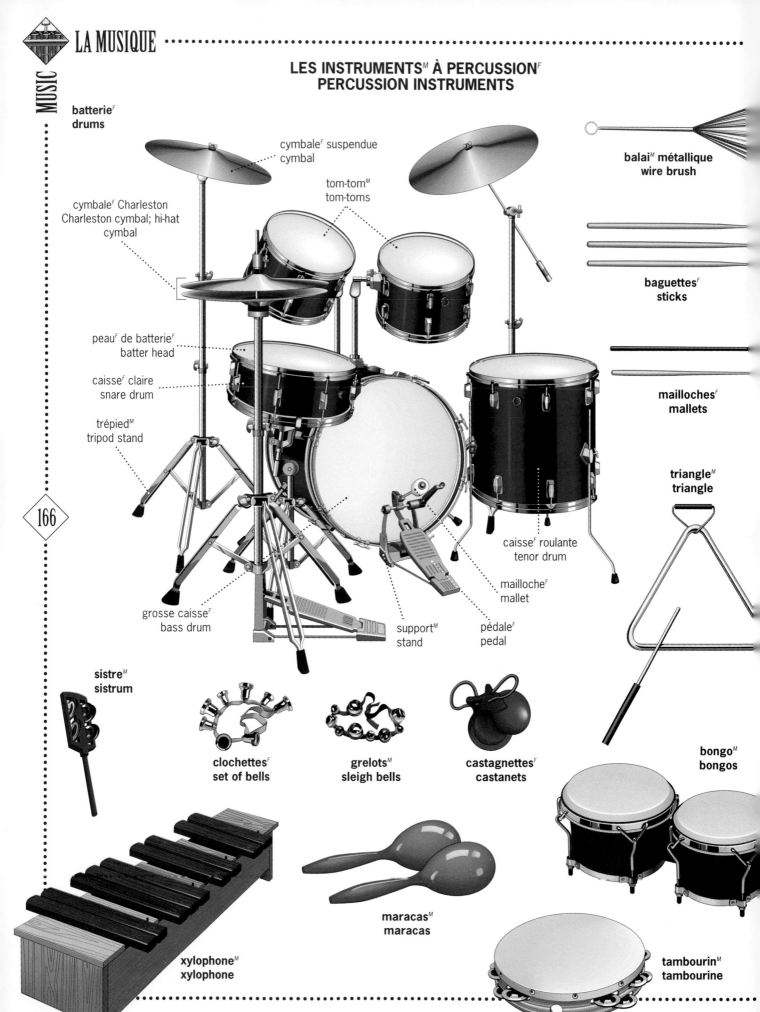

LES INSTRUMENTS^M À PERCUSSION^F
PERCUSSION INSTRUMENTS

batterie^F
drums

cymbale^F suspendue
cymbal

tom-tom^M
tom-toms

cymbale^F Charleston
Charleston cymbal; hi-hat
cymbal

balai^M **métallique**
wire brush

peau^F de batterie^F
batter head

baguettes^F
sticks

caisse^F claire
snare drum

mailloches^F
mallets

trépied^M
tripod stand

triangle^M
triangle

caisse^F roulante
tenor drum

166

mailloche^F
mallet

grosse caisse^F
bass drum

support^M
stand

pédale^F
pedal

sistre^M
sistrum

bongo^M
bongos

clochettes^F
set of bells

grelots^M
sleigh bells

castagnettes^F
castanets

maracas^M
maracas

xylophone^M
xylophone

tambourin^M
tambourine

L'ORCHESTRE^M SYMPHONIQUE
SYMPHONY ORCHESTRA

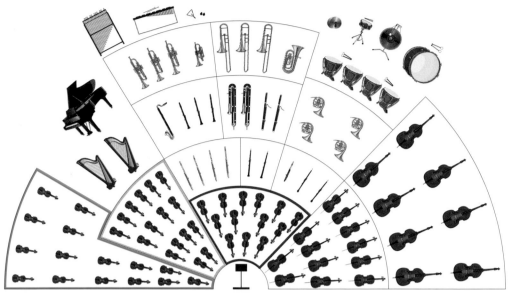

pupitre^M du chef^M d'orchestre^M
conductor's podium

carillon^M tubulaire
tubular bells

xylophone^M
xylophone

grosse caisse^F
bass drum

harpe^F
harp

piano^M
piano

flûte^F
flute

hautbois^M
oboe

piccolo^M
piccolo

cor^M anglais
English horn

premier violon^M
first violin

second violon^M
second violin

alto^M
viola

violoncelle^M
cello

contrebasse^F
double bass

clarinette^F basse
bass clarinet

clarinette^F
clarinet

contrebasson^M
contrabassoon

basson^M
bassoon

cor^M d'harmonie^F
French horn

cornet^M à pistons^M
cornet

trompette^F
trumpet

trombone^M
trombone

tuba^M
tuba

triangle^M
triangle

caisse^F claire
snare drum

cymbales^F
cymbals

castagnettes^F
castanets

timbale^F
kettledrum

gong^M
gong

LE BASEBALL^M
BASEBALL

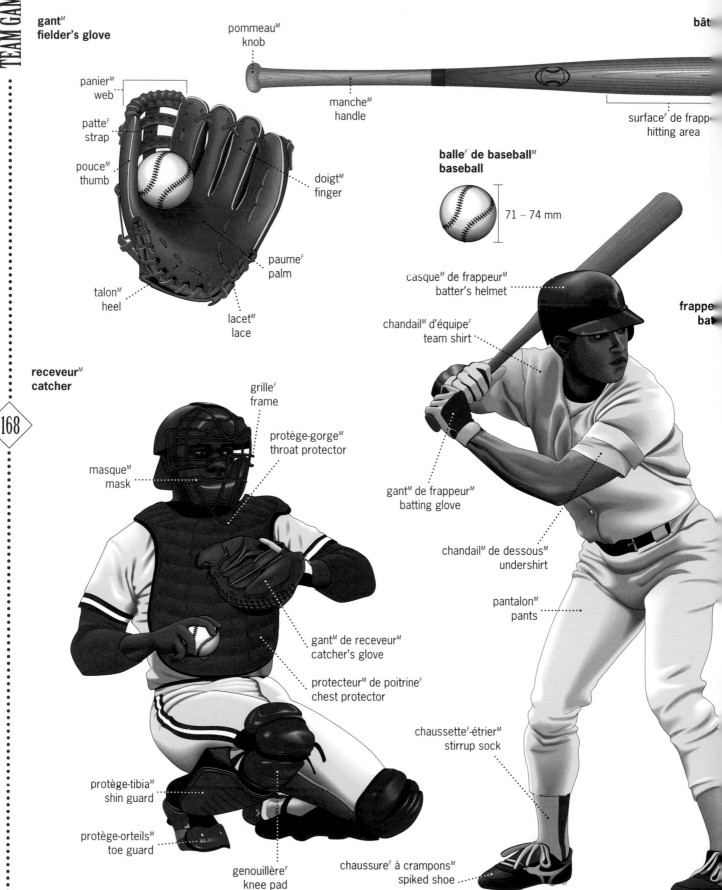

gant^M
fielder's glove

panier^M
web

patte^F
strap

pouce^M
thumb

doigt^M
finger

paume^F
palm

talon^M
heel

lacet^M
lace

pommeau^M
knob

manche^M
handle

bât

surface^F de frapp
hitting area

balle^F de baseball^M
baseball

71 – 74 mm

casque^M de frappeur^M
batter's helmet

chandail^M d'équipe^F
team shirt

frappe
bat

gant^M de frappeur^M
batting glove

chandail^M de dessous^M
undershirt

pantalon^M
pants

chaussette^F-étrier^M
stirrup sock

receveur^M
catcher

grille^F
frame

protège-gorge^M
throat protector

masque^M
mask

gant^M de receveur^M
catcher's glove

protecteur^M de poitrine^F
chest protector

protège-tibia^M
shin guard

protège-orteils^M
toe guard

genouillère^F
knee pad

chaussure^F à crampons^M
spiked shoe

168

arrêt-court[M]
shortstop

champ[M] centre[M]
center field

voltigeur[M] de centre[M]
center fielder

voltigeur[M] gauche
left fielder

deuxième-but[M]
second baseman

champ[M] gauche
left field

piste[F] d'avertissement[M]
warning track

voltigeur[M] droit
right fielder

ligne[F] de jeu[M]
foul line

champ[M] droit
right field

27,4 m

troisième-but[M]
third baseman

premier-but[M]
first baseman

troisième but[M]
third base

premier but[M]
first base

rectangle[M] des instructeurs[M]
coach's box

avant-champ[M]
infield

deuxième but[M]
second base

cercle[M] d'attente[F]
on-deck circle

abri[M] des joueurs[M]
dugout

marbre[M]
home plate

lanceur[M]
pitcher

frappeur[M]
batter

plaque[F] du lanceur[M]
pitcher's plate

receveur[M]
catcher

monticule[M]
pitcher's mound

arbitre[M] en chef[M]
home-plate umpire

TEAM GAMES

LE FOOTBALL^M AMÉRICAIN
AMERICAN FOOTBALL

footballeur^M
American football player

casque^M
helmet

jugulaire^F
chin strap

numéro^M du joueur^M
player's number

chandail^M d'équipe^F
team shirt

bracelet^M
wristband

ballon^M de footb
footl

279 – 286 mm

équipement^M de protecti
protective equipm

casque^M
helmet

masque^M
face mask

épaulière^F
shoulder pad

pantalon^M
pants

plastron^M
chest protector

brassard^M
arm guard

protège-côtes^M
rib pad

coudière^F
elbow pad

protège-hanche^M
hip pad

protecteur^M lombaire
lumbar pad

coquille^F
protective cup

cuissard^M
thigh pad

chaussette^F
sock

chaussure^F à crampons^M
cleated shoe

genouillère^F
knee pad

170

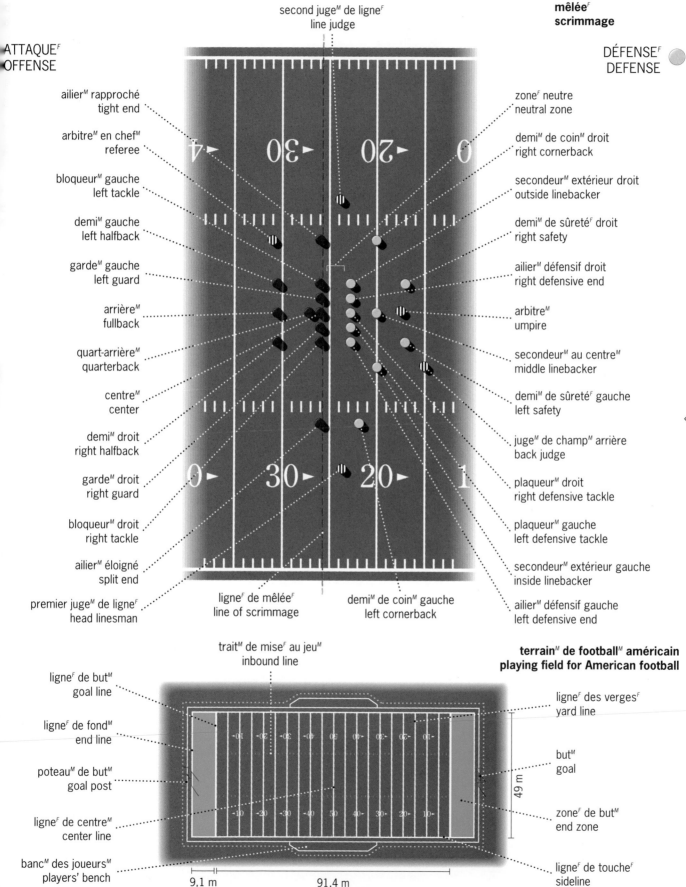

second juge M de ligne F
line judge

mêlée F
scrimmage

ATTAQUE F
OFFENSE

DÉFENSE F
DEFENSE

ailier M rapproché
tight end

arbitre M en chef M
referee

bloqueur M gauche
left tackle

demi M gauche
left halfback

garde M gauche
left guard

arrière M
fullback

quart-arrière M
quarterback

centre M
center

demi M droit
right halfback

garde M droit
right guard

bloqueur M droit
right tackle

ailier M éloigné
split end

premier juge M de ligne F
head linesman

zone F neutre
neutral zone

demi M de coin M droit
right cornerback

secondeur M extérieur droit
outside linebacker

demi M de sûreté F droit
right safety

ailier M défensif droit
right defensive end

arbitre M
umpire

secondeur M au centre M
middle linebacker

demi M de sûreté F gauche
left safety

juge M de champ M arrière
back judge

plaqueur M droit
right defensive tackle

plaqueur M gauche
left defensive tackle

secondeur M extérieur gauche
inside linebacker

ailier M défensif gauche
left defensive end

ligne F de mêlée F
line of scrimmage

demi M de coin M gauche
left cornerback

terrain M de football M américain
playing field for American football

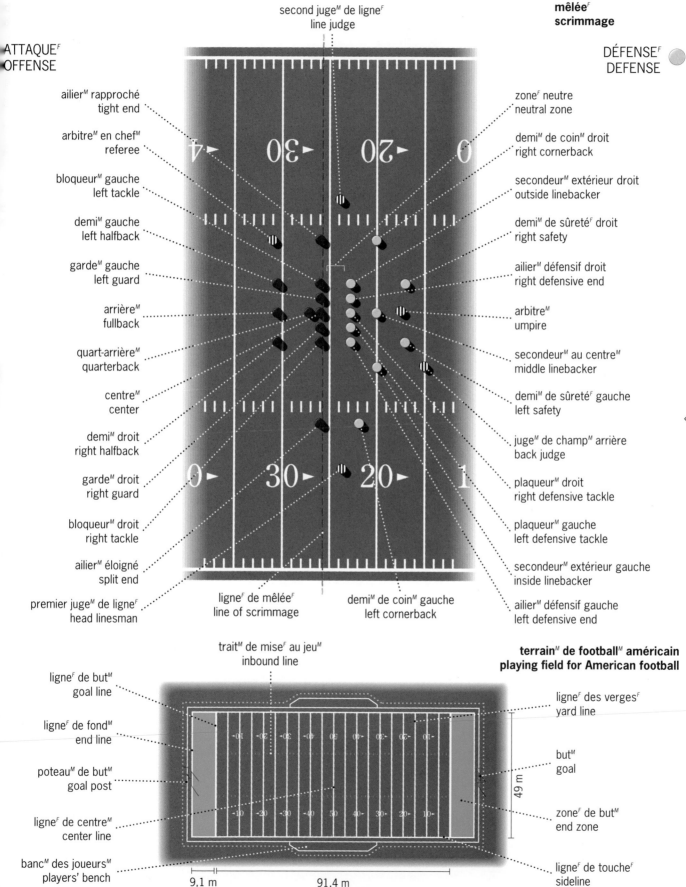

trait M de mise F au jeu M
inbound line

ligne F de but M
goal line

ligne F de fond M
end line

poteau M de but M
goal post

ligne F de centre M
center line

banc M des joueurs M
players' bench

ligne F des verges F
yard line

but M
goal

zone F de but M
end zone

ligne F de touche F
sideline

9,1 m   91,4 m   49 m

LE FOOTBALL^M
SOCCER

footballeur^M
soccer player

ballon^M **de football**^M
soccer ball

chandail^M d'équipe^F
team shirt

218 mm

172

short^M
shorts

protège-tibia^M
shin guard

chaussure^F de football^M
soccer shoe

crampons^M interchangeab
interchangeable studs

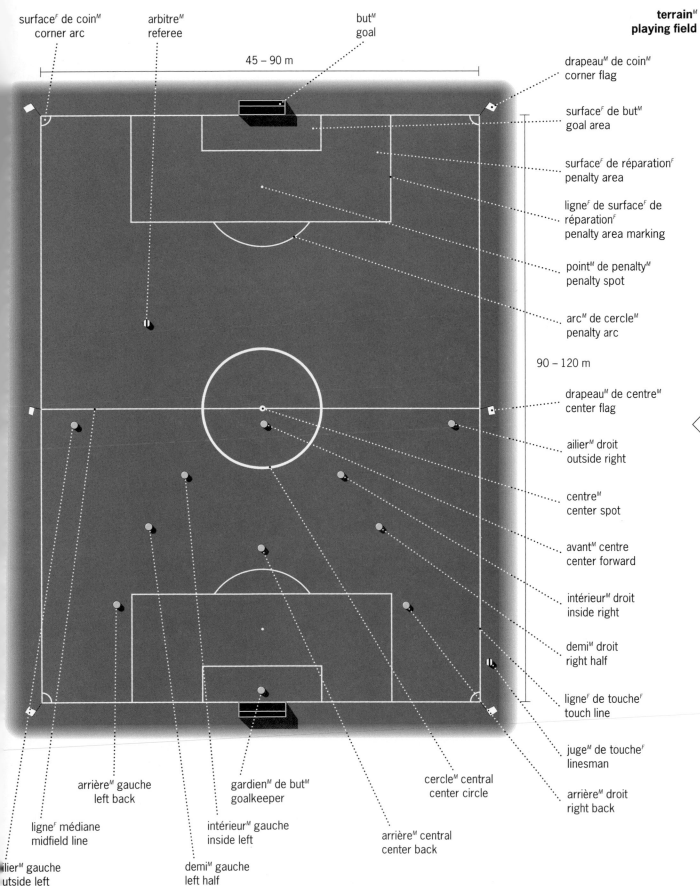

surface^F de coin^M
corner arc

arbitre^M
referee

but^M
goal

45 – 90 m

terrain^M
playing field

drapeau^M de coin^M
corner flag

surface^F de but^M
goal area

surface^F de réparation^F
penalty area

ligne^F de surface^F de
réparation^F
penalty area marking

point^M de penalty^M
penalty spot

arc^M de cercle^M
penalty arc

90 – 120 m

drapeau^M de centre^M
center flag

ailier^M droit
outside right

centre^M
center spot

avant^M centre
center forward

intérieur^M droit
inside right

demi^M droit
right half

ligne^F de touche^F
touch line

juge^M de touche^F
linesman

arrière^M droit
right back

arrière^M gauche
left back

ligne^F médiane
midfield line

ailier^M gauche
outside left

gardien^M de but^M
goalkeeper

intérieur^M gauche
inside left

demi^M gauche
left half

arrière^M central
center back

cercle^M central
center circle

LE CRICKET^M
CRICKET

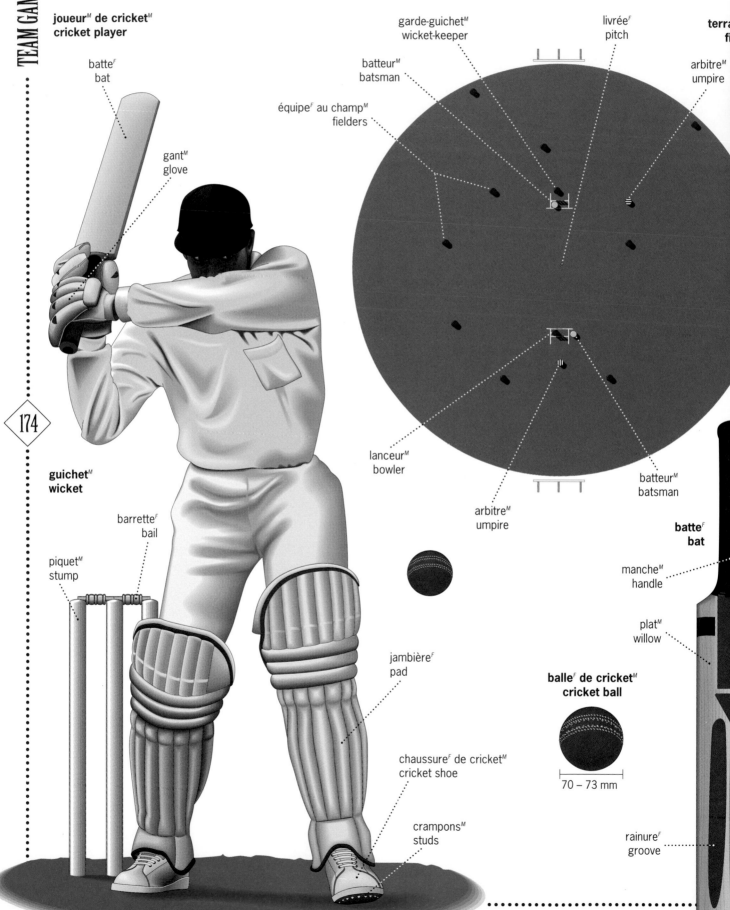

**joueur^M de cricket^M
cricket player**

batte^F
bat

gant^M
glove

garde-guichet^M
wicket-keeper

batteur^M
batsman

équipe^F au champ^M
fielders

livrée^F
pitch

arbitre^M
umpire

terra
fi

lanceur^M
bowler

batteur^M
batsman

arbitre^M
umpire

**guichet^M
wicket**

barrette^F
bail

piquet^M
stump

jambière^F
pad

chaussure^F de cricket^M
cricket shoe

crampons^M
studs

**batte^F
bat**

manche^M
handle

plat^M
willow

**balle^F de cricket^M
cricket ball**

70 – 73 mm

rainure^F
groove

174

LE HOCKEY^M SUR GAZON^M
FIELD HOCKEY

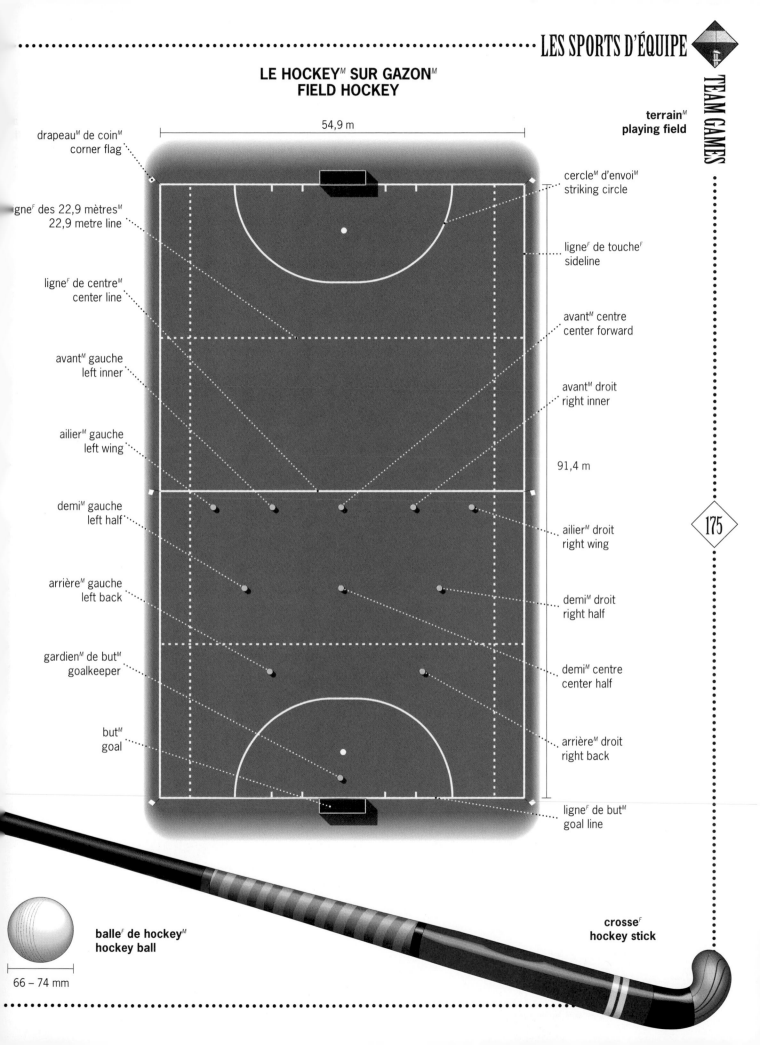

terrain^M
playing field

54,9 m

drapeau^M de coin^M
corner flag

cercle^M d'envoi^M
striking circle

gne^F des 22,9 mètres^M
22,9 metre line

ligne^F de touche^F
sideline

ligne^F de centre^M
center line

avant^M centre
center forward

avant^M gauche
left inner

avant^M droit
right inner

ailier^M gauche
left wing

91,4 m

demi^M gauche
left half

ailier^M droit
right wing

arrière^M gauche
left back

demi^M droit
right half

gardien^M de but^M
goalkeeper

demi^M centre
center half

but^M
goal

arrière^M droit
right back

ligne^F de but^M
goal line

balle^F de hockey^M
hockey ball

66 – 74 mm

crosse^F
hockey stick

LE HOCKEY[M] SUR GLACE[F]
ICE HOCKEY

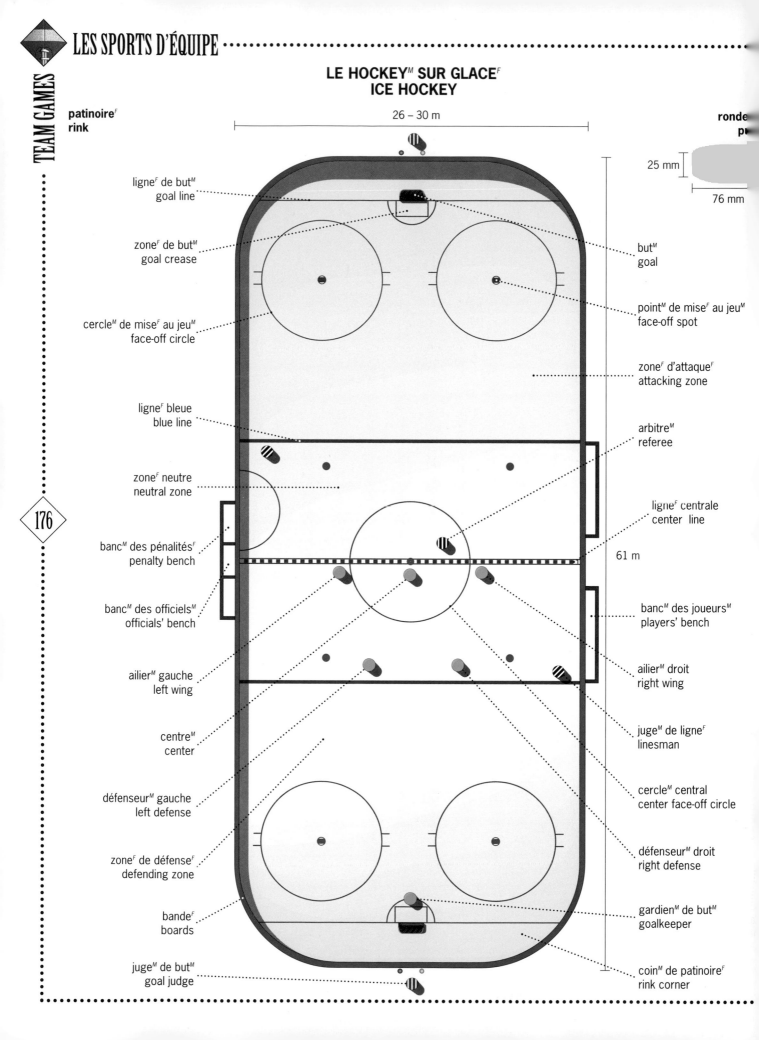

patinoire[F]
rink

26 – 30 m

ronde
p

25 mm

76 mm

ligne[F] de but[M]
goal line

but[M]
goal

zone[F] de but[M]
goal crease

point[M] de mise[F] au jeu[M]
face-off spot

cercle[M] de mise[F] au jeu[M]
face-off circle

zone[F] d'attaque[F]
attacking zone

ligne[F] bleue
blue line

arbitre[M]
referee

zone[F] neutre
neutral zone

ligne[F] centrale
center line

61 m

banc[M] des pénalités[F]
penalty bench

banc[M] des joueurs[M]
players' bench

banc[M] des officiels[M]
officials' bench

ailier[M] gauche
left wing

ailier[M] droit
right wing

juge[M] de ligne[F]
linesman

centre[M]
center

défenseur[M] gauche
left defense

cercle[M] central
center face-off circle

zone[F] de défense[F]
defending zone

défenseur[M] droit
right defense

bande[F]
boards

gardien[M] de but[M]
goalkeeper

juge[M] de but[M]
goal judge

coin[M] de patinoire[F]
rink corner

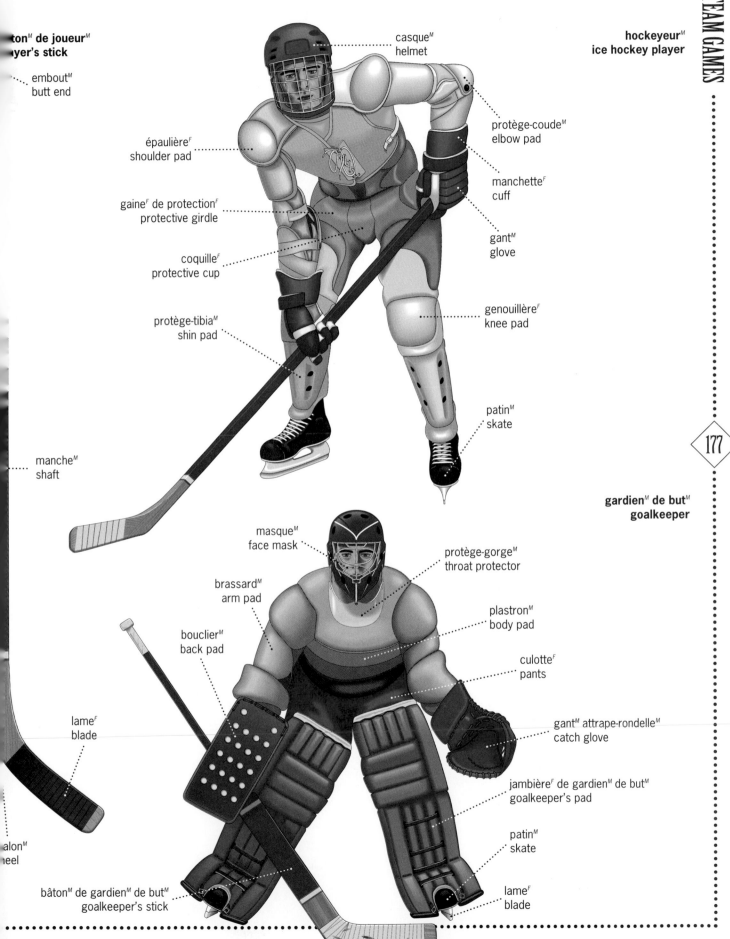

hockeyeur^M
ice hockey player

ton^M de joueur^M
ayer's stick

embout^M
butt end

casque^M
helmet

protège-coude^M
elbow pad

épaulière^F
shoulder pad

manchette^F
cuff

gaine^F de protection^F
protective girdle

gant^M
glove

coquille^F
protective cup

genouillère^F
knee pad

protège-tibia^M
shin pad

patin^M
skate

manche^M
shaft

177

gardien^M **de but**^M
goalkeeper

masque^M
face mask

protège-gorge^M
throat protector

brassard^M
arm pad

plastron^M
body pad

bouclier^M
back pad

culotte^F
pants

lame^F
blade

gant^M attrape-rondelle^M
catch glove

jambière^F de gardien^M de but^M
goalkeeper's pad

patin^M
skate

alon^M
eel

bâton^M de gardien^M de but^M
goalkeeper's stick

lame^F
blade

LE BASKETBALL[M]
BASKETBALL

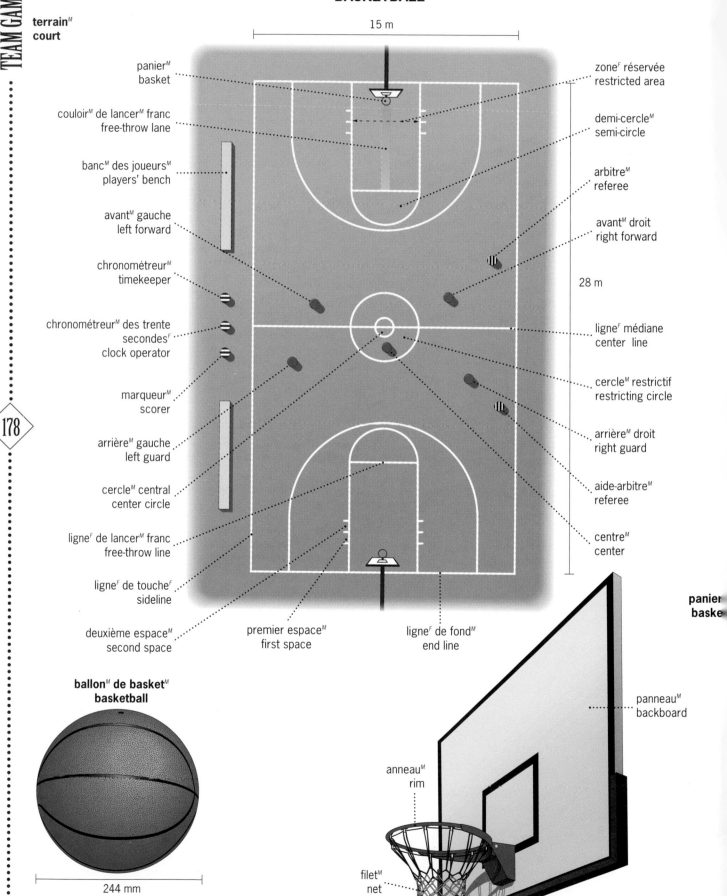

terrain[M]
court

15 m

panier[M]
basket

couloir[M] de lancer[M] franc
free-throw lane

banc[M] des joueurs[M]
players' bench

avant[M] gauche
left forward

chronométreur[M]
timekeeper

chronométreur[M] des trente
secondes[F]
clock operator

marqueur[M]
scorer

arrière[M] gauche
left guard

cercle[M] central
center circle

ligne[F] de lancer[M] franc
free-throw line

ligne[F] de touche[F]
sideline

deuxième espace[M]
second space

premier espace[M]
first space

ligne[F] de fond[M]
end line

zone[F] réservée
restricted area

demi-cercle[M]
semi-circle

arbitre[M]
referee

avant[M] droit
right forward

28 m

ligne[F] médiane
center line

cercle[M] restrictif
restricting circle

arrière[M] droit
right guard

aide-arbitre[M]
referee

centre[M]
center

ballon[M] **de basket**[M]
basketball

244 mm

panier[M]
baske

panneau[M]
backboard

anneau[M]
rim

filet[M]
net

178

LE VOLLEYBALL^M
VOLLEYBALL

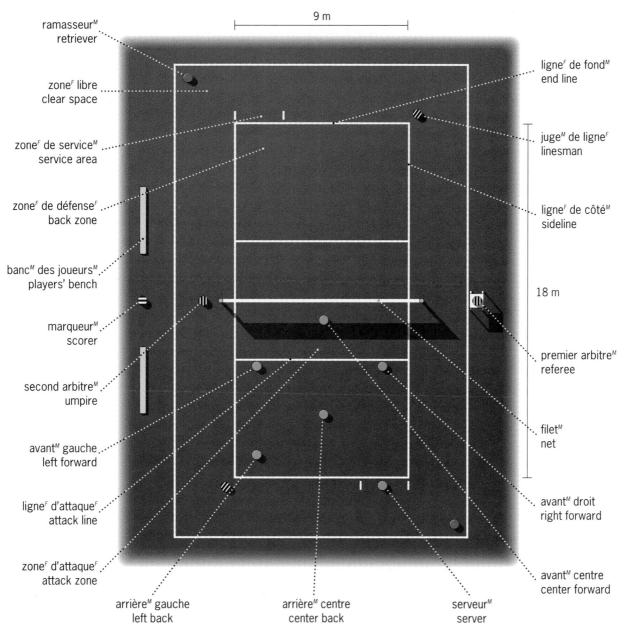

9 m

ramasseur^M
retriever

zone^F libre
clear space

zone^F de service^M
service area

zone^F de défense^F
back zone

banc^M des joueurs^M
players' bench

marqueur^M
scorer

second arbitre^M
umpire

avant^M gauche
left forward

ligne^F d'attaque^F
attack line

zone^F d'attaque^F
attack zone

arrière^M gauche
left back

arrière^M centre
center back

serveur^M
server

terrain^M
court

ligne^F de fond^M
end line

juge^M de ligne^F
linesman

ligne^F de côté^M
sideline

18 m

premier arbitre^M
referee

filet^M
net

avant^M droit
right forward

avant^M centre
center forward

filet^M
net

ballon^M de volleyball^M
volleyball

206 – 213 mm

bande^F verticale de côté^M
vertical side band

bande^F horizontale
tape

antenne^F
antenna

poteau^M
post

LE TENNIS^M
TENNIS

terrain^M
court

8,23 m

juge^M de ligne^F
linesman

marque^F centrale
center mark

ligne^F de fond^M
baseline

receveur^M
receiver

ligne^F de service^M
service line

arrière court^M
backcourt

juge^M de service^M
service judge

avant court^M
forecourt

ligne^F médiane de servic
center service line

ligne^F de simple^M
singles sideline

23,8 m

arbitre^M
umpire

juge^M de filet^M
net judge

court^M de service^M gauche
left service court

filet^M
net

couloir^M
alley

court^M de service^M droit
right service court

serveur^M
server

juge^M de faute^F de pieds^F
foot fault judge

ramasseur^M
ball boy

ligne^F de double^M
doubles sideline

11 m

filet^M
net

sangle^F
center strap

poteau^M de simple^M
singles pole

bande^F de filet^M
net band

poteau^M de double^M
doubles pole

le^F de tennis^M
nis ball

64 – 68 mm

joueuse^F de tennis^M
tennis player

bandeau^M
headband

polo^M
polo shirt

bracelet^M
wristband

raquette^F de tennis^M
tennis racket

talon^M
butt

poignée^F
handle

181

jupette^F
skirt

manche^M
shaft

cœur^M
throat

épaule^F
shoulder

tête^F
head

chaussure^F de tennis^M
tennis shoe

cadre^M
frame

chaussette^F
sock

tamis^M
strings

LA NATATION^F
SWIMMING

bassin^M de compétition^F
competitive course

chronométreur^M principal
chief timekeeper

juge^M de classement^M
placing judge

enregistreur^M
recorder

mur^M d'extrémité^F
end wall

arbitre^M
umpire

juge^M de nages^F
stroke judge

bassin^M
swimming pool

repère^M de virage^M de dos^M
backstroke turn indicator

couloir^M
lane

juge^M de virages^M
turning judge

chronométreur^M de couloir
lane timekeeper

juge^M de départ^M
starter

numéro^M de couloir^M
lane number

plot^M de départ^M
starting block

50 m

mur^M latéral
side wall

ligne^F de fond^M
bottom line

corde^F de couloir^M
lane rope

mur^M de virage^M
turning wall

23 m

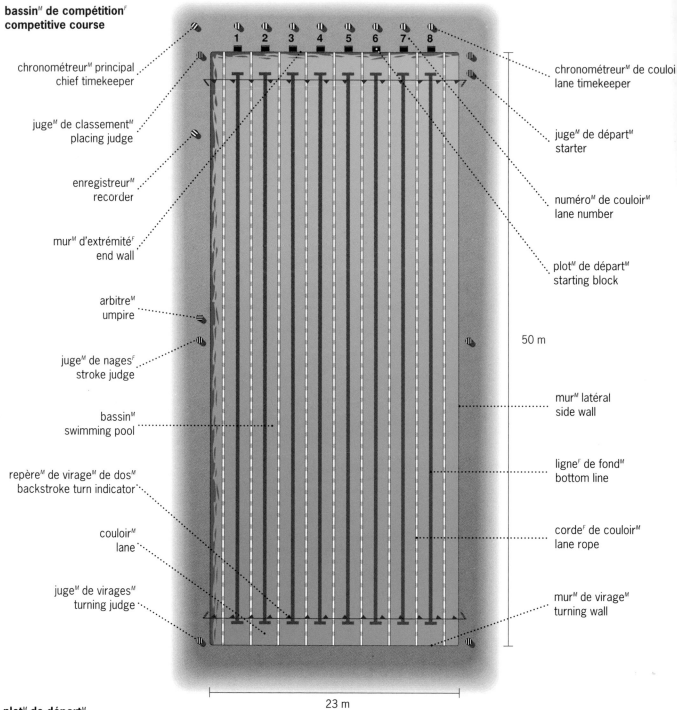

plot^M de départ^M
starting block

plate-forme^F
platform

colonne^F
column

barre^F de départ^M (dos^M)
starting bar (backstroke

mur^M de départ^M
start wall

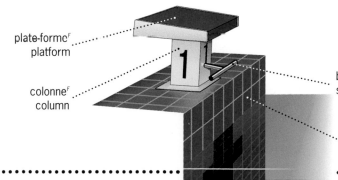

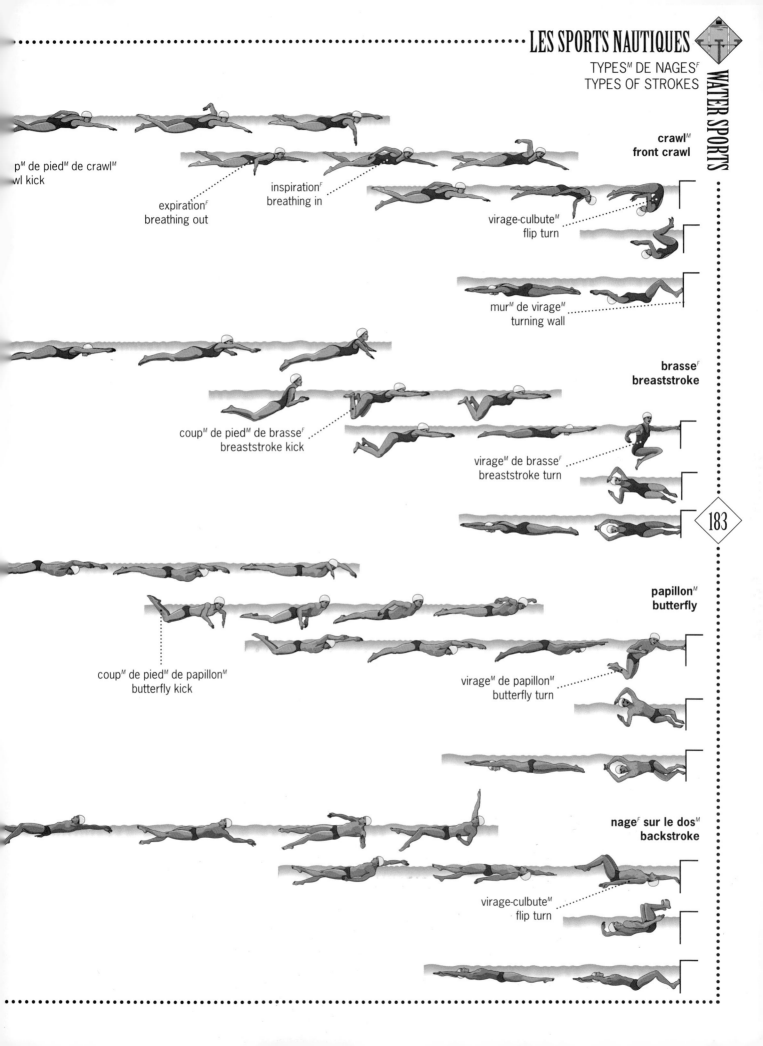

crawl^M
front crawl

p^M de pied^M de crawl^M
wl kick

expiration^F
breathing out

inspiration^F
breathing in

virage-culbute^M
flip turn

mur^M de virage^M
turning wall

brasse^F
breaststroke

coup^M de pied^M de brasse^F
breaststroke kick

virage^M de brasse^F
breaststroke turn

183

papillon^M
butterfly

coup^M de pied^M de papillon^M
butterfly kick

virage^M de papillon^M
butterfly turn

nage^F sur le dos^M
backstroke

virage-culbute^M
flip turn

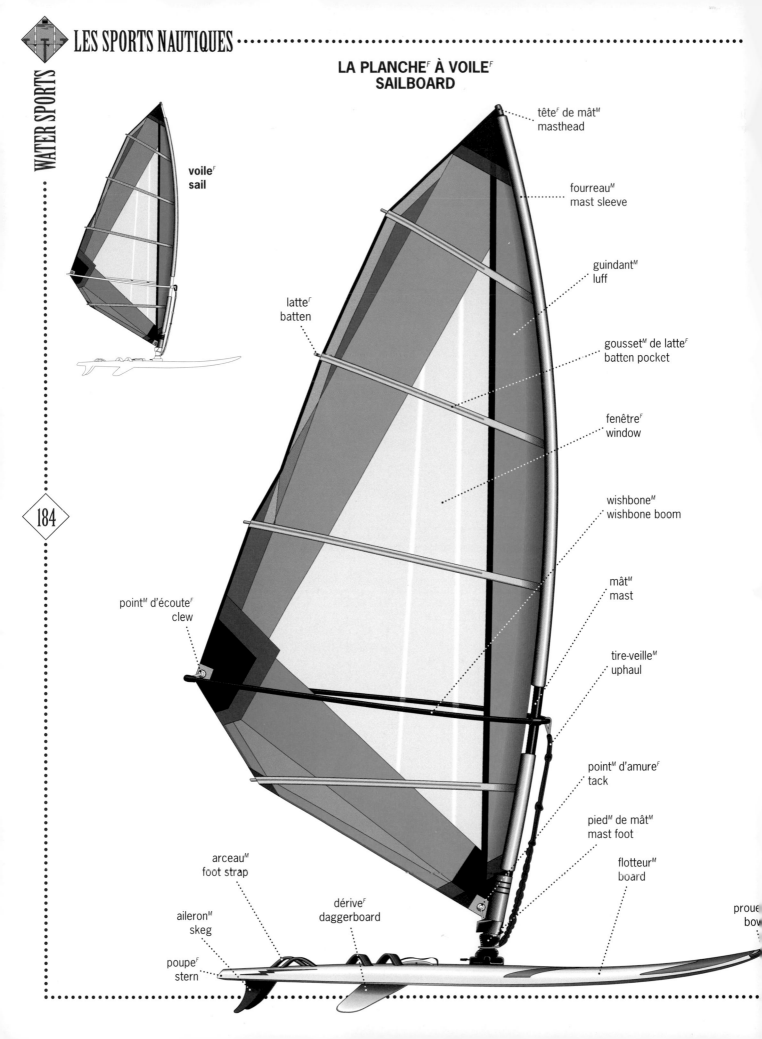

LA PLANCHEF **À VOILE**F
SAILBOARD

voileF
sail

tête F de mât M
masthead

fourreau M
mast sleeve

guindant M
luff

latte F
batten

gousset M de latte F
batten pocket

fenêtre F
window

wishbone M
wishbone boom

mât M
mast

point M d'écoute F
clew

tire-veille M
uphaul

point M d'amure F
tack

pied M de mât M
mast foot

arceau M
foot strap

dérive F
daggerboard

flotteur M
board

aileron M
skeg

proue
bow

poupe F
stern

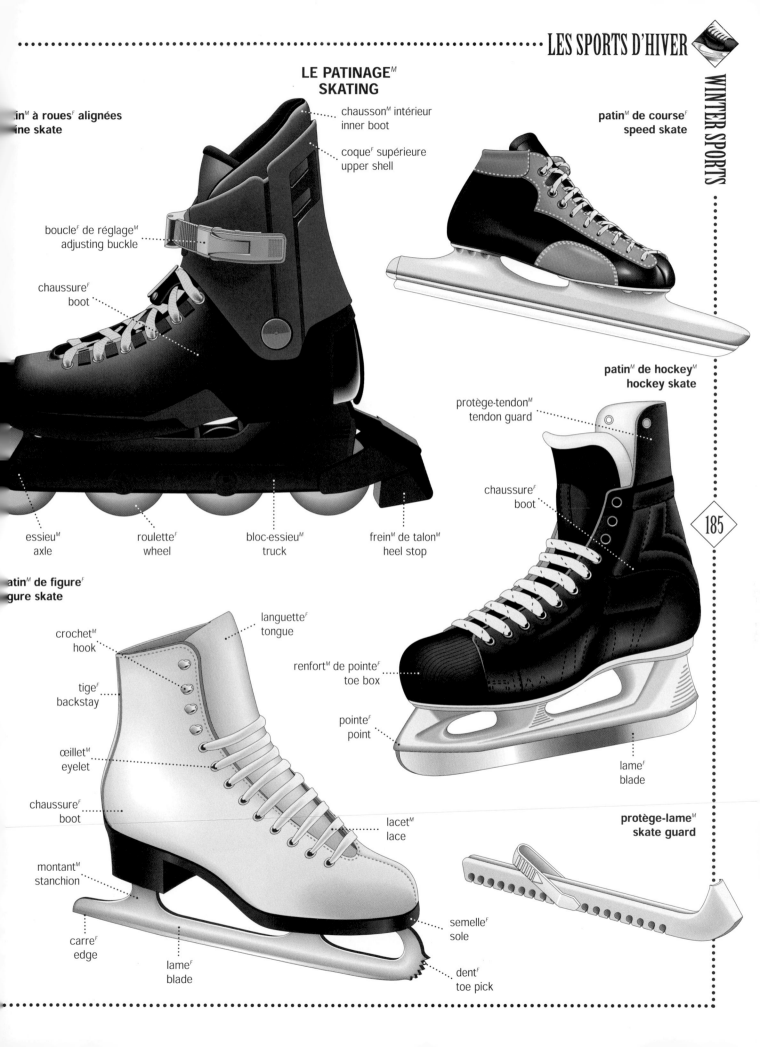

LE PATINAGE^M
SKATING

in^M à roues^F alignées
ine skate

chausson^M intérieur
inner boot

coque^F supérieure
upper shell

boucle^F de réglage^M
adjusting buckle

chaussure^F
boot

essieu^M
axle

roulette^F
wheel

bloc-essieu^M
truck

frein^M de talon^M
heel stop

patin^M de course^F
speed skate

patin^M de hockey^M
hockey skate

protège-tendon^M
tendon guard

chaussure^F
boot

renfort^M de pointe^F
toe box

pointe^F
point

lame^F
blade

185

atin^M de figure^F
gure skate

languette^F
tongue

crochet^M
hook

tige^F
backstay

œillet^M
eyelet

chaussure^F
boot

montant^M
stanchion

carre^F
edge

lame^F
blade

lacet^M
lace

semelle^F
sole

dent^F
toe pick

protège-lame^M
skate guard

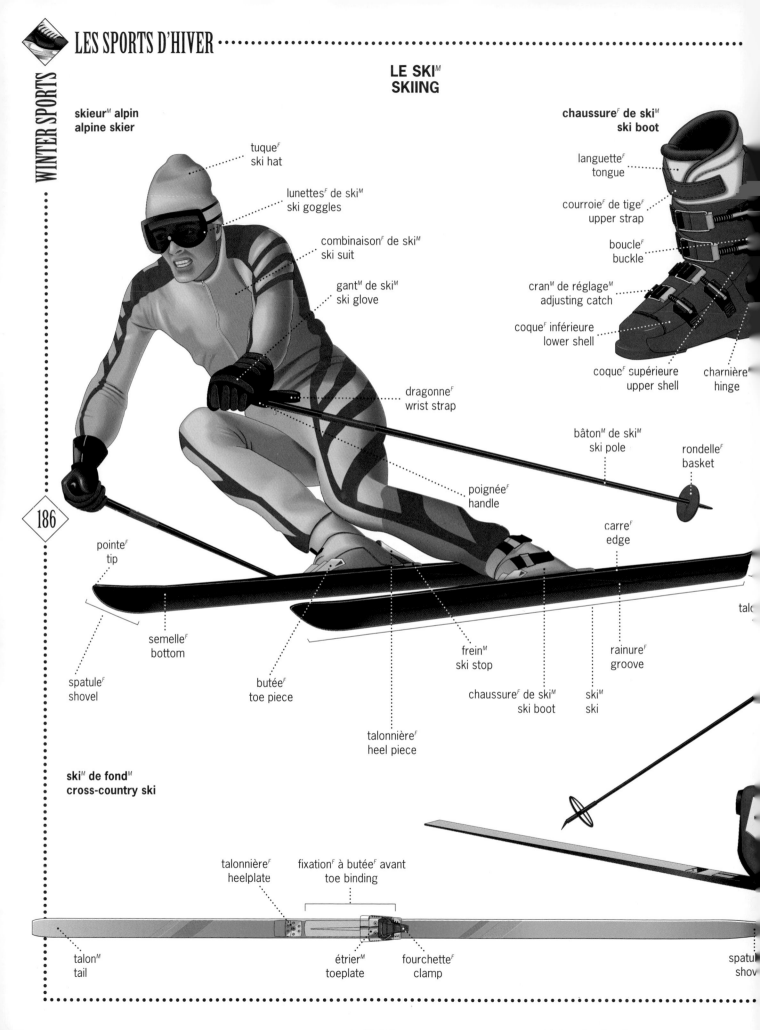

LE SKI^M
SKIING

skieur^M **alpin**
alpine skier

tuque^F
ski hat

lunettes^F de ski^M
ski goggles

combinaison^F de ski^M
ski suit

gant^M de ski^M
ski glove

dragonne^F
wrist strap

poignée^F
handle

chaussure^F **de ski**^M
ski boot

languette^F
tongue

courroie^F de tige^F
upper strap

boucle^F
buckle

cran^M de réglage^M
adjusting catch

coque^F inférieure
lower shell

coque^F supérieure
upper shell

charnière^F
hinge

bâton^M de ski^M
ski pole

rondelle^F
basket

carre^F
edge

pointe^F
tip

semelle^F
bottom

spatule^F
shovel

butée^F
toe piece

frein^M
ski stop

talonnière^F
heel piece

chaussure^F de ski^M
ski boot

ski^M
ski

rainure^F
groove

talo

ski^M **de fond**^M
cross-country ski

talonnière^F
heelplate

fixation^F à butée^F avant
toe binding

talon^M
tail

étrier^M
toeplate

fourchette^F
clamp

spatu
shov

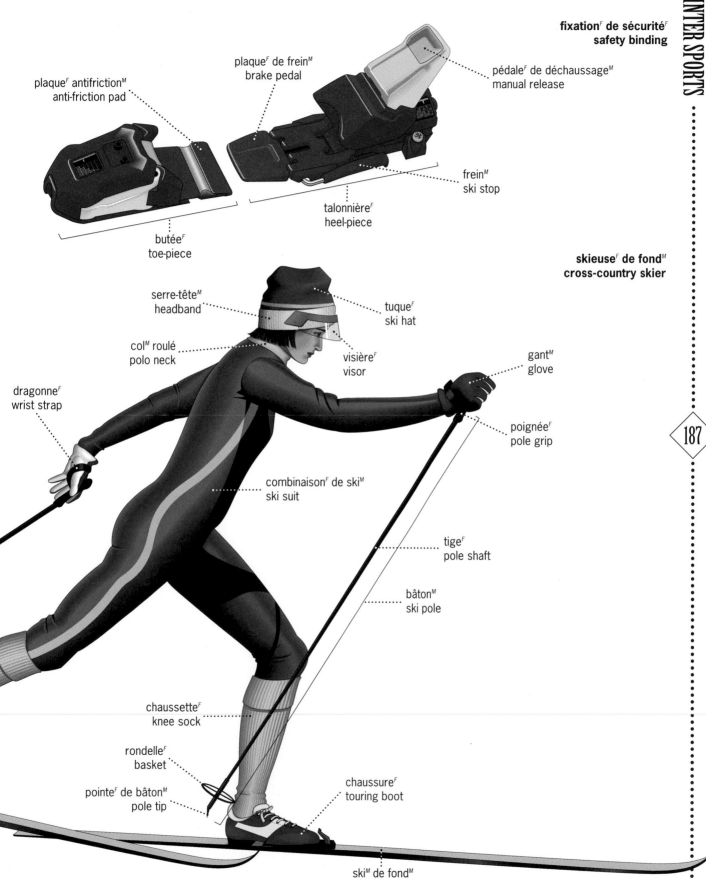

fixation^F de sécurité^F
safety binding

plaque^F antifriction^M
anti-friction pad

plaque^F de frein^M
brake pedal

pédale^F de déchaussage^M
manual release

frein^M
ski stop

talonnière^F
heel-piece

butée^F
toe-piece

skieuse^F de fond^M
cross-country skier

serre-tête^M
headband

tuque^F
ski hat

col^M roulé
polo neck

visière^F
visor

gant^M
glove

dragonne^F
wrist strap

poignée^F
pole grip

combinaison^F de ski^M
ski suit

tige^F
pole shaft

bâton^M
ski pole

chaussette^F
knee sock

rondelle^F
basket

chaussure^F
touring boot

pointe^F de bâton^M
pole tip

ski^M de fond^M
cross-country ski

187

LA GYMNASTIQUE^F
GYMNASTICS

cheval^M d'arçons^M
pommel horse

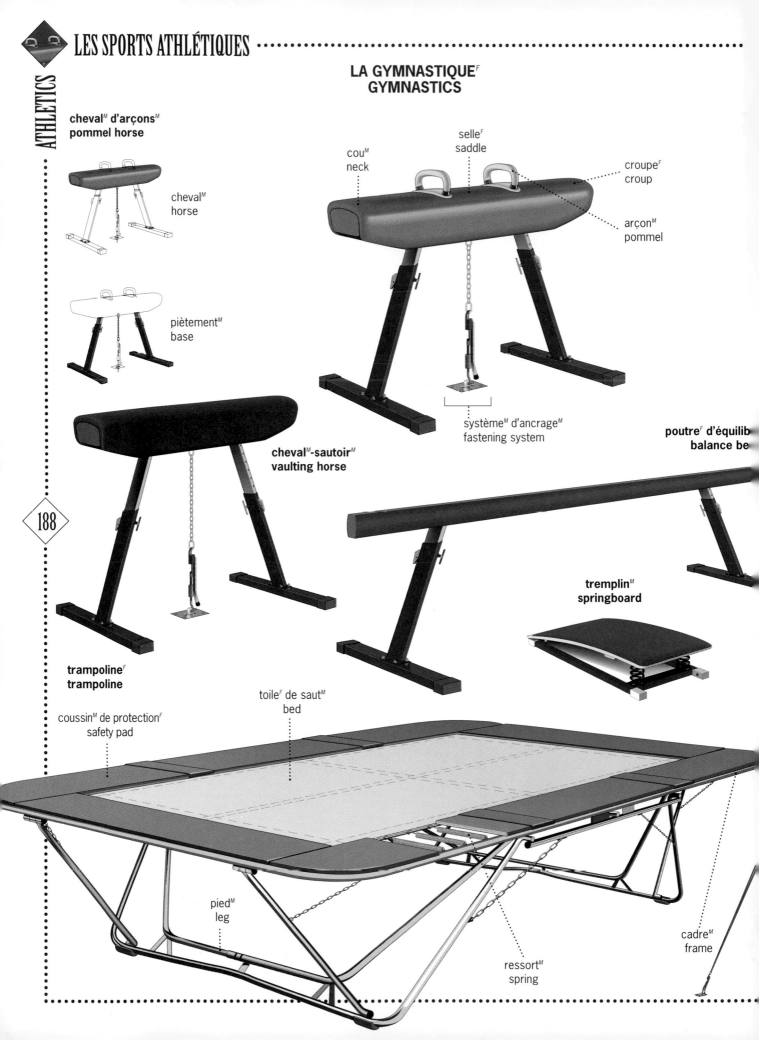

cheval^M
horse

cou^M
neck

selle^F
saddle

croupe^F
croup

arçon^M
pommel

piètement^M
base

système^M d'ancrage^M
fastening system

poutre^F d'équilib
balance be

cheval^M-sautoir^M
vaulting horse

tremplin^M
springboard

trampoline^F
trampoline

toile^F de saut^M
bed

coussin^M de protection^F
safety pad

pied^M
leg

cadre^M
frame

ressort^M
spring

res^F asymétriques
mmetrical bars

barre^F fixe
horizontal bar; high bar

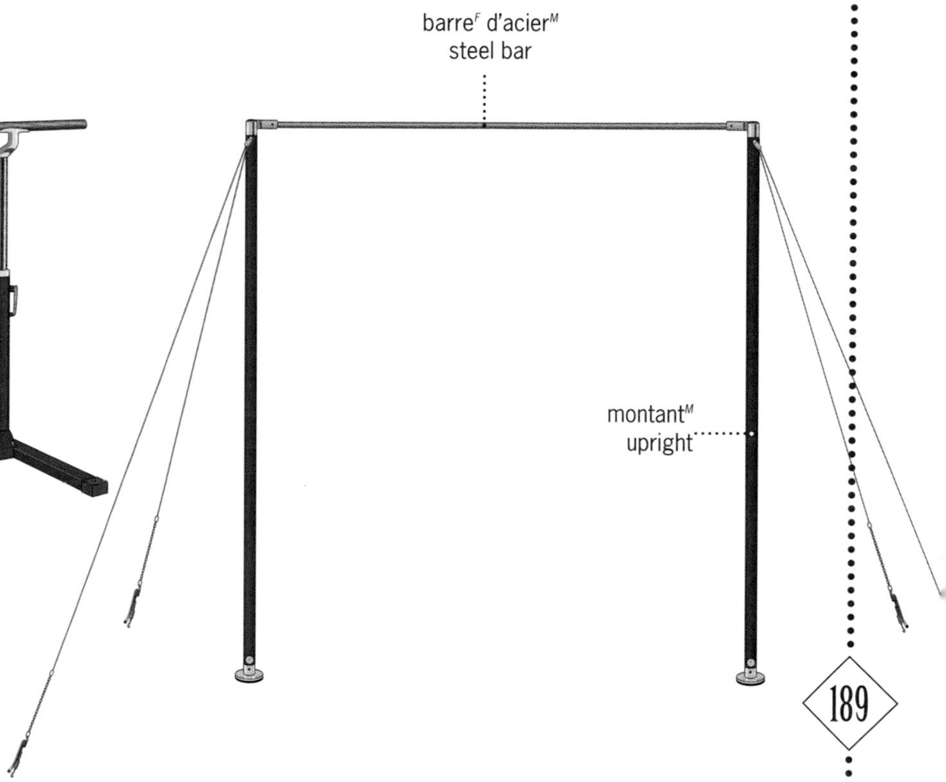

barre^F d'acier^M
steel bar

montant^M
upright

neaux^M
gs

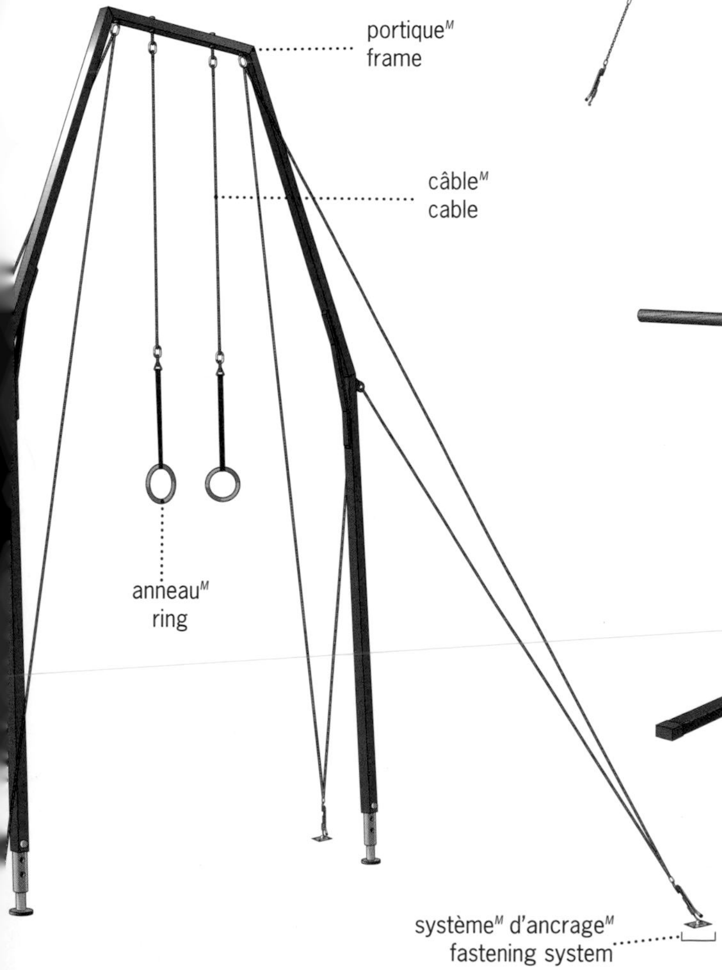

portique^M
frame

câble^M
cable

barres^F parallèles
parallel bars

anneau^M
ring

système^M d'ancrage^M
fastening system

189

LES TENTES^F
TENTS

tente^F deux places^F
two-person tent

double toit^M
rainfly

porte^F
door

auvent^M
awning

hauban^M
guy line

piquet^M
stake

tendeur^M
strainer

fermeture^F à glissière^F
zipper

tente^F intérieure
inner tent

190

PRINCIPAUX TYPES^M DE TENTES^F
MAJOR TYPES OF TENTS

tente^F grange^F
wagon tent

tente^F rectangula
wall tent

tente^F canadienne
pup tent

tente^F dôme^M
dome tent

tente^F igloo^M
pop-up tent

tente^F familiale
family tent

tente^F individuelle
one-person tent

L'ÉQUIPEMENT^M DE COUCHAGE^M
SLEEPING EQUIPMENT

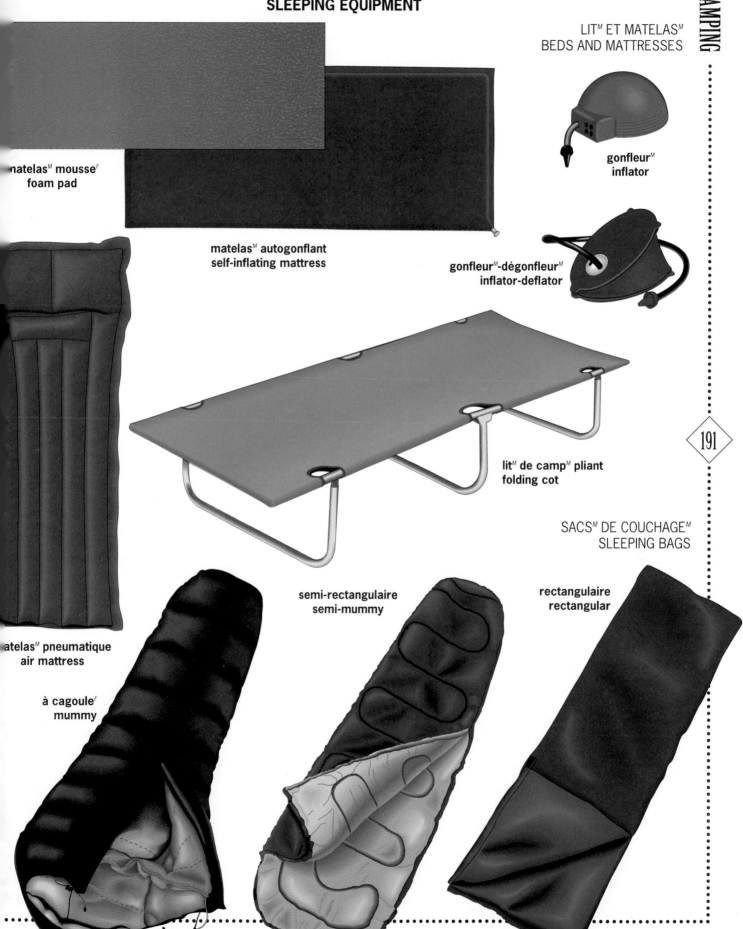

LIT^M ET MATELAS^M
BEDS AND MATTRESSES

matelas^M mousse^F
foam pad

gonfleur^M
inflator

matelas^M autogonflant
self-inflating mattress

gonfleur^M-dégonfleur^M
inflator-deflator

lit^M de camp^M pliant
folding cot

SACS^M DE COUCHAGE^M
SLEEPING BAGS

semi-rectangulaire
semi-mummy

rectangulaire
rectangular

matelas^M pneumatique
air mattress

à cagoule^F
mummy

**LE MATÉRIEL^M DE CAMPING^M
CAMPING EQUIPMENT**

**couteau^M suisse
Swiss army knife**

ciseaux^M
scissors

règle^F graduée
ruler

loupe^F
magnifier

écailleur^M
fish scaler

lime^F
file

petite lame^F
small blade

tournevis^M cruciforme
cross-tip screwdriver

décapsuleur^M
bottle opener

tournevis^M
screwdriver

tournevis^M
screwdriver

grande lame^F
large blade

onglet^M
nail nick

poinçon^M
awl

tire-bouchon^M
corkscrew

ouvre-boîtes^M
can opener

**étui^M de cuir^M
leather sheath**

**couteau^M
knife**

**lampe^F de poc...
flashlight**

**hachette^F
hatchet**

**gaine^F
sheath**

POPOTE^F
COOKING SET

**assiette^F plate
plate**

**cafetière^F
coffee pot**

**poêle^F
frying pan**

**tasse^F
cup**

**gourde^F
canteen**

**queue^F
handle**

**faitout^M
saucepa...**

sac^M à dos^M
backpack

rabat^M
top flap

bretelle^F
shoulder strap

sangle^F de compression^F
side compression strap

armature^F intégrée
internal frame

ceinture^F
waist belt

boucle^F de réglage^M
tightening buckle

passe-sangle^M
strap loop

sangle^F de fermeture^F
front compression strap

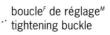

◇ 193 ◇

trousse^F de secours^M
first aid kit

boussole^F magnétique
magnetic compass

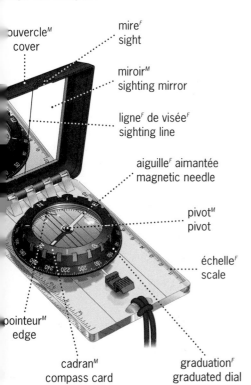

couvercle^M
cover

mire^F
sight

miroir^M
sighting mirror

ligne^F de visée^F
sighting line

aiguille^F aimantée
magnetic needle

pivot^M
pivot

échelle^F
scale

pointeur^M
edge

cadran^M
compass card

graduation^F
graduated dial

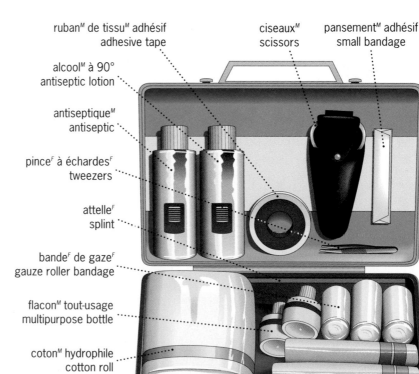

ruban^M de tissu^M adhésif
adhesive tape

ciseaux^M
scissors

pansement^M adhésif
small bandage

alcool^M à 90°
antiseptic lotion

antiseptique^M
antiseptic

pince^F à échardes^F
tweezers

attelle^F
splint

bande^F de gaze^F
gauze roller bandage

flacon^M tout-usage
multipurpose bottle

coton^M hydrophile
cotton roll

compresse^F stérilisée
sterile dressing

INDOOR GAMES

LES CARTES^F
CARD GAMES

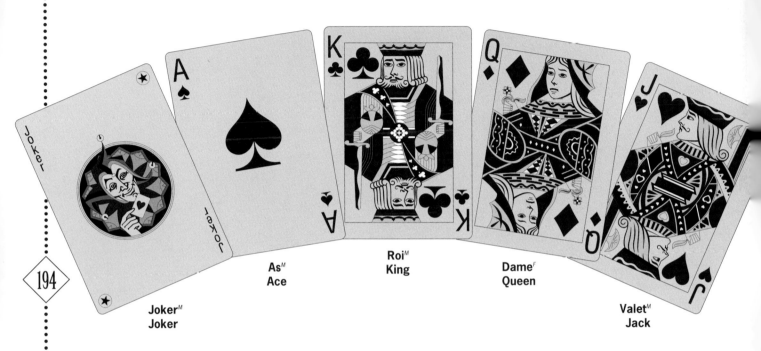

cœur^M
heart

carreau^M
diamond

trèfle^M
club

pique^M
spade

Joker^M
Joker

As^M
Ace

Roi^M
King

Dame^F
Queen

Valet^M
Jack

194

LES DÉS^M
DICE

dé^M à poker^M
poker die

dé^M régulier
ordinary die

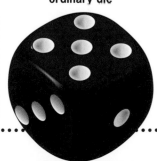

LES DOMINO
DOMINOE

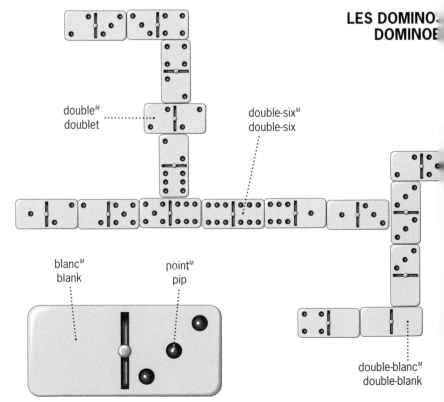

double^M
doublet

double-six^M
double-six

blanc^M
blank

point^M
pip

double-blanc^M
double-blank

LES ÉCHECS^M
CHESS

Échiquier^M
Chessboard

PIÈCES^F
MEN

aile^F Dame^F
Queen's side

aile^F Roi^M
King's side

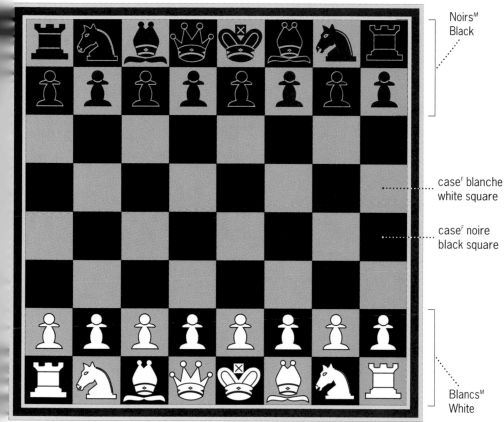

Noirs^M
Black

case^F blanche
white square

case^F noire
black square

Blancs^M
White

a b c d e f g h

notation^F algébrique
chess notation

Pion^M
Pawn

Cavalier^M
Knight

Fou^M
Bishop

Tour^F
Rook

types^M de déplacements^M
types of movements

déplacement^M vertical
vertical movement

déplacement^M diagonal
diagonal movement

déplacement^M en équerre^F
square movement

déplacement^M horizontal
horizontal movement

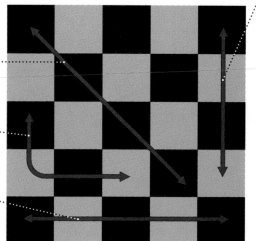

Dame^F
Queen

Roi^M
King

LE JACQUET^M
BACKGAMMON

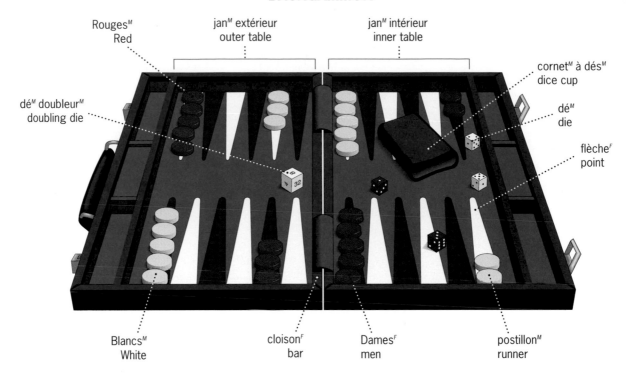

Rouges^M
Red

jan^M extérieur
outer table

jan^M intérieur
inner table

cornet^M à dés^M
dice cup

dé^M doubleur^M
doubling die

dé^M
die

flèche^F
point

Blancs^M
White

cloison^F
bar

Dames^F
men

postillon^M
runner

LE JEU^M DE DAMES^F
CHECKERS

Dame^F
checker

damier^M
checkerboard

LE SYSTÈME^M DE JEU^M VIDÉO
VIDEO ENTERTAINMENT SYSTEM

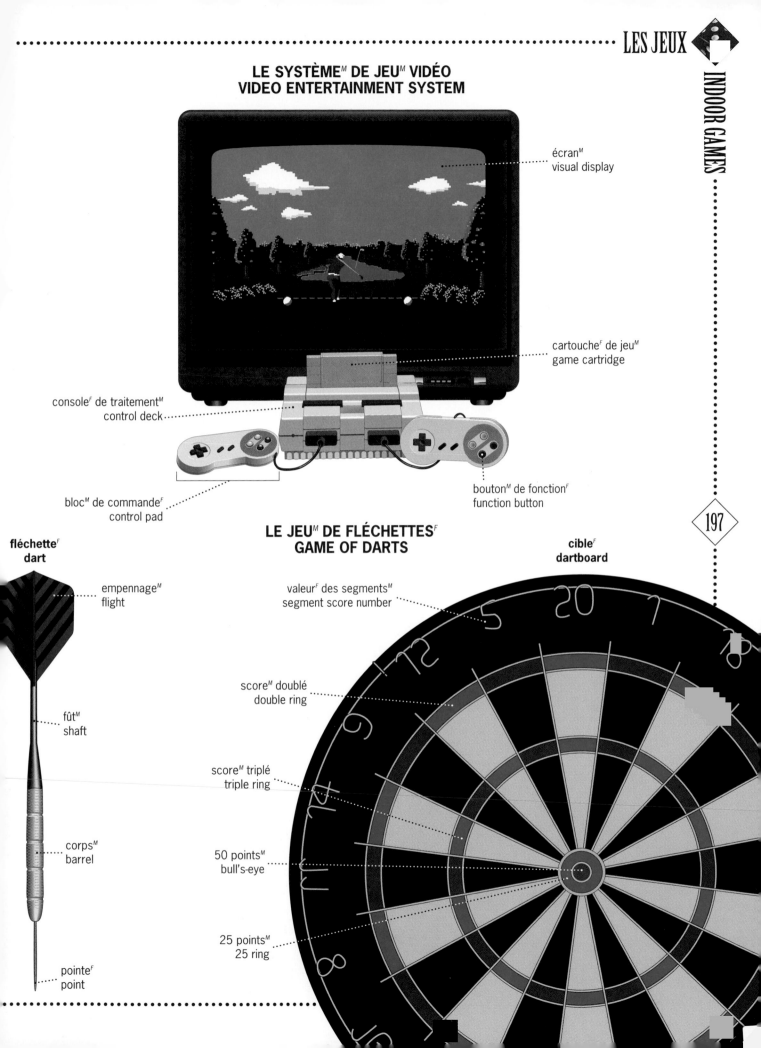

écran^M
visual display

cartouche^F de jeu^M
game cartridge

console^F de traitement^M
control deck

bouton^M de fonction^F
function button

bloc^M de commande^F
control pad

197

LE JEU^M DE FLÉCHETTES^F
GAME OF DARTS

fléchette^F
dart

cible^F
dartboard

empennage^M
flight

valeur^F des segments^M
segment score number

score^M doublé
double ring

fût^M
shaft

score^M triplé
triple ring

corps^M
barrel

50 points^M
bull's-eye

25 points^M
25 ring

pointe^F
point

LA MESURE^F DU TEMPS^M
MEASURE OF TIME

chronomètre^M
stopwatch

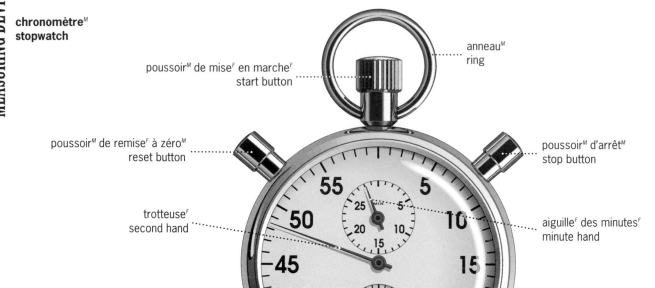

poussoir^M de mise^F en marche^F
start button

anneau^M
ring

poussoir^M de remise^F à zéro^M
reset button

poussoir^M d'arrêt^M
stop button

trotteuse^F
second hand

aiguille^F des minutes^F
minute hand

aiguille^F des dixièmes^M de seconde^F
1/10th second hand

boîtier^M
case

montre^F **à affichage**^M **analogique**
analog watch

cadran^M
dial

minuteur^M
kitchen timer

sablier^M
egg timer

montre^F **à affichage**^M **numérique**
digital watch

cristaux^M liquides
liquid crystal display

style^M
gnomon

ombre^F
shadow

cadran^M
dial

cadran^M **solai**
sundi

LA MESURE^F DE LA TEMPÉRATURE^F
MEASURE OF TEMPERATURE

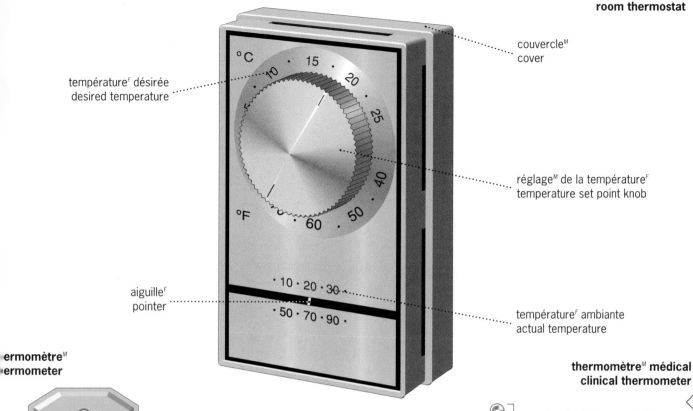

thermostat^M d'ambiance^F
room thermostat

couvercle^M
cover

température^F désirée
desired temperature

réglage^M de la température^F
temperature set point knob

aiguille^F
pointer

température^F ambiante
actual temperature

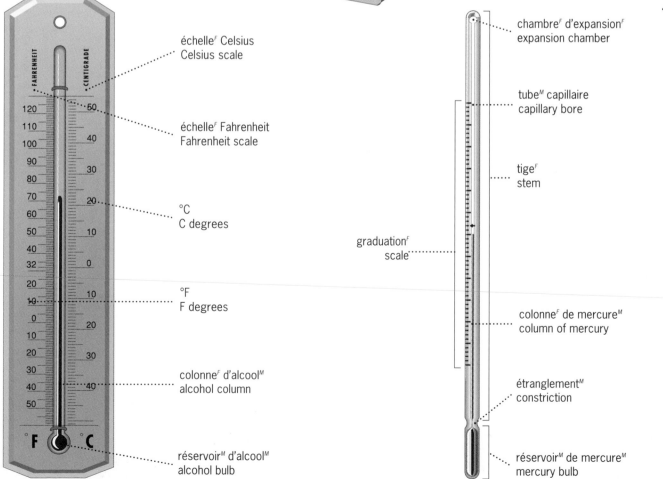

ermomètre^M
ermometer

échelle^F Celsius
Celsius scale

échelle^F Fahrenheit
Fahrenheit scale

°C
C degrees

°F
F degrees

colonne^F d'alcool^M
alcohol column

réservoir^M d'alcool^M
alcohol bulb

thermomètre^M médical
clinical thermometer

chambre^F d'expansion^F
expansion chamber

tube^M capillaire
capillary bore

tige^F
stem

graduation^F
scale

colonne^F de mercure^M
column of mercury

étranglement^M
constriction

réservoir^M de mercure^M
mercury bulb

LA MESURE^F DE LA MASSE^F
MEASURE OF WEIGHT

balance^F de Roberval
balance

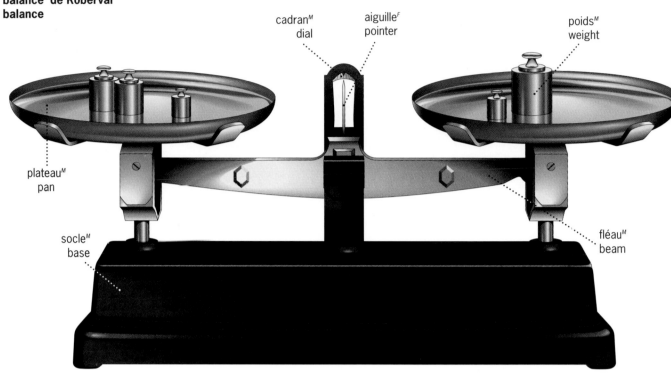

cadran^M
dial

aiguille^F
pointer

poids^M
weight

plateau^M
pan

socle^M
base

fléau^M
beam

200

balance^F romaine
steelyard

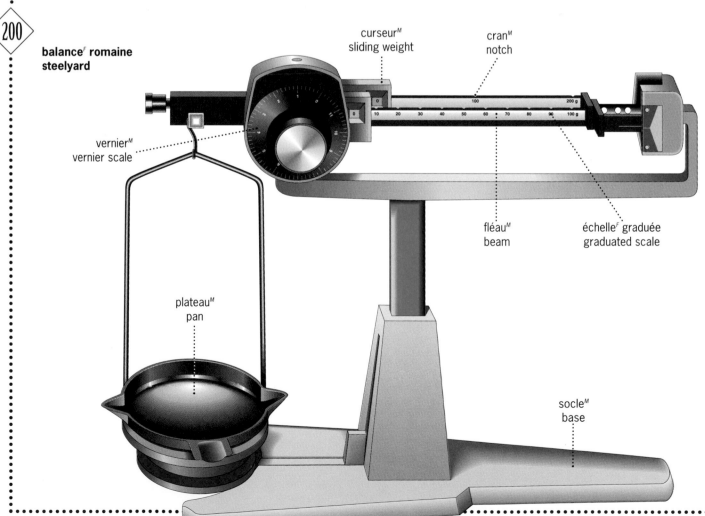

curseur^M
sliding weight

cran^M
notch

vernier^M
vernier scale

fléau^M
beam

échelle^F graduée
graduated scale

plateau^M
pan

socle^M
base

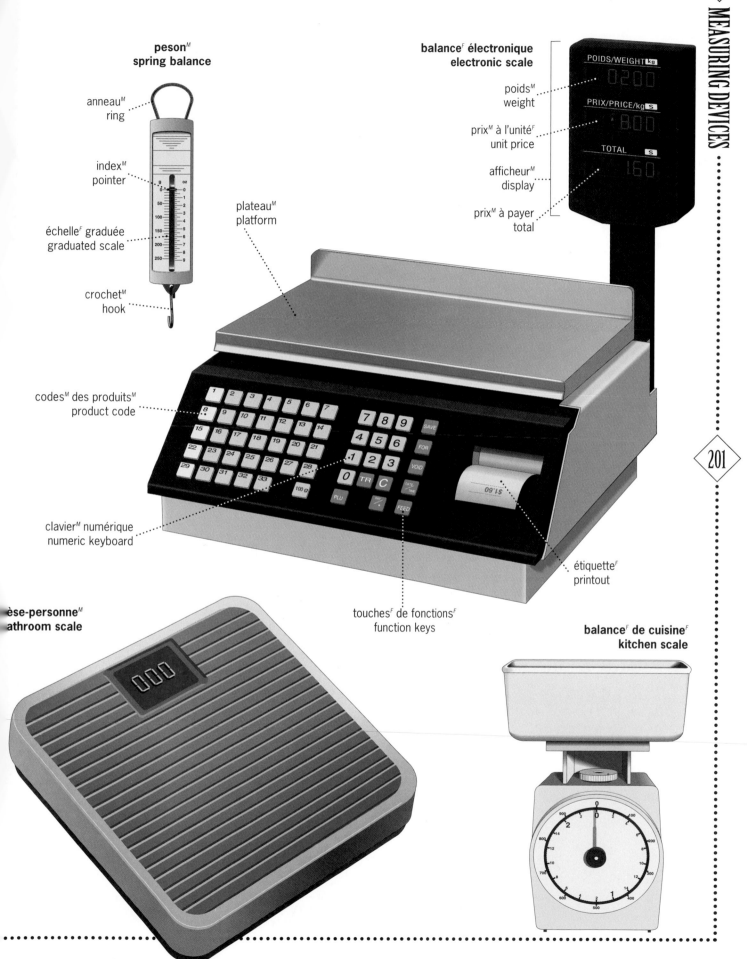

peson^M
spring balance

anneau^M
ring

index^M
pointer

échelle^F graduée
graduated scale

crochet^M
hook

plateau^M
platform

balance^F **électronique**
electronic scale

POIDS/WEIGHT kg

0.200

poids^M
weight

PRIX/PRICE/kg S

8.00

prix^M à l'unité^F
unit price

TOTAL S

1.60

afficheur^M
display

prix^M à payer
total

codes^M des produits^M
product code

clavier^M numérique
numeric keyboard

étiquette^F
printout

touches^F de fonctions^F
function keys

èse-personne^M
athroom scale

balance^F **de cuisine**^F
kitchen scale

LE PÉTROLE^M
OIL

LE PÉTROLE^M

TRANSPORT^M TERREST
GROUND TRANSPO

oléoduc^M
pipeline

PROSPECTION^F
PROSPECTING

**prospection^F terrestre
surface prospecting**

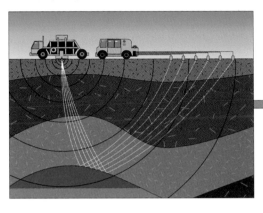

FORAGE^M
DRILLING

**appareil^M de forage^M
drilling rig**

semi-remorque^F citer
tank trai

**prospection^F en mer^F
offshore prospecting**

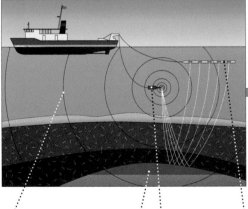

**plate-forme^F de production^F
production platform**

TRANSPORT^M MARITIM
MARITIME TRANSPO

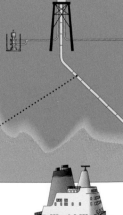

onde^F de choc^M
shock wave

enregistrement^M sismographique
seismographic recording

gisement^M de pétrole^M
petroleum trap

charge^F explosive
blasting charge

oléoduc^M sous-marin
submarine pipeline

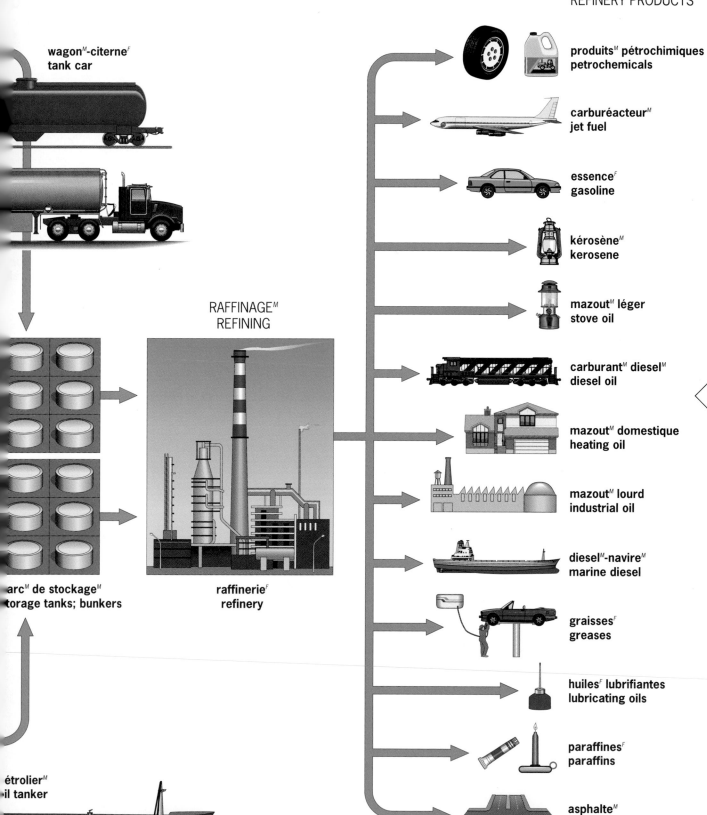

PRODUITS^M DE LA RAFFINERIE^F
REFINERY PRODUCTS

wagon^M-citerne^F
tank car

RAFFINAGE^M
REFINING

arc^M de stockage^M
torage tanks; bunkers

raffinerie^F
refinery

étrolier^M
il tanker

produits^M pétrochimiques
petrochemicals

carburéacteur^M
jet fuel

essence^F
gasoline

kérosène^M
kerosene

mazout^M léger
stove oil

carburant^M diesel^M
diesel oil

mazout^M domestique
heating oil

mazout^M lourd
industrial oil

diesel^M-navire^M
marine diesel

graisses^F
greases

huiles^F lubrifiantes
lubricating oils

paraffines^F
paraffins

asphalte^M
asphalt

L'ÉNERGIE^F HYDROÉLECTRIQUE
HYDROELECTRIC ENERGY

complexe^M hydroélectrique
hydroelectric complex

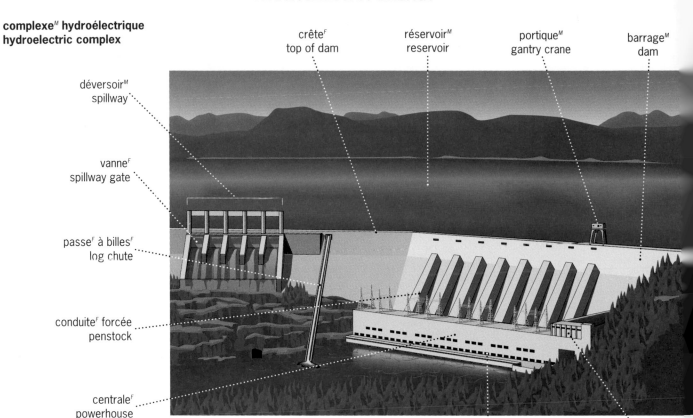

déversoir^M
spillway

crête^F
top of dam

réservoir^M
reservoir

portique^M
gantry crane

barrage^M
dam

vanne^F
spillway gate

passe^F à billes^F
log chute

conduite^F forcée
penstock

centrale^F
powerhouse

salle^F des machines^F
machine hall

salle^F de commande
control room

coupe^F d'une centrale^F hydroélectrique
cross section of hydroelectric power station

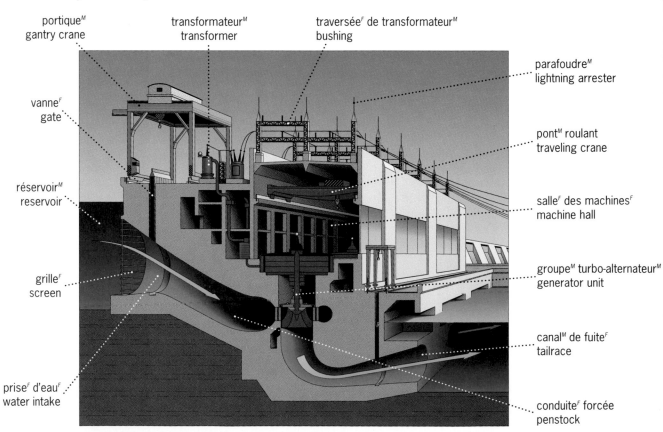

portique^M
gantry crane

transformateur^M
transformer

traversée^F de transformateur^M
bushing

parafoudre^M
lightning arrester

vanne^F
gate

pont^M roulant
traveling crane

réservoir^M
reservoir

salle^F des machines^F
machine hall

grille^F
screen

groupe^M turbo-alternateur^M
generator unit

canal^M de fuite^F
tailrace

prise^F d'eau^F
water intake

conduite^F forcée
penstock

204

circuit^M électrique
electric circuit

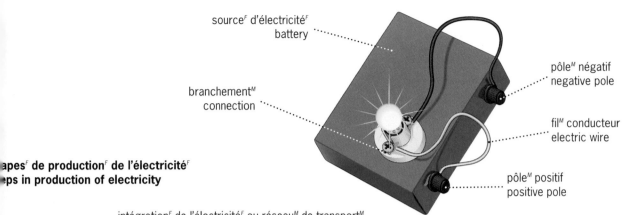

source^F d'électricité^F
battery

pôle^M négatif
negative pole

branchement^M
connection

fil^M conducteur
electric wire

pôle^M positif
positive pole

étapes^F de production^F de l'électricité^F
steps in production of electricity

intégration^F de l'électricité^F au réseau^M de transport^M
energy integration to the transmission network

production^F d'électricité^F par l'alternateur^M
production of electricity by the generator

provision^F d'eau^F
supply of water

élévation^F de la tension^F
voltage increase

transport^M de l'électricité^F à haute tension^F
high-tension electricity transmission

abaissement^M de la tension^F
voltage decrease

transport^M vers les usagers^M
transmission to consumers

205

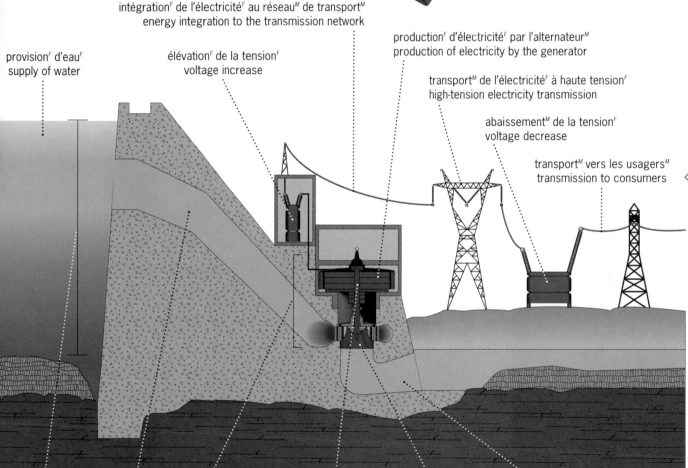

hauteur^F de chute^F
head of water

évacuation^F de l'eau^F turbinée
turbined water draining

eau^F sous pression^F
water under pressure

transmission^F du mouvement^M au rotor^M
transmission of the rotative movement to the rotor

conversion^F du travail^M mécanique en électricité^F
transformation of mechanical work into electricity

mouvement^M rotatif de la turbine^F
rotation of the turbine

L'ÉNERGIE^F NUCLÉAIRE
NUCLEAR ENERGY

centrale^F nucléaire
nuclear power station

vanne^F d'arrosage^M
dousing water valve

réservoir^M d'arrosage^M
dousing water tank

générateur^M de vapeur^F
steam generator

pompe^F de caloportage^M
heat transport pump

bâtiment^M du réacteur^M
reactor building

piscine^F de stockage^M du combustible^M irradié
spent fuel storage bay

réacteur^M
reactor

piscine^F de déchargement^M du combustible^M irradié
spent fuel discharge bay

bâtiment^M de la turbine^F
turbine building

transformateur^M
transformer

salle^F de commande
control room

alternateur^M
generator

cuve^F du réacteur^M
calandria

turbine^F
turbine

réchauffeur^M
reheater

machine^F à combustible^M
fueling machine

sortie^F de l'eau^F de refroidissement^M du condenseur^M
condenser cooling water outlet

entrée^F du reflux^M du condenseur^M
condenser backwash inlet

sortie^F du reflux^M du condenseur^M
condenser backwash outlet

entrée^F de l'eau^F de refroidissement^M du condenseur^M
condenser cooling water inlet

oduction^F **d'électricité**^F **par énergie**^F **nucléaire**
oduction of electricity from nuclear energy

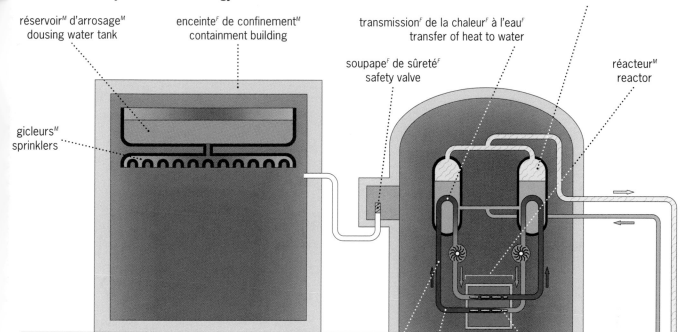

réservoir^M d'arrosage^M
dousing water tank

enceinte^F de confinement^M
containment building

transmission^F de la chaleur^F à l'eau^F
transfer of heat to water

transformation^F de l'eau^F en vapeur^F
water turns into steam

soupape^F de sûreté^F
safety valve

réacteur^M
reactor

gicleurs^M
sprinklers

acheminement^M de la chaleur^F au générateur^M de vapeur^F par le caloporteur^M
coolant transfers the heat to the steam generator

fission^F de l'uranium^M
fission of uranium fuel

production^F de chaleur^F
heat production

207

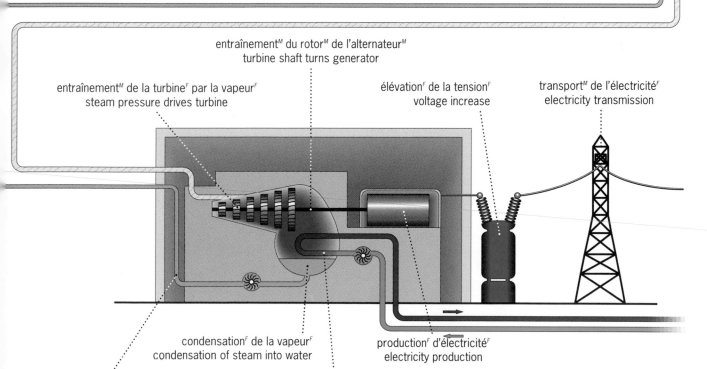

entraînement^M du rotor^M de l'alternateur^M
turbine shaft turns generator

entraînement^M de la turbine^F par la vapeur^F
steam pressure drives turbine

élévation^F de la tension^F
voltage increase

transport^M de l'électricité^F
electricity transmission

condensation^F de la vapeur^F
condensation of steam into water

production^F d'électricité^F
electricity production

retour^M de l'eau^F au générateur^M de vapeur^F
ater is pumped back into the steam generator

refroidissement^M de la vapeur^F par l'eau^F
water cools the used steam

L'ÉNERGIE[F] SOLAIRE
SOLAR ENERGY

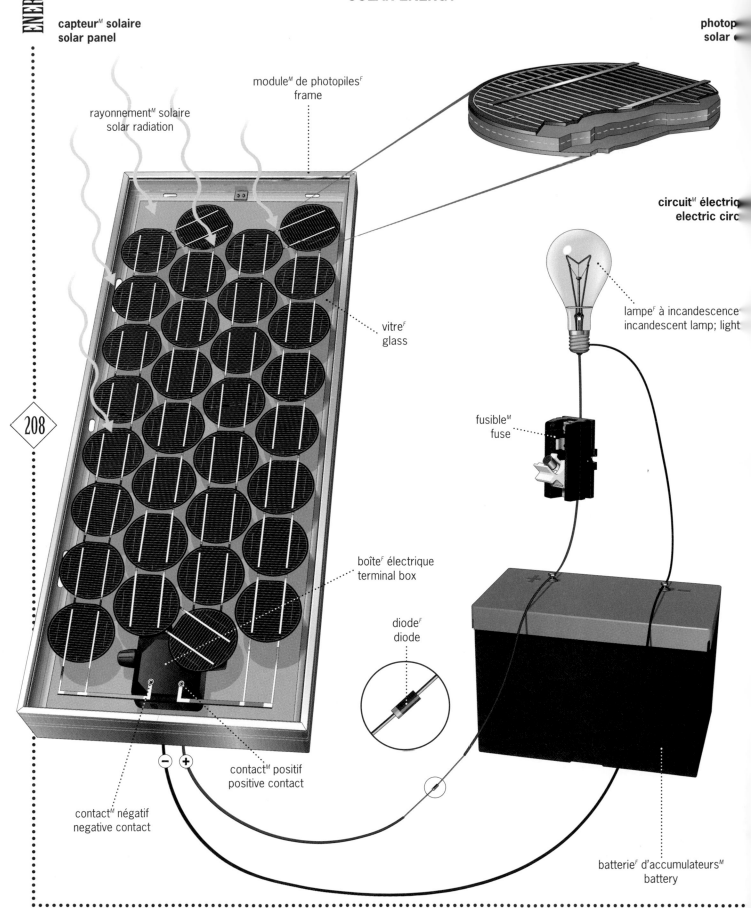

capteur[M] solaire
solar panel

module[M] de photopiles[F]
frame

rayonnement[M] solaire
solar radiation

photop
solar

vitre[F]
glass

circuit[M] électriq
electric circ

lampe[F] à incandescence
incandescent lamp; light

fusible[M]
fuse

boîte[F] électrique
terminal box

diode[F]
diode

208

contact[M] positif
positive contact

contact[M] négatif
negative contact

batterie[F] d'accumulateurs[M]
battery

L'ÉNERGIE[F] ÉOLIENNE
WIND ENERGY

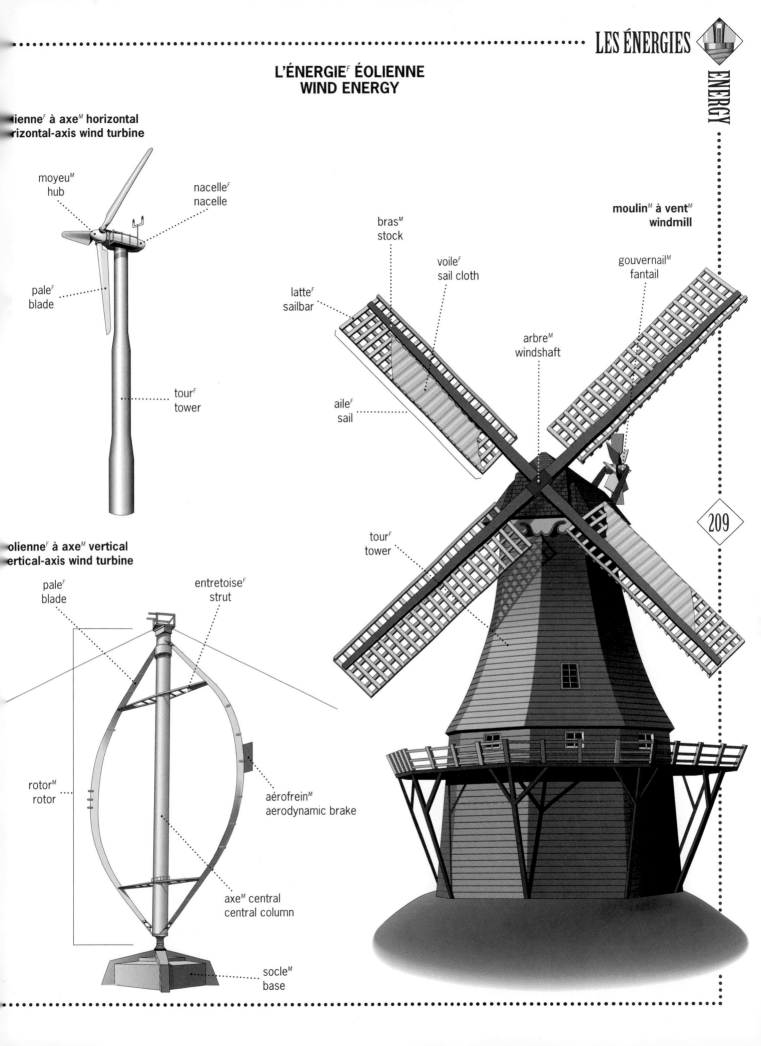

éolienne[F] à axe[M] horizontal
horizontal-axis wind turbine

moyeu[M]
hub

nacelle[F]
nacelle

pale[F]
blade

tour[F]
tower

moulin[M] à vent[M]
windmill

bras[M]
stock

voile[F]
sail cloth

gouvernail[M]
fantail

latte[F]
sailbar

arbre[M]
windshaft

aile[F]
sail

tour[F]
tower

éolienne[F] à axe[M] vertical
vertical-axis wind turbine

pale[F]
blade

entretoise[F]
strut

rotor[M]
rotor

aérofrein[M]
aerodynamic brake

axe[M] central
central column

socle[M]
base

209

LA PRÉVENTION^F DES INCENDIES^M
FIRE PREVENTION

tuyau^M de refoulement^M
fire hose

extincteur^M
portable fire extinguisher

borne^F d'incendie^M
fire hydrant

carré^M de manoeuvre^F
operating nut

prise^F d'eau^F
water supply point

bouchon^M
cap

colonne^F
upright pipe

grande échelle^F
fire engine

tourelle^F
turntable mounting

flèche^F télescopique
telescopic boom

vérin^M de dressage^M
elevating cylinder

projecteur^M orientable
spotlight

coffre^M de rangement^M
storage compartment

orifice^M d'alimentation^F
hydrant intake

stabilisateur^M
outrigger

panneau^M de commande^F
control panel

gaffe^F
pike pole

sapeur-pompier^M
fire fighter

bouteille^F d'air^M comprimé
compressed-air cylinder

hache^F
fire fighter's hatchet

casque^M
helmet

masque^M complet
full face mask

appareil^M de protection^F respiratoire
self-contained breathing apparatus

arc^M à échelles^F
wer ladder

tube^M d'alimentation^F en air^M
air-supply tube

gyrophare^M
flashing light

échelle^F de tête^F
top ladder

avertisseur^M sonore
warning device

lance^F à eau^F
ladder pipe nozzle

vêtement^M ignifuge et hydrofuge
fireproof and waterproof garment

botte^F de caoutchouc^M
rubber boot

LA MACHINERIE^F LOURDE
HEAVY VEHICLES

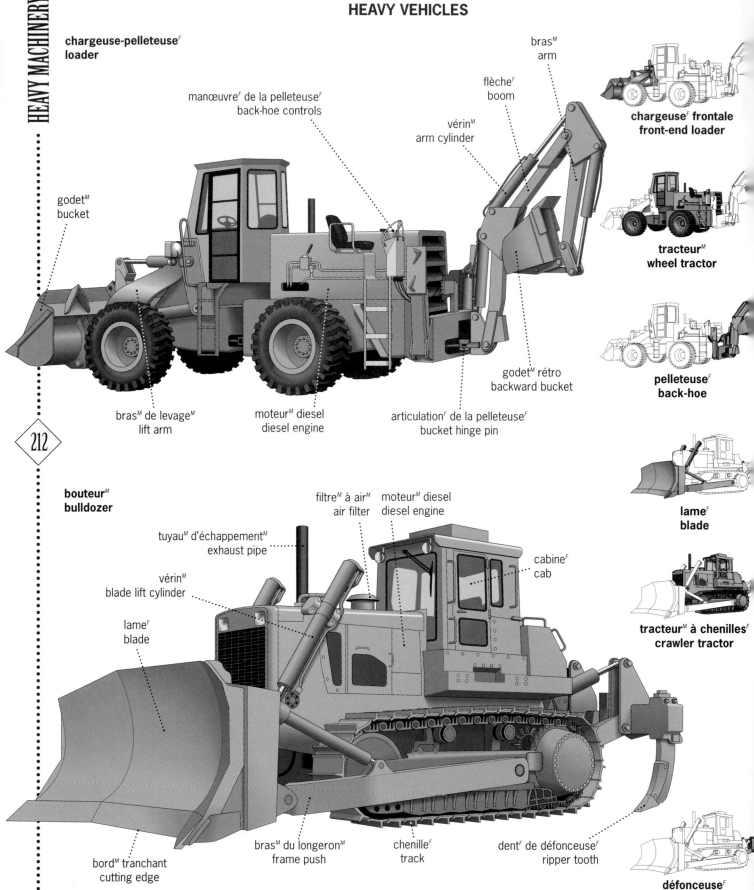

chargeuse-pelleteuse^F
loader

manœuvre^F de la pelleteuse^F
back-hoe controls

bras^M
arm

flèche^F
boom

vérin^M
arm cylinder

godet^M
bucket

chargeuse^F **frontale**
front-end loader

tracteur^M
wheel tractor

pelleteuse^F
back-hoe

bras^M de levage^M
lift arm

moteur^M diesel
diesel engine

articulation^F de la pelleteuse^F
bucket hinge pin

godet^M rétro
backward bucket

bouteur^M
bulldozer

filtre^M à air^M
air filter

moteur^M diesel
diesel engine

tuyau^M d'échappement^M
exhaust pipe

cabine^F
cab

vérin^M
blade lift cylinder

lame^F
blade

lame^F
blade

tracteur^M **à chenilles**^F
crawler tractor

bord^M tranchant
cutting edge

bras^M du longeron^M
frame push

chenille^F
track

dent^F de défonceuse^F
ripper tooth

défonceuse^F
ripper

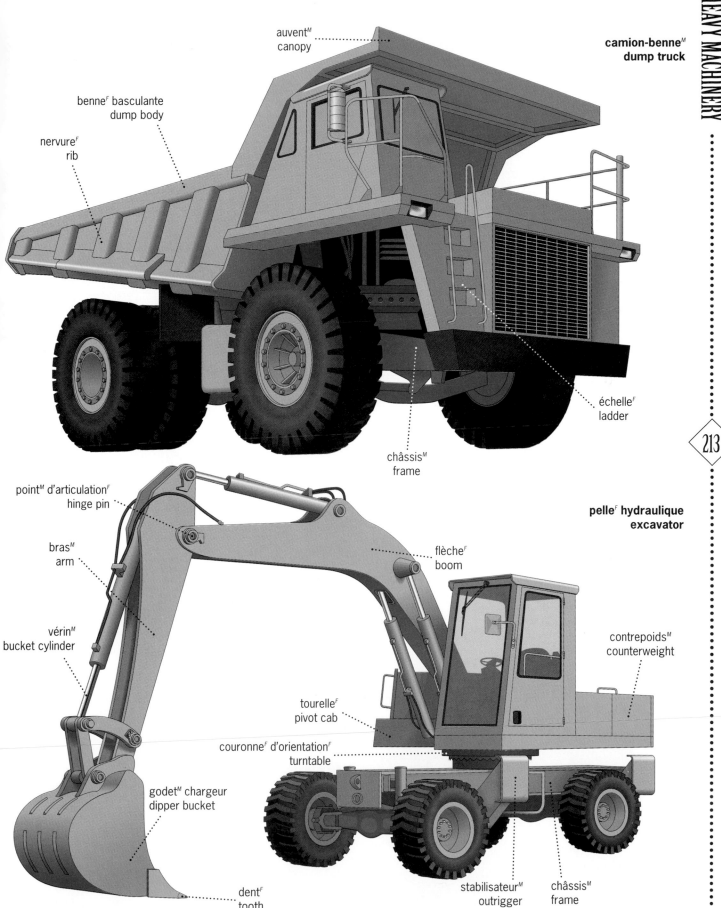

auvent^M
canopy

**camion-benne^M
dump truck**

benne^F basculante
dump body

nervure^F
rib

échelle^F
ladder

châssis^M
frame

point^M d'articulation^F
hinge pin

**pelle^F hydraulique
excavator**

bras^M
arm

flèche^F
boom

vérin^M
bucket cylinder

contrepoids^M
counterweight

tourelle^F
pivot cab

couronne^F d'orientation^F
turntable

godet^M chargeur
dipper bucket

dent^F
tooth

stabilisateur^M
outrigger

châssis^M
frame

LA MACHINERIE^F LOURDE
HEAVY MACHINERY

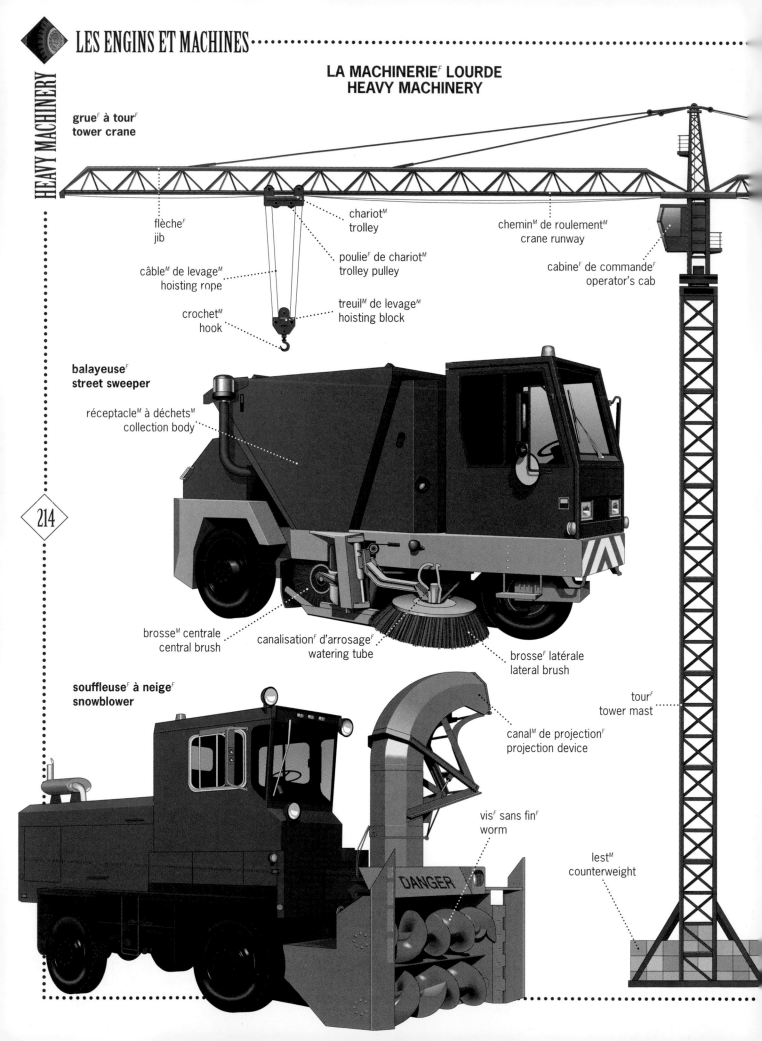

grue^F à tour^F
tower crane

chariot^M
trolley

chemin^M de roulement^M
crane runway

flèche^F
jib

poulie^F de chariot^M
trolley pulley

cabine^F de commande^F
operator's cab

câble^M de levage^M
hoisting rope

treuil^M de levage^M
hoisting block

crochet^M
hook

balayeuse^F
street sweeper

réceptacle^M à déchets^M
collection body

brosse^M centrale
central brush

canalisation^F d'arrosage^F
watering tube

brosse^F latérale
lateral brush

tour^F
tower mast

souffleuse^F à neige^F
snowblower

canal^M de projection^F
projection device

vis^F sans fin^F
worm

lest^M
counterweight

DANGER

214

tirant^M
jib tie

contrepoids^M
counterjib ballast

benne^F tasseuse
packer body

camion^M à ordures^F
sanitation truck

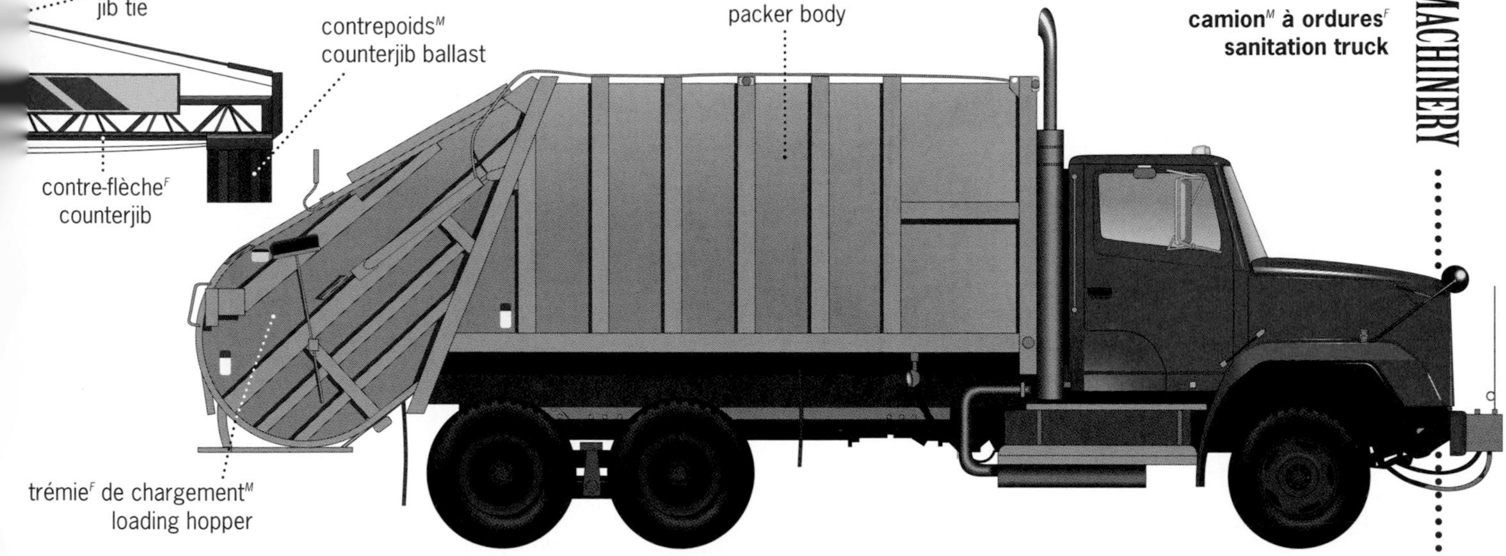

contre-flèche^F
counterjib

trémie^F de chargement^M
loading hopper

grue^F sur porteur^M
truck crane

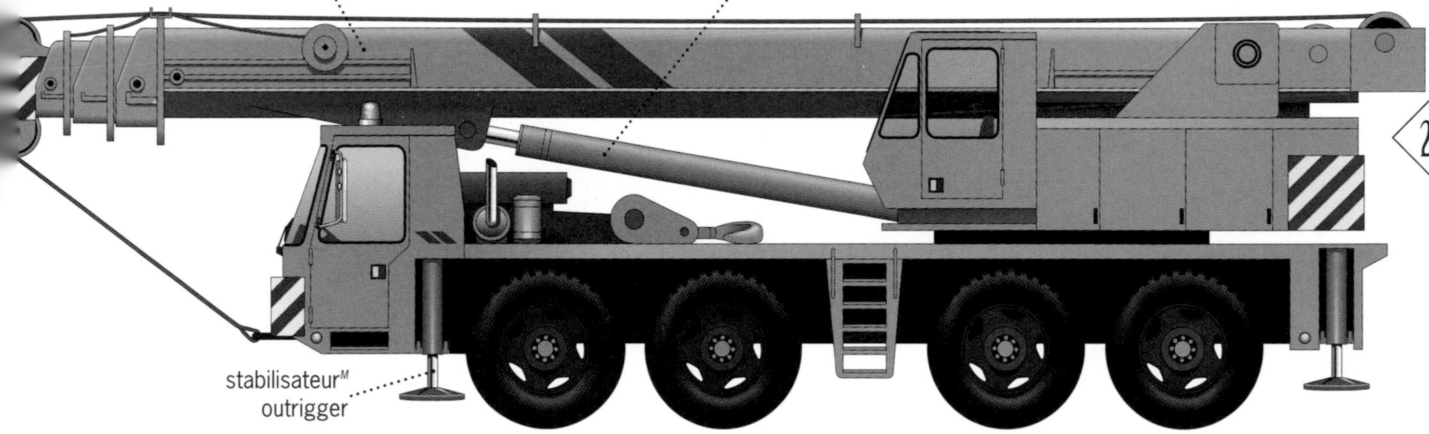

flèche^F télescopique
telescopic boom

vérin^M de dressage^M
elevating cylinder

stabilisateur^M
outrigger

215

poutre^F de levage^M
boom

vérin^M
elevating cylinder

treuil^M
winch

dépanneuse^F
tow truck

câble^M
cable

crochet^M
hook

ositif^M de remorquage^M
towing device

commandes^F du treuil^M
winch controls

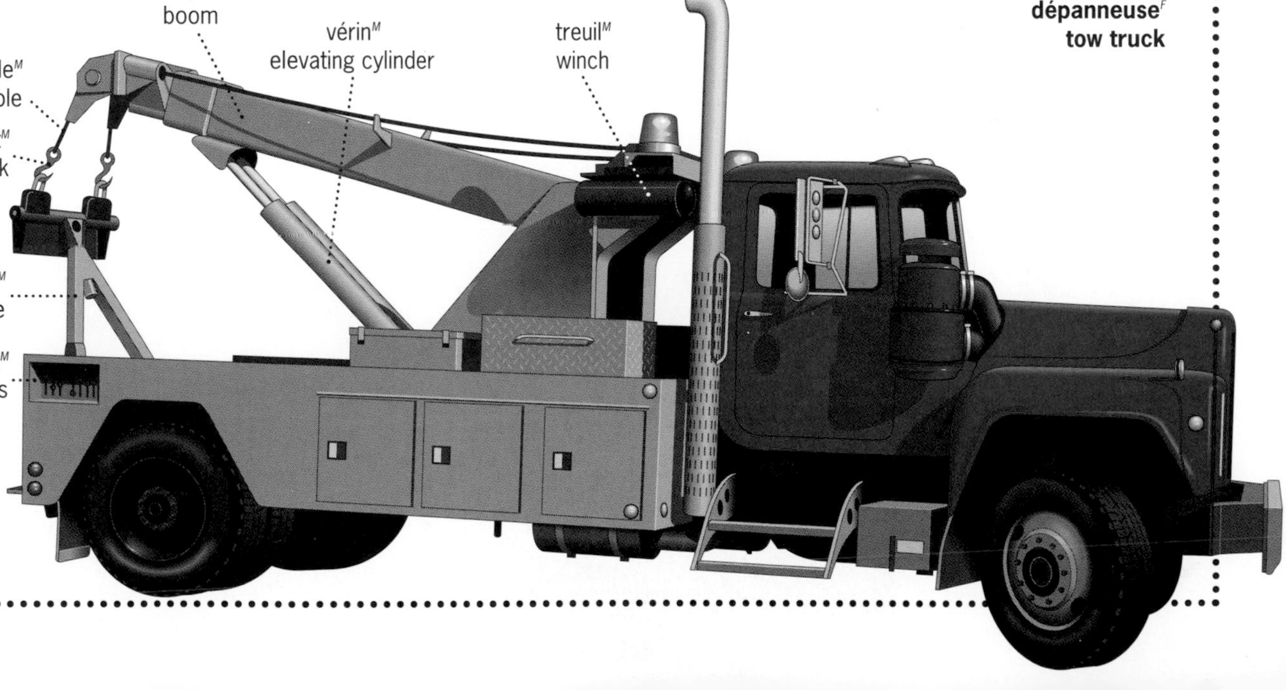

LES SYMBOLES^M D'USAGE^M COURANT
COMMON SYMBOLS

toilettes^F pour dames^F
women's rest room

toilettes^F pour hommes^M
men's rest room

accès^M pour handicapés^M
physiques
wheelchair access

hôpital^M
hospital

téléphone^M
telephone

défense^F de fumer
no smoking

camping^M
camping (tent)

camping^M interdit
camping prohibited

arrêt^M à l'intersection^F
stop at intersection

LES SYMBOLES^M DE SÉCURITÉ^F
SAFETY SYMBOLS

matières^F corrosives
corrosive

danger^M électrique
electrical hazard

LES SYMBOLES^M DE PROTECTION^F
PROTECTION

protection^F obligatoire de la vue^F
eye protection

protection^F obligatoire de l'o...
ear protection

216

matières^F explosives
explosive

matières^F inflammables
flammable

protection^F obligatoire de la tête^F
head protection

protection^F obligatoire des m...
hand protection

matières^F radioactives
radioactive

matières^F toxiques
poisonous

protection^F obligatoire des pieds^M
foot protection

protection^F obligatoire des
voies^F respiratoires
respiratory system protecti...

...s termes en **caractères gras** renvoient à une illustration, ceux en CAPITALES indiquent un titre.

Les termes en **caractères gras** renvoient à une illustration, ceux en CAPITALES indiquent un titre.

219

Les termes en **caractères gras** renvoient à une illustration, ceux en CAPITALES indiquent un titre.

s termes en **caractères gras** renvoient à une illustration, ceux en CAPITALES indiquent un titre.

Les termes en **caractères gras** renvoient à une illustration, ceux en CAPITALES indiquent un titre.

223

...s termes en **caractères gras** renvoient à une illustration, ceux en CAPITALES indiquent un titre.

Les termes en **caractères gras** renvoient à une illustration, ceux en CAPITALES indiquent un titre.

225

The terms in **bold type** correspond to an illustration; those in CAPITALS indicate a title.

The terms in **bold type** correspond to an illustration; those in CAPITALS indicate a title.

The terms in **bold type** correspond to an illustration; those in CAPITALS indicate a title.

229

The terms in **bold type** correspond to an illustration; those in CAPITALS indicate a title.

◇ 231 ◇

..he terms in **bold type** correspond to an illustration; those in CAPITALS indicate a title.

The terms in **bold type** correspond to an illustration; those in CAPITALS indicate a title.